P9-CDA-728

EXIT
STRATEGY

EXIT
STRATEGY

A NOVEL
CHARLTON PETTUS

HANOVER
SQUARE
PRESS

HANOVER
SQUARE
PRESS

Recycling programs
for this product may
not exist in your area.

ISBN-13: 978-1-335-01692-8

Exit Strategy

For questions and comments about the quality of this book, please contact us at
CustomerService@Harlequin.com.

HanoverSqPress.com
BookClubbish.com

Printed in U.S.A.

AP
LVM

EXIT
STRATEGY

BEFORE

As Jordan saw it there were only three options: nothing, the pills or the number. If he did nothing, he knew exactly how it would go. First he'd lose the company, then the house and finally his family, assuming you didn't count them as lost already. In a few months everything he loved would be gone.

Option B, then, the pills. Dr. Rosen had written the prescriptions after they'd lost the baby. (Say her name. Elizabeth. Her name was Elizabeth.) Zoloft for Stephanie and sleepy red Seconal for Jordan. Steph had taken hers dutifully, almost mechanically, until the day she'd simply stopped. Jordan had hoarded. He rolled the little bottle appreciatively in his hand. A dense solid sound, no hollow space for capsules to tumble. That good night held no terrors, far from it, but there were issues. The generous policy on his life wouldn't pay out in case of suicide, or as they euphemistically put it, "Intentional Self-Destruction." The unraveling would carry on without him. Just another mess for someone else to clean up.

Which left only the number. Jordan smoothed out the piece of paper. It had been tucked in his wallet so long the creases had taken on a feathered, leathery permanence. In Dr. Rosen's neat, even hand: "Exit Strategy" and the number. He typed the ten digits into the phone. They hovered on the screen, bland and banal. The clock said 12:34. Good omen. He pressed the green icon.

With that simple motion a cascade of chemical reactions started in his nervous system. Time seemed to slow to a near standstill; his ears buzzed and flushed. He had the distinct sensation of floating just behind and slightly above himself, tinglingly aware and alert but, at the same time, apart. Everything would be all right.

After what seemed like a very long time there was a click on the line as the connection was established and then the ring. It sounded hollow and distant like an overseas call but the ringtone was definitely American. His hands, without any conscious thought, had begun to deftly refold the paper, crimping here, creasing there. The ringtone stopped. Silence. "Hello?" Jordan said. His voice sounded odd in his ear. Then there was a quick series of electronic beeps and the line went dead.

He stared at the phone in his hand until the operator's voice came, loud and metallic. "If you'd like to make a call..." Redials produced nothing but a busy signal. For a long time he just sat. When he finally left the office, the heavy wood door shut with a muted click. The pills were shoved deep in his pocket and a tiny origami possum lay on its side on the desk. It was cold already. Boston winters started in August and ended in July. He should have worn a sweater.

A van was blocking the alley, its exhaust billowing. The driver, a solid man with an ex-jock's belly squeezed into a tight blue jacket, had gotten out and was complaining loudly on his phone. Jordan tried to engage the slender, vaguely foreign-looking man in the passenger seat but he just stared straight ahead. Swearing under his breath, Jordan walked around the back of the van. As he rounded the corner he caught a glimpse of blue jacket and heard a door open behind him. Then there was a brilliant flash of light that didn't seem related in any way to the heavy impact on the back of his head. As his knees buckled he thought he felt a hand on his back, then nothing.

The van pulled out onto Dunster Street, made the left on Comm. Ave., then merged into the northbound flow on Storrow Drive. Jordan's Prius followed several car lengths behind with the slender foreign man at the wheel. Neither vehicle ever exceeded the speed limit.

1

SCHRÖDINGER'S CAT

"But, Dr. Parrish, that is absurd. The cat can't be alive and dead at the same time."

Dr. Stephanie Parrish smiled. The corners of her eyes crinkled and her mouth turned up gradually as if against her will. She glanced at the speaker's name tag.

"Of course you're right, Mr. Edelman, but that was Schrödinger's point, reductio ad absurdum. We talk a great deal about the wave function of a particle, the *probability* of its state. It is only the act of observation that finally forces the particle, or the cat in this case, into one state or the other. *Our* curiosity kills the cat. You see?"

Edelman laughed loudly. He had been drinking steadily during the speeches and was now feeling every inch the magnanimous donor of the university's shining new Edelman Library. "Not at all! More confused than ever. Try again." As one of Harvard's more profligate benefactors, Lawrence Edelman felt absolutely justified in monopolizing the junior professor's time.

Stephanie Parrish was, at thirty-eight, in his view, without question the most beautiful woman in the room and so, by rights, his for the evening. Long brown hair streaked with gold framed a delicate oval face with eyes that hinted at gray, green and blue without, appropriately, he supposed, committing to any.

"There you are." Stephanie leaned back slightly to admit Alex Prenn into the conversation. "Larry, how are you?" Alex asked, clapping an arm around Edelman's meaty shoulder. "Good turnout. I'm afraid I'm going to have to borrow Dr. Parrish for a bit." He nodded to the podium at the front of the ballroom. "Don't worry, I promise to bring her back."

Edelman murmured something not quite intelligible and steadied himself against a large column.

"Thank you," Stephanie whispered into Alex's ear as he guided her between tables of well-heeled donors and university dignitaries interspersed with second-tier local politicians and a sprinkling of ferret-eyed Big Pharma flacks.

Prenn had a military carriage; people often assumed, incorrectly, that he was ex-army or navy. His short-cropped hair was receding slightly and gray at the temples. He gave her a gentle squeeze as they wove toward the dais. "He had his turn."

She smiled and leaned into him.

"Ladies and gentlemen, if I could intrude on your patience one last time…" Alex paused to let the conversational walla subside. There was a clattering of dishes and a shriek of laughter cut short.

"I'd like to introduce you all to Dr. Stephanie Parrish. As most of you know, she is Jordan's widow and a long-standing member of the physics department here at Harvard." Warm applause. Sympathy applause. She felt their eyes on her as she stepped to the podium. The genius's widow. They had heard the rumors. Craning to see the wreckage. She felt her face begin to set into the cool indifferent expression she wore to keep gawkers at bay, but forced a smile.

"Thank you so much. Happy holidays to you all. I promise

I won't take too much more of your time. You have been very patient and very generous. I know Jordan would have been incredibly moved." She glanced at the blown-up photo on its flimsy easel. It was an old picture, from Genometry's early days, probably before the kids were born. His eyes still shone with the fierce intelligence and determination she had fallen in love with.

"My husband's work was so important, and by endowing this chair in his name, all of you have ensured that it will go on, that a new generation will have the tools to pick up the torch." She paused and laughed. "Sorry, that was awful. I'm new at this kind of thing. I can't imagine what kind of tools would be appropriate in torch lifting." Ripples of laughter, generous; they were on her side.

She pushed on. "Jordan always dreamed of a world without disease, of a world where our bodies repaired themselves. Today, thanks to you, we are a step closer to realizing that dream. So, thank you." More applause, sustained now. At the back, people were standing, nodding toward the tables in front where senior executives from Genometry and Pfizer clapped politely, basking in the acknowledgment of their largesse with as much grace as they could muster.

"Was it horrible?" Stephanie asked, sliding into her seat.

"Pitch-perfect," Alex said. "Short and sweet. Totally natural." He squeezed her hand.

"I should have said more…"

"No, it was right. They've heard plenty. You just needed to bring it all back to Jordan. It was great. Simon, back me up."

Simon Perry sat on Stephanie's left. He looked up from the plate where he'd been distractedly pushing quartered roast beets through a sea of baby greens dotted with bergs of purple-stained chèvre. "Oh, yes, no, absolutely. Just the right tone." He was an angular, nervous man with a prominent Adam's apple and short gray-bordered hair that receded steeply from the center of his forehead. His mother was Jamaican and his father Senegalese, but Simon's upbringing had been quintessentially British. He spoke with a deliberate, considered accent, its edges dulled by decades in America but the Eton provenance still evident. He started to say something else, then shook his head as if to himself and returned to his beets.

"Thank you, Simon," Stephanie said finally, "for being kind, if not entirely honest."

After a moment, "He would have hated it, y'know."

"Sorry?"

"This." He swept his hand sloppily to include the whole room. "These people—" he pointed to the adjoining tables "—he used to call them Pfuckers, Pfools, Pfilistines and any other silly *Pf* thing he could come up with. Hated the lot of them. Press, too. Thought it was all crap. Where were they when it would have helped?"

"I'm sure you're right," Stephanie said with a tight smile. "The socializing alone would have made him completely miserable." She thought about it for a moment, then leaned in as if she was sharing a secret.

"Let's be honest, Simon, he never would have come. He would have found a reason to be somewhere else. Anywhere."

2

SENSES WORKING OVERTIME

In the darkness Jordan pressed his left palm to the sole of his right foot, gently evening them up. He measured carefully. The foot was exactly one hand plus a hair under an index finger long. The lights would come on soon with their dull green buzzing. He had adapted to the cycle of light and dark even though he was pretty sure it had no correlation with night and day. When they came on he'd measure again just to be sure. Then he'd pace off the room. He was sure it was shrinking. He was careful, very precise, heel to toe, heel to toe, always patient, always certain the second toe met the heel squarely. For a long time, wall to wall had measured thirty-six of his feet plus a bit, but yesterday it had been thirty-five and a half. He'd checked and rechecked. Thirty-five and a half. There was no mistake. He'd studied the way the wall met the floor. It was perfect. No sign of how such a thing might be done. He'd used his spoon to scratch the tile right at the join. If the marks were gone, he'd know. Unless they were shrinking the whole room somehow.

He should measure the height. No, that was crazy. He wasn't crazy.

A pride of lions, a murder of crows, a crash of rhinos, a fesnyng of ferrets, a pity, no, a piteousness of doves, a memory of elephants, an ascension of larks. He wasn't crazy. He'd measure and check the marks, then maybe they'd let him fold for a while.

Alex was awake. He lay still and listened. Breathing, a light rustle of sheets. That's right, there was a girl. He'd texted Vanessa after the fund-raiser, feeling celebratory and a little drunk, and she'd sent her over. Allegedly Russian, though Alex thought more likely Polish. She had a softness to her, a plushness. Alex opened an eye and slowly turned his head. She was still asleep, puffy lips parted so he could just see the tips of her two front teeth. A tousled blond mane framed her face and fanned out over the pillow. Alex smiled to himself. Exquisite as promised, young Bardot. Winter sun shone through the blinds striping the bed. From the angle he guessed noon or a bit after.

He reached for his phone on the bedside table, careful not to wake the girl. Sixty-seven new emails and a dozen texts. He flipped through. Mostly congratulations. One of the Pfizer PR minions had forwarded a post from an apparently influential investment blogger.

Our little birds tell us a deal is apparently close for drug behemoth Pfizer (PFE) to acquire tiny Cambridge-based Genometry (GNM). Pfizer shares were off nearly three-quarters of a point in after-hours trading as speculation swirled at a heavily attended gala celebrating a newly endowed chair in memory of Genometry founder Jordan Parrish. GNM has been trading in the penny stock range on the Hong Kong Exchange after several years of disappointing trials for their proprietary protein modeling software; however, share price is up today nearly two hundred percent (!) on the rumors. If the deal goes through, GNM shareholders could find themselves awash in bargain basement shares of the world's largest drug maker so Genometry is our #TwitPickoftheday.

He nodded, not bad. People were doing their jobs. And then there was a text from Stephanie.

> Thank you for last night. And for everything. You have been a good friend. I wouldn't have made it through without you. (I guess you can apply that to last night or the last year, ha, ha.) Anyway, I talked to the kids—if you don't have plans we'd love to have you join us for Christmas lunch (but of course totally understand if you can't). Invitation—not pressure. :) Lmk.
> Annnnnd, yes to Gardner outing. Wed.? Xo, S

The girl yawned, arching her back and rolling her head gently from side to side. Alex was transfixed by the way the sun caught the impossibly fine hairs on her arms and upper thighs. He leaned over and breathed in. Soap and sex and a hint of lavender, and something else, something tangy and slightly sour like buttermilk. He ran a finger lightly down her stomach, leaving a goose-bump wake.

She made a sound like a great cat purring and tugged at her right wrist, which was still tied to the bedpost with Alex's blue-and-yellow-striped necktie. Her eyes half-open, she fixed him with a petulant stare. He smiled and moved closer. He opened the Sonos app on his phone and pulled up the song running through his head. XTC, off *English Settlement*. He turned up the volume and rich sound filled the bedroom and then Andy Partridge's glottal whine.

Hey, hey, The clouds are whey.
There's straw for the donkeys,

And the innocents can all sleep safely,
All sleep safely.

She frowned and pulled again on the tie, shaking the bed frame so it knocked against the wall.

My, my, sun is pie.
There's fodder for the cannons,
And the guilty ones can all sleep safely,
All sleep safely.

He ran his tongue down her arm as his hand opened her legs. An infinity of smells but only the four, no, five tastes. He ticked them off out loud as he discovered them.

"Sweet. Sour. Salty. Bitter. Umami…"

And all the world is biscuit-shaped.
It's just for me to feed my face,
And I can see, hear, smell, touch, taste.

And I've got one, two, three, four, five senses working overtime.
Trying to take this all in...
Trying to taste the difference 'tween a lemon and a lime,
Pain and pleasure, and the church bells softly chime.

3

OAKRIDGE

A great deal of thought had gone into the decor. The principal's office managed to successfully interweave the potentially discordant strands of its nuanced message. A clutch of framed diplomas from esteemed colleges was balanced by a beaded deerskin certification from the Narragansett Tribal Authority. The bookcase gave agonizingly balanced time to progressive staples like Spencer, Steiner and Montessori, classical works from Virgil to Shakespeare and global fiction from Bolaño to Walker. Photographs on her walls and desk firmly established Margot's bona fides as both a compassionate caregiver and a responsible custodian to her precious charges.

"Stephanie. Thank you for coming."

Margot came around from behind her desk, hand extended with a broad smile only partially dampened by the concerned, vaguely regretful furrow of her brow.

"Can I offer you a tea? Water? Yes, I know we should be using glass, but I'm always afraid someone's going to cut themselves," she said, nodding to the neat stack of water bottles on the tea table.

Oakridge had been Jordan's choice. He would never have admitted it but the private school was a yardstick of his own success. Toward the end when the fiscal levee was starting to crumble, he had put the Oakridge bills on a credit card.

"I wondered if you and I might catch up a bit before I have Sophie join us." It came across as a question.

"Of course."

"How have things been, at home?" Margot leaned back in her chair and interlaced her fingers over her expansive chest. Her expression was open, expectant, patient, supportive and utterly free of judgment. Christ, she was good, Stephanie thought.

"Fine. I mean, obviously it's been a little…challenging for all of us, but fine. Sophie has seemed—" she floundered for a moment before concluding helplessly "—fine." Margot nodded sagely but said nothing. Waiting.

"She lost her father. I can only imagine how a ten-year-old processes something like that."

"Of course." Silence. She would need more. Gossip was the currency here. Yes, your child may stay at our prestigious institution despite beating the crap out of some tormenting bitch, but only if you pay the toll in full. Stephanie sighed.

"I'm sure you've heard the stories."

Nothing.

"Jordan, my husband, had been having an affair. Apparently for some time." Margot's expression subtly softened and became more attentive. *That's it. Now we're getting somewhere.*

"I never knew about it, but it seems he'd kept an apartment on Marlboro Street. He and this…this woman had been on the way back from the Cape together when the accident happened. Her car rolled down an embankment into a pond. They both drowned. Most of it was kept out of the news but the police were not so discreet. Sophie heard it all. She loved her dad very much. It was terrible for her, particularly for her." Stephanie glanced up. Confirmation of rumor but no fresh product. She'd need more.

"We weren't allowed to see him, even the funeral was closed casket. The bodies were in the water for a while and apparently… Well, they wouldn't let us see the body. I think that was the worst—there was no real closure and Sophie had nightmares for weeks. You know, her father as some hideous bloated zombie lurching out of the water…"

"How awful," Margot said, shaking her head with an expression of deepest sympathy. She pressed the intercom on her phone. "Would you send Sophie in, please?"

On the way home Sophie sat sullenly in the backseat even though her mother had been letting her sit up front for months. "You can't keep doing this sort of thing, you know." Stephanie glanced at her daughter in the rearview mirror.

"She started it."

"Yes, but you escalated—Christ, you literally beat her up. We're lucky they're letting you come back."

Sophie didn't say anything else for a while. She just looked out the window. When she followed them just with her eyes the trees seemed to whiz by so fast but when she moved her whole head they slowed down so they almost stood still. "I'm not like you," she said quietly. "I can't just pretend everything's all right all the time."

The only light in the cell was from the large screen mounted high on the wall. Jordan's arms were raised like a conductor's. All of his attention was focused on the two long cylinders, one tan and one green, twisted together like snakes in a can. Moving his hands in the air, he rotated the image so he could see it from every angle. Finally he brought his hands slowly together, folding the animated protein on the screen into a position where hydrogen bonds held it in place. He clicked the green "done" button on the lower right corner, and the protein disappeared with a cheap digital fanfare and a new puzzle took its place.

4

LAMENTATION

Alex rang the bell again. He didn't hear anything; it could be broken. Stephanie's car was in the driveway. He tried the knob. Unlocked. He eased the heavy door open. It groaned in protest. "Hello?"

"Hey, Alex," Stephanie called from upstairs somewhere. "Come on in. There's coffee, help yourself. I'll be down in a minute." Alex dumped his coat over the radiator in the front hall and went into the kitchen. The sun was reflecting off the snow in the yard, filling the room with a cool blue light. The sink was full of breakfast dishes, and the tang of souring milk mixed with the smell of burned toast and overcooked coffee gave the house a feel of rumpled normalcy. He took the spare key to Jordan's old office off his key ring and laid it on the counter.

"Sorry," she said brightly, coming into the kitchen, wiping stray wisps with the back of her hand. "Just trying to pull things together a little here before I go attack the office." She was wearing a pair of blue Patriots sweatpants, tube socks and a white

T-shirt. Her face was flushed and lightly beaded with sweat. Her hair was in a high ponytail. She looked, Alex thought, save a few fine lines around the mouth and eyes and the odd strand of gray, just like the incandescent sophomore he had first met almost two decades before.

Jordan and Alex had shared an apartment on Exeter Street in Back Bay after college. It abutted a parking lot and a gay disco whose steady thump had lulled them to sleep most nights. Alex had a theory about fetal memory of the mother's heartbeat, which he trotted out whenever an overnight guest complained. Jordan waited tables at the Harvard Bookstore Café on Newbury Street to make rent while he did his doctoral work at MIT. Alex was getting his hours as a pilot and making and losing little fortunes, never more than a few hundred dollars either way, trading penny stocks. This left a lot of time for lounging around the apartment listening to late Miles Davis and Ornette Coleman. On summer nights when the little place was insufferably hot and the disco pulse particularly irritating, Alex would walk around the corner to the café and sit at one of Jordan's outdoor tables. He would troll the bookstore for a particular sort of pretentious philosophy book and the earnest undergraduate coeds who often read them. If he found either, he could return to his table and while away the evening sipping from a cup Jordan kept filled with coffee or white wine as the pace required. One muggy August night he was sitting at his usual table with a collection of enticing books arranged to catch the eye—*The Dancing Wu Li Masters*, *The Tao of Physics*, *The Tao of Pooh* (in case a little levity was called for), *Theosophia Practica*, *The Secret Teachings of All Ages: An Encyclopedic Outline of Masonic, Hermetic, Kabbalistic and Rosicrucian Symbolic Philosophy* and, finally, *The Riddle Wrapped in Enigma*. He was sipping a cup of the house white and thumbing through *The Tao of Physics*, trying to look thoughtful when a beautiful brunette in black pants over a black leotard—maybe a dancer, he thought—approached the table and considered him for a moment.

"Excuse me," she said.

"Yes," Alex said, looking up, every inch the intellectual disturbed at his study.

"Are you reading this one?" the girl asked, picking up *The Riddle Wrapped in Enigma*.

"Not at this moment but it looked quite interesting."

"Yes, I rather thought so, too, and it seems you have the last copy," she said, regarding him coolly, a little smile playing around the corner of her mouth. She waited to see if he would offer her the book but he just smiled back up at her.

Finally he said, "I was going to buy it but, please, have a seat, read away, see if it speaks to you." With a little laugh and a nod, the girl pulled out a chair and sat down.

"Thank you..." she said, holding out her hand.

"Alex, Alex Prenn."

"Thank you, Alex Prenn. I'm Stephanie." She took up the book and started flipping through the index. Without raising her eyes from the page, she said, "What was it about this one that appealed to you, Alex?"

"Oh, I'm just a seeker, I guess," he said, sweeping his arm over the little collection of books. "I'm fascinated by life's mysteries, its enigmas."

"I see," she said. "I don't think you'll care for this one much, then."

"Why not?" he said.

She turned the open book so Alex could see the page. There were columns of numbers with a single letter at the bottom of each column; it was gibberish. "This book is a technical treatise on the Enigma code machine used by the Nazis in the Second World War. Pretty dull reading for a seeker, don't you think?" Alex laughed out loud.

"Is that really what it is?"

"Yup," she said. "You know what I think?"

"No, what do you think?" Alex asked.

"I think you wander around in there, pick out a bunch of titles that you think will catch the eye of any earnest girl with a newly discovered sense of her own worldliness and intellectual depth and you bait your web with them like a patient old spider."

"Who are you calling old?" he cried with mock indignation. "All right, take your silly code book, then. Run along, little fly."

"No need to get huffy—" she smiled "—and besides, I'm still not sure there's any new stuff in this one. I think I'll sit for a while and skim."

"And ruin my chances with any other eager seekers who may wander by."

She laughed, a throaty, husky sound, like a habitual smoker's, though Alex would have bet his next month's rent she didn't smoke. He drained his cup and gestured to Jordan, who was just clearing off another table. When he came over Alex waved a hand over his empty cup and said, "Refill, please, and a cup for my friend. Jordan, this is Stephanie. Stephanie, Jordan."

"Delighted," Stephanie said, shaking Jordan's hand, "but I'll pass on the coffee, thanks. Bit late."

"Pay no attention to her, J." And then to Stephanie, "The coffee here is special." Jordan returned in a moment with a coffee cup filled with white wine, which he placed in front of her with a little pitcher of cream for appearances.

"Ah, I see," said Stephanie. "I suppose not so late after all."

After her second cup, Stephanie said, "He's sweet...your friend the waiter, shy, though."

"Jordan? No, not really shy. He's a genius, a real genius. I think a lot of the time he's just in his own head, off in Geniusville, you know?"

"No," she said, "I don't. What kind of genius?"

"Tough to explain. He's kind of a whiz with figuring out how a chain of amino acids is going to fold up to make a protein. Something to do with alpha helices and beta sheets. Did I lose you yet?"

"No. Not yet. It sounds cool actually. I'm physics but I have a bit of bio."

"Ah, right, you're way ahead of me, then. Bottom line, he's a total fucking genius and when he finishes his doctorate we're going to start a company and save the world."

She smiled.

When the restaurant closed, Jordan took off the tan-and-burgundy apron and joined them, pouring himself a glass of wine and smoking a cigarette as he counted his tips. Alex noted that Stephanie's nose wrinkled at the cigarette smoke but she didn't say anything about it. She asked Jordan about his thesis. He was awkward at first, but as he began to talk about it and realized she genuinely understood and was interested in what he was saying he became more and more animated, the passion illuminating his face. They were absorbed in each other, and when the manager came to lock the front door, Alex passed him his pile of books and made his excuses.

He was happy for his friend. Alex had plenty of girls but Jordan was a loner. Alex knew he'd gone out with a couple of mousy studious types at Harvard but nothing serious, and at grad school the lab had been his only love. Stephanie was hot and smart and funny. If she was into Jordan, Alex was willing to let this one go. Stephanie turned to him, face flushed, a little tipsy, and said, "Good night, Alex Prenn. To the seekers." She raised her cup and drained it.

"Come on," she said to Jordan, "walk me home." And she grabbed an open bottle of wine from the ice bucket at the waiters' station. Alex smiled and raised his cup to them as they wove unsteadily down Newbury Street and out of sight.

5

CLEANING

Stephanie let herself in with Alex's key. The office was unnervingly quiet. It had an odd abandoned quality like pictures she'd seen of Hiroshima after the blast, life suddenly interrupted. It had snowed overnight so the light Sunday-morning traffic sounded woolen and distant. The little reception area, cluttered in faded yellow and pink Post-its, was bitter cold, but inside Jordan's office it was uncomfortably warm and close. The radiator by the window sputtered and spat, blustering through the unnatural quiet. As she struggled with the swollen window, she could smell the rust coughed up from deep in the old building's respiratory system. Then the window gave with a sudden shriek. Dry cold air swirled in and the room seemed to shake itself awake.

She had bought a stack of moving boxes and a tape gun from the U-Haul in Central Square. She leaned the stack up behind the door and opened and taped three boxes. The sensible plan seemed to be to start just inside the threshold and work her way clockwise around the room. With a black Sharpie she labeled one box Books, one Papers and one Stuff. She took the Sunday *Globe* and spread out the sections, opening up the automotive and style pages first. As she took each diploma or photograph from the wall, she wrapped it in two sheets of newsprint. She quickly filled her first Stuff box, taped it shut and made a new one.

When she came to the bookcase, she took all the files and loose papers and dumped them indiscriminately in the Papers box. Then she started with the books, quickly filling two boxes and half of a third. She was sweating now and flushed. Progress. Order out of chaos. A postponement of the inevitable victory of entropy.

She felt numb as she filed her dead husband's life away; it didn't feel like any of this was really his, even the family pictures seemed somehow at a remove from the man. It was remarkable that he could have spent so much time in this little room without leaving more of himself behind. It was all just paint and paper. The phone rang once in the outer office and the ancient machine picked up but the caller left no message.

Stephanie surveyed her progress. Not bad for a couple of hours. There were six sealed boxes ready to go and three more in progress. She was two-thirds of the way around the room with nothing major left except the desk. She toyed with the idea of plowing ahead to the end but her lower back was killing her and her stomach was grumbling.

She threw her coat back on and, without really thinking about it, walked around the corner to Oggi for a roast beef sandwich. Oggi had been their go-to in Genometry's early days when she and Jordan had met for lunch whenever their schedules allowed. She sank into the familiar booth as the lunch rush bustled and simmered around her. Through the window she watched the students and early Christmas shoppers, eyes squinted against the blowing snow, as they struggled upstream with their bags and backpacks. She nursed a second cup of coffee and let the muffled clatter of dishes and murmur of conversation envelop her like a warm bath.

An hour later as she paid the check and pulled her coat tight, she noticed how dark it had become. The sun seemed low and impotent already, though it wasn't yet two. When she got back to the office it seemed changed. The cold air had overwhelmed the radiator and the room seemed suddenly bare and freezing. Stephanie shut the window, leaving just a crack at the bottom.

She dragged the open boxes over and sat down at Jordan's desk. Part of her mind romanticized the heaps of notes and intricately folded papers as a snapshot of his last hours or days but a cooler bit reminded her that the police had been through the office multiple times and that the particular disorder in front of her was no doubt more a result of their ministrations than her husband's. All the loose papers went into a box. She rescued an old snapshot of herself with Haden on vacation in Hawaii. Haden was pointing at a rainbow and laughing. Another lifetime. Jordan had written "S&H, Paia" on the back in his familiar angular scrawl. She slipped it into her purse.

There was a stack of software manuals at the back of the desk. As she tossed them in the current Books carton something fluttered to the floor. Stephanie picked it up. One of Jordan's origami doodles. A tiny baby rat—no, a possum. She smiled and flipped through the manuals looking for more. He usually made them in bunches. He'd offer them up with the appropriate collective noun: a murder of little paper crows, a paddling of Post-it ducks. If there were more, she couldn't find them. She tucked it into her purse with the picture.

When the desktop was cleared she moved on to the drawers. Pens and pencils, trash. Old phone logs, trash. She flipped through them first, not that she expected to see "Call back mistress re: early dinner and a quick fuck" written anywhere. All the other bills, receipts, letters and miscellany of life went into a Papers box, probably never to be seen again.

Halfway through the middle drawer on the right side she saw a faded bit of lined paper that looked familiar, like a favorite T-shirt from high school that turns up unexpectedly in a suitcase after a visit home. She pulled it out. It was a faded green and tattered at the top where it had been ripped out of one of the steno pads Jordan and Alex had used for phone messages at their Exeter Street apartment nearly twenty years before. On it, in her own neat and boxy hand, was written "TGG TGG! CTG GTG, ATG."

She gasped for air as the sob rose from deep in her lungs and ripped through her. Tears filled her eyes and rolled unobstructed down her face as she sat silent and perfectly still at her husband's desk, clutching a decades-old note from herself. The grief that had never seemed to come, through the search, the recovery, the funeral and the countless earnest whispered condolences, now inexplicably burst inside her, racking her body in shuddering waves.

It was dark when she finally locked up and left. Everything that had been in Jordan's office, all that was left of him, was now stacked in nine sealed boxes in the hall except for a single photograph, one sheet of green lined paper and a tiny origami possum.

6

Stephanie woke up from a catnap. Jordan lay beside her, watching. The room was streaked with sunlight coming through the slat blinds. She must have dozed off after making love for the second, or fourth, time depending on how you looked at it. They had come home late and pretty tipsy to find the apartment empty. The roommate, Alex, had left a message on the machine. People were laughing and yelling in the background so it was difficult to hear what he was saying but they did catch "New Hampshire" and "Monday." That meant the place was theirs for two whole days. The goal was to christen every piece of furniture in the apartment. They had passed out in each other's arms as the sun came up. She had woken up a few hours later with Jordan's fingers delicately tracing the contours of her belly. She didn't speak or move but her breathing betrayed her. They both held perfectly still at the end, trying to prolong the moment. After, Jordan had ordered breakfast from the Greek diner around the corner. It had come in minutes.

The delivery boy—just a kid, fifteen or sixteen—had stared wide-eyed from the doorway as Jordan, wrapped in a sheet, fumbled through his jeans pockets. When he'd gone they'd burst out laughing and devoured the containers of scrambled eggs with soggy hash browns, bacon and French toast. Full and content, they had begun a patient and scientific exploration of each other's bodies, which at some point had lost its clinical detachment. And then she must have fallen back to sleep.

"Good morning," he said, seeing her stir.

"Hmm…closer to evening it looks like," she said.

"Do you know why you're beautiful?"

"What time is it?"

"I've been studying you and I think I've figured it out."

She propped herself on one elbow and studied him; his face was completely serious. "All right, Dr. Parrish," she said, "let's hear your theory—Darwinian bullshit, I'm sure."

He allowed himself a half smile. "No, I know better. This is a purely aesthetic epiphany with, I humbly suggest, profound and far-reaching implications."

"Oh, then, by all means."

"Okay, we'll start easy. What is your most attractive feature?"

"Ugh, please don't say my eyes, that would be—"

"Oh God, no, I know," he interrupted, "and false. That's not where I'm going. Science. Come on, most attractive feature?"

"Are you being smutty and vile? I am a modest and delicate flower, Doctor, and won't have you speak to me that way."

"Freud was right. You're all harlots!"

She smacked his arm. "Fuck Freud! I'm not playing." Then after a minute of feigned sulk, "Okay, what is my best feature, then, smart-ass?"

"Not best, most attractive. Pay attention."

She groaned. "Stop milking it—you do have a point, right?"

"Your knee. Specifically your left kneecap."

She burst out laughing. "Oh my God, you are so full of shit.

Okay, I have a real theory. Ready? You know how most of your DNA is junk—it just sits there doing nothing. It doesn't code for blue eyes or lovely kneecaps or anything—it's just there? Huge waste, right? But wait..."

"No, you wait," he said, "you're dismissing my epiphany! I'll spell it out in little words so you can understand. It's all about curves and straight lines."

"Deep. So anyway, what if God or aliens or people from the future or whatever hid secret knowledge in our DNA. You know, like in code. Like the monolith on the moon in *2001*. So when we were sophisticated enough to read it we could find it."

"It *is* deep," he said. "Look at your knee. See how the top is almost a straight line, then it curves into sides that are totally straight but then underneath totally curved." He traced the movement with his finger. "And the muscle of your thigh where it follows and exaggerates the arc of the knee… That's beauty. It's the balance between the curves and the lines, like a perfect tooth, straight yet bowed as a full sail. Or your cheekbone, a gentle arc that falls into a hard line, then softens and turns under at the jaw, another straight edge. And the collarbone— oh, the collarbone!—that little pocket between the collarbone and shoulder, a perfect half sphere formed by two straight lines. How can you not see it? It's obviously an evolved aesthetic. You know, fitness, sexual maturity, all that stuff. There is clearly an ideal ratio of curves to straight lines in a physically fit, fertile, yet not over-the-hill woman, and that ratio is what we perceive as beautiful."

He rolled on, encouraged by her arch smile. "You ever play that game with yourself? 'At what age do I look most like me? As a child, an old woman?' Of course as babies we all kind of look the same, like babies. Neoteny, Bambi, big eyes, little chins. And ditto when we're old—eventually time takes similar liberties with everyone, right? But in between, where is the moment? You could argue for forties or fifties but I would say at that point your face is more a record of the life you have lived than an expression of ultimate you-ness. I think that at that knife's edge between the curves of youth and the brittle lines of age there lies a moment of both greatest expression of your genetic essence and greatest beauty." She rolled her eyes. He ran his fingers lightly down her entire length, sweeping around the curves and hollows for emphasis. "And for you, Ms. James, that moment is right now."

Suddenly self-conscious, she pulled the sheet around her. "Nice. Used that one before?"

He held her eyes. "Never thought it."

After a silence, she said, "Did you hear a word of my brilliant DNA as alien code hypothesis? I should warn you, mock at your peril, I got an A on it sophomore year."

"Every word." He smiled. "Junk DNA is really a hidden instruction manual from God or Xenu, right?"

"Exactly. Genius, huh?"

"No comment."

"Good answer. I know it sounds pretty nutty but there are fascinating parallels out there. You know anything about kabbalah, or the sefirot? Numerology of the Hebrew alphabet?"

"Absolutely nothing," he said with some satisfaction.

"Heathen. Well, I know you know how the four letters of DNA—G, A, T and C—code for the twenty amino acids that make us, right? So, what if you think of those amino acids as letters?"

"Okay," he said, watching her lecture with a smirk.

"So, you'd have a twenty-letter alphabet, basically all the consonants without the vowels, an abjad like Biblical Hebrew. Then it's like those posters on the subway—wait…" She grabbed the steno pad and a pen from the table and wrote out "f y cn rd ths y cn mk gd mny." "Get it? You just have to plug in the vowels. Are you with me?"

Jordan took the pad. "I think so. So, alanine would be *A*…"

"No vowels, remember."

"Right, right, okay. Alanine is *B*, cysteine *C*, aspartic acid *D*..."

"What a quick student you are." She stood up, dropping the sheet, and walked across the bed to press his head to her belly.

"This is kind of kinky, in a hot-for-teacher kind of way," he said, voice muffled in her abdomen as he pulled her down.

Later, as he lay curled beside her, one leg between hers, twirling the fine hairs on the back of her neck around his index finger, he said, "I think I might be falling in love with you, Ms. James."

For a while she was silent, then a sleepy and contented voice murmured, "What do you mean 'might'?"

She woke in the dark. The clock said just before five. She slipped from the bed and dressed. She needed to protect this new happiness she carried like a water droplet swollen to its bursting point. She grabbed the discarded steno pad and quickly scribbled him a note. "TGG TGG! CTG GTG, ATG." She folded it once and placed it on the pillow before soundlessly letting herself out.

When he woke, hours later, it took Jordan a couple of minutes to work out the letters *WW! LVM*, but most of the day to convince himself it could only mean "Wow! Love, Me."

7

DAYS

The two men sat together watching the closed-circuit feed from the Kinect. Jordan was folding, intent, hands manipulating invisible shapes, mouth working as if he were talking. He seemed to be staring straight at them.

"How's he doing, Dennis?" asked the older man. He had black horn-rims and wore his graying hair swept over to one side in a style that would have looked right at home in an early '70s Brylcreem ad.

"Lousy," Dennis said with an edge to his voice. Since picking Parrish up one hundred and nine days ago he'd been on twenty-four-hour call. "He's burned."

"Mmm," the older man said vaguely.

Dennis pushed his chair back with a shrill scrape.

Of course it was all wrong, Jordan thought. The side chains were too close together and there weren't enough hydrogen bonds to secure the backbone. But he was hungry. He clicked

Done and swiped his hand impatiently to bring up the next puzzle. The door opened with a bang. Jordan flinched but forced himself not to turn. The puzzle flickered and was gone. He stood completely still until he heard the sharp clatter of the tray on the table.

One Miss'ippi, two Miss'ippi, he counted in his head. Then out loud, "Thank you, Dennis." He didn't move until he heard the door close and lock. Plain white soup and plain white bread.

There had been potatoes involved, and maybe some kind of albino winter vegetable. Like those fish that live too deep to be bothered with pigment. Schools of the blind. No glint of goldfish. No shoal of shads, or was it *shad*?

Still hot. He blew on it and his breath made a flapping pocket. He felt the heat of it all the way down.

When Dennis came back the man with the horn-rims was scrolling back through the logs and shaking his head.

"He's working you."

"What do you mean?" Dennis asked, leaning over to read along.

"See here?" the man said, his finger tracing several points on the graph. "We were stretching him, nearly twenty-eight-hour days here, but then—" he traced the line back down "—mid-November the error rate starts to go up at specific intervals. You see?"

Dennis nodded. His eyebrows furrowed as he scanned the chart and his jaw bunched.

"And now," the man went on, "we're back under twenty-five hours."

"I followed protocol. When he started messing up—"

"No, I know, I know. I get it. But so does he." He shook his head with a rueful smile. "He's working you."

Stephanie was instantly wide-awake. She didn't think there'd been any sound; the house was certainly deathly quiet now.

Outside she heard the constant buzz of the streetlight but nothing else. It was completely still. No breeze rattled the frozen yews beneath her window. But her nerves were electric; she was in full fight-or-flight. Someone was there. She could feel the presence as her fully dilated pupils swept the room. Then she saw it. A lumpy shadow in the corner by her door swayed slightly, then steadied itself. Stephanie's heart was thudding in her chest; her mouth was dry and her ears were ringing as she strained all her senses toward the shadow.

"I'm sorry, Momma."

"Sophie? Are you okay?" She tried to keep the hysterical edge out of her voice. Sophie stepped out of the shadow and approached the bed, head bowed, face hidden by her bangs. She was dressed in oversize green plaid pajamas and clutching a tattered stuffed rabbit.

"I'm sorry, Momma," she said again. As she stepped into the light from the window Stephanie could see her face and realized she wasn't really awake. She had a furrowed brow and her mouth was working as if she were chewing on a piece of fish, feeling for hidden bones. Her eyes were open but she wasn't seeing anything. Stephanie got up and gently guided her around the bed and helped her in. As Sophie's breathing settled into a slow, shallow regularity, Stephanie cradled the head of thick brown hair, wishing she could draw her daughter back inside and protect her from the hurt that was beginning to reshape her sweet and gentle nature.

When Stephanie woke again the sun was shining clear and strong through the windows and Sophie lay pressed against her, chin slack and mouth open. Her cheeks were flushed and the sour heat of her breath, halfway between the milky sweetness of a child's and the ripe funk of an adult's, blew damp on Stephanie's cheek. Haden lay across the foot of the bed, wrapped awkwardly in the bottom third of the duvet. She hadn't heard him come in.

Their orbits were decaying. The loss of his father had made Haden fearful. He wouldn't go anywhere alone. He made Sophie or his mother go with him everywhere, even to the bathroom. Sophie had been a champ. Without being told anything she had seemed to understand and had become her little brother's constant guardian. She would take his hand and walk back up the stairs to get his favorite Red Sox hat or run back outside to the car with him if he forgot his knapsack. He had started sleeping on the trundle in her room but seemed to end up in his mother's bed most nights. Stephanie never said anything, and even though he was a fitful bundle of pointy knees and elbows, she slept better when he was there.

She knew she needed to do something, to begin the climb back to normalcy. She couldn't just let it all fall apart. She was the center; the holding started here. She wanted to hate Jordan, to curse him for dying, for abandoning her, for fucking someone else, for leaving his children to grow up without a father, but she couldn't. She was stuck in the first stage according to the cheesy little pamphlet Father Gil had pushed on her. Denial. Not just a river indeed. Didn't Kübler-Ross end up spending her final years trying to contact the dead, mediums and that sort of nonsense? It was all bullshit, Stephanie thought. She just needed to pull herself together, accept that he was gone and get on with it. And she would. The annus horribilis was winding down. Good riddance.

She reached over and gently brushed the hair from her daughter's face. "Wake up, sweet girl. It's time." As Sophie stretched and yawned Stephanie rubbed Haden's back and began easing him, too, toward wakefulness.

8

ISABELLA

The Isabella Stewart Gardner Museum was a mile and a half from the house, and yet, despite having driven past it thousands of times, Stephanie had never been. From the outside it didn't look like a museum at all; if not for the discreet painted wood sign she would have simply assumed it was a private house. Inside she passed through a narrow, dimly lit walkway of arched brick. On her left, infrequent small windows revealed nothing of the house's dark interior, but to her right the hallway suddenly opened onto a spectacular courtyard whose roof of leaded Victorian glass filled the space with a palpable winter light. She heard mizzling water and a Gregorian murmur of voices in the air. The walls rose four stories with balconies all around overlooking the garden and its massive tiled floor. All around the central mosaic were little walkways and statues, a mix of Asian and classical. At one end a pair of stone staircases rose to meet at a second-floor balcony thrusting into the courtyard like a pul-

pit. Gothic moldings in marble and stone adorned every available surface.

"Oh my God," she whispered as she gazed up at nasturtium
vines cascading down the side wall.

Alex was waiting. He said something to the girl in the green
blazer manning the admissions desk and she hastily unhooked
the rope and motioned Stephanie through.

She started to rummage through her purse to pay.

"I'm a member," he said, taking her arm. "You're my guest."

"It's beautiful."

"You've never been? How is that possible?"

Stephanie shook her head as she continued to take in the garden. Stone benches habited by engrossed couples, solitary readers and breathless tourists ringed the courtyard.

"I don't know," she said. "I guess I just never did." Looking
up, she could see people passing through hallways and pausing
on balconies on the upper floors. She thought of the Escher print
that had hung in the kitchen of her parents' house. Faceless men
purposefully navigating stairways that defied gravity and Euclid.

They crossed the hall into what a small placard indicated was
the Gothic Room. "Isabella." Alex pointed to a life-size portrait
of a woman in the corner of the room. She wore a simple black
velvet dress and her hair was pulled back in a bun. No jewelry
except a plain pearl choker with a ruby at the throat and a silver
chain belt around her waist. Her skin was like marble, pale and
luminescent. Her eyes looked straight ahead.

"Sargent—she was a fan."

"Beautiful. She looks so…sure."

"Apparently she had a motto, as I guess one did back then." He
cleared his throat dramatically. "'Win as though you were used
to it and lose as if you enjoy it.'" He smiled. "Pretty good, huh?"

Stephanie turned to look at him. "Someone's got a little crush,
I think."

"Oh, absolutely." He held Stephanie's eyes until she looked away.

"And how exactly did you two meet?"

"Well, there was this girl, also named Isabella as it happened, and apparently all Isabellas get in for free, part of the bequest."

Stephanie raised an eyebrow. "Really," he insisted.

They did a circuit of the Gothic Room. Stephanie paused to admire a Giotto painting and a wood carving of the Trinity but she was struck most by the room itself. The pale light was warmed by the stained glass of the rose window and scattered by dark tile and burnished hardwood so it glowed muted and reverent.

He followed her eyes. "Dutch light," he said.

"Mmm." She nodded.

"She had several Rembrandts but they were stolen. You must have heard of it. It was quite a thing at the time. Early '90s, I think."

Stephanie cocked her head. "That does sound familiar… Cops, maybe?"

"Sort of. They posed as cops and fooled the security guards. Took a bunch of Rembrandt and Degas paintings. Never caught, never recovered."

"That's crazy," Stephanie said quietly. They stood in silence.

Alex tipped his head to the portrait of Isabella. "You remind me of her, you know." He was standing close. "She was incredibly alive, so much energy."

"Ha. That's me, all right," Stephanie said with a bitter smile.

He took her arm. "Come on, I want to show you something."

He led her back down to the ground floor and halfway around the courtyard to a room called the Spanish Cloister. One wall was dominated by a Sargent painting called *El Jaleo*. In it a flamenco dancer, right hand gathering her voluminous skirts, left delicately extended, dances across the room as a dour group of black-jacketed musicians play against the back wall. She's in profile, fairly crackling with vitality and sensuality. Alex swept his hand over the scene. "What do you see?" he said.

"I see her. I see Isabella, her spirit."

"She bought this painting just after losing her son. He was two."

"Jesus," Stephanie said. Her belly clenched.

"Her only child," Alex went on. "She never had another."

Stephanie studied the painting, all somber blacks and whites save a stroke each of red and orange, scarves on two seated women at the far right, almost off the canvas. Like the first tulips of spring.

Neither spoke and Stephanie was uncomfortably aware of his hand still resting lightly on her arm.

She stepped away and turned to face him with a mock pout. "You never answered my quite sincere Christmas invitation."

Alex laughed. "Appalling manners. I'm sure there's nowhere I'd rather be."

The lights came on suddenly. Too early, too bright. Jordan struggled to clear his head. He'd been dreaming. The door was open and a man was coming toward him. Not Dennis. Jordan sat up, pulling the thin blanket up to his chin protectively. He blinked to focus as his eyes adjusted. The man was slighter, older. He had gray hair, glasses with dark frames and JC Penney clothes—khaki slacks, some kind of wrinkle-resistant synthetic, light blue button-down tucked in, brown belt and a cream windbreaker. And his shoes, not quite sneakers, sensible, functional; they made only the slightest dull sound of compression as he crossed the room. Everything about him was ordinary, neither so very much any one thing or another. He was almost invisible, the kind of person your eye would track past on a city street without retaining any impression. He was carrying a folding metal chair. He opened it at the foot of Jordan's bed and sat down.

"Hello, Dr. Parrish," the man said. His voice, too, was neutral, steady. It conveyed benevolence without judgment like an old family doctor or a very expensive lawyer. "Call me Sam."

9

JESUS, TAKE THE WHEEL

As Jordan struggled to clear his head Sam watched him with a bemused smile, as if remembering a droll aside from an intimate gathering the night before.

Finally he said, "What do you want, Dr. Parrish?"

Jordan stared, uncomprehending, blanket pulled tight. He was cold.

"How do you see your future? What do you imagine will happen? What do you *hope* will happen?"

Jordan stuttered, "I—I w-wa…" His mouth felt dry, tongue swollen and uncooperative. He swallowed, willing saliva. "I want to go home."

"Ah, home," Sam said, nodding. "Such a romantic idea, home. But so hard to pin down? Wouldn't it be fair to say that this—" he swept his arm around the room "—is your home now?"

"I just want to go home."

Sam nodded again as if ticking an item off a list. He crossed his legs and leaned forward in his chair. "Let's refine that idea,

Jordan. When we say home we don't mean a place, do we? We mean family, and this is the crux of the problem. You *have* no family and, ergo, no home."

Jordan's face went ashen and he struggled to speak, head twisting from side to side. "What did you do?" he croaked.

"Don't worry, your wife and children are fine, better, really. It's you, Jordan. *You* are dead. Dead and buried, mourned after a fashion, but absolutely and permanently gone from their world." He leaned back and spread his hands on his lap as if he were laying out a winning straight. "Let me tell you a story.

"There was a man. He struggled, struggled with his wife and children, struggled with his job. He was unhappy. Everything he touched turned rotten. But then he met a girl—let's call her Hailey. She was young, quite young. But she admired the man, his intelligence, his suffering. They fell in love. The man would meet her at an apartment he kept."

Jordan's brow furrowed. "No..."

Sam put a finger up. "Wait. Things went on this way for some time. Then there was an accident. The man and the girl were driving. Police supposed they were coming back from a romantic getaway. The car was discovered in a lake. The bodies, though badly disfigured, were eventually identified—fingerprints, dental records, that sort of thing."

"How?" Jordan blinked furiously.

"Records can be changed," Sam mused almost to himself. "At any rate, the case was closed and the man was buried, small private ceremony, somewhat sparsely attended, I'm sorry to say. But then something rather remarkable happened. Remember I told you everything the man touched turned rotten? Well, what do you suppose happened once the man was gone?"

Jordan shook his head.

"No guesses? Well, it turns out our friend was quite well insured and the family's financial situation, which had been, I must tell you, rather bleak, took a striking turn for the better. And his company, which had been foundering, had a few successes and began to rebound rather vigorously. The man's wife paid off both the mortgages on their house and I'm told is now considering moving to a bigger one. An uncharacteristically happy ending, wouldn't you say?

"Our man turned out to be a far more capable provider in death than he had ever been in life." Sam sat back and regarded Jordan coolly.

"It's a lie."

Sam looked surprised. "Yes, I suppose it is, but a kinder, gentler one, wouldn't you say? Imagine the story without the fiction, without sweet Hailey. How would the plucky little family ever pull together and move on? And if they thought the paterfamilias was a suicide, how would that play out? No insurance. No money. Think of the guilt, the decades of therapy. What kind of man would wish that on his heirs? Only a petty and selfish one. I don't think you're that sort of man, Jordan. Am I wrong?"

"Let me go," Jordan said in a small voice, barely audible.

"Go? Where would you go? *Home?* So what? So you could ruin their lives all over again? And what about us? Your miraculous reincarnation would raise many awkward questions. We have responsibilities. I can assure you, our other clients have no ache for home. Most would be sent back to face firing squads or worse. No—" he shook his head "—there is no back. There's only forward."

Almost a whisper, "I would never tell."

Sam sighed. "What changed, Doctor?"

"What do you mean?"

"I mean, you called us. What changed between that call and when Dennis picked you up just a few hours later? Or between then and now?"

"I—I don't know," Jordan stammered. "I mean, nothing, but everything. I can't really describe it. Everything just seemed different." His mouth had gone dry again.

"Let me give you my theory, Dr. Parrish," Sam said, leaning back in his chair and steepling his fingers. "What changed was the call itself. You were desperate. You asked for help. In programs to treat addiction you often hear the phrase, 'Let go. Let God.' You've heard that before, haven't you? You hear the same thing from people who have suddenly found religion, born-agains or evangelicals. They all tell the same story. They were at rock bottom, their lives were all messed up, maybe drugs or alcoholism, maybe financial crisis or the loss of a loved one, whatever, you know the story. Then there's a moment, an epiphany, literally like Saul on the road to Damascus, a moment where they ask for help, a moment where they acknowledge their inability to solve their problems alone, a moment where they put their fates in someone else's hands."

He was warming to his subject, his hands active like small birds. "Do you remember that song 'Jesus, Take the Wheel,' Dr. Parrish? I always loved that song. Remember? She's a young mom, maybe unwed, too, I forget, but she's driving her car on the ice and it starts to skid out of control and she just throws her hands up and says, 'Jesus, take the wheel.' It gives me goose bumps." Sam's eyes glistened behind his glasses. "That was you, Jordan. When you made that call, when you acknowledged you could not carry your burden alone, that admission freed you. You no longer felt hopeless because suddenly there was hope. You no longer felt helpless because you knew help was out there. You were no longer alone."

In the other room Dennis watched the performance on the monitor with a smirk. He had to admit it. Sam was good. The man should have been a preacher.

"You can't think of this as an ending," Sam was saying. "This is a new beginning for you, Jordan. Think about it. Things will get better. We're going to move you out of here. In a while you're going to be somewhere far away, new town, new life, new you. You'll have money in the bank, nice place, no bills—

it's every guy's secret dream." He leaned in conspiratorially. "Imagine it. No one's going to know you from Adam. You're whoever you say you are. All the baggage you've carried with you from childhood, the little humiliations, the fights you ran away from, the touchdown passes you dropped, the girls you were too chicken to ask out, none of it happened. Tabula rasa. Blank slate. It takes a while to adjust but you will. Maybe there will be other women. You're a good-looking guy, maybe they'll be young. Tell me you've never had the fantasy. You'd be the first." He sat back and waited.

Jordan struggled to keep the panic out of his voice. "I'm sure that for most of the people you deal with this is the best option they have but it's not the same with me."

"And how is it with you, Dr. Parrish?" Sam asked pleasantly. His eyes had lost their glistening intensity. It seemed as if he'd lost interest in the conversation but continued to listen out of politeness.

"I have a life, a family. I can't leave them. I can't just disappear. I'm not running away from anyone or anything. You need to understand. This has been an awful misunderstanding. A moment of weakness. Just let me go. I'll go home and it will be like this all never happened."

Jordan spoke almost in a whisper. "I would never tell."

Sam stood and sat beside Jordan on the bed. He took his glasses off and turned them over in his hands as he continued, his face a foot from Jordan's. "I need you to understand and to accept that this is the way it will be, Doctor. In my business the absolute security of my clients and their secrets is everything. There are times when a man has second thoughts. I understand that. But this is not the kind of decision you can take back. Do you understand? You can't unjump out of the airplane, you can't unpull the trigger. If you ever make any attempt whatsoever to contact anyone you know, you will be killed. And so will they. And so will your family. I will be forced to assume that they know about us and that is unacceptable. Do you understand, Dr. Parrish? This is important." Jordan nodded numbly. "Good. I know it may seem a bitter pill right now, but trust me, it is for the best. The world that led you here is unchanged. Your problems weren't going anywhere. Now your family will be very well provided for. You've done the right thing, Jordan." Sam replaced his glasses. "We'll talk again," he said as he pushed to his feet, glancing pointedly at the camera above the door.

"I wouldn't," Jordan was trying to yell, but it seemed so hard to make his voice any louder.

The door opened just as Sam reached it.

"I'd never tell." A hoarse croak, voice echoing flatly, no air.

Sam slipped out between Dennis and the other man coming in. Jordan recognized him as the skinny passenger from the van the night he was taken.

Dennis carried a tray of food and his mouth was set in a hard line. Jordan struggled to disentangle himself from the blanket and stand. Dennis reached him just as he got to his feet. Jordan took the head butt just above the bridge of his nose. His vision exploded in a flash of yellow light. He heard the tray clatter against the floor and a dish shatter, pieces skidding across the floor. He fell back. He blinked against the trickle of blood running into his eye. Dennis's forearm caught him in the throat and snapped his head back hard against the wall.

"Do not fuck with me." His voice was close. Jordan thrashed his head, trying to see.

Something hit him hard in the side, knocking the wind out of him. He gasped for air as he was hit again. The pressure on his windpipe got worse. And then things seemed to tumble away. He heard a snuffling, bubbling sound. Blood in his nose. Darkness. And suddenly the pressure was gone. He fell onto one side on the bed. He saw the skinny man picking up pieces of broken crockery. The image flopped sideways as if the man were crabbing along the wall.

"Leave it, Manny." Dennis pulled his partner by the shoulder and they crossed the wall together to the door on the ceiling. It closed with a bang and the lights went out.

10

SWEET DREAMS

Alex didn't want to go. It would be awkward—it always was. But he couldn't get out of it now. His father would hold it against him for years, not that he had any real desire to see Alex, either. It was just how it worked. He picked the suit for its structured sense of impenetrability. Armor.

Dreaming. Stephanie. Hair roped in thick sun-streaked tendrils. Before Haden had been born.

So young. Her skin soft and slick in the warm seawater, legs wrapped around his waist, arms about his neck. Then the sun growing brighter and brighter, a supernova of fizzy green. The lights. Buzzing. For a moment Jordan hung on the edge between the dream and reality but then Stephanie sank away and he was awake and alone, shivering on the narrow steel bed. It occurred to him that he was almost always middream when the lights came. They were stealing even that.

He turned his head to face the camera and raised his middle

finger as he deliberately mouthed the translation. For a while nothing happened. And then the lights snapped off. Jordan held his breath, listening and waiting. Nothing. Silence and darkness. Absolute.

Most of the monitors in the observation room showed only grainy gray with sparkles of analog distortion, but on one a thermal image of Jordan's head rolled from left to right in vibrant oranges and yellows. The eyes were closed but the lids rippled as the pupils beneath darted back and forth. REM sleep.

"Why not just kill him?"

"You know why. Golden goose."

"Don't you mean 'robin'?"

"Ha, ha. We'll see."

It was their bedroom, brown walls, before the repaint. Stephanie was screaming, clutching her belly, swollen with their child. (Elizabeth. Her name was Elizabeth.) She stared past him, unrecognizing, animal in her pain. He carried her to the Subaru, Sophie and Haden, eyes wide with fright and the strangeness, clutching at his pants, threatening to trip him, pull them all down.

The hospital. Stephanie panting, raw and ragged. Iodine target for the epidural, brown like dried blood. Doctors huddled in hallways, something about the cord. Danger to the mother. Pitocin-induced birth that wasn't any birth at all. (Her name was Elizabeth.)

Jordan's face was wet in the dark and he knew he was awake and not alone. He heard movement. Close. Then Dennis's voice in his ear, hissing.

"Is this what you wanted me to see?"

Steel fingers pried open Jordan's balled fist, found the middle finger and bent it back hard. Pain, excruciating. Jordan screamed as the gracile bone snapped. His stomach lurched and he vomited in the dark. As he fainted he heard Dennis swearing.

He came to with a gasp of pain as the jagged edges of bone ground together. The finger was roughly set and taped to its neighbor.

Dennis's voice hot in his ear. "Sweet dreams, Doc."

11

CHRISTMAS EVE

The Prenns' house was straight out of Bedford Falls central casting. Standard white colonial with black shutters, and in rural Concord, when they said *colonial* they meant it. It had been originally built in 1673 for the Reverend Thomas H. Puckett, according to the prominently affixed historical landmark plaque, though Alex was certain it had been expanded a bit in the intervening centuries. The snow was a couple of days old but deep enough still that the bushes lining the walk were reduced to little humps in the general whiteness. The path had been cleared with professional efficiency and there was a large, immaculately groomed wreath with a bright red bow on the front door and candles flickering in every window.

His stepmother, Shanisse ("Like Chez Panisse," she always said when she met people), opened the door. "Alex!" She dragged out the first syllable. "You made it." She motioned him inside. "I'm so glad. Were the roads just horrible?" *She doesn't age*, he thought. Mrs. Prenn 2.0 wore a floor-length black satin dress with a high slit that proffered a decidedly unmotherly view. She flung her arms around his neck and her voice was warm in his ear. "Merry Christmas, darling. I really am glad." Alex closed his eyes and breathed in the smell of her. Just the same—the hair, the perfume, whatever it was, undertones of almond and cocoa butter. Eau-de-stripper. That epiphany had come later, in his midtwenties. No one had ever said it but it certainly seemed plausible.

Shanisse had been twenty-two to Alex's seventeen when she'd married his father. Fortunately, Alex had stayed in the shitty two-bedroom in Brookline with his mother, and had only had to grapple with the oedipal monsters every other weekend.

"Everyone, Alex is here!"

"Hey, Alex." A half note rest, then, "Merry Christmas." This in virtually perfect singsong unison from his two half siblings, Serena and Moses. They looked almost identical; both had the good fortune to favor their mother except in the eyes, which were the same pale blue as Alex's own. After this perfunctory greeting they returned their attention to Moses's phone. As he followed Shanisse into the living room Alex did the calculation in his head. Serena would have to be a junior at Vassar now and that would make Moses what? A freshman? God knew where, the same probably.

"Merry Christmas. Bet you're happy to be home for a while."

"Yeah," without looking up, heads together, laughing.

"Alex! Merry, merry. What can I get you?" said Martin Prenn as he handed his wife a flute of champagne. He wore a cream-colored linen shirt unbuttoned to the crest of his round belly. With his longish white hair and deep off-season tan he looked like a European tourist at a Caribbean singles resort. In his other hand he balanced a cloudy martini with two olives.

"You, too, Dad," Alex said, awkwardly half embracing his father, careful not to jostle the glass. "Actually, a dirty martini sounds pretty good."

Shanisse's throaty laugh was accompanied by a theatrical wink. "Doesn't it?" Alex felt his face go warm.

"Sure, I'll make another batch," Alex's father said, taking a generous swallow and fishing out an olive as he headed back toward the kitchen. Alex saw he was barefoot. The soles of his feet were tan. "Gin, right?"

"If it ain't gin, it ain't a martini," Alex recited.

"It's just cold vodka," his father finished from the hall.

Sam walked briskly around Jordan, snapping his face from every angle and chatting amiably. "You know, the thing with facial recognition is, on the one hand, it's infinitely better than we are at flipping through millions of images to find a match, but at the same time it completely lacks our ability to deal with small changes in fundamental topography." He studied Jordan's swollen nose with a professional thoughtfulness, head cocked to one side.

"So, let's say a person's eyes were too wide or closer together, or their chin were slightly fuller, or the cheekbones… Well, you and I would still think, *Man, that guy looks familiar*, but not software. On the other hand, hair, wigs, makeup, none of that stuff fazes it much anymore." He flipped through the pictures he'd taken and seemed satisfied. "You don't have to do much but some of it does need to be structural."

"What are you going to do to me?" Jordan asked in a small voice.

"Do you know what day it is, Jordan?"

Jordan shook his head.

"It's Christmas, Ebenezer. Christmas Eve actually. A night of great hope, wouldn't you say?" Sam smiled. "Why do you suppose I am so interested in your face, in its trackability? No guesses? You're going to be leaving us soon. Very soon."

"I don't understand."

"Your new life awaits, Jordan. New man, new life, new world, eh?" Jordan started to say something but Sam waved him off. "It was always going to be this way, and the time seems right. New year, new you."

"What about you, Mom?" Haden said.

"No, I'll wait. I only have a couple of things, anyway." She saw the expression and before he could say anything she went on. "Besides, it's not really about grown-ups."

"Come on. Please? It'll be more fun." He pushed a small, perfectly wrapped box into her hands.

"Okay, okay." She laughed. "You win. But you guys first. One each."

Sophie picked through the pile of presents around the tree in a distracted way, occasionally opening the card on a box to see who it was for before tossing it back on the pile. There were too many, Stephanie thought. She hadn't remembered buying so much. And there were almost as many more again in the closet waiting for the children to go to sleep. Sophie hadn't believed for years but she wasn't sure about Haden; he'd never said. She hoped he still did. Take innocence wherever you find it. So many, though. Was it compensating? Or just having money for a change?

It was so quiet. The street was empty and the snow muffled the sound of the occasional cars down the hill. Stephanie got up and turned on the radio. *The Messiah* spilled out into the dark corners and made the house feel a little less empty, a little more like Christmas.

Alex was drunk. Not sloppy or slurry drunk, just two martinis and a bottle of wine at dinner, everything-bright-and-fuzzy-at-the-edges drunk. Shanisse was hanging up a pair of enormous red stockings with Serena's and Moses's names embroidered in gold thread.

"You really won't stay? I'm sure I could find a stocking for you somewhere." The image came instantly and unbidden, her fingers undoing the clasp and slowly peeling off a sheer black stocking. Was it really in her tone or just a product of his own dormant issues?

"No, I can't. It's getting late. I should get going."

"I hear work's going well," his father said.

"Yeah, it's pretty good right now," Alex said, getting up a little unsteadily.

"About time. Good for you." Martin nodded to himself as if that settled something.

"Oh, you can't go yet," Shanisse protested, pulling him back toward the sofa. "We never see you anymore. I need stories. Are you happy? Are you terribly in love?" She wouldn't let go of his hand. She'd taken her shoes off and tucked one foot underneath like a schoolgirl. "Martin, make him stay."

Alex pulled away. "Really, I can't."

It was a perfectly clear night, diamond-strewn black velvet sky, breath billowing cold. Alex started the car and turned on the seat warmer. He texted the Russian. where r u? The heater struggled to get a toehold on the chill.

Stupid party

come over

Can't. Sorry :(

where is it? i'll come

Private, downtown

i got you a present

Can't. Tomorrow

    now

She didn't answer. He cradled the phone, waiting. Message delivered.

Okay.

And an address on Milk Street.

Stephanie couldn't sleep. Her brain wouldn't shut down. She didn't know how to do this. Any of it. It wasn't as if Jordan had ever participated much, but his just being there, occupying space, had made the geometry work; it had defined her role. She had known what to say, what to do.

Now everything felt wrong.

Sophie had opened a tiny cat charm for the bracelet she'd been adding to since she was six.

It was too young; Stephanie sensed her disappointment. Then Haden had opened what was supposed to be a small gift but it hadn't been the one she'd thought and, of course, the Xbox controller gave away tomorrow's big surprise—0 for 2. And then it had been her turn. A gift-boxed perfume from the mall. Opium. She had laughed. She hadn't meant to, she'd just been surprised; it was so improbable. She'd recovered but there were bruised feelings—more harm done. Trifecta.

Looking back, of course, it made sense, a first stab at grown-up gift giving. She could imagine them together at Macy's trying to figure out what to buy Mom now that handmade gifts from school seemed childish. Or was there a deeper message? Get it together, get on with it, get out there, get a life?

★ ★ ★

i'm here

Alex got out of the car, rubbing his shoulders vigorously against the cold. He could hear the dull thump of the party from somewhere above. It was a desolate part of downtown, all offices, deserted except for the one soiree. Must be one of the big hedge funds, Alex thought, if they were bringing in the most expensive call girls in Boston for the Christmas party.

A light came on in the lobby of the Dunham East Building and a bulky figure, backlit by the open elevator, tottered toward the door. She was wrapped in a full-length fur coat, white and gray—wolf, maybe, if such a thing were legal. Her hair spilled out in pale wisps between the collar of the coat and the bottom of the matching hat, an ushanka right out of *Doctor Zhivago*, pulled so low only the tip of her nose and a glimpse of her eyes were visible.

She took his arm. "You look like a bear." He laughed.

She shook her face clear of the coat's collar so he could see the pout. "Not nice."

"A very beautiful bear." She tried to pull her arm away but he held on. "Come on, walk with me. Not a bear, an exotic Slavic goddess, a Tolstoyan vision from the steppes."

They turned down Oliver and walked past the Langham. Except for a lone doorman out front clapping his hands together and stomping his feet to keep warm, all was quiet.

"How is your party?"

"Stupid. Horrible people, all drunk and stupid."

"You have to go back?"

She shrugged. "I think so. Big client. Vanessa would be pissed."

She held his arm a little tighter. They turned left on Franklin. The wind from the river funneled up the narrow street and whipped at Alex's ears and cheeks. He gasped. The girl wriggled her face lower into her collar.

"So delicate," she said, pulling him toward a little alley between the brick side wall of Shea's Pub and an office building with two-story black windows surrounded by marble ledges. She stepped up into one of the windows and pulled Alex after her.

"Better?" He could see the fine powder of snow blowing down Franklin but the recessed window was a perfect windbreak. She pushed him back against the glass and opened her coat to envelop them both.

"I'll keep you warm, *bednyaga*, poor baby." She lifted her face and he felt her body press against him. He brushed the hair away with his glove, revealing pale, laughing eyes.

"Tell me about this present," she said. "No, wait, let me guess. Is it something you know I will like?" Her eyebrows arched up innocently as she wriggled her arms out of the sleeves. He shivered as her hands began to roam over his body.

"It must be here somewhere." She searched his pockets.

"Ah, what's this?" Her fingers traced his zipper. "I should unwrap it now?"

Over her shoulder he saw movement down the alley. He heard a clattering, shuffling sound and a homeless man wearing a filthy red parka over a couple of other coats and a blue wool cap came pushing an old shopping cart with a giant trash bag full of empty bottles through the snow.

Alex exhaled as her hand tugged his zipper. "If it doesn't fit, I can return it?"

She leaned in and stretched up on her toes and then he was inside her. It didn't seem possible with the coats and muddled layers of clothing, like landing a jet on a tiny strip of runway halfway around the world. Every part of his body felt different from every other. His face was still numb from the cold wind but his neck was flushed. His feet felt heavy with a dull ache in the big toes. His back was tight and cold from the glass, and his thighs burned.

"It's perfect," she said. "How did you know?" She arched herself against him. The homeless man had stopped and was watching them. It was hard to tell what he knew or what he thought. His beard was wild and matted with frozen spit or snot. His eyes were dark and animal, assessing. He was almost certainly crazy, one of the deinstitutionalized thousands.

The girl buried her head in Alex's chest and her fingers clutched at the back of his shirt. Her eyelids fluttered and she made a small sound. Alex and the homeless man held each other's eyes until it was over, then the man shrugged and continued up the alley toward Franklin, one wheel spinning in lazy circles in the snow.

The girl's voice was far away. "Santa…"

12

HOME

Jordan sat at a small round table at the Taza Café in the Hamburg airport, absently stirring an espresso. He wore an opaque pair of aviators and had a small bandage taped over the bridge of his nose. The nose appeared slightly swollen still and there was fading yellow bruising. He wore a cheap brown wool suit, identifiably Eastern European in a Soviet Ostalgie sort of way. In his lap he held a ticket stub and a passport in the name of Dieter Boll whose pages he absently riffled. He had flown the Lisbon–Hamburg leg after an overnight Dulles to Lisbon via Heathrow and was pretty glazed.

"*Guten tag*, Herr Boll. May I?" the stranger said in heavily accented English as he pulled up a chair and sat down at the table. "We will change here, all right?"

As he spoke he slid an envelope into Jordan's hand and took the passport and ticket, tucking them into his folded copy of *Die Zeit*. He pushed back his chair and stood with a curt nod, saying, "Have a pleasant flight, Mr. Kramaric."

Leaving a couple of euros on the table, Jordan walked to the restroom. He locked himself in a stall and opened the envelope. Inside was a round-trip coach ticket to Hong Kong along with a well-worn Croatian passport and a credit card. The credit card and passport were in the name of Antonin Kramaric. He crumpled the envelope and threw it in the trash. He washed his hands and dabbed at his face with a wet paper towel. His nose still hurt like hell and his eyes burned. He gingerly took off the shades and studied his face in the mirror. Where the nose had been broken there was now a pronounced Roman dip. Also his eyes were now a little wider and larger and subtly sloped down at the outside, giving him a vaguely morose Slavic look. The skin was still puffy and red at the corners where the lids had been cut and sutured. Taken with the short, short hair and the scruffy facial growth, the cumulative change was substantial. If a former colleague had passed him in the airport, Jordan doubted he would have looked twice.

"What's Parrish's status?" Sam asked, brushing the rain from his jacket with a glove before folding it neatly over the back of a chair.

"So far so dull," Dennis said without looking up from the screen. "Manny put him on the Lisbon flight. All the hand-offs have been clean." He selected several files, double-checked against a list, then hit Delete. He exhaled and sat back in his chair. "I still think it's an excess of caution."

"I'm sure you're right," Sam said.

"No one's looking."

"No, I suppose not. But even so, well, it would be irresponsible to lead anyone to our doorstep. Better part of valor, right?"

"Sure." The chair creaked in protest as Dennis pushed back. "Server's clean. He was never here."

"Thank you. As you say, excessive. But I appreciate it. Going soft."

Dennis smiled. "Well, if it all plays out…"

"Big if."

"Sure. But *if*... Tuscany, maybe. Little palazzo with a garden to putter around in, maybe a vineyard."

Sam laughed drily. "Your lips to God's ear."

The woman in 19C had the longest fingernails Jordan had ever seen. She was playing a game on the touchscreen monitor at her seat. It looked like a Japanese mash-up of sudoku and Scrabble. There was a row of kanji characters in a little box at the top of the screen and the woman would select them one at a time with the curved bright purple nail of her left index finger and drag them sharply across to make words on the line below. Each time a word was complete, she'd tap a blue box with her right pinky nail and the letters would fly back to the top with a cheerful puff of animated smoke. She seemed to be doing very well. Jordan was in 20D, one row behind and across the aisle. The man in the seat next to him was sharply thin and smelled terrible. He kept falling asleep, then jerking awake every time his head lolled forward. The elderly woman in the window seat was visibly outraged and had pressed herself against the bulkhead. There was a tourist group filling the front third of the plane and a young boy directly behind Jordan's seat who took a break from kicking it just often enough to make the resumption doubly irritating.

He'd been traveling nonstop for almost two days now, over thirty hours in the air and another fifteen in airports across Europe and Asia. At every stop he had been met by someone new who had given him new tickets and documentation. A blur. He had sunk into the rhythm of flight. It felt like he was traveling in his own little bubble of space-time like the stick man in a freshman physics lecture, little chalk rocket, alarm clock.

The immigration hall at Narita was mobbed. Two or three international flights must have landed within minutes of each other. Jordan shuffled through the serpentine queue for foreign nationals. He glanced quickly at his current passport to refresh himself on the particulars. Gordon Patterson, thirty-nine. Seattle. As the line switched back around the stanchions, he filed past the same twenty or thirty faces again and then again. Most looked as tired and rumpled as he felt. He tried to remember if he'd seen any of them before the last flight. He didn't think so. Would someone be following him? Were they watching now? He had to assume yes.

And then he was next. The immigration officer waved him forward with a desultory flap of his hand. He wore white cotton disposable gloves. He thumbed open Jordan's passport with a deliberate casualness.

"Business or pleasure, Mr. Patterson?"

Right now. He could do it right now. End it, jump off the carousel. He imagined himself saying the words in hushed urgent tones: "You need to contact the American Embassy right now. I am not Gordon Patterson. My name is Jordan Parrish and I have been kidnapped. People are threatening my family. Pick up the phone, call the embassy, take me into custody." The nightmare would be over. But then what? Sam would know. He'd kill them all. Jordan believed it absolutely.

"Pleasure," he said, and the full weight of it fell on his shoulders, the impossibility of escape, the terrible senseless loss. His vision misted over as the officer's stamp thudded twice.

"Enjoy your stay in Japan."

He was met in baggage claim by a driver with the lithe build and precisely tousled mop of a young Paul Weller. The traditional black jacket was worn over a casually underbuttoned white shirt and jeans and loafers that would have looked right at home at the Bridgehampton Polo Club. He was holding a sign that said Patterson and he nodded when his eyes caught Jordan's. "Hey, Mr. Patterson, how was your flight?" When Jordan looked at him blankly he went on. "Any checked bags, sir?"

"Oh. No, I don't think so," Jordan mumbled thickly.

"Okay, sir. Follow me. Car's just outside." Taking Jordan's battered carry-on, he waded into the mass of humanity flowing like tar toward the exits.

Jordan sank into the plush gray wool-upholstered seat in the back of the Toyota Century. The car's V12 purred with understated power. The driver, who had introduced himself as Kai, drove without speaking, a small creased chauffeur's cap perched on the back of his head. Tokyo at night was a bewildering maze of narrow wet streets and sweeping thoroughfares all dazzlingly lit by the ubiquitous illuminated billboards and video screens. Times Square would be just another intersection here. That old movie *Blade Runner* captured the feeling pretty perfectly, Jordan thought, the cacophony of light as whirling, pulsing greens, reds and whites competed with one another for the eye's attention. The frenetic saturation was so complete that a simple black-and-white billboard of a grizzled Scott Glenn, in a tieless tux, hawking Suntory Whisky, held his eye like the horizon on a heaving sea. The hint of a smile playing at the corner of Glenn's mouth seemed to confirm the absurdity of Jordan's situation, just as the rheumy blue eyes acknowledged its tragedy.

The route seemed to wind and double back on itself as the driver whipped down narrow side streets and alleys that suddenly burst out into riotous intersections. Jordan couldn't tell if Kai was worried about being followed or was just showing off, but he sat back passively as the city unfolded itself through his window. A red-and-white metal tower rose up in the distance, a garishly overdressed twin of Eiffel's original in Paris. In the foreground a massive shopping complex shone in gleaming curves of steel and glass. They drove on past expensive retail stores and down narrow roads choked with people streaming in and out of bars and clubs.

Kai grinned in the rearview mirror, speaking for the first time since they had gotten in the car. "Roppongi. This is where all the gaijin come. Good time." The venom in his voice belied the wide smile in the mirror. They continued up a gradual hill and the bright neon gave way to dull cinder-block buildings with only token bits of tile work to differentiate them from all the other grim functional structures that had sprouted like mushrooms from the rubble of the Second World War.

At the end of a little cul-de-sac the car stopped in front of a plain brown structure, one of a set of conjoined triplets, with the number 47-2 painted in white on the door. Kai switched off the car and said, "Here we are, Mr. Patterson. Welcome home."

13

GAIJIN

Jordan pushed open the apartment door. The air smelled stale, like no one had been there for a while. To the left there was a narrow kitchen with a small sink, portable stove top, microwave and a rice cooker along the back wall. A half-size washer-dryer and a minifridge were tucked into an alcove opposite. Straight ahead was the living room—small black leatherette sofa, glass coffee table, tatami floor mat and a TV, no room for anything else. A sliding screen led to the bedroom with a single bed and closet. Jordan dropped his bag on the floor. The shower and toilet were off the bedroom. The toilet, a beige Toto with a tiny sink built into the top of the tank, was in a space so small you couldn't shut the door from the inside.

The bedroom window overlooked the parking lot behind the building. Jordan slid it up, then closed it quickly as a reek of rotting fish and shit wafted up from the alley. It was freezing. He began to shiver uncontrollably. He found a built-in air-conditioning and heating unit mounted on the living room wall. White plastic. All the labels were in Japanese. He pushed every possible combination of buttons and spun the two dials. The appliance came to life with a shuddering sputter of dust and a blast of frigid cold. He twisted both dials the opposite direction and pushed more random buttons, eventually managing to coax out a grudging stream of warmish air.

He grabbed the comforter off the bed and, wrapping it around himself, curled up on the couch under the heater with his feet hanging completely off one end and his arm on the floor. His eyes stung. His stomach was bloated and empty; he felt vaguely nauseated. It was the middle of the night. As tired as he was, sleep seemed hopelessly improbable. It wasn't just the jet lag, though that was bad enough. He couldn't still the relentless chatter of voices in his head, but neither could he extract any clear thought from the babble. He found the remote and turned on the TV, an ancient Sony with a CRT that hummed to life with a pinpoint of light and a static electricity sizzle. He flipped through several badly dubbed American shows before settling on a bizarre game show—or was it a talk show?—with a braying toothy host and three giggling girls in matching pigtails and schoolgirl uniforms. He turned the sound up loud enough to compete with the inner chorus, shoved his balled fists between his knees and rocked back and forth, counting down from a thousand as the couch thudded dully against the hollow wall.

The silence woke him. The television was off. Someone was there.

"Wakey, wakey, Gordo. Half eleven. Lag'll kill you if you sleep all day." Booming voice, Australian accent. Jordan opened an eye. Fuzzy shadow, a big man backlit in the doorway. His mouth was so dry.

"Come on, mate, shake it off."

Jordan forced his eyes open. His whole body felt swollen,

pumped full of extra fluid. He struggled to a sitting position and took the proffered hand. It was enormous.

"Who are you?"

"Terry Allison. Good to know ya, Gordo. I'm gonna be your new best mate." Jordan took in the thick neck, rugby build and the open, acne-scarred face framed in gray-streaked sandy curls and doubted it. "Here, try this," Terry said and tossed him a little vial. It looked like a bottle of nail polish remover. The only English on it was the one word *Cool* written in a flowing blue script.

"What is it?" Jordan asked thickly.

"Eye drops. Go on. Wake you right up." Jordan just looked at him. "Seriously," Terry said.

The guy seemed sincere and watched him expectantly. His expression had an openness, a lack of apparent guile, that made him totally unreadable. Jordan couldn't tell if he was putting it on or not. He loosened the cap and Terry smiled and nodded encouragingly.

"That's it, go on, mate." It came out "gwanmay."

He watched the drop fall between blurred, fluttering lashes. The first sensation was cool, then almost immediately it started to burn. He screwed his eye shut and grunted, rubbing at the eye with his fist. He heard Terry's booming laugh and thought of Dennis. Would they really have him pour acid in his own eyes just for the hell of it?

"Wait for it." Still laughing. The burn was fading to a stinging tingle. He blinked several times and looked around. Not blind. Everything looked brighter. Clear.

"Fucking awesome, right? Menthol or something. Wakes you up, makes 'em white, too. Gooks're nuts for the stuff. Go on, do the other one." Jordan did and held out the vial. "Nah, keep it. Got shelves of it. Got more goodies for you, too."

He tossed a white envelope on the coffee table. "Gordon P" was written on the front in a blocky childlike hand.

Jordan tore it open with puffy fingers and tipped out the contents, a wad of thousand-yen bills, an HSBC ATM card, a laminated ID and a brass key.

"PIN's first four of your name—probably want to change that. Key opens front door and the trash thing." He gestured toward the lot behind the building. "Try not to lose the ID— they're real pains in the ass about it." Jordan picked up the ID. His face, looking startled, deer in the headlights. Gordon Patterson, and the logo was *JET* in pale blue letters with a silhouette of an adult holding hands with a child wearing a backpack.

"What is this—" Jordan started to say.

"Japan Exchange and Teaching. You'll be teaching English. It's a piece of piss."

"I don't—"

"Sure you do. Come on, take a walk with me. Help you stay awake and we can get acquainted." Without waiting for a response he threw open the front door and strode out. Freezing air swirled into the stuffy room and startled Jordan to his feet. He stuffed the money, key and bank card into his pocket and, grabbing his coat from the floor, followed Terry out.

They walked fast, downhill, through a maze of small streets that suddenly opened up onto a major road with an elevated freeway running overhead. Jordan was assaulted by the bustle and reek of the city. There was a pervasive smell of dry cleaning, bleach, steam and fish that seemed to leach out of every doorway and grate. He felt like he was walking in mud while all around him cars and bicycles swerved and gyred. Terry talked as they walked.

"A lot of gaijin in Roppongi all the time—that's why we put our people here, blend right in."

"Gaijin?"

"Yeah, that's us. Sort of gook for *foreigner*. Not exactly *foreigner*, more like *outsider*, or *other*." He thought a second. "*Alien*, that's more the sense of it. Anyway, if we put you in Shibuya, you're gonna be noticed, but here you're Susan Fucking Storm." Jordan looked at him blankly. "You're invisible, mate."

They came to an intersection where three roads converged and passed under the freeway. "So here's how it goes. Think of this like purgatory. You do a year here working for JET, establish a little history, figure out who you are, who you want to be. Then you move on. On to the good stuff. It's a small life here, but it's manageable. Most clients settle right in." They joined the crush crossing diagonally to the far corner dominated by a cotton-candy-pink café called Almond with pink-and-white-striped awnings.

"When we first started out we lost a couple. We used to set 'em up nice from the get-go—you know, fancy apartment, access to all the money—and they'd go crazy—hookers, drugs, buying everything." He leaned in with a confidential whisper. "Arabs and Africans, mostly. Anyway, one fella OD'd and another got arrested and eventually sent home." He drew a finger across his throat with a wicked smile.

"Sam brought a shrink in and she had this whole spiel about rebuilding the superego from scratch or some pile of horseshit like that." The smile again. "But it works. You'll see."

He took Jordan by the elbow and steered him through a knot of people to a low wrought-iron section of fence along the curb. He raised his arm and a black taxicab appeared out of nowhere. Terry opened the door and helped Jordan in.

He spoke to the cabbie in rapid Japanese and sat back with a sigh. They drove in silence for a while. The driver wore white cotton gloves and handled the cab with brisk precision as they hurtled through roundabouts and down side streets.

"And what about you?" Terry said. "I'm told you're not exactly happy to be here. You know that's a first—most of 'em, it's us or dead in a ditch somewhere."

"That was the idea," Jordan said under his breath.

"What, dead?"

"Too chicken."

Terry nodded. "Well, you chose right. This is take two. You get to start over, do it all better. Maybe start a family."

"I have a family," Jordan muttered. His eyes were shining.

Terry covered Jordan's hand with his own; his eyes had gone hard and still. "No, mate. You don't. That's important."

Abruptly the cab pulled up at one end of a sprawling urban park. Terry paid and they got out.

"You gotta see this," he said, the moment forgotten, all hail-fellow-well-met again. "Happens every Sunday. I come whenever I can. It reminds you of where you are."

Jordan sullenly followed him up the service road ringing the park, assaulted by a din he couldn't make any sense of. There was a muted roar of machines with dissonant shrieking in the distance and, between, something that sounded as though it may have been music once. As they rounded the corner Jordan saw beyond the overhanging trees to a packed road jammed with Japanese teens in costume. There were ersatz punks with towering pink Mohawks, Elvis impersonators with slicked pompadours, kilted rockers, safety-pinned, parachute-panted '80s kids in pale face paint with weeping mascara, and then there were the bands. Every ten feet another stage was set up.

Each was powered by its own gas generator. A punk band, then three girls playing ska, then a greaser howling out "Hound Dog" over a karaoke track and four transvestites playing heavy metal. There must have been a hundred bands ringing the park. Many had little clusters of fans in front; some played with furious abandon to empty space. It was as if every cliché of Western popular culture had come out to vie for supremacy in a medieval melee.

They walked past thirty or forty stages until the crush finally thinned out to a last couple of Elvises, one white pantsuited, the other young, sneering black-leather-clad. When they had passed and conversation was finally possible, Terry said, "Another fucking planet, right? And remember, *you're* gaijin."

14

OMISOKA

Alex had bailed on Christmas but he'd insisted on New Year's Eve at his place. Just the four of them. Stephanie accepted. It would be easier. What else would they do, sit at home watching Times Square on TV or, God forbid, going down to the Charles to huddle in the cold with all the happy revelers, all the intact families and young people in love? She was surprised he wouldn't be out at some glittery party. Probably had invitations but was taking the hit out of guilt over Christmas. Mercy invite. Fine, she'd take it.

Jordan heard the front door open. He was folding. The television was set up with an Xbox and Kinect just like the one in his cell in what he now thought of as the dark time. He didn't turn around. It could only be Terry. He registered the heavy breathing, tried to guess the time. Hard to say; it seemed like it was nearly always dark outside and his internal clock was still completely scrambled. Concentration creasing his brow, he slowly brought his hands together, guiding two strands of the animated protein on the screen until the hydrogen bonds held with a satisfying click.

"They told me about your little game," Terry said in the doorway. "But I don't get it. What's the point? You play 'GTA'?"

Jordan shook his head and rotated the puzzle on the screen, chewing on his lower lip.

"Don't know what you're missing, mate. That's a proper game. Steal cars, ram the cops, bang hookers, shoot 'em after for extra points. Wicked."

Jordan nodded his head and zoomed in on one dangling chain. Terry sighed in exasperation.

"It's just a puzzle," Jordan said. "But a very beautiful one." He heard Terry unzip his coat and, a moment later, heard it hit the chair and then slide with a soft hiss to the floor. Something was set down on the kitchen counter and the cupboards were opened.

"Where are your plates? Never mind." Clattering of dishes.

"No, it's lovely," Jordan said almost to himself. Terry was opening a bag and serving something out. "Life is proteins." Jordan's voice took on a rolling meter, as if he were lecturing to a room full of freshmen. "They are literally magical microscopic machines that perform all the functions of life. The mystery is how they form. They're these long strands of amino acids chained together single file like a string of buoys that magically fold themselves into the exact right shape to work as a pump or a switch or an assembler of other machines. It seems like they should clump up in an infinite number of ways but they don't. They follow rules, some of which we understand but most of which we don't." As Jordan twisted the strand on the screen, red arrows started to flash and there was a dissonant buzzing sound. Jordan shook his head.

"We're competing with nature and she always wins. Then again, she has a big head start."

Terry strode over to the TV and hit the input button. The puzzle disappeared and the screen filled with an image of dozens of girls dressed all in red, singing a shrill Japanese pop song.

"What are you doing?" Jordan protested.

"It's Omisoka, mate. New Year's Eve," Terry said. "Over here that means toshikoshi noodles and *Kohaku Uta Gassen* on the telly." He passed Jordan a plate of soba noodles with scallions and sat down on the couch. Terry overwhelmed the sofa and there was nowhere else to sit so Jordan awkwardly sat on the floor.

"It's their Christmas, Easter and Thanksgiving in one, the big holiday. Everyone watches this shit—" he jerked his chin at the television where the girls had finished and three boys in white were coming out "—or goes out to the shrines." He shoveled a mound of glistening noodles into his mouth, lipping them in as he spoke.

"*Kohaku*'s a singing competition, kind of team *American Idol*, boys versus girls. I don't really get it but they've been doing it forever. Crazy for it."

Jordan was transfixed. A round-faced man with a porkpie hat was singing and playing a tiny stringed instrument while dancers in traditional Japanese costume high-kneed around him, hitting tiny taiko drums. Then another girl group, indistinguishable from the first. And then it seemed like the finale. Over a hundred men and women were on the stage; it looked like the climax of an opera or Broadway musical. There was a group of women in sleek gray '30s suits, a dozen men dressed like country-fair barbershop quartet singers and, behind them all, a massed choir of men and women dressed in lavender robes. An older man with a few wisps of combed-over gray hair was singing with a querulous vibrato as a young girl gazed up at him in solemn, dewy-eyed admiration. Finally they all burst into song together, bowed to thunderous applause and it was over. The image jumped to a news reporter outside a shrine. People were milling around seemingly aimlessly. There was a shaky shot of a huge bell.

Then it rang. It sounded like it was just outside. Jordan jumped. The bell rang again, a little farther away, then immediately again closer. Jordan realized bells were ringing everywhere, on TV and all over Tokyo. The bells went on and on. After several minutes Jordan looked quizzically at Terry, the last of his noodles forgotten.

"A hundred and eight. Once for each of our earthly desires, the causes of all our suffering." Terry smiled broadly. "Extra points if you can name them all."

15

ONE

Stephanie stood in the sunken living room of Alex's apartment looking out over the city. In the reflection she saw herself and the apartment behind her suspended over the city in ghost form. She found that by focusing her eyes she could make one world, the city or the apartment, more real and substantial and push the other into a tenuous limbo. She saw the long U-shaped couch behind her to the right. Sophie and Haden looked tiny on it. Each had claimed a limb of the U, and both, despite Haden's bold predictions earlier over homemade pizza and furtive sips of prosecco, were curled up sound asleep. Ryan Seacrest's cloyingly youthful face rippled in front of her, reflected in the glass as his voice rose in anticipation behind. The city sparkled, distant fireworks briefly painting the mirrored side of the Hancock Tower.

A lone set of headlights caught her attention, pulling her focus to the world outside as they wound their way up the hill across the city in Charlestown. It seemed like no one else was on the road. Late to their New Year's Eve party. Stephanie was rooting for them. *Come on, you've got time*, she thought as the lights darted forward, then stopped at another interminable and pointless red light.

The countdown had started on the TV. "Nineteen! Eighteen…" The glittering Times Square ball twinkled, its reflection suspended like a hologram over Back Bay. In the mirror world of the apartment she saw the man in the kitchen dry his hands and walk toward the woman standing motionless inches in front of her.

"Fifteen! Fourteen!"

The car was moving again, and as her eye followed it the city below came into focus and the mirage apartment faded. There was a sudden intake of breath, like a little cry from the sofa. She turned her head and watched Haden turn over and settle back into deep sleep.

"Ten! Nine!" She turned back to the window and the superimposed realities. The man was right behind the woman; he put his hands on her shoulders.

"Make a wish," Alex said. The ball was going down, yet appeared to hang motionless, shimmering in air.

"This is going to be a good year for you. You'll see." His hands gently squeezed her shoulders. "You're due." In the reflection he smiled. In Charlestown the headlights stopped and winked out. They'd made it.

"Four! Three!" The crowd in Times Square had trebled in intensity for the last ten. "One…"

Car horns started sounding from below. Did she imagine the slightest increase in pressure from his right hand and corresponding decrease from his left, Ouija board pressure, or was it her own impulse that caused her to turn around into the hard warmth of his chest and tip her head back as he kissed her? It was like falling and being held at the same time. It had been a very long time. Stephanie couldn't remember if she'd made a wish.

On the sofa, Sophie frowned and closed her eyes tight.

16

JET

The children sat in even rows, their mouths open in perfect round Os as they sang. Row, row, row your boat. Rows of Os. Jordan suppressed a smile. The primary consonant was a struggle, though certainly not reduced to the *L* of stereotype. Jordan had been nervous at first—how was he supposed to manage a room full of seven-year-olds without speaking a word of Japanese?—but it had been fine. His students had turned out to be polite, attentive and unflaggingly earnest. He told them stories—it didn't seem to matter whether or not they understood him—and he taught them songs. He remembered more songs from Haden and Sophie's childhood driving playlists and inane television shows than he would have imagined. And when that well ran dry, he pulled out the pop songs. His older class loved to sing the old Kelis song "Milkshake" at the top of their lungs. No one ever asked what it meant.

He taught three classes on Mondays, Wednesdays and Fridays and two on Tuesdays and Thursdays. Two weeks in, he was getting the hang of it.

"Merrily, merrily, merrily, merrily…" That was a tough one. "Life is but a dream."

"Very good, everybody, very good. That will do for today. I'll see you all…" He rummaged around through his papers as if he was looking for something. "When will I see you?"

"Monday!" the children answered in one voice, some giggling; it was a popular game.

"When?"

"Monday!"

"Ah, that's right. Thank you. Monday. Have a lovely weekend, everybody."

There was a muted scraping of chairs and rustling of paper as the children gathered their things.

"Thank you, Mr. Patterson."

Jordan looked down. A boy was standing just in front of Jordan's desk with his hands nervously crossed one over the other, plaid knapsack hanging off one shoulder. Like all of the students he wore a white button-down shirt with short sleeves and a black tie. The tie was loose and inexpertly knotted and the shirt was coming untucked on one side.

"Thank you, Mr. Patterson," the boy said again, slowly with some emphasis. He'd clearly practiced it. He bowed.

Jordan was at a loss. "You're very welcome…" He scanned the seating chart but couldn't place the kid in the room.

"I'm sorry, what was your name?"

The boy dipped his head again. "I am Ryuichi, Mr. Patterson. You are best English teacher." His ears flushed red. With a final bow Ryuichi backed up a couple of steps, turned and left, joining the rearguard of the general exodus.

Something was happening in Jordan's head; he felt it. His breathing was rapid and shallow.

What was it? His eyes were watering and his chest felt tight. He never thought of them as individuals, only as the group,

parts in a homogenous whole. Ryuichi. Almost the same age
as Haden.

He shoved his papers in his blue JET-issue drawstring bag and
stumbled out the door of the classroom. He bumped hard against
a woman who was coming in. He could barely see.

"*G-gomennasai,*" he stammered as he strode down the hall and
out the double doors into the frigid afternoon. It was already
nearly dark. He walked down the hill to the subway. Shinjuku
Station. Four stops to Roppongi and home. Home, that was a
fucking good one.

Haden would be taller. What would his hair be like? He had
been talking about cutting it short. Jordan rode the escalator
down into the station. It was early rush hour. He hugged the
right side as salarymen pushed by on the left. He felt their irritation at his bulky foreignness and hated them for it. As he
neared the platform he heard three rising electronic tones. The
train would be entering the station. A woman's voice, calm and
efficient, came over the intercom.

Haden. Eventually his voice would drop and he'd sprout the
wan beginnings of a mustache and start to smell. And Jordan
wouldn't be there. He pushed forward blindly toward the car. It
looked completely full, yet he knew they'd pack dozens more in
before the doors slid shut. The press was total as they funneled
into the car. Jordan's toe caught on the threshold as he crossed
the gap. He felt the white-gloved hands of the oshiya steady him
from behind. He turned his body slightly, easing into the space
as efficiently as he could. He must be in direct physical contact
with at least a dozen people, he thought, and yet utterly alone.

And Sophie. Jesus, ten! Already she was a wry, articulate little girl with opinions and humor and style, a girl who would
grow older, fall in love, get married, have a family, a life. And
he would miss it all. He let his body go, collapsing against the
bodies around him. They were packed so tight it made no difference. No one noticed that the big American with tears running

down his cheeks had lost the will or the ability to hold himself upright. There was nowhere to fall.

He got off at Roppongi and pushed through the crowd pouring out of the station. He felt like he was going to explode.

He needed to be away from people. He heard someone protest as he elbowed past but ignored them. He walked hard up the hill toward his house, head lowered, shoulders hunched awkwardly forward. His eyebrows were bunched and he hissed to himself.

"No one else's fault. You did it. Feeble fucking pussy." Traces of spit blew back in his face. He struggled with the key in the lock. Steam roiled off his head. He dropped the key. "Fuck!" Strangled, choked back.

Finally open. He slammed the door behind him, threw the bag of papers in the corner and tore off his jacket and dropped it on the floor. He was bathed in sweat. He pulled his shirt over his head and threw it at the wall. He stood there, fists clenched at his side as he scanned the tiny apartment. This was it. His life. He was shaking.

The rice cooker with its smiling elephant logo. He grabbed it and, ripping the cord from the wall, flung it across the room. It exploded against the washer-dryer. Day-old rice and shards of white plastic. This just made him angrier. He pulled the coffee maker, teakettle and dish rack to the floor in quick succession. Water and coffee sluiced together underfoot. He kicked at the kettle, sending it spinning against the cupboard.

He screamed. No words, just an inchoate howl of rage and pain. His head swung around looking for the next enemy. He grabbed a flimsy pot from the stove and hurled it at the television at the far end of the living area. It bounced off with a harmless ping. This seemed an unbearable affront. He bellowed and charged the TV, grabbing it by the corners and pulling it over. It hung up for a moment, caught on the cords from the Xbox but then its inertia shifted and it swung to the ground, just missing Jordan's leg. The curved front exploded with a bright pop followed by the tinkling of countless slivers of delicate glass. Jordan kicked at it and a sharp pain shot through his foot. He screamed again, his throat raw and burning.

He barked his shin on the coffee table. He grabbed the glass top and awkwardly flipped it toward the bedroom. It cracked into three pieces; one leaned upright against the doorjamb. Then he turned his rage onto the sofa. With a grunt and throbbing pressure in his temples he ripped the fake leather of the cushions open and tore out the white stuffing. It felt coarse and unnatural on his fingers, and where particles of it stuck to the sweaty skin of his back and chest it itched.

As he looked around, panting heavily, the front door swung open. Dennis stood in the doorway with a grim smile, surveying the wreckage.

"You," Jordan said, still holding the last eviscerated cushion in one hand.

Dennis's eyes flitted from Jordan's face to the cushion to the room beyond. He gave a small shake of his head. "Enough."

17

KIDS

Terry had a broom, which seemed woefully inadequate to the task of steering the river of water and coffee toward a similarly overmatched dustpan. He had arrived moments after Dennis and had taken charge of cleanup. Dennis sat on what was left of the ruined couch, making little piles of glass with the toe of his shoe.

"So what happened today?"

"Nothing," Jordan said. "I just can't do this."

"Nothing?" Dennis said with a raised eyebrow. Jordan couldn't look directly at him. There was something utterly primal in the fear Dennis instilled in him.

"There was a kid," he said after a minute. His eyes were cast down and his posture conveyed total submission.

"Ah." Dennis nodded.

"How did you…" Jordan started to say.

Dennis reached into his pocket. Jordan flinched, then relaxed when he saw the phone. Dennis flicked his finger over the screen, tapped a couple of times and handed it to Jordan.

The screen was divided into six panels. On each a tiny video feed played. As Jordan leaned his head closer, he saw the movement recapitulated with a half second's delay on two of the feeds. They were streams of the apartment from different perspectives. One, a flickering view of the ceiling, he realized was from the Kinect, which was lying on the floor where it had fallen when he had destroyed the TV.

"Jesus," he said.

Dennis took the phone and slipped it back into his pocket.

"I came to check on you," he said. "Word was you were good." He glanced at Terry, who gave a rueful shrug.

All the fight had drained out of Jordan. He felt cold and his skin prickled where the bits of white stuffing and specks of glass clung to it. He felt like he was supposed to say something but he just stared at the floor. The only sound was the swishing of Terry's broom.

Dennis finally put his hands on his knees and pushed himself to his feet. "Okay. Here's what's going to happen. You're going to clean this place up, and you're going to get your shit together. Monday we start you somewhere else. Got it? No more crazy. You lose it, the consequences are on you."

Jordan felt the familiar clench of fear at the word *consequences*. "Okay." Barely a whisper.

"Good," Dennis said, moving to the door. "Come on." This to Terry, who leaned the broom against the counter and followed. "See you around."

"No kids," Jordan said.

Dennis turned and looked at him. Then he nodded. "No kids."

18

:)

Alex paged quickly through the data. Six months in and the cumulative results were still barely better than random. And ROBIN was at eighty-plus percent, which meant the rest were shit. Pfizer was losing patience. He needed to lean on Chun. They needed a working model of ROBIN. His phone vibrated on the desk. Stephanie.

U there?

    yup

Need a huge favor

    k

Department meeting tonight, forgot about it. Need someone to stay w kids.

sure

Really?

absolutely

Thank you so much!! They get home a few minutes after 4. I should be back by 6:30

no problem

You're sure?

totally. don't worry. on it.

I owe u. Xx

:)

19

BEST FRIENDS

He heard them coming up the walk. Haden was talking fast
and loud, trying to explain something he'd just figured out in
"Clash of Clans." Sophie was clearly uninterested and irritated.
Alex took out his phone and flipped through his messages. He
thought it would seem more casual if he was doing something,
not just sitting there, waiting. Haden burst through the front
door.

"Mom!" he yelled, dropping his knapsack by the radiator and
heading for the kitchen.

He stopped when he saw Alex in the living room.

"Hey, Uncle Alex, what are you doing here? Where's my
mom?"

Sophie appeared behind her brother. "Is she okay?" she said,
worry creasing her brow.

"Hey, guys, Mom's fine. She had to work late and asked me
to come over so you wouldn't come home to an empty house."

"Cool," Haden said. "Hey, do you play 'Clash of Clans'?"

Sophie rolled her eyes and said, "I'm going upstairs."

"Hang on, Soph," Alex said. "Listen, you guys want to surprise your mom? I thought we could make dinner." Haden and Sophie looked at each other dubiously.

"Come on, it'll be fun. Blitz shopping, come back, throw it together. Piece of cake."

After a glance at his sister, Haden said, "Okay. What would we make?"

"Well, I thought we'd keep it simple. Spaghetti, grilled chicken paillards, a little Broccolini with garlic, maybe. How does that sound?"

Haden wrinkled his nose. "I don't know if I like garlic. But spaghetti sounds good."

"Okay, great. How about you, Soph, are you in?"

"Yeah, I guess," Sophie said.

"What's a chicken pie yard?" Haden asked.

The shopping was quick and efficient. Alex knew what he wanted and where to find it. For the kids it was completely unlike their occasional Stop & Shop outings with Jordan, who would inevitably become distracted poring over nutritional information labels and buying new cereals and exotic sauces that would languish for months in a cupboard until Stephanie threw them out.

Back at the house Alex turned on the old KLH radio in the kitchen and tuned it to WBUR. As meandering piano snaked through the kitchen he put Haden to work washing Broccolini while Sophie peeled and sliced garlic. He put a large pot of water on to boil, started a quick tomato sauce of canned San Marzanos with sautéed garlic and olive oil and pounded out the chicken breasts.

"So, how has school been?" he said.

"Okay, I guess," Haden said.

"What are they teaching you?"

"Nothing. I don't know." After a pause, "Were you and my dad really best friends in school?"

The question caught Alex by surprise. He put down the pepper mill. "Yeah, I guess we were."

"Then why are you trying to steal his family?" Sophie asked without looking up from her slicing. Haden's wide eyes jumped from his sister to Alex and back to his sister. The only sound in the room was the steady click of Sophie's knife on the cutting board and Satie's gentle piano arpeggios rolling on unperturbed.

The question hit Alex like an openhanded slap. He felt his face flush and his ears started ringing. He breathed slowly to hold down the surge of temper he felt stirring in his chest.

"Why do you say that, Soph? What do you mean?" He tried to keep his voice steady; it felt like he was about to strike a match in a gas-filled room.

"You know what I mean," she said. She stopped slicing garlic and looked up at him. She held the knife tilted up in her hand and tears had started to spill over. Her lip shook as she spoke.

"I know you like my mom and now you think you can come in here and take my dad's place but you can't. You think we're going to forget him and like you but we won't." Her voice had risen to a near shriek as she threw the knife in the sink, shattering a glass, and ran from the room crying. She pounded up the stairs and her bedroom door slammed a couple of seconds later.

Alex let out his breath and turned to Haden. "Do you feel like that's what I'm trying to do?" he said.

"I don't know. I mean, no, I guess," Haden said.

Alex squatted down and looked him in the eye. "It's not. I'm trying to help."

Haden nodded and looked down.

Alex took a moment and looked around the kitchen. "This has been a horrible, horrible year. Right?"

Haden nodded.

"You lost your dad. I lost my best friend. It's about the worst thing that could ever happen. But we're still here. We have to wake up and go to school and go to work. Life doesn't stop. Do you understand?" Haden nodded again. His eyes were still big. Alex put his hands on the boy's shoulders. "You're a great kid, Haden. I know you've been really strong for your mom, she's told me. If you're okay, I'm going to go try to talk to your sister. You can come if you want."

Alex knocked on the door, noticing the fresh chips of paint on the floor. "Sophie, can I come in?"

"Go away!" from inside, through a pillow it sounded like.

Alex sat down next to the door, his back against one wall, his feet angled against the other, knees bent in the narrow hallway. Haden sat a few feet away, watching.

There was a spot on the wall where a nail hole had been filled with spackle and painted over, and from where he sat Alex could see a difference in the finish. It looked like the walls had been done in an eggshell and the repair in a flat, but the brown of the walls looked like a custom color so that didn't seem likely. Why would they even have flat if the walls were all eggshell?

Maybe it was something about the unsanded patch that dulled the finish on the touch-up. Alex pulled himself back into the moment. "Can I tell you a story about your mom and dad?" he asked the door. When it didn't answer he went on. "I actually met your mom before your dad did. She was really cool. I know that's probably hard to imagine for you, but she was. She was so confident she just walked up to me and started talking. She was like you that way, Sophie. She wasn't afraid of anybody.

"Anyway, I introduced them and you know what? It was crazy, I swear I knew the second they met they were going to get married and have kids, the whole thing. I just knew it. And it's not like they were a couple you'd expect to be together— they were pretty different. Your dad was really shy and your mom was the kind of girl who would scare him usually, but somehow it worked. They just fit."

Alex thought a moment, then said, "You don't mind me talking about this, do you?" The door remained silent and Haden shook his head.

"When your parents moved in together they lived in this little apartment on Queensberry Street over on the other side of the Fens. It was a strange little place. The kitchen looked out over Fenway Park and whenever there was a night game the lights from the stadium blasted into the apartment and you had to close all the windows if you wanted to talk because the crowd was so loud. This was right when Genometry was starting up. Your dad was working in a lab at MIT and he was there pretty much all the time. He would even sleep there sometimes on the couch in the lounge. It was rough. Anyway, your mom came to see me one day. She was crying, really upset. They had just gotten Darwin. He was a puppy, six weeks old. He was cute. He used to trip over his own ears and then look around to see if anyone saw." Haden laughed.

"Anyway, apparently your mom had gone home for Thanksgiving and when she got back Darwin was all alone in the apartment with no food or water. He was frantic. He'd pooped and peed all over the apartment and had turned over the garbage, probably looking for food. Your dad had stayed at the lab and obviously just forgot about him. He was pretty forgetful when he was working. Your mom was really pissed. She was going to take Darwin and go back to her old place and never talk to your dad again. I told her that he was under a lot of pressure, all my fault. It took some pretty smooth talking but eventually I calmed her down. Then I moved us out of the school lab and got the place on Dunster Street so your mom could always come by if she wanted. And a year later you were born, Sophie. And really, that's why I'm your godfather. You wouldn't have happened without my help."

"Gross," Haden said, wrinkling his nose.

"I'm not telling you this so you'll think I'm so great or anything, I just want you to know how important your family is to me. I would do anything for you guys. Anything. I need you to know that." Alex struggled to his feet. The door opened slowly. Sophie stood, shoulders hunched. Her face was red and her eyes glistened.

"I'm sorry," she said, sniffling.

"It's okay," he said, holding out his hand. "Friends?"

"Friends." She took his hand and they shook formally as though agreeing to terms after a long negotiation. They heard the front door close downstairs and Haden jumped up.

"Mom!" he yelled and ran down the stairs two at a time, his hand squeaking on the banister.

"Hey, guys. How are we all?" she asked as Alex and Sophie came down the stairs.

"We're good," Alex replied, "but you're early. Dinner's not done."

"Dinner? What's going on here?" Stephanie laughed, following them into the kitchen. "Oh my God, look at all this. You guys did this?"

The children nodded. "I helped a little," Alex said as he casually picked the bits of broken glass out of the sink and dropped them in the trash.

"Really," Stephanie said, regarding her children, her eyes lingering a moment on her daughter's puffy eyes. "It all looks amazing." She turned off the flame under the pot of water. "Let's finish and eat. I'm starved. Alex, are you joining us?"

Before he could answer Sophie cut in, "He can't, Mom. He said he has to go out tonight. He was just waiting for you to get home."

Alex caught her eye over Stephanie's shoulder.

"Oh," Stephanie said, "I'm sorry. That would have been fun. Maybe next time."

"I'd love that, I really would," he said, giving her a quick hug. "I wish I could have gotten out of my thing tonight, but you know how it is." He winked at Sophie and tousled Haden's hair. "Good night, Parrish people."

Outside Alex released his breath with a sigh. He texted Vanessa. is the russian available?

She replied immediately. Da. A quelle heure?

now

20

KNOW YOURSELF

The phone was in the coffee cup on Jordan's desk to make it louder and help the bass. Old Drake song. Moody synth, stuttering syncopated kick drum, Auto-Tuned vocal.

Jordan paused the track and looked around the room at the fifteen expectant faces. They ranged from early twenties to one grandmother who must have been eighty.

He let out a breath with puffed cheeks and shook his head.

"No idea," he said. "I mean, woes are sorrows." Blank looks all round. "You know, sadness, ah, things you feel sad about." Better, some nods, murmured consultations in Japanese.

"But what is 'the six'?" Kimiko, the owner of the phone asked.

He shook his head again. "No idea but let's let it play, gather some context clues…" He emphasized the last two words. It was a running theme in the class, a couple of appreciative groans and mock eye rolls.

He played a bit more of the song.

"Ok," he said, pausing the phone. "A little background, so, you

all get that there's an element of braggadocio, of boasting or bragging, in rap culture, right? Like gangs, or cowboys..." He was
floundering. "So Drake is counting his money, in other words,
he's hugely successful and he's praying 'the real,' in other words
him and his crew, live forever and 'the fakes,' i.e. other competing rappers, get exposed, shown to be the impostors that they
are. Does that make any sense?"

The younger students, particularly the girls, hung on to his
every word but he was losing the forty and ups. It had seemed
like a great idea to have them bring in American music to open
up the idiomatic English discussion, he had pictured himself
like Robin Williams in *Good Morning, Vietnam*, winning hearts
and minds with good old American rock and roll. He hadn't
counted on how completely out of touch with contemporary
pop music he was. Or how completely dependent it was on a
shared common culture.

"I think I found it," a girl named Ayumi piped up, holding
out her phone. "'The six' is Toronto in Canada, where Drake
grew up. The phone code. It means *home*."

21

IT HAPPENED

"Sophie hates me." Alex's voice echoed from the kitchen.

"No, she doesn't. She's just having a hard time." Stephanie sighed and looked out the window at the city below. "She's angry. Half the time I feel like she hates me, too."

"No, it's different. She thinks I'm trying to take Jordan's place. She said so." Stephanie shook her head. "Do you think that?" Alex said as he stepped down into the living room, a sweat-beaded glass of straw-colored Chablis in each hand.

"Of course not. Jesus." She looked at him and started pacing, her stockinged feet etching a lazy lemniscate in the thick carpet. Their dirty plates from lunch were on the coffee table.

"What *do* you think?" he said, setting down the glasses. She was aware of his eyes on her. He came around the table. Her loops became smaller as he cut the room down. She smiled to herself and stopped with her back to the window.

"I think," she said, eyes dancing, "that you are herding me, Mr. Prenn."

He laughed. A warm, genuine laugh. She liked it. She placed her hands on his chest. It felt hard under the crisp blue shirtfront. "And I think I don't entirely mind."

He leaned in slowly and kissed her, tentatively at first. He studied her face, his own betraying nothing, then kissed her again, harder this time. Her back was pressed against the glass and she felt as though she were tipping backward. Then her eyes fluttered closed and she heard a low sound that seemed to come from deep in her chest.

After a while he pulled back to look at her again, gently brushing a wisp of hair from her face. Then he began to undress her. His hands were immaculately groomed. She tried to picture him at the manicurist and the idea seemed sweet and vulnerable somehow. He didn't say a word as he unbuttoned, unhooked and deftly peeled away, only watched her face with the same solemn concentration. When he was finished he let his eyes freely wander over her body with an expression of subdued wonder. Stephanie's skin tightened in little goose bumps and her breathing quickened. As his fingers began to delicately explore she grabbed him by a handful of shirtfront and began to fumble with the buttons.

Matthew Chun couldn't believe his eyes, so he ran the numbers again. Same result. Matthew was the lead researcher on the PEREGRINE team. He and his staff at Litton Labs were tasked with verifying and trying to duplicate the protein folding predictions from ROBIN. It was a double blind, so neither team had any interaction with the other. Genometry, with a pile of Pfizer cash, was funding both groups along with competing teams QUAIL, SWALLOW and THRUSH. Supposedly the bird theme was chosen because all the teams were pursuing strategies based on FINCH, Genometry's first big breakthrough in the neural network approach.

According to these numbers, ROBIN was averaging over

eighty percent on secondary structure prediction. That was huge, new territory. He sent a quick email. Please confirm newest ROBIN data.

Didn't want to break out the champagne too soon.

Alex was asleep; his head gently rose and fell on her belly. His features had softened, lost some of the tightness of his waking expression. He looked like a little boy, Stephanie thought.

Chun stared at his screen and refreshed the mail again. The suspense was killing him. Three months to the next CASP. Jesus.

The Critical Assessment of Protein Structure Prediction was held every two years and was basically the Super Bowl of the field. All the big players would take a shot at a mystery amino acid sequence. It would be a protein that was about to be mapped by X-ray crystallography so all the predictions could be compared to the real thing. If ROBIN was as good as it was looking, Genometry was going to blow away the field and Pfizer shares were going to go through the roof. They'd all be rich.

"Of course, being a woman, I do have questions," Stephanie said. She was on one elbow, looking down at him.

He smiled but didn't open his eyes. "How did you know I was awake?"

"You can tell. The grown-ups were back."

"Mmm," he said with a tiny nod. "Okay, shoot."

"The usual. What now?"

"Ah, now," he said. "Well, the wine's probably gone warm but I could pour those out and grab more from the fridge."

She punched him lightly on the chest. "Don't be an idiot."

He opened his eyes, blinked a couple of times and looked up at her. "It's true. It really is you. I was afraid it couldn't be," he said.

"Answers," she said with a smile.

He stretched and turned his neck with a crack and his voice

took on a more serious tone. "What happens? Nothing. Anything. Whatever you want, whenever you want. No pressure, no expectations." Her fingers traced the vein down his neck as he talked and trailed over his chest. "I get it. The last thing I want is to make your life more complicated. Mine is simple. Really simple. It's just me. So whatever you need, whatever you want, or don't want, I'm good."

"Yes, you are."

She swung her leg over and sat up, straddling him. Her hair cascaded forward as she leaned her face toward his and they didn't talk anymore.

22

M'BUTE

Abdi Samuels sat erect in the uncomfortable metal chair. The Belgravia police station was relatively quiet in that lull between the last of the night's drunken punch-ups and the commencement of the next day's parade of petty thieves and indigents. His feet were square on the floor and his meaty hands rested on his knees. Strong, thick hands. The skin was a deep ebony except for the knuckles, which were scraped an ashy gray and spotted with the occasional surprisingly vivid blots of red blood. Abdi couldn't tell if it was his own or the girl's. The solicitor was still talking but Abdi paid no attention. His body felt heavy. He had put on weight here. He was still strong but carried an extra stone of soft flesh. His face conveyed, he knew, the right sort of imperious indifference to whatever trifling details were being sorted out between his solicitor and the policeman. Then the conversation stopped and they were both looking expectantly at him.

"Mr. Samuels?" Abdi looked up. The policeman had a sour expression and the solicitor was smiling, a tight, nasty smile.

"You're free to go, sir. There's a car waiting." He leaned in with a deferential inclination that almost hinted at a bow and swept an uncalloused hand toward the exit. Abdi nodded and pushed himself to his feet. The flimsy chair grated loudly in the quiet of the station.

The solicitor held the door as Abdi eased his bulk into the back of the gray Bentley Mulsanne. He sighed as he sank into the tan calfskin seat.

"Ah, Sam." Abdi smiled.

"General," Sam said with a tight nod. His face was blank except for perhaps a note of disapproval in the corners of the mouth. "Are you uncomfortable here?"

Abdi shook his head. "No. Not at all."

"Does the climate not agree with you?"

Abdi laughed as the car pulled away from the police station. "You are angry, Sam. I make too much trouble for you."

"And what about Natalie? Adjusting?"

"Yes. She likes it very much, I think."

"These sorts of things can't happen, General. If your face gets in the press, someone *will* recognize you. People who have assumed you are dead will realize that you are not. You understand what that will mean? They will come. I won't be able to protect you."

The man who had been General Obah M'Bute closed his eyes and leaned his head back with a deep exhalation. "Yes, yes, I understand, Sam."

23

CHURCH AND STATE

It could easily become a habit, she thought. She seemed to make it to Alex's more days than not.

"I'm actually playing hooky. I had Reina cover my particle theory class."

"I was going to ask."

"Seemed a shame to waste such a lovely day teaching sophomores."

"I love that I only see you in the daytime," he said.

"You mean you hate it."

"No, I don't. I get it. Kids, school... I like it."

Stephanie pulled the comforter up self-consciously and studied his face. "I don't think I've ever actually seen you with a woman."

"What are you suggesting?" Alex smiled. "There have been a few."

"Clearly." Stephanie returned the smile. "And, of course, it's none of my business..."

"None." He laughed. "But it's okay, no big secret." He looked at her. "No judgments?"

"No judgments."

"Okay. I guess I would say I'm a practicing believer in the separation of romantic church and state."

Stephanie laughed. "I'm sorry, that may be a little too cryptic for me."

"Right. Maybe better to say I'm a sexual pragmatist." Stephanie snorted but he held up a palm. "Hold on. I know, I know. I'm getting to it." He considered the backs of his hands.

"You know, this whole dating thing is based on the idea that we're all spouse shopping, or mating-partner test-driving and that's just not where I'm at. I'm not looking. Kids, marriage, picket fences, they just aren't part of the program."

Stephanie nodded, encouraging him, face serious but eyes still twinkling.

"Sex for me is just…sex. I suppose it's a kind of barter system. I like pretty women and I'm not naive—I know I'm not exactly Brad Pitt. So if I don't want to mislead people about my intentions, and I don't, I have to offer some other kind of value. To wit, I'm a very generous date—excellent dinners, gifts, the occasional shopping spree, that sort of thing. But I'm always clear up front—no commitments, no expectations, no future. That seems to work fine with a certain type of woman, but in fairness, they're not always the type you want to bring to corporate dinners or the office party. Sends the wrong message. So, I keep it separate. Church and state."

He glanced up at her. "How am I doing? Too seedy?"

She smiled and ran her hand through his hair. "Not at all. Honest. I think a lot of men want the same thing and just lie about it."

She thought for a moment.

"I am a little fuzzy on where *this* fits in, though. I hope you're not offering to take me shopping."

"Oh God, no. This is totally different. Completely unrelated. Church and state."

"Hmm...so..."

"Don't think too much. No pressure, no expectations. I just want you to be happy."

She kissed his forehead. "Mission accomplished."

24

BREAKFAST

Kimiko and Ayumi had invited him to breakfast. "*American* breakfast," they'd said with emphasis. They had come together to see him after class and, with lots of giggling behind open hands and consultations in Japanese, formally issued their invitation. They were both in their midtwenties. Ayumi was the more confident and did the bulk of the talking. Kimiko barely looked at him and Jordan suspected she might be harboring a little teacher crush. She had long bangs and almost always covered her mouth when she spoke.

Rocket Pajamas was exactly as advertised. The menu was right out of Arnold's Drive-In from *Happy Days*. It was cheeseburgers and fries, chocolate malts, banana splits and breakfast served all day. Pancakes, waffles, hash browns, bacon or sausage, eggs any way you like. There were a couple of American tourists sitting at a booth in the back, but the rest of the diners were young well-dressed Japanese kids. The decor was entirely pink plastic and glass. The waitresses wore uniforms that looked like a cross between a vintage stewardess outfit and Jane Fonda's getup in *Barbarella*.

The hostess, her hair in two long pigtails wearing pink fluffy pajamas and huge bunny slippers, squealed and embraced Ayumi and Kimiko before leading them to a choice corner booth with a view of the whole space.

The girls both ordered the silver-dollar pancakes and Jordan risked the recommended scrambled eggs and bacon with hash browns.

Conversation was stilted and awkward, Ayumi single-handedly carrying most of it. Everyone was relieved when the waitress returned with their orders. She placed Jordan's in front of him with a little flourish.

"Wow" was all he could manage. The eggs were a muted green and smelled of smoke and the sea. The bacon looked more like fatty bologna and the hash browns were pale white and flecked with something artificially orange.

"Special for you," the waitress explained with a little smile at Kimiko, who was blushing and studying her pancakes.

"Wow," he said again. "Thank you." The waitress smiled and topped off his coffee. He had only drunk a couple of sips as it managed to be weak and bitter all at once. The creamer had given up its oils, which now swirled around the surface in a glistening slick. The girls were ignoring their tiny pancakes drowned in syrup and watching him expectantly. He took a forkful of eggs and hash browns and chewed thoughtfully without breathing through his nose and made appreciative sounds and nodded to their evident relief.

When they started to eat and confer, he carefully let a trickle of air pass through his sinuses. Fish eggs and seaweed. He ordered a side of toast and just about made it through.

25

ENTANGLEMENT

hey

    Hey

what ya doing?

    Nothing. Sitting in my office staring out the window. U?

just finishing up a call. lunch?

    Mmm…is that what we're calling it? Sorry I can't today.

no i mean actual lunch. food. sandwich, salad…

    Haha still can't.

k :(
you all right?

> Yeah.
> No, not really
> Bad morning.

sorry. how come?

> Doesn't matter.

come on.

> Ugghh. Just mad…mad at him, mad at me. I don't know, just mad.

why mad?

> Arguably cycle related.
> I'm so stupid. How could I not have known?

known what?

> Known anything! How could I have not known he was fucking that cunt? How could I have not known ghe was lying about everything. He** (duh).

how could you have? he fooled us all. he was a good liar.

> No he wasn't. That's the thing. He was terrible. I always knew. He got pale whenever he tried. And he talked too much.

or he lied well when it suited him and badly when he wanted you to see through it?

Maybe… I dont know.
You know what entanglement is?

i dont

It's a quantum thing, spooky action at a distance?

sorry. no bells

It doesnt matter

come on

Okay, basically you have pairs of particles and no matter how far apart they are if you change one of them the other one changes at the same instant, even if it's at the opposite end of the universe.

that seems impossible–speed of light…

It's a puzzle, but apparently true. Anyway, we always joked that we were entangled

meaning?

Meaning, how could he just fucking die and I not know!! Not feel it, not KNOW IT!! Not know anything!???

sorry.
steph?
u there?

Yeah.

I'm sorry.

it's okay.

No it's not. It's not fair to drag you into my shit. I just don't know who else to talk to. Pathetic.
I should go. I'll call u later.

okay.
steph, it's going to be okay.

26

GREEN FAIRY

Jordan started when the doorbell rang. It made a cheap digital chiming noise that seemed to be coming from the kitchen somewhere. This was the first time he'd ever heard it. When it rang a second time he jumped up from the couch where he'd been sitting for he didn't know how long. Minutes, hours? There was an open *International Herald* on the floor but he didn't remember reading any of it. "Just a minute." He opened the door and admitted a broadly smiling Terry Allison.

"Hey, Gordo, how ya goin'?" Terry boomed, surveying the apartment. Jordan saw his eyes rest momentarily on the menagerie of strange anthropomorphic trees and creatures folded from old newspaper and paper bags that huddled beside the new modest flat screen. He didn't ask.

"Okay, n–nothing," he stammered, waving vaguely toward the open paper. "Just catching up."

"Well, leave it," Terry said. "We're going out."

"Why?"

"You've graduated. We've got to celebrate. Come on, don't you have any decent clothes?"

Jordan looked down at his black discount-store sneakers and jeans and winced. "Not really. What do you mean graduated?"

"All in good time, my son. Patience is a virtue much to be admired." Terry strode through the tiny apartment to Jordan's bedroom and started rifling through his closet. "Fucking right you don't. Your wardrobe is shit. You really don't get out much, do ya?"

"No."

"Right, no worries. Come over to mine. We'll kit you out." Terry tossed Jordan his coat and opened the front door with a flourish.

Terry's place was just around the corner, the parking lot actually backed onto Jordan's. It wasn't very big, Jordan thought, barely bigger than his own. The decor was well-traveled frat boy, some unframed photos from exotic locales and a stunningly comprehensive collection of third-world beer bottles. Jordan obediently followed his host and allowed him to hold various garish and oversize garments up to his body while pursing his lips and shaking his head, casting the rejects aside until finally settling on a simple white button-down and a tailored black leather jacket. It was an outfit Jordan would never have chosen but, particularly considering most of the alternatives, it could have been much worse.

"Better," Terry said, surveying his handiwork. "Let's hit it. First stop, the hub of the known universe."

The hub turned out to be the Hub of Roppongi, an English pub five minutes' walk down the hill. The entrance was a couple of steps down from street level and, had Terry not guided his head under the lintel, Jordan was certain he would have knocked himself out cold.

"Terry, you sorry sack of convict semen and Aboriginal ova,"

roared a voice with a damp north London accent from somewhere behind the semicircular bar.

"Alan, you fat cunt," Terry cheerfully returned as a moun-
tainous man with disheveled black hair and riotous eyebrows
and beard emerged and embraced him warmly. "This is Gordon, new guy. Gordon, this repulsive hillock of flesh is Alan,
our proprietor."

"Good to know you, Gordon," Alan said with a wicked smile
and an enveloping handshake. "I won't hold him against you."
He disappeared behind the bar as Jordan and Terry sat down at
a dark wood table with a sticky plastic cover protecting a collection of faded Guinness coasters. Almost immediately a sour-
looking older Japanese man in a tight pink Never Mind the
Bollocks T-shirt set down two tumblers of a pale, sickly yellowish liquid and a plastic bucket of ice. Terry dropped a handful
of ice in each of their glasses and Jordan saw milky clouds roll
off the cubes and drift through the liquor.

"*Kampai,*" Terry said, raising his glass.

"Cheers," Jordan replied. "What is it?"

"Green Fairy. Bottoms up," the Australian said, emptying his
glass. No more enlightened Jordan shrugged and knocked back
his own. It tasted familiarly of licorice or anise.

"Pernod?" he said, swirling the milky residue.

"Not exactly," Terry said as he waggled his empty glass toward the bar. "Close, though." The waiter came back with a
half-empty bottle, which he slammed down on the table with
a disgusted look before walking away muttering to himself in
Japanese.

"Absinthe," Terry said, showing Jordan the label quickly before
refilling both of their glasses.

"Right," Jordan said. "Toulouse-Lautrec, crazy artists..."

"Yeah, that's the one." He took a languorous pull on his glass.
"Made a bit of a comeback, you know, craft cocktails, all that
bullshit. Alan swears this one's the only one with the histori-

cally accurate amount of wormwood and whatever other crap they put in it."

Absinthe was the only English word on the label; the rest was in a belle epoque–infused kanji that Jordan found completely un-intelligible. Terry drained his glass and Jordan tried to keep up.

"What did you mean by graduated?" he asked.

"I mean the babysitter's gone. Your mate Dennis took off this morning," Terry said with a conspiratorial smirk. "That leaves me in charge, lunatics running the asylum."

He poured two more generous shots. "It's good. It means they think you're okay, you're not going to do anything weird. It all gets easier from here on out, my friend. Long leash." Terry saw Jordan wince at the metaphor. "Look, no point trying to pretend a thing's not a thing, right? A cage is still a cage but it doesn't have to be the fucking zoo. I cut the camera in your bedroom today. A man needs *some* privacy, right?" He raised the glass. *"Kampai."*

They emptied the glasses twice more in silence. Jordan was feeling it now. It was warm but edgy. There was none of the self-pity and justification of the brown alcohols, nor the furry conviviality of vodka. He felt alive and invulnerable and something else, something that felt a little like what bag-pipes must have felt like to a Scot following William Wallace across Stirling Bridge.

Terry stood up suddenly, his chair shrieking on the floor. He stoppered the bottle and left it on the table as he headed for the door, Jordan in his wake. "Cheers, you fat cunt," he bellowed to no one.

"Good riddance, convict," echoed the bar.

27

LEXINGTON QUEEN

The air was bracing cold. It stung Jordan's cheeks as he pulled his coat tighter. The neon and fluorescence of Roppongi had a garish sparkle. Terry led him straight across the street, ignoring peevish honks from a green-and-white taxi. They walked down half a block before Terry ducked into a doorway overhung with an unmarked blue awning.

The sushi bar was not much bigger than Jordan's bedroom. There were half a dozen somber, nattily dressed men seated at the bar. They looked up when the gaijin entered, but the sushi chef greeted Terry with a familiar nod and the men went back to their conversation.

They took two available seats and almost immediately a large Asahi and two sakes appeared. Terry served Jordan, who reciprocated in the traditional ritual. The chef placed a wooden platter with six pieces of pinkish-white sashimi between them.

"You feel lucky?" Terry said.

"What do you mean?"

"Fugu, puffer fish. You ever had it?"

Jordan shook his head. "I've heard of it, though. I thought it was poisonous."

"Lethal, mate, but only if they cut it wrong."

"So, illegal?"

"Not illegal, just has to be prepared by a certified guy and there aren't too many of those."

"How many's not too many?"

"No idea, but I doubt Ochi's one of them." Terry tipped his head toward the chef, who was deftly peeling a daikon radish into long curled sheets. "But don't worry, I'm pretty sure he knows what he's doing. Did you catch the fellows at the bar?"

"Yeah," Jordan said.

"They're all chimpira, low-level yakuza. They trust him— Ochi is the best. Come on, try it before he gets pissed off."

Jordan broke apart his chopsticks and rubbed them against each other to smooth off the splinters. Terry poured a splash of shoyu in the little ceramic bowl and stirred in a lump of wasabi. "After you, mate."

Jordan picked up a slice of the glistening fish and dredged it lightly through the soy, then, with no more than a blink's hesitation, popped it in his mouth. It had an odd texture, firm and mushy at the same time. The taste was salty, yeasty soy in front with an almost tangy, delicate sweetness behind. Jordan didn't chew the fish but compressed it between his tongue and the roof of his mouth, enough to make the tender sashimi disintegrate. He smiled and looked straight into Terry's eyes as he swallowed. What did he care? He was dead already.

"Not bad," he said, taking another.

Terry laughed and said, "Slow down, sport," diving in himself.

Jordan felt exhilarated and reckless; maybe it was the risk, or maybe it was the freedom of being with the one person with whom he could be relatively honest. His lips felt a little numb and tingly. He refilled Terry's sake cup and looked at him expectantly. Terry took the cue and served him, then they both drained and served and drained again.

"I got a little graduation gift for you," Terry said as the waitress cleared the empty sake tokkuri and went off to get another. He took something that looked like a hardcover book in a pink plastic bag out of his knapsack and slid it across the bar. "Not much of a wrapping job, I'm afraid."

Jordan picked it up. Not a book; the weight was wrong and the edges were too rigid. He reached into the bag and pulled out a little netbook, a cheap Toshiba with a blue brushed-metal case. He looked at Terry, puzzled.

"Outside world, mate. It's the beginning." Jordan flipped open the screen and hit the power button. A splash screen came up with the JET logo spinning slowly on its axis. "All the teachers get one when they start. We just waited awhile on yours, you know, until we thought you were ready. It's had a little work done," he added as he saw Jordan rub at some scratches on the case. "We had to tweak the network setup a little. It will only connect to the router in your apartment and all of your activity will be logged on the server at mine. No email, please, except JET business, and needless to say no contact of any sort with anyone or anything from your previous life. Fair enough, right?"

Jordan nodded mutely. His head was a little fuzzy and he couldn't organize his emotions. It seemed like this must be a good thing but he didn't really feel much about it one way or the other. The waitress returned with more sake and two bowls of steaming miso soup. Jordan shut the netbook and pushed it across the table.

"Shall I hang on to it for the night, mate?" Terry said, sliding it back into his shoulder bag.

"Yeah, thanks," Jordan said, filling Terry's cup, relieved to be back on the emotionally surer ground of food and drink. Twenty minutes later they were back on the street. Jordan no longer felt the chill as he followed Terry through a narrow alley and down a short flight of stairs.

There was a long line at the Lexington Queen but the Japanese doorman, a pumped-up bodybuilder in a gray suit with Oakley's, acne scars and slicked-back hair nodded to Terry and opened the velvet rope to admit them.

Inside the music was booming. A repeating six-note phrase filtered up from murky rumble to angry hornet as a tight kick drum thudded relentlessly. They passed through a narrow hallway escorted by the doorman, past a throng of well-dressed club kids waiting to pay. The dance floor was a couple of steps down on the left and the bar ran along the wall to the right. The doorman led them right into the crush of dancers. The lights were spinning and pulsing in time with the music through a haze of smoke-machine fog that smelled vaguely chemical and felt cool on Jordan's face. As he stooped to push his way through the crowd, the press of bodies made him feel claustrophobic and anxious, but he realized if he stood up straight, he could see across the tops of the dancers' heads rolling and heaving around him.

The doorman led them to an elevated section in the middle of the club separated by another velvet rope that a shaved-headed bouncer opened as they approached. The VIP section was empty and surrounded on all sides by kids craning to ogle the new arrivals. A cocktail waitress in a short black skirt and stockings with pronounced seams up the back arrived just as they sat down on a low brown velvet sofa. She put two glasses down. "Whiskey," she said as if it was a question, and then she was gone.

Jordan took a sip. It was indeed whiskey, albeit not a very good one and pretty watered-down. He raised his glass to Terry and drained half of it. Talking was out of the question over the music so he leaned back and watched the dancers. After what felt like a few minutes but could have been quite a bit longer, the doorman returned with three girls. They were in their early twenties and, even by Lexington Queen standards, provocatively dressed,

Jordan thought. They arranged themselves on the only other sofa in the VIP area and carried on an animated conversation, laughing loudly and frequently glancing over at Terry and Jordan. The waitress brought them a bottle of Chivas along with glasses and a bucket of ice. Terry stood up and leaned into Jordan's ear. "Come on, mate. Nampa time. Let's meet the neighbors." Jordan finished his drink and obediently followed.

The girls spoke almost no English and Jordan's minimal Japanese had fallen victim to the music and alcohol. He sat in one of the two black leather chairs facing the sofa and watched Terry work. Jordan had seen nampa boys at the school. They always dressed flashily, sometimes rat-pack-gangster chic, sometimes garish Ed Hardy T-shirts and True Religion jeans. They usually hung out by the train station, coming on hard to every attractive girl that walked by. The whole nampa idea—they were players, pickup artists—ran completely counter to the stereotypical Asian reserve, and yet it had a certain respectability. Like drunken karaoke, it was socially accepted. Terry was a master, and a fluent gaijin to boot. He was aggressive without being threatening; he was funny, yet not without a hint of danger. Within twenty minutes he was kissing one girl while his hand worked its way up the thigh of another. The girls were laughing and the Chivas was nearly gone.

Jordan felt like the whole improbable scenario was unfolding at a remove, like a Bergman movie playing out on the back of a headrest somewhere over Omaha. He watched with a half smile playing on his face, scotch perched perilously on the edge of his armrest. Suddenly the third girl stood up and grabbed his glass. She sipped, watching him over the rim with a sly smile, then placed it on the table and held out a hand. "Miki." Must be her name, he thought. "Dance?"

Jordan shook his finger no, but she took his wrist and pulled him to the dance floor. The bouncer opened the rope and shut it behind them, his expression never wavering. Without releasing her grip on his wrist, the girl led him away from the VIP dais into the thick of the crowd. He felt foolish and awkward, aware of his height and the stupid smile he couldn't seem to turn off. The girl wore a gold dress of draping metallic fabric that left her back completely open. In the front the coverage was better, but in a way that suggested it could be brushed aside with the lightest of touches. When she stopped and turned around Jordan just stood in place, an improbable island in the tossing sea. She smiled and pressed herself against him, rocking gently in half time with her arm encircling his back. Jordan's eyes fluttered closed. The smell of her hair and skin, expensive shampoo with traces of jasmine perfume and cigarettes, flooded over him. It was dark. The music was far away. Her hand tentatively pressed on his back; he put his arm around her. They both tensed at the unexpected skin on skin. She leaned into him, her head buried in his chest as his hand, flexed wide and with only the most tenuous of contact, explored. He felt her press hard into his thigh. She lifted her face and looked up at him with dancing eyes and smiled as she pulled his head gently to her own. Jordan marveled at the perfect undented oval that was her upper lip, and as he tentatively kissed her, his hand slid down the back of her dress to find that beneath it she was wearing nothing at all.

She pulled him toward the exit. Jordan turned back and saw Terry, head and shoulders above everyone in the club. Terry smiled and shooed him out with a conspiratorial thumbs-up. Moments later, in the back of a cab, ignoring the reproving glares of the cabbie in the rearview mirror, the girl slipped out of her shoes and straddled him, kissing him hard as her bare feet wriggled against him. The taxi stopped at a brown marble-faced building with no windows on the upper floors and a confusing redundancy of entrances. The girl hurriedly pulled him in one door. They stood in a small vestibule with a machine that looked like an ATM. She took a credit card out of her purse and swiped it, then touched the screen next to a picture of a small room dominated by a king-size bed with red satin sheets and a massive reproduction of an Edo-era woodcut of what appeared to be a woman having sex with an octopus.

A plastic card key came out of the machine and the far door hissed open to reveal an elevator. They went in and up; Jordan couldn't tell how high as the elevator barely felt like it was moving. He had no sense of time. When the door opened he followed the girl into the room from the picture. She shrugged her shoulders and the dress spilled to the floor. Standing there in white heels, the dress puddled at her feet, the girl seemed much younger. The lipstick had been kissed away and she looked like an adolescent caught trying on her mother's things. She stepped toward him, reaching for his hands, but Jordan turned away and murmuring a slurred *"Gomennasai"* and stumbled out the door.

There was a taxi stand at the corner. As the cab sped through the empty city, the horizon started to glow a dull gray. He felt sick to his stomach. He smiled, a tight grim line. Street cleaners washed the sidewalks clear with orange buckets of water and straw brooms. When Jordan got out at his apartment, the sun was nearly up. The porch light seemed feeble and unnecessary. On the top step a huge beetle lay on its back, legs flailing in a lazy, almost pro forma way. Jordan kicked it off onto the little patch of grass with his toe and opened the door. Inside he pulled all the curtains and undressed. The pink plastic bag with the computer was neatly centered on his bed next to an unopened bottle of absinthe. He put them on the desk and, pulling the covers up over his eyes, curled up tight and rocked himself into a fitful sleep.

28

THE DARK WEB

Two nights later, the memory of the girl's skin teased at the periphery of his awareness. The smell of her. The image of her lips when the lipstick had been rubbed away. Jordan sat at his little table and opened the bottle. He inhaled the familiar waft of licorice and herbs and the skin on the back of his neck prickled expectantly. He poured it over ice and watched the clouds billow like cigarette smoke through the pale green. While he still didn't exactly like the taste it gave him a sense of anticipatory wellbeing with the first sip, a foreshadowing of how he knew he would feel as the green fairy worked her charms. He opened the Tor browser on the laptop. He had tried to download the more familiar Chrome but a system-level app had blocked the download. Sam didn't trust him enough to let him loose on the internet with a traceable IP. Fair enough.

He paused with the cursor blinking in the address box, wrists on either side of the touchpad, fingers in the air like a pianist about to begin. He typed the address almost unconsciously.

The internet was built on porn. Some staggering percentage of all the data flowing around the globe was dedicated to endless images, moving and still, of the same basic bits of human anatomy engaged in roughly the same small collection of familiar activities. He clicked on a thumbnail and poured a glass. Then another, and another, but even as the absinthe dulled his senses and spread through his body like a warm wave, the pornography left him cold. It didn't awake anything but a vague sense of disgust.

He closed the window and opened a fresh one. He opened a Google News page and scrolled down. Usual shit. Korea, Israel, Iran, sports and celebrity scandal, neutrino discoveries at CERN. Then his eye snagged on a little story near the end of the business section: Pfizer Stock Price Battered by Ill-Advised Acquisitions, RoDacin and Genometry.

He clicked on the link. A new tab opened with a short story in a web letter called *FiercePharma*.

RoDacin and Genometry, two CASP front-runners picked up by Pfizer in December, have failed to deliver on early promise, dragging down the parent company's share price.

That was it. There was a small picture. Jordan refilled his glass. The ice had long melted. He clicked on the picture and it opened in a separate window. A table in the foreground, men in suits and women in pricey frocks applauding. In the background, slightly out of focus, a woman was speaking at a lectern. He zoomed in. He couldn't breathe, something in his chest was hammering to get out. He couldn't feel his legs. He zoomed in more; the picture was low-res, just fuzzy pixels. As the cursor hung over his wife's blurry face, her name came up. Tagged. Dr. Stephanie Parrish. He clicked on it and it jumped him to a string of search results.

Connect with Dr. Stephanie Parrish on LinkedIn.

Follow Dr. Stephanie Parrish on Twitter.

Do you know Dr. Stephanie Parrish?

Share pictures with Dr. Stephanie Parrish on Instagram.

He clicked.

This user account is private. Log in to access or request to follow.

Without thinking Jordan typed in his old Instagram credentials. She had only posted one picture. The sun was catching coppery highlights in her hair and her mouth was turned up in the merest hint of a smile. Her eyes danced, though she was trying to look very stern. Haden had his arms wrapped around her neck and was trying to pull her down while Sophie stood just off to the side with a shy smile, watching. Hawaii. The Nelsons' place in Paia. He remembered.

Jordan gasped, realizing he had stopped breathing. His vision pointillized and his throat ached. He zoomed in and ran the arrow of the cursor delicately over her face, tracing the jawline and the arc of her neck. He hadn't thought he'd pushed on the track pad, but suddenly a graphic of a heart swooshed through the frame and the "likes" incremented from zero to one.

The phone vibrated on Stephanie's desk, jarring her out of her fugue state, staring out the window watching the powder-fine grains of snow flowing up and around in eddies created as the wind swept across the slate roofline. She glanced at it. Instagram notification. Nothing.

29

SAM I AM

What the fuck had he done? There was a loud buzzing in Jordan's ears and his face felt like he'd been shot with Novocain. Adrenaline. Breathe. They'd see he'd been on the page. They'd see he'd "liked" the picture. He hadn't meant to. Jesus, Jesus. Sam had said he'd kill them all. He couldn't. Not for this; it had been a mistake. Stupid. Stupid. He looked around the room. Struggled to clear his head. The bottle was nearly empty. Idiot. He opened his eyes as wide as he could and swallowed hard to pop his ears. Think.

He could fix it. He had to. He looked in the Tor browser history. The three last entries were all Instagram. He ticked the boxes and deleted them. Cleared the cache, restarted the browser and checked again. Gone. But the backup on Terry's computer, shit—Instagram.com/stephaniejparrish—no one was going to miss that. Stupid. So stupid. He checked the clock in the kitchen. Almost two in the morning. Terry was probably still out; he burned both ends pretty hard. Maybe it could still be fixed.

Jordan closed the front door with a firm click and ran lightly along the side of his building in the shadow of the roofline before cutting through the parking lot to Terry's. From the outside it looked just like Jordan's. There was a small window in the bathroom, over the walkway that ran along the side of the house. He wheeled a squat green trash bin underneath the window. Every sound seemed deafening; the scrape of the wheels on the gravel was going to rouse the neighborhood. Jordan carefully stepped up on the bin. The screen came out easily when he pulled but the window was locked. Fuck. There were four small panes on one side and a large pane with wires crisscrossing through it on the other. His ears strained in the darkness for the approaching sirens he knew must come. Repeating a string of whispered obscenities under his breath, Jordan wrapped his right fist in his bundled sleeve, then coughed loudly as he punched one of the small panes hard. The glass broke cleanly and he held his breath. The whole world seemed to buzz and hum but no one stirred in the houses. Gingerly he reached his hand in and found and released the window catch. It slid open easily and he was able to wriggle through.

He was headfirst, so his hands found the floor and felt around for space as he pulled his legs through. His foot caught a jar of something that crashed to the bathroom floor but didn't break. He didn't turn on the light. He thought he remembered the layout pretty well. The bathroom led into the kitchen and the living room was on the other side. Sure enough, as he felt along the wall, he saw the faint light from the living room under the door. His hand was on something smooth…glass. It wobbled as his hand brushed over it. Reflexively his hand jerked to right it. As he did, as if in a dream, he remembered the vast beer bottle collection in Terry's kitchen, bottles from every corner of the globe, tiny American minis to huge Belgian bottles, the beer equivalents of Jeroboams and Nebuchadnezzars. Then a delicate tinkling sound seemed to come from everywhere at once, ahead of him and behind, as bottles started to fall. The first few didn't break when they hit the floor but, like perfectly struck bowling pins, the subsequent bottles spread the collapse and a second later it sounded as if a bomb had gone off in a glass factory.

Bottles exploded on every side, each fresh wave louder than the one before. Jordan heard frightened Japanese voices from upstairs and next door and a dim light filled the kitchen as a neighbor's lights came on. Broken glass was everywhere, and as the last two bottles rolled around, their tightening spirals sounded louder in his ears than all the violence that had preceded them.

Then it was suddenly completely still. Jordan walked quickly to the living room, broken glass crunching underfoot. He scanned the room for the server. He tore through it all—the closets, the rooms—nothing. There was only the cheap laptop on the desk. He tapped the track pad and the screen came to life with a swirling JET logo. The cursor blinked patiently in the password field. Shit. *Think.* He had to get out of here. The server had to be on the laptop.

He snapped it shut and tucked it under his arm. Any cameras? He doubted it, didn't see any obvious ones. Fuck it. It could be a robbery, right? Totally random. He pulled out drawers as if he'd been a thief looking for cash, stuffed a chunky-looking watch into his pocket and ran.

He cut through the parking lot, pulse pounding in his neck. At his front door he struggled with the key, swearing under his breath, then the door just swung open; he hadn't locked it. He slammed the door, threw the dead bolt and looked around the stale-smelling space. It was still. He held his breath; he heard his own chest thumping dully and some muffled voices from the direction of Terry's but nothing here. He was alone. Well, not entirely. He looked up at the light over the stove. One of the cameras was in there. There was another one, he was pretty sure, in the microwave but he'd never studied it too closely. He wondered if anyone was watching; he hoped not. Dennis was gone and Terry was either out still or on his way home. He sank to a squat on the kitchen floor. He cradled his head in his hands and squeezed as hard as he could. *Think, think.* He desperately wished he were sober. They would know it had been him at Terry's. He needed to figure this out. He needed time. He needed to get out of there.

He had some cash in the desk, not enough to get far but something. He grabbed the stack of bills and shoved it into his pocket. His adrenaline level was spiking, but everything seemed to be happening so slowly. His eyes felt like the pupils had dilated all the way, like a cat's when it's about to pounce. Clothes. He pulled his school knapsack out of the closet and dumped its contents on the floor; ungraded tests and papers drifted lazily down as he grabbed a couple of clean T-shirts and pairs of socks from the dresser and stuffed them in the bag.

"Sam," he said toward the camera over the stove, "this isn't what it looks like. I'm not running. I just need a minute to clear my head. To get it straight. I know the rules. I promise. I won't do anything stupid." Well, anything else. He had to go. They'd be coming. What else did he need? Nothing, got to go. He shoved Terry's laptop in the bag. He'd figure out what to do with it.

"I can't eat fish and fat noodles three times a day. I can't eat green fucking eggs." He started to giggle, a little hysterically. "I do not like green eggs and ham, I do not like them, Sam I am."

They were coming. Time to go. He ran, leaving the front door lazily swaying on its hinges.

30

ONE LIKE

Stephanie lay in bed, too much chatter in her head to sleep. The kids. Alex. Where was it all going?

She couldn't seem to get the gears to engage. She felt like a passive observer, swept along in the momentum of life around her.

She picked up her phone to make sure the alarm was set. She needed to prep for her superstring lecture early before she woke the kids. Never enough time.

The Instagram icon, kind of a cute animated version of an old Kodak Instamatic, had a red one on it. She remembered the notification and opened it.

She clicked on the heart icon to see current activity and there it was.

Jordanparrish99 liked your picture.

Goose bumps sprang up on her arms and the back of her neck and she felt a chill run through her entire body. It reminded her of one of those silly horror movies when a ghost passes through someone. She felt her throat tighten. She clicked on the picture. Her and the kids on the beach in Hawaii. The only picture she'd ever gotten around to uploading. She and Jordan had signed up when Sophie had become an obsessive Instagrammer.

Obviously it was a mistake, either an ancient "like" that got stuck in electronic limbo and suddenly resurfaced or, more likely, a side effect of some old email address getting hacked by spammers. Still, she couldn't shake the ridiculous thought that it was somehow Jordan's ghost reaching out from the ether.

"Stupid," she whispered out loud as she logged out of the app and rechecked the alarm. She clicked off the screen and pulled the comforter up under her chin.

She didn't fall asleep until the first gray light was already glimmering sullenly around the edges of the curtains.

31

EYES WIDE OPEN

Jordan counted the money again. He had almost fifty thousand yen, around five hundred dollars. That was the maximum he'd been able to take from the ATM in a day and he was pretty sure by tomorrow the account would be closed. He was in the common area of a capsule hotel in Akihabara. There were a couple of salarymen in suits waiting to check in. Check in was at 5:00 and even if you stayed multiple days you had to check in again every day. Jordan had already put his shoes in the shoe locker and given the key to the man at the front desk. He had paid for the night in cash—four thousand yen—and been given his locker key.

Finally the man at the desk glanced up at the clock, which said just after five, and gave a curt nod to the men, ignoring Jordan completely. Jordan followed the salarymen to the elevator. He got off at the sixth floor. As the elevator door swished shut he heard the men, who had been silent the whole time he'd been there, start an animated conversation. Their laughter faded quickly away as the elevator rose.

The hallway was bathed in a soft yellowish glow. The light came from the open capsules, stacked two on either side of the narrow corridor. It was like a cross between the world's longest sleeper car and a futuristic mausoleum, more like the latter if he was honest with himself. He found his capsule toward the end of the hall on the left. It was number 637 in the upper row. He pushed the knapsack in and, slipping off the tan sandals, climbed up using the narrow black plastic steps affixed to the side of the lower compartment.

The interior was seamless white fiberglass with a thin mattress covering the floor. There was a television just inside the entrance, which caught Jordan behind his left ear as he wriggled awkwardly into the narrow space. Cursing under his breath, he worked his way in and sat up as high as he could. The capsules were clearly designed for smaller people more accustomed to limited personal space. If he lay flat, Jordan's feet hung out the entrance into the hall, and if he sat upright, his head was pressed against the ceiling. He managed to close the brown fabric curtain over the entrance and arrange himself in a semireclined slump that offered some stability and put his knees at the right angle to support the laptop. Other than the television, the only furnishing was a narrow shelf along the right side with a control panel beneath it. There were controls for the TV, radio and air conditioner and dimmers for the two lights recessed into the ceiling. The only decoration was a universal no-smoking sign, which had begun to peel away at one corner.

It was surprisingly quiet. Jordan had become inured to the constant noise of the city, but now the silence was shocking; he realized how much of a numbing assault the constant clamor and din had become. He found a setting for the vents that reduced even the muted white noise of the circulating air to a pursed whisper.

He opened Terry's laptop and the spinning JET logo came up and dissolved into the bland, infuriating password prompt. God forbid anything be easy. *Okay, Terry Allison, let's start obvious*—Terry wasn't the most complicated guy. Jordan tried every permutation of Terry's name he could come up with in four-, five- and six-letter versions, with numbers at the end. Nothing. He couldn't remember if Terry had ever talked about any family. He didn't think so and, really, couldn't picture Terry picking some little niece or nephew as his password, anyway. A lot of people used numbers— old phone numbers, important dates. Jordan had no clue where to start so he started at the beginning—0-0-0-0, 0-0-0-1, and so on.

He fell into a bit of a fugue state as he began cycling through the ten thousand four-digit possibilities. He tried to calculate how many five- and six-digit ones there were, and that was without letters. Small blessings department: at least he wasn't being locked out for too many bad guesses. When 4-4-4-4 was rejected he took a deep breath and flexed his neck, which had begun to ache and cracked loudly as he twisted it from side to side. He realized his fingers were stiff and his legs were cramping, as well. He needed to take a break. The capsule hotels were intended for sleep, not for semiupright work; for that matter the occupants were usually completely drunk and exhausted after missing the last train home at the tail end of a rousing night of karaoke or clubbing. He shut the computer and slid it under his pillow, taking the knapsack with him down to the communal baths on the second floor.

Access to the baths was through the locker room. The lockers were numbered the same as the capsules. Jordan found 637 and opened it with the key around his wrist. He took out the folded robe and pushed in the knapsack, piling his dirty clothes on top. He cinched the belt on the yukata, whose sleeves rode halfway to his elbow, and headed into the bathing area. A few early arrivals were chatting in the hot tub and one older man, who seemed stupefied with alcohol despite the relatively early hour, was sitting on a plastic stool in one of the shower stalls, head lolling on his chest as water cascaded down his creased back.

Jordan hung up his robe and eased into the scalding water of the tub. The conversation stopped and the room went silent except for the stream of water and the muffled groans of the old man in the shower. Jordan let his head lean back against the side and his eyes fluttered shut. He had been going for over thirty-six hours now. After leaving his apartment, he had ridden the subway for hours, circling the city until finally getting off at Shinjuku and mingling with the tourists. He was exhausted. The adrenaline that had kept him going was ebbing and he felt shaky. He needed to eat but didn't think he had the strength to go out. He'd grab something from one of the vending machines in the common room and call it a night. The shower turned off. Jordan looked up; the bathing area was deserted. He laughed; he'd driven them all out just by showing up. Fine, fuck 'em. He lay back and closed his eyes. The drips from the shower hit the tile in little clusters, tapping out bursts of rhythm. His eyes began to flit back and forth beneath his eyelids as he drifted away.

He was in the summerhouse in Maine, thirty years ago, rain on the kitchen roof, even though part of his mind was still here, still leaning back on the tiles of an empty hot tub in a Tokyo capsule hotel where he was hiding from men who were hunting him because he had to conceal the capital crime of looking up a picture of his own family on an abandoned Instagram page in the hinterlands of the worldwide-fucking-web. It was insane.

Suddenly he opened his eyes and sat up. The rhythm. He had seen Terry log on to his computer at school a hundred times. Not from the keyboard side, but he remembered the rhythm, *tik-a-da-tik*. Four letters, or numbers, very quick. And typed with one hand he was almost positive. The left hand. So not numbers unless it was 1-2-3-4 or something like that. Four-letter word. He laughed out loud. That sounded like Terry.

32

FUCK, SHIT, COCK...

"Fuck, shit, cock, twat, suck, bitch." No, *bitch* was five... He had been absolutely sure. It seemed so right but now the certainty was fading. "Ass1, ass2, ass3..." He stared at the keys, focusing on the left side—*q-w-e-r-t-a-s-d-f-z-x-c-v*—then he saw it. He knew it was right even before he typed it. He entered it fast with his left hand: *a-r-s-e, tik-a-da-tik*. The JET logo spun apart and he was at the desktop, a picture of Terry and five smiling JET teachers standing in front of the Hub of Roppongi. He was in.

The apartment door was unlocked so she walked in. Alex was sitting at the kitchen counter with a man Stephanie had never met. He was attractive in a doughy, bland, older sort of way, friendly face. Alex looked pale and a little tired but he smiled when Stephanie came in.

"Hello, stranger," he said, pushing back his chair. "I'm sorry.

Dr. Stephanie Parrish, this is…" The other man stood up and came around the counter with a warm smile, hand extended.

"Delighted to meet you, Dr. Parrish. Please call me Sam."

Buried alive. The dark was total. He reached his hand out and felt the sides of the casket, oddly smooth and hard. He sensed the weight of the earth above and all around the box. How did things like that happen? Weren't you supposed to make sure the guy was finished, properly DOA, before you planted him? Then he heard them, like dozens of little bellows wheezing and blowing each in their own rhythm. He reached out with his toe and found the soft woven curtain and pushed it open. A dim light illuminated the interior of his capsule. He wriggled around and stuck his head out into the hallway. The sound of the men snoring all around him was louder now.

Pairs of feet stuck out of the occasional curtain and one man was passed out on his knees with only his head in his capsule, looking for all the world as if he had just been guillotined and the executioner was waiting for the torso to fall before presenting the severed head to the howling mob.

Jordan had fallen asleep with the computer on and the battery had died. He'd have to get a charger. Akihabara was the electronics center of Tokyo, so he could grab one as soon as the stores opened. His watch said almost five in the morning. He should try to go back to sleep. His mind wouldn't stop, though. He'd excised the offending entries from the server log but he couldn't tell if the information had been backed up anywhere else.

He needed a story. Why had he run? Why had he broken into Terry's place? Why the fuck did he have the computer? He needed something plausible and soon. The longer he was off the reservation, the more dangerous it got for Stephanie and the kids. Jesus, what had he done?

Before the battery had died he'd gone through Terry's calendar. Last Friday: "D gone. Out w GP. Book M plus two.

50thou. Lex?" D, Dennis. GP, that was him. M, Miki, the girl. She was a hooker. Of course she was a hooker. It was all part of Terry's grand unified theory. Jordan was furious with himself. How fucking naive could he be, how racist, really? How else could you explain believing that this beautiful young girl was ready to fuck some middle-aged gaijin she'd just met? On Thursday there had been an entry that read "Pull GP bedroom," so it looked like Terry had been as good as his word about the camera in the bedroom, anyway. There was a lot of JET stuff—new teachers' evaluations, report deadlines. All in all, it was a surprisingly dull schedule for a guy working as a facilitator for mass murderers and mobsters trying to flout international law and maybe defraud a few insurance companies in the process.

Jordan had no memory of falling back to sleep. He was wide-awake now so he decided to check out early. It was probably good to keep moving and keep as low a profile as he could.

They could be out there, looking for him. He needed to know what else was on the laptop. He slipped out of the capsule and walked down the narrow hallway. The televisions had been left on in a few capsules and laugh tracks and muted dialogue mixed with the noises of drunken sleep. The air smelled of stale alcohol and cigarette smoke, mixed with locker room and morning breath, and underneath it all, a sour hint of vomit. Jordan breathed through his mouth until the elevator started down. He was the only one in the bathroom as he showered and changed into fresh clothes. At the front desk he traded the locker key for his shoes and walked out into the gray early morning.

Akihabara was ablaze with garish neon and massive vertical anime posters. Directly across from the hotel a shop was just opening its doors. It was on the ground floor of a building that went up twenty stories, all electronics and home theater shops. There was a massive pink-and-green banner over the entrance with kanji that Jordan didn't understand but he could see the

racks of cheap consumer gear, some unboxed and haphazardly
piled up in plastic bins. He went in and quickly found a universal power adapter with tips in every conceivable shape and size.
He paid in cash and tucked it into his knapsack before heading
west down a narrow street that threaded its way between the
fragile towers of steel and glass that leaned out over the street
like gangly mantises peering down at their scuttling prey.

Within a few blocks the sky appeared overhead as the towers
gave way to modest two-story residential buildings and then a
long wall of perfectly stacked brown sheets of slate behind which,
Jordan saw through an iron gate that punctuated the stone, slum-
bered a medieval monastery with great sweeping roofs of black
tile and immaculately tended gardens. Ahead an older man in a
rumpled black suit, with a sparse black comb-over and a briefcase swinging jerkily at his side, kept his face buried in an illus-
trated paperback and muttered aloud to himself as he hiked up
the gentle grade, completely monopolizing the sidewalk. Jordan
was forced to slow down, and after a couple of throat clearings
went completely unacknowledged, he stepped over the low iron
railing and into the street to make his way around.

The taxi came from nowhere. It rounded the corner fast and
swerved just in time. Jordan saw the driver's face seemingly frozen in a grimace, caught midexpletive, as the cab passed within
inches. He only heard the blare of the horn afterward, though
he thought it must have come before and just taken longer to
penetrate. Then everything went quiet except for the clatter of
bamboo from the monastery garden. The man was staring at
Jordan with an annoyed expression, still clutching his book. Jordan looked away, throat dry, heart thumping in his chest, and
stepped back onto the sidewalk.

He walked faster, head down, his back and shoulders beginning to ache from the constant weight of the knapsack. At the
top of the rise he walked under a bridge just as a red commuter
train burst from a tunnel below him, headed for the station at

Akihabara. The noise startled the pigeons nesting in the girders and they fluttered their wings in protest. There was a large apartment building on the right when he came out from the underpass. People were hurrying down the steps of the boxy, postwar structure. No one looked at the pale American as they hurried to the subway or the underground parking.

Jordan crossed the street. The city was waking up. The sidewalk was wide and bordered a narrow park whose trees overhung the low wall. The buildings ahead got bigger and taller as the road widened into a main boulevard with traffic coming in at each roundabout, flowing west toward Shinjuku. Ahead on the right he saw a stream of schoolkids dressed in gray uniforms heading into a tall marble-and-glass-fronted building. Beyond the school to the left he saw an enormous wheel and the edge of a roller coaster.

Jordan knew where he was now. He picked up his pace and, rounding the corner, saw the huge silver bubble of the Tokyo Dome rise up behind the Ferris wheel. There was a whole shopping complex built around the dome and foreigners flowed in and out all day.

Once inside, Jordan felt safe and unremarkable as he sat in one of the overstuffed white chairs in the Festa Café sipping on a scalding milky latte, waiting for the laptop to charge.

33

RUN

In college Jordan had taken a class on political thought to fulfill his liberal arts requirement. There had been a section on the Holocaust. Hannah Arendt's description of the banality of evil had struck him as fundamentally wrong. He'd argued heatedly with the grad student teaching the recitation. He couldn't believe that people could commit evil acts while thinking they were decent and right. It went against the ingrained New England Protestantism in him. Evil was an absolute; it was part of our nature, something to be resisted and fought at every turn. But now, poring over the minutiae of Terry Allison's life, he wasn't so sure.

Terry's in-box was a random mix of JET business, inane forwards, spam and the occasional Exit Strategy communiqué. Hidden in plain sight, Jordan supposed. Who would think to look?

The majority of the emails were so dull and the ES stuff so cryptic, even if someone did happen to stumble on his open mail, they'd think nothing of it. There was one strange thing about the ES emails; they sounded to Jordan as though they were all from Sam but the sender was different for every one—different names, different domains. Jordan figured they must be spoofing the addresses. That would explain why Terry had so much junk; any decent Bayesian spam filter would probably strip out half of his most important emails.

Patiently going through the last month's mail, Jordan found several that related to him. There was a recent conversation discussing reimbursement for the money Terry had spent on their night out. Terry implied that Jordan had slept with the girl; hard to tell if he knew better or not. Going back, Jordan found a couple of routine status reports ("All good, not very social, seems to accept things") and one interesting missive from a few days before Jordan's arrival in Tokyo. This one alerted Terry to Gordon Patterson's imminent arrival and included a link to his personal file. Without thinking, Jordan clicked on the link. A web browser opened and a screen filled with kanji came up. There was a button at the lower right and Jordan clicked on it. A new window opened saying, "DNS error—page not found," and a second later, with a swooshing sound like a loud sigh, a Skype chat window popped up from MAS799. Where are you, Gordon?

The cursor blinked expectantly in the reply window. Jordan stared at it. He was such an idiot. They knew where he was now. How long? He scanned the shoppers and tourists, expecting to see armed thugs surrounding him already. No one seemed to be paying him any attention. He typed, Who is this?

The reply was immediate. You know who it is. Stay where you are, we want to help you. Seconds later, Your family.

What about my family? he answered.

We want to help them, keep them safe. You've put them in a great deal of danger.

Leave them alone. I haven't told anyone.

It isn't safe for them, Gordon. The tone, it had that same silky menace, and the answers came so quickly.

Sam?

Sam is not here right now. But he knows we are in contact. He was very concerned about you and your family.

Leave my family out of it!

It doesn't work that way, Gordon. Stay where you are.

Suddenly he felt overwhelmingly tired. His shoulders slumped. Okay, he typed, I'm at the Tokyo Dome.

We know. Stay where you are.

MAS799 signed off. Jordan looked around. The amusement park was opening. Lines were starting to form at some of the popular rides. Jordan took a sip of his now-cold coffee. He quit Skype and came back to Terry's in-box with the dead link to his file. Last looks, he thought.

Maybe Terry had downloaded it. He searched for "Patterson." The search returned a couple of calendar hits and one email attachment. He opened it. There he was. Gordon Patterson, thirty-nine, male, Caucasian. Corporate-relo. Invol. Family: wife, two kids. High IQ. Special abilities. Referred APrenn, 6–13.

Jordan felt like he was rushing through a tunnel; his ears went dull and felt like they needed to pop. The room seemed to fall out of focus as it surged toward him from all sides. That was impossible. Alex...6–13? Years ago? It didn't make any sense. Dr. Rosen had given him the number in the darkest days after they lost Elizabeth (say her name). Only to be used in the direst need. If you knew you were going to harm yourself. A permanent solution, but better than dead.

But who had recommended Dr. Rosen?

The last years played back in his mind. Snapshots jumped unbidden into the frame. Alex shutting a laptop when Jordan came in or abruptly getting off the phone, his increasingly infrequent appearances at the Dunster Street building and one image he'd completely forgotten from almost two years ago.

Every year on April 1 Genometry had their annual Fool's Errand party. It was a tradition that had started when Alex and Jordan were still in school. It was usually a fun night of sophomoric pranks and too much alcohol. This particular party had been a good one. All the research assistants were there with their dates and friends. A couple of new investors had just come in so there was fresh money, Jordan's research had turned a promising corner, so spirits were high. Alex had actually relaxed. He'd had a few beers while helping clean up the office the afternoon of the party, then he'd done tequila shots with one of the investors, a young Korean kid from San Francisco.

Later that night Jordan had gotten into a long debate with one of the researchers about the implications of some of Ventner's work. He'd gone to refill his beer from the keg in the lab and had seen Alex with his arm draped familiarly around Stephanie's waist, deep in conversation with some VC guys from New York. There was nothing overt but something about the casualness, the ease of his posture, the possessiveness of the way he held her, cut like a razor through whatever alcohol Jordan had consumed and set off small alarms deep in the oldest part of his mind. At the same instant Alex saw him and smiled, waving him over. The moment had passed. Jordan told himself he'd imagined it but now he wondered. Alex, Stephanie, Sam…how did it all fit together?

A loud scream brought him back to the present. There was a rushing sound and more screaming. He looked out the window.

There was a steel tower one hundred and eighty feet high and twenty-four people were strapped into harnesses and hurtling down the vertical coaster's front track in free fall. He needed more time. He needed to figure this out. Something stank.

He shut the computer and grabbed the power supply, wrapped both in some dirty shirts and jammed them in the bag. He ran out of the coffee shop and toward the escalator. He got on behind a family with a stroller. Halfway down he saw a small disturbance below, at the line for one of the rides. A bulky man in a familiar tight blue windbreaker, standing a head taller than the thronged Japanese, was wading through the queue, pushing people aside while scanning the park. Jordan tried to shrink down behind the family but it was too late. Dennis's eyes met his and the recognition was instant. He yelled and tore for the up escalator.

Jordan swiveled and forced his way through the knot of people behind him. He saw Dennis pushing people aside and taking the escalator steps three at a time. His face was bright red and he was yelling into his phone. Jordan ran in the other direction, frantically scanning the concourse for somewhere to hide. The shops were nearly empty; the only crowded areas were the lines for the rides. The most crowded was for the Thunder Dolphin, the biggest coaster at the park. Jordan threaded his way into the middle of the serpentine line, mumbling apologies in his most formal and apologetic Japanese. People gave him dirty looks but no one pushed him out of the line. He stooped as low as he could and shuffled along with the group. He heard Dennis pass, feet away, twice, still barking into the phone. Finally Jordan's cohort passed into the enclosed loading area and he was able to stand without fear of being seen. He scanned the area, looking for another way out but there wasn't one. The only way out was up.

Jordan hated roller coasters. Haden had fallen in love with the Matterhorn at Disney World on a long-ago trip and Jordan had ridden it with him over and over again. Thunder Dolphin made the Matterhorn look like a backyard play set. It rose two hundred and sixty-two and a half feet into the air, all twists and loops of spidery steel like a suspension bridge that had been uprooted and splattered across downtown Tokyo in an old *Godzilla* movie. It arched over the Spa LaQua building, whipped through a hole cut in another steel building and finally shot right through the center of the great hubless Ferris wheel, the Big-O. With a resigned sigh, Jordan took a seat in a middle car, slumping as low in the seat as he could, the backpack clutched to his chest.

The train glided smoothly out into the sunshine. As unobtrusively as he could, he scanned the area but saw no sign of his pursuers. The cars made the steep ascent effortlessly, with none of the clatter and sway he remembered from Disney World. The track was narrower than the car, so when Jordan looked down over the side all he saw was the park and the dome receding at a horrible vertiginous rate. Looking out he saw all of Tokyo unfolding as the coaster rose. He could see the tall needles of Akihabara and the Mori Tower beyond and all around the skyscrapers and motorways that seemed to aimlessly sprawl in every direction.

From the top he could see to the harbor and beyond. He felt it in his stomach. The first couple of cars had crested the top and only the weight of the rest kept them from hurtling straight down. As the last car came up the rise, there was that moment of suspended gravity, of utter weightlessness, before the plunge. This was the part he hated most. Then with a sickening falling away, they were over and beginning the acceleration down. The incline seemed impossibly steep. Jordan couldn't help but press himself back into the seat with all his strength, fighting the car's seemingly inevitable need to flip slowly over and crash to the ground, killing them all. Then they were falling; his body floated away from the seat no matter how hard he tried to press it down.

His heart seemed to swell in his chest as he willed himself to give in to the momentum of the ride. It felt like the train had completely separated from the tracks in that first plunge, then with a hydraulic whoosh and a stiff shudder of rubber on steel it surged up again and into the sky, lunging over the spa building and sweeping around in a wide-banked turn where the car turned almost upside down before heading for a solid steel wall that only revealed its opening at the last possible moment. The cars streaked through the gleaming circle, then plunged to the bottom again for a pair of rapid twists that surely should have thrown the train from the rails before pressing the riders back against the seats for a straight vector right through the center of the massive Ferris wheel. Riders in the Ferris wheel were laughing and pointing at the coaster as it came. Suddenly Jordan become aware of one man on the Ferris wheel, who was staring straight at him and screaming into his phone. As the car streaked past, ten feet from the man, Jordan recognized Manny.

Shit! He had to get out before the ride was over. He'd be a sitting duck once it came in. He scanned ahead. There was no way; he'd be killed. The train finished its last swerving run and Jordan felt the braking mechanism engage. They were heading into the loading area. He pulled the knapsack out from under the restraint and realized he had enough room now to squeeze his shoulders through. The other three riders in his car looked at him in shock and some fear as he twisted free of the padded restraint. Slinging the knapsack on his back, he stood up. Twenty yards until they passed into the loading building. With a deep breath he climbed onto the back of his car and jumped to the next. The riders were yelling at him and waving him away with their hands but he paid no attention and stepped over them from seat back to seat back before jumping to the next car and then the last. He jumped off the back of the last car and onto the track as the train disappeared into the darkness. Hanging on to the track he lowered himself as far as he could, then started to make his way hand over hand to the next stanchion. Then there was a bellow from above.

"Down there!" Jordan didn't need to look. He let go and dropped the ten feet to the cement below. He tried to roll but the impact knocked the wind out of him and shuddered his shins and knees. He hobbled to the elevator bank and pressed the up and down buttons. When the first one came he pressed the button for the lower parking lot and jumped back out. He waited for the second one and took it back up to level three. Down was out; he hoped they'd assume he'd gone that way.

When he got out at three, he looked around; it seemed clear. He needed somewhere to hide. Staying as close to the wall as he could, he limped around the retail level.

From his left he heard the yell. "Manny, over there!" He saw Dennis on the up escalator, pointing straight at him, then he heard pounding feet coming from around the corner. He was trapped. He heard singing. The Wonder Drop flume ride ran through the middle of the mall and there was a blue canoe with three schoolchildren heading for the big waterfall drop-off. Manny had rounded the corner and had slowed. His mouth was set in a tight smile.

"Come on, Gordon," he said. "No more running, okay?"

Dennis had reached the top of the escalator and was closing from the other side. His face was bright red and he looked pissed. The canoe was wriggling into its slot before taking the plunge. Manny followed Jordan's eyes. His smile faded and he sped up. Jordan climbed onto the railing; his legs were shaking. The canoe paused at the top of the falls and began to slip over.

"No!" Manny yelled, breaking into a sprint. Jordan jumped. It was farther than it had looked and he was a couple of feet short. He hit hard on the back of the canoe, one foot in and one out. His knee exploded in pain where it had slammed into the hard molded plastic. The schoolchildren screamed. Jordan held on for dear life as the canoe made the three-story drop and slammed into the pool at the bottom. Jordan was knocked clear by the impact. He flapped to the edge of the shallow pool and dragged himself out. Bystanders were staring in stunned silence. His eyes met Dennis's three stories up, peering over the railing. Dennis shook his head. A hint of a smile played at the edge of his mouth for a split second, then his eyes went hard and he turned toward the escalator.

At his first step, pain shot from the knee all the way through Jordan's jaw. Limping and soaking wet, he made for the exit. The commuter train was just at the corner. If he could make it there. The crowd parted for the madman and Jordan hopped and hobbled across the plaza and down the stairs. He made it down into the train station without hearing any pursuit. He swiped his commuter pass and let himself be swept into the late rush hour herd as it funneled up to the platform. The train came quickly. It looked completely full but Jordan knew better. When the doors opened the oshiya in their black uniforms started pushing people onto the train. Some used long staffs, others their gloved hands and shoulders. It never ceased to amaze Jordan how many people they could pack into an apparently full train. He let himself go slack as the oshiya did their job. He was pressed into the car and arranging his limbs as more passengers were packed in front of him when he heard a loud grunted "Fuck" from the far end of the car. The last few riders were shoved in and the doors were starting to close.

Pitching his voice as high as he could, Jordan cried out, *"Chotto matte kudasai, chotto matte,"* and waved his hand at the oshiya at the nearest door. The guard reached in and pulled Jordan from the car as the doors shut. Already people were lining up for the next train. Water puddling at his feet, Jordan watched the train slowly glide by, picking up speed. Dennis's face was pressed to the window, sweat streaking the glass. He saw Jordan and he smiled grimly and shook his head.

34

FRIENDS

"Nice to meet you, too, Sam," Stephanie said, shaking the proffered hand. She felt like she'd met him before but she couldn't place him. Just a regular guy, kind of like a high school chemistry teacher with his sensible rims and the dated hair. He pulled out a chair for her and she sat down.

"I'm sorry, I should have called," she said to Alex. "I can come back."

"No, no," Sam said. "I was just leaving. Alex and I had our little catch-up. He's all yours. By the way, Dr. Parrish, I have to say, I knew your husband and I am so sincerely sorry for your loss. Jordan was a remarkable man."

Stephanie flushed scarlet around her neck and jaw. She looked down at the table. "Th-thank you," she stammered. There was an uncomfortable silence. She felt Sam watching her. "How did you know him?" she asked finally.

"We did some security upgrades on the Cambridge office a few years back. I remember your husband being pretty annoyed when I kicked him out of his lab." Sam smiled. "But he managed to be gracious in the end."

"Mmm." She nodded. "So, security? That's what you do, then?"

He smiled. "I know, sounds racy, doesn't it?" he said. "It's actually pretty dull, though. We put in fancy locks and alarms, sometimes cameras. Not quite Q Division."

She laughed. "And how do you know Alex?"

"I've known this young man since he was a boy. His father and I were friends a long, long time ago. I still try to check in whenever I'm in town." He smiled at Alex, who nodded and looked away. "Anyway, hate to meet and run but I've got to hit the road. Plane to catch. Always seems to be these days." He stood up, smoothing his hair over in a reflexive gesture and slipping into his overcoat.

"Say, could you do me a favor?" he said, fumbling in the coat pocket. He pulled out his phone and passed it to Stephanie with raised eyebrows. "I should bring back a picture of Alexander for the wife. She'll let me hear it if I don't."

"Of course," Stephanie said. Sam walked around the table and put an arm around Alex, smoothing his hair again. "Alex, smile," Stephanie said as she centered the image on the display. She took three shots and proclaimed the second the best.

"Thank you so much," Sam said, taking the phone. "Hey, can I get one with you, too? Wind the wife up a little? Add it to my story."

"Not even sure what that all means, but sure." Stephanie laughed.

Sam put his left arm around her shoulders and held the phone up in his right. The screen flashed once. He checked the result and smiled. "Perfect. She'll be outraged. Thank you, you're a trouper. Should I tag you?"

"Oh, I don't do all that stuff. My daughter does but I'm useless."

Sam smiled again and slipped the phone into his pocket. "Never mind, then. Probably for the best. Stay in touch, Alex," he called breezily over his shoulder as he closed the door behind him.

"He seems nice," Stephanie said when they were alone.

"Sometimes."

She looked at him. "You look tired."

Alex grimaced. "Glass houses, my friend."

She laughed. "I know. I couldn't really sleep, then early morning. Blah, blah, blah."

"Why not sleeping?"

"I don't know. All right, that's not true, of course I know. Too many plates, spinning plates… Kids, you…"

"I told you, I don't want to—"

"And you haven't, you aren't. You've been perfect. But I still have to figure out me, what I think, what I'm feeling. And then there's Jordan."

"Right." Alex nodded.

"I keep having these things, these feelings, it's stupid. It just feels so…so unresolved. I keep feeling like it would have been easier if I had seen his body."

"No, it wouldn't have been. Believe me."

"Maybe it would feel more real, more final. I feel like it would make me more clear about what I feel for you. I'm sorry. I'm just tired."

He shook his head. "No, it's okay. I get it. One day at a time." He smiled and held out his hand. "Friends?"

She took it tenderly, rubbing the ridge of his knuckles with her thumb. "Friends."

35

PLAN

He needed answers. And he needed a better plan. Twenty thousand yen gone already, thirty thou left; at this rate he'd be broke in less than a week. And that was living on a bowl of ramen a day and sleeping in capsule hotels. Jordan didn't think he would survive on the street. Not here. He didn't speak the language; he couldn't even read the signs. Dumpster diving took on a whole new risk factor when you couldn't tell if the food was spoiled or if it was supposed to smell like that. They were going to find him, that seemed inevitable. Why didn't he just turn himself in, walk into the JET office and wait? They might kill him but that was far from the worst thing that could happen. He'd made peace with the idea, at least to a point. Protecting Stephanie and the kids, that was the big thing. Were they in more or less danger with him running around loose? For now, less. At least, he hoped so.

He had spent most of the last couple of days deliberately going through every file and email on Terry's laptop. He copied all of the interesting links and addresses into a little notebook, one of those top-bound flip pads you could tuck into a back pocket. He had decided against getting a Go phone. Too risky; he was sure they'd figure out how to track him. He wouldn't let the laptop online again, either. He'd take the whole list to an internet café or the library, log on at a public computer and print out whatever he found. He was becoming a necessary Luddite; all this interconnectedness had a downside.

He had learned a little. Apparently there were two ES offices, one in Washington—he assumed that was where he had been originally taken—and one in London. The one in Washington was on Mass. Ave. on Embassy Row, and in London they had a building on Hoxton Square. The Washington office seemed to deal primarily with incoming clients and the often complex negotiations between them and the countries they had squeezed dry and were now compelled to flee. Once successfully relocated, clients dealt almost exclusively with the office in London. It seemed like most of them ended up living there; London was cosmopolitan, diverse and sophisticated, offering ample distractions for wealthy men who preferred to keep a low profile. Jordan assumed that's where he would have eventually ended up if he'd played along.

Jordan returned repeatedly to the email that had prepped Terry for his arrival. "Gordon Patterson, thirty-nine, male, Caucasian. Corporate-relo. Invol. Family: wife, two kids. High IQ. Special abilities. Referred APrenn, 6–13." He tried futilely to come up with an alternate explanation for the last detail but there wasn't one, nothing plausible, anyway. Occam's razor. When presented with multiple possibilities, go for the simplest one. It had been Alex—Alex had sold him out. If he started there, so many other little things—comments, looks, intangible feelings—began to fit into place. It seemed inconceivable that his friend would betray him but it fit the data. He'd gotten the number from Dr. Rosen, the therapist. *Alex's* therapist. As a scientist you learned to trust the method.

Pose a hypothesis, no matter how improbable, then try to tear it down.

But why? Didn't there have to be a reason? People always had reasons; they were unscientific that way, not like Nature, capital *N*, where often things just were. Then he remembered Alex with Stephanie at the party again and thought back on the history of the company, how Alex seemed to have ended up with everything. Love and money. Two of the oldest reasons in the world.

Jordan felt sick. He needed air. He was staying at the Rainbow Inn in Kabukicho. It was 1:30 in the morning but he knew the neighborhood would be jumping for hours yet. Kabukicho was Tokyo's biggest red-light district. When Jordan walked outside, the street was packed with young men in sharkskin suits and wraparound shades trying to herd the late-night postkaraoke salarymen into the string of massage parlors and hostess clubs that lined the block. Young girls in outfits that ranged from provocative to preposterous sashayed through the crowd. As Jordan pressed down the block, a man in improbable Sean John sweats with a wired earpiece yelled after him, "Hey, Captain, hold up, my girls gonna love you long time." He reached for Jordan's arm but Jordan hunched deeper into his coat and tacked into the center of the street. He walked two more blocks east, then cut into a narrow alley. The riot of neon and sex gave way to a seedy nobility that seemed transported from an earlier era.

The Golden Gai, a maze of narrow lanes and alleys on the edge of the Kabukicho district, was essentially unchanged since the 1970s. After the Second World War it had been a center of the blossoming sex trade, but in the '60s the brothels had moved out and the warren had been taken over by radicals and intellectuals who had converted the tiny rooms to nomiya, counter bars.

The alley had dim streetlamps spanning the gap between the long sheds that ran down either side. Each had been subdivided into dozens of bars. The walls were made from an impossible gumbo of building materials—brick, corrugated tin, wood, shoji screens and newspaper—all taped, glued and hammered together into a massive collage. A couple of the newer bars had signs but most had no obvious visible markings. The air was rich with cigarette smoke, cooking smells and the concerted babble of dozens of intimate conversations and heated debates, laughter and scraps of music from every country on earth.

Jordan peered through a grimy pane of glass in a red wooden door in the middle of the block and tapped lightly. The bar woman waved him down the side of the building. He squeezed through the narrow gap as she opened the side door and ushered him in. He peeled off his sneakers and put on the traditional house slippers. The mama-san greeted him warmly and gestured up the steep wooden staircase. Jordan climbed to the cramped upstairs room, which was completely filled by the two occupied chairs around a plain wooden table and another empty chair with a wine case beside it. A young Japanese man dressed all in black with a ribbed turtleneck and a tiny dot of hair on his lower lip was arguing in heavily accented English with a somewhat older, severe-looking woman who sounded Dutch or Swedish and with whom, notwithstanding her apparently grossly misguided views on contemporary animation, he seemed to be in absolute sartorial agreement.

Jordan took the last chair and nodded to the couple, who looked up for only an instant before returning to their debate. Even though he understood the words Jordan couldn't make anything of what they were saying; the language just washed over him and got entangled in the scratchy flamenco that floated up from the lower level. A dusty guitar and a faded bullfighting poster decorated the wall behind the art house gladiators and a striped serape hung over the back of Jordan's chair. The mama-san brought up a plate of just-fried soba and cold sliced omelet with a glass of ice and Jordan's bottle, a Yamazaki eighteen-year-old single malt.

He'd never have been able to justify squandering money on something like that now, but when he'd first come to Red Bar a week and a half ago, the bottle had seemed a permissible luxury. And now here it was, paid for and waiting patiently for his return. He was a little surprised the proprietress had recognized him, but then again, not many gaijin came here and the place probably couldn't hold more than ten people, upstairs and down combined.

He swirled the scotch in the glass. The ice was an aesthetic disappointment. The cubes in Japanese whiskey ads and billboards were sublime, perfectly cubical, yet rough-hewn and unique as though each had been hand chiseled from a glacier by a master craftsman. And of course they were absolutely clear while the pedestrian cubes in Jordan's glass were frosted and opaque. But the scotch was superb, less peaty and smoky than its Scottish counterparts, but mellow and complex with a warmth that radiated from his belly to the tips of his fingers.

Jordan emptied and refilled the glass before devouring the noodles and egg. He hadn't realized how hungry he was. He sipped the second glass of whiskey more patiently, sinking into the chair and letting his body relax and take in the warmth of the room. He was suddenly aware of the silence. The couple beside him had stopped speaking and were looking at him expectantly. He looked from one to the other, and the man repeated the question, "Are you American?" Without knowing why, Jordan shrugged and shook his head as if he didn't understand.

"English?" the man tried.

"Sorry," Jordan mumbled with what he hoped was a passable generic Eastern European accent and looked away. After a moment the conversation picked up again, now discussing Jordan's possible provenance and the lack of decent manners in Europe generally.

★ ★ ★

It had been during the worst of it. Dr. Rosen had asked Jordan to come alone, in addition to the twice-weekly joint sessions with Stephanie.

"I've canceled your prescription, Jordan."

"Why?"

"Because I don't think you're taking them, and honestly, that concerns me."

"Why do you think that?"

"Am I right?"

Jordan shrugged noncommittally. "What did you want to talk about?"

"Whatever you'd like."

"I mean, without Steph—why just me?"

"Because I think you are on very different paths right now. I thought it might be helpful for you to talk alone."

He nodded but didn't say anything. Finally he laughed and put his hands on his thighs to stand up. "I don't have anything."

"To say?" she asked.

"Yeah, that, too," he said, standing up.

"Jordan, wait," she said.

"Why? This is pointless. We both know that. Nothing is going to change. It's all gone."

"What's gone?"

"Come on. Everything. The marriage is over—I know you see it. They'd all be better off without me."

"Jordan, sit down." Her voice took on an edge he'd never heard before. He sat.

"Listen to me," she said. "I know where you are right now things may seem…difficult, maybe even hopeless, but you have to try and get some perspective. It *will* get better."

His voice was tight and low. "Yeah, I know that's what you people are supposed say but it's not always true. Sometimes people's lives are just fucked. Elizabeth is dead. She's not coming back. The company is dying. I'm broke. I can't even take care of my family anymore. The harder I try to fix one thing, the worse it is for the others. My kids barely know me. Stephanie blames me for all of it, and she's right. I can see the future, Dr. Rosen, and you can, too. It's shit. It's all shit."

"You know the saying, Jordan. 'Suicide is a permanent solution to what may turn out to be a temporary problem.'"

He shrugged. "Still, a solution."

Dr. Rosen tore off a small sheet of paper from the pad on her desk. She wrote something and folded it over. "Yes, but there are others. There are always others." She slowly twirled the sheet on the smooth desk. "We always have choices."

She slid the piece of paper across the desk but kept her finger on it as though she were unwilling to let it go. Finally she said, "Jordan, I have a great deal of ambivalence about this, but if you ever feel like you are absolutely committed to the idea of harming yourself and see no other way forward, please call this number first. Mind you, only as a last resort. They can help you but it will be permanent. Be sure. But if you are, remember, there is always another way."

Jordan was brought back to the present by the gentle touch of the mama-san's hand on his arm. He looked up. He was alone in the bar. They were closing. He murmured apologies and left a couple of one-hundred-yen coins on the table. The bottle was almost empty. He made it down the steep stairs without injury and passed into the night. The alley was empty except for a cat that was perched on the fence opposite, cleaning itself. Even Kabukicho was relatively still. A trio of girls in matching bob wigs—one platinum, one black and one pink—were sharing a cigarette outside one of the hostess clubs as an old man tried to sweep up around them. Back at the hotel Jordan climbed into his cubicle and pushed the laptop to the wall before curling up and falling soundly asleep.

Sometime later—he had no idea how long—he was awakened

by a familiar ding. His eyes flew open. It was the laptop's new-mail alert. How could there be mail? He had never logged on; he wasn't that stupid. He grabbed the laptop. In the upper right corner the Wi-Fi icon showed full bars and connected. His mind raced through possibilities. Terry must have stayed here and logged on and now the computer had automatically joined the familiar network. That meant he'd probably been on for hours. He command-tabbed to the mail program. One new mail. No subject. He clicked on it. The screen filled with a photograph of Dr. Stephanie Parrish, smiling broadly. A man had his arm around her and was staring straight into the camera, also smiling. The flash reflected off his horn-rimmed glasses. His gray hair was swept neatly over to one side.

36

PICS

What about pictures? The police must have pictures?

probably. but you don't want that in your head.

Yeah, but at least Id know. Id FEEL it.

entanglement?

Exactly. :)
I'm going to call the detective. I have his card somewhere.

don't do that. it was him steph. i saw him. not that you could really tell by then. but the prints, dna, medical records, dental records, they looked at everything it was him. i know it.

But I don't.

honestly i don't think the pictures will help.

They might.

can't tell anything.

I could.

37

TRUST

As Jordan stared at the picture of his wife and Sam, trying to make sense of it, a Skype chat window opened with a sigh. MAS799. You're awake. Not a question. A statement. The cursor blinked patiently in the reply field.

Jordan twisted around in his capsule. He was startled by a sudden movement, then realized it was his own grossly distorted reflection in the black TV screen whirling to meet his frightened gaze.

Where are you? he typed.

We are here.

"Do you trust me?" Alex asked.

"What do you mean?" she said.

"Do you trust me?" The girl was lying on the bed in Genometry's apartment on Marlboro Street. It was the lower floor of a mid-nineteenth-century brownstone with elegant bowed windows in the living room and a small garden off the kitchen in back. The police had done some damage to the floors and closets after Jordan's disappearance when they had traced the apartment back to him. It hadn't been repaired but Alex had had the cleaning service in that morning before texting the Bolshy to say it was hers for as long as she wanted it.

"Of course I trust you, Alex," she said. Her eyes were half-closed and her mascara was smudged. She managed to always look like she'd just woken up, he thought. Literally bedroom eyes.

"You say that," he said, "but do you mean it?" He took hold of one wrist and roughly pinned it to the bed over her head. She watched him with a bemused smile. She was naked from the waist up; her thick blond hair covered part of one breast and fanned out around her head like a Raphaelite halo. He brought her second wrist to the first and clamped one hand around them both. She was wearing a billowy white peasant skirt and discordant black cowboy boots. He ran his tongue up the side of her rib cage and her armpit, inhaling deeply. She smelled of talc with a hint of sour milk, no stubble even under her arms. When his tongue reached her tricep he bit down hard and continued into the damp crook of her elbow. She let out a breath of air but didn't cry out. When he looked up her eyes were dancing. She knew this game.

"Do you trust me?" He was still completely dressed. His blue-and-white oxford was untucked over new jeans.

"I trust you."

He released one wrist and pulled her to the top of the bed. He reached back under the mattress and pulled out a black leather cuff with fleece lining and a metal buckle. Her eyes widened almost imperceptibly but she didn't look away. She opened her hand and watched him secure the strap. She was breathing deeply and slowly. She reached her free hand to his chest but he knocked it aside and walked around to the other side of the bed. She extended her arm as he prized out the other cuff. Her eyes assented as he tightened the strap and tucked the end under the roller buckle.

"Do you trust me?" he said.

"I trust you."

He went to the foot of the bed and pulled off the boots. He put them side by side in the closet, white socks hanging out. Her toes tasted briny, like olives, and she clenched them in his mouth but didn't pull away. He pulled the skirt off by the hem. She wore nothing underneath. She was tidy, nearly hairless. Recently waxed, he thought. He could see, too, that she was aroused. He ran the backs of his fingertips up the front of her thighs. Her eyes closed and she arched her back slightly, pushing herself onto his hand as it reached the top but he pulled back and stepped away.

She pouted and let out a little whimper. Playful. He crossed to the far closet and came out with a black duffel bag.

"Do you trust me?"

She nodded, her hips twisting, arms splayed over her head, eyes fixed on him. He put the bag down on the floor and she heard a heavy zipper, then he stood up with what looked like a stainless-steel curtain rod with leather cuffs for finials. He cuffed one ankle and again looked to her for permission before attaching the other. She blinked her assent. He tightened the second cuff, then pressed a small spring-loaded catch on the rod and spread it, forcing her legs farther and farther apart until, satisfied with the geometry, he released the catch with a solid click. He grabbed the bar and tugged down, stretching her arms and pulling on her shoulders. She gave a guttural groan. He smiled and crawled beside her on all fours and tasted, smelled and bit his way around her body. She twisted her head to kiss him but he slapped her hard, leaving an angry red mark on her cheek. She didn't turn away but her eyes took on a stony hardness and her lip tensed.

"Do you trust me?"

"I trust you." Her voice was thick and her breathing quicker and shallow. Alex took a dull metal briefcase out of the duffel and opened it on the bed. She couldn't see what was inside; the lid of the case blocked her view. He studied the contents for a moment before making his selection. She heard something slide, then click into place. Alex took the object from the case with him and plugged it in next to the bed before laying it gently on the floor. He crossed to the window and pulled the heavy drapes. Then he hit the light switch and the room became totally dark. She heard his steps as he crossed the room, brisk and sure.

There was a dull click and an almost-neon purple glow illuminated the side of the bed. She turned her head. She saw his face, still impassive, lit by the glow coming off the mushroom-shaped tip of the object Alex held in his hand. It looked like a big brown electric toothbrush except the brush part was glass, glowing violet and flared at the top. It made a low surly buzzing sound, like an old record player before the music starts. He moved it closer to her body and she heard the buzzing change as it got closer. Another hum came on top of the first and rose in pitch as it neared her skin. As he held it just over her breast all the tiny hairs stood straight up. She felt a tingle on her skin. Then he lowered the wand and a spark jumped from the tip to her skin. She cried out and looked at him with fear for the first time. His eyes were steady and he allowed a trace of a smile. She kept her eyes on his as he played the wand around her nipple. The little sparks were continuous now and not so much painful as intensely effervescent. "Champagne," she said, her eyes swimming shut as he traced his way down her stomach.

She smelled ozone as if a lightning storm had just passed. Alex wrapped his hand around the glowing end of the wand. She thought he'd be shocked but he wasn't. He adjusted something on the handle and the humming got higher in pitch as he reached his left index finger to her lips. She raised her head to kiss it but when her lips got close a spark arced from his finger and shocked her hard.

Whatever part of his body came near hers brought the current now. The tips of his fingers snapped and burned her; his tongue gave a softer, tingling sensation except when it brushed against her sex with an overpowering jolt as painful as it was pleasurable. He constantly adjusted the intensity of the instrument, raising the intensity gradually until she cried out, then backing it off to a tingling tease before building up again. She lost track of the time, yearning for and dreading each new touch.

He had his mouth on her, gradually raising the voltage. Her fingers convulsively flexed as her knees shook, fighting the restraints. It hurt. She was sobbing, words in Polish he couldn't understand. The pitch of the machine grew higher and more insistent. Her sobs came in a constant panting rhythm. She smelled ozone and sweat bitter with fear. Suddenly he pulled away. She hung on the precipice, her eyes pleading with his. He went to the case and took out a large silo-shaped dildo of black rubber with gleaming metal contacts at the head and along the base, and as he attached it to the power supply, he said gently, "Do you trust me?"

Her fingers still clutching, eyes closed, tears trickling down her mascara-streaked face, she managed to say, in no more than a whisper with a voice cracking and dry, "I trust you."

38

STRANGE ACTIONS AT A DISTANCE

"Shit," Jordan said. He slammed the laptop and shoved it in his knapsack with the dirty clothes he had spread out in the pod to air out. His chest felt like someone was squeezing him hard and his pulse thudded in his ears. His mouth had gone sour. He scrabbled backward out of the capsule, dragging the bag. Suddenly strong hands grabbed him and jerked him out. His head slammed against the edge of the opening, filling his eyes momentarily with a bright yellow light. He had bitten down and tasted blood but felt no pain either from his tongue or the golf ball budding on the back of his head. The knapsack was ripped away and his head was slammed against the wall.

"That won't be necessary, Dennis" came from behind him in a familiar, gentle, bemused voice. The hands let him go. Slowly Jordan turned around. His cheek still stung where it had pressed against the wall. Dennis stood a couple of steps away, his bulk filling the hallway, the knapsack still swinging in his hand. At the end of the hall on the other side Manny leaned against an open capsule, picking at his teeth with a grubby fingernail.

"I'm sorry about that, Jordan," Sam said. He was sitting on the edge of the capsule opening on the lower level across from Jordan's. "Let's take a walk, shall we?"

Outside Sam led the way and Dennis and Manny trailed several yards behind. "This hasn't worked out entirely, has it?" Sam looked at him with an easy smile. Jordan didn't say anything; his mind was racing a dozen directions at once but couldn't seem to fix on any one thought. "You know," Sam went on, "usually the change of venue works for people. It makes the idea of starting over more...I don't know...more reasonable." He raised his eyebrows as though it were a question.

"Not so much for you. I've thought about it a bit and my theory is that it's because you had some ambivalence about leaving your past behind. As you can imagine that is not generally the case with our clients." Here he gave Jordan a knowing smile. "In any case, that ambivalence has made it more difficult, no?"

Jordan tried to read the expression but Sam was inscrutable.

"Yes. We know about the Instagram account. And the unfortunate events of the other evening."

Blood hammered in his ears.

"But don't worry. As you know I have seen Dr. Parrish and the incident seems to have passed without undue notice."

"You mean..." He didn't dare say it, even hope it.

"I mean, she seems unaffected. I got the impression she's not much of a social media person. There seemed to be no need to take any kind of, shall we say, corrective measures."

They walked in silence for a minute. Sam wasn't going to hurt his family. That was as much as Jordan could understand. He felt the panic fade away into a dull distant toothache of simple fear. He wrinkled up his nose as they walked over a subway grate.

Sam arched an eyebrow.

"How do you stand it?" Jordan asked. "It's like rotting fish over raw sewage."

Sam smiled. "Honestly, I never noticed. I'm anosmic." Jordan looked at him blankly.

"No sense of smell. Silver lining, I guess."

"What are you going to do with me?"

Sam smiled again. "We're not going to do anything. We're going to move you somewhere more pleasant, somewhere I think you'll be much happier—at least, I hope so." They had arrived at a tan Toyota sedan. Sam opened the front passenger door. Jordan got in as Manny and Dennis squeezed into the back. Sam drove effortlessly through the chaotic Tokyo afternoon traffic, eventually merging onto the Keiyo Toll Road toward Narita.

39

DNA THEN

Ok, DNA then. I can have Simon run it.

    maybe.

They'd still have it right?

    i would think so. let me ask my guy.

I can call the police. He was my husband.

    no! don't call police. if they reopen the case it will be a mess. insurance
    company will freeze everything, may fuck up pfizer deal. all bad. copy?

Copy.

    for real ok? i promise i'll get something. my guy is high up.

Ok thank you

40

22 RUE BONAPARTE

Jordan looked up: 22 rue Bonaparte had a simple facade, pale gray stone with minimal ornamentation save the pairs of tall windows on each floor. Each had faded white shutters and a small wrought-iron railing on the outside. One window on the second floor was slightly open, revealing long heavy curtains that luffed gently in the breeze. Dennis was struggling with the key that opened the heavy black wooden outer door. He cursed under his breath, and then, with a creak, the lock surrendered and the door swung in. They entered a dim foyer with two narrow staircases on the right and a heavy oak door on the left. Dennis led the way up the far staircase, carrying the larger of Jordan's two bags. Two flights up he used the same key to open the door to the apartment.

Jordan blinked as his eyes adjusted to the light. The ceilings were high with ornate rosettes anchoring the light fixtures and rococo moldings around the borders. The furnishings were spare but tasteful. The living room had a sleek modern white sofa broken up by a pair of Jonathan Adler pillows with swirling designs in vivid green and orange. A massive chrome lamp arched over the back of the couch, casting a warm pool of light on a glass bowl filled with smooth black stones and a red plastic Pernod ashtray on the coffee table, a maple Louis XV with tiger-stripe figuring. A pair of black armchairs and a bookcase against the opposite wall completed the room.

"I told you it was nice," Sam said, crossing to the windows. His footsteps echoed in the open space. He flung open the heavy curtains, which pooled onto the floor, and the daylight flooded in. "One of our first clients bought this place for a girl he was seeing, beautiful girl. It turned out she was screwing some young writer when he wasn't around. It got messy. Very unpleasant. Anyway, it's been empty since. Lovely neighborhood, though. Les Deux Magots is just around the corner."

Sam opened the windows. They swung in and a rush of cold air stirred the pages of the old fashion magazines on the coffee table. There was a muffled ring and Sam dug out his phone. "I'm sorry, I have to take this," he said. "Why don't you put your bag in the bedroom and give yourself the short tour? I won't be a minute." He gestured with his chin at the French doors and answered the call.

Jordan went into the bedroom and threw his knapsack on the bed while Dennis sat on the sofa and began idly flipping through magazines. The bedroom was decorated as minimally as the living room. The bed was covered in a simple white comforter and faced an antique armoire.

There was a small writing desk and a table with a flat-screen TV and a telephone. On the wall was a framed poster for the Luc Besson film *Le Grand Bleu* and a photograph of a laughing Josephine Baker with a martini in one hand and a cigarette in the other. A doorway opened to a bathroom with an old claw-foot tub and a pyramid of stacked white towels. Jordan crossed back through the living room and the connected dining room

with its farmhouse table and orange-and-red globed chandelier, to the kitchen. It was small but efficient, tiled entirely in
black and white squares. He heard Sam approach like a nurse
on her ward.

"You should be comfortable here for a while, wouldn't you
think?"

"Y-yeah, it's fine," he stammered. "I mean, it's certainly better."

"You speak any French, Jordan?"

"No, not really, little grade school stuff. I can count to twenty,
I think."

"Don't worry about it. They all speak English. They'll pretend they don't just to be shits but they do. Especially around
here. Saint-Germain is pretty high-end. All the shops cater to
rich tourists. You'll be fine."

"How long am I here for?"

Sam looked surprised by the question. "Up to you, really. If it
works out, indefinitely. You can have a good life here, Jordan."
He pulled out one of the dining room chairs and sat down, mo-
tioning for Jordan to join him.

"Dennis, would you see if there's any wine in the fridge?
Thank you." Dennis heaved himself up with a grunt.

"Look," Sam said, spreading his hands on the table and af-
fecting to study his cuticles, "this is new for me, too. I'm not
sure I've ever had a client who didn't want to stay lost before. It
presents some challenges. I've decided to skip ahead a bit. We're
going to cut right to the point where I turn over access to some
of your money and you do what you want."

"What money?" Jordan said.

"Your company insured you for a great deal, Jordan. You were
their primary asset. That payout has allowed them to carry on
in your absence. If it were to be suspected that your demise was
suspicious or, God forbid, fraudulent, they would find themselves in a very compromised position indeed."

Jordan studied him like a venomous spider he had just recognized by its distinctive markings.

"Fortunately, they were sensible enough to invest part of their windfall with us to ensure that never happened."

"Blackmail," Jordan said.

"I prefer to think of it as an insurance policy on their insurance policy. Risk mitigation," Sam said, looking up as Dennis placed two glasses of white wine on the table. Sam raised one and silently toasted Jordan as Dennis sulkily returned to the sofa.

"We're going to back off. No cameras in here, long leash. I'm trusting you. I'm trusting that you understand and accept my one absolute ironclad condition—Jordan Parrish is dead. That means your past has to remain in your past. It has to be this way. You do understand that, right?" Jordan nodded as the cool Chardonnay slipped down. Definitely French, steely compared to the oaky Californians Stephanie liked.

"Excellent. Then you are free to live here, or anywhere you like in France for that matter, with no restrictions. In the due course of time, who knows, you may find love again, you may even remarry. You never know how life turns out."

"What about my family?" Jordan said.

"I will keep an eye on them. They will be taken care of. For you they cannot exist. There will be no repeats." Sam looked at him and Jordan saw that subject was closed.

He nodded.

"One more thing," Sam said, "we are going to have to tag you. It's not terribly pleasant but it's the price of freedom. It keeps us apprised of your whereabouts without having to constantly intrude on your privacy." He nodded to Dennis, who quickly crossed to Jordan's other side.

"There may be some discomfort but there won't be any pain as long as you cooperate," Sam said as Dennis handed him a black zippered nylon pouch about the size of a sandwich. He unzipped it and laid it on the table. "Remove your shirt, please."

Jordan's vision tunneled; everything seemed to be happening very fast and his head felt fuzzy. He looked at the empty wineglass.

"Sorry," Sam said with a little shrug.

Dennis pulled Jordan's shirt over his head and hung it over the back of the chair. Sam had a square of gauze stained a rusty brown, which he wiped around Jordan's right chest and shoulder, staining the skin. Then he took a long thin needle from the pouch and threaded it onto a syringe. From a vial he drew a good amount of a clear liquid and squirted a little out the tip. Jordan smelled a familiar hospital smell that made his already swimming head even worse. He wanted to get up and run or at least put up a struggle but his body wasn't responding. He felt like he was trapped behind thick glass, watching, unable to resist.

Dennis pinioned Jordan's forearm to the arm of the chair as Sam brought the needle to a little hollow just below the end of the clavicle at Jordan's right shoulder. "Probably best if you don't look," he said as he firmly pressed the needle through the skin. There was a momentary sharp pinch, then he felt the smooth steel pass through the soft tissue and suddenly his right middle finger started convulsively twitching as if it were flicking a switch. Sam gently shifted the angle of the needle, and first Jordan's index finger, then his thumb, started to jump with each probing twist of the needle's tip. A muscle in his forearm started to convulsively bunch and release then, and Sam made a small sound of irritation and repositioned the needle again. Finally when Jordan's first two fingers clenched together in a palsied spasm, Sam seemed satisfied and pushed in the plunger. Jordan felt an unpleasant fullness as the syringe emptied; it made his lower back tighten and arch as his head twisted to one side and he groaned involuntarily.

"Almost done," Sam said, and a second later he withdrew the needle, eliciting a deep slumping exhalation. A single drop of blood formed at the exit point and then mixed with the sweat beading Jordan's chest and ran down in a streaky rivulet. Jordan felt warmth and a prickling sensation work its way slowly down his arm.

Sam took a small plastic cylinder out of the pouch and unscrewed the lid. He scooped out a glob of clear jelly with what looked like a glass grain of rice with some tiny electronics and a wound coil inside. "This is the Angel," he said, laying it on a clean piece of gauze. "Can you flex your hand for me?" Jordan tried to move his fingers but only managed a little twitch of the ring finger. Sam nodded. "Almost ready." On a fresh length of gauze he laid out a scalpel, a pair of forceps with handles like scissors and a curved needle and poured alcohol over them. Jordan began to breathe more quickly. His arm felt completely numb now. He tried to move it but couldn't. It felt improbably heavy. He remembered a night in Tokyo when he'd passed out with his arm off the sofa and had woken up with it completely asleep, seven and a half pounds of meat and bone, deadweight.

Sam pulled on a pair of latex gloves and picked up the scalpel. "Okay," he said. Dennis took a long piece of the gauze and folded it over several times to make a square. He put the square on the table and placed Jordan's hand on it, holding it firmly at the wrist. Jordan felt the pull on his body as it moved but felt nothing at all from the arm. Nor did he feel anything when Sam made an inch-and-a-half-long incision between the metacarpals of his middle and index fingers. Blood immediately filled the cut and began to run down his wrist but Dennis dabbed it away with fresh gauze. Jordan felt like he was going to faint. Sam glanced at him.

"Don't pass out on me. Close your eyes, hang your head down, breathe deep and slow." Jordan did and felt his blood pressure stabilize a little. He tried not to think about the cause of the tugging sensation in his right shoulder. "Count to a hundred," Sam said. At seventy-three, he said, "Done."

Jordan opened his eyes. The back of his hand was neatly sutured with clear thread. The pad was stained with a fair amount of blood but the hand was clean. It was a professional job. "Can you stand?" Sam asked.

"I think so," Jordan said, but he stumbled as he tried to get to his feet. Sam took his left elbow and Dennis put an arm around him and, supporting the useless right arm, they helped him to the sofa.

"You should probably take it easy for a while," Sam said. "The sedation will wear off in a couple of hours, but honestly, I'd relax for the rest of the day. Tomorrow you'll be good as new. The hand's going to hurt a little but it shouldn't be too bad. I'm going to leave you these—" he held up a vial of pills and then put them on the coffee table "—to make sure your body doesn't reject the Angel. I would definitely take them until they're gone. Much easier going in than coming out. The stitches will dissolve in a week or so."

He sat down and looked Jordan in the eye. "This is goodbye for us, Jordan. The Angel is powered by your muscle movement, so it should run for many years, and as long as it's going we shouldn't need to see one another. I know you'll miss our little chats," he said with a wry smile, "but I'm sure you'll get over it. Dennis has left you a care package. The usual things—ID, phone, bank card. If you are reasonable, the money will last for quite a while. The phone has the game you like on it. My little gift to you. There is also a number if you ever need to contact us, not that I expect you will." He put his hands on his thighs and pushed up from the couch.

"So, best of luck, and remember the rules. And, Jordan, this is important—please don't think about removing the Angel. If it touches the air, it sends an alarm and, well, that would be bad."

"Oh, yes, almost forgot." Dennis handed him a small envelope and Sam plucked a few strands of Jordan's hair and put it in the envelope.

"What's that for?" Jordan said, rubbing his scalp.

"Just a DNA sample," Sam said. "Open, please." He scraped

Jordan's cheek with a long Q-tip and put that in another envelope and sealed it.

"Why do you need my DNA?"

"Just in case."

"In case of what?"

"In case there are ever any questions, I suppose."

Jordan thought for a second, struggling to think clearly. "So someone isn't buying it. Who is it? Insurance? Stephanie? Police?"

"Just a precaution," Sam said calmly.

"If it's Steph, she'll know." Adrenaline cut through the fog. Maybe there was a glint of daylight. Not hope but a tiny step on the road to hope.

"Why do you say that?" Sam said nonchalantly, continuing to repack the nylon bag.

"The sample won't have decayed right? It's called necrotic decay. When you take a DNA sample from someone who's dead, there's a predictable degeneration of the sample. Most forensic labs won't look for it. They're just looking for correlation with the control. But if Stephanie was looking, she would catch it immediately." He looked from Sam to Dennis and back. Both were impassive. Jordan's heart was hammering but he kept his voice steady. "I could fix it. I could make it look like it was from someone who died when I supposedly did."

"I see," Sam said, zipping up the bag. "Well, as I say, it's only a precaution. I don't think we have to worry about it too much. Goodbye, Jordan. Come, Dennis, let's let Mr. Butler get some rest."

When the front door closed the pressure made the windows to the street swing wide-open and a pool of bitter cold air swirled through the room. Jordan pushed himself awkwardly to his feet, his right arm flopping at his side, and went to shut the windows.

Glancing down he saw Sam and Dennis getting into the car. Sam was on the phone, and as he closed his door he snapped, "Well, find out!" and ended the call with an abrupt stab of his thumb.

41

LE POULET

Alex walked down the stairs of the Marlboro Street apartment. It was the quietest hour of the morning. The night owls had gone to bed and the early birds were not yet stirring. He was pretty sure the Bolshy was sleeping, though he had considered the possibility that she was faking. Their relationship had become more complicated lately.

The phone vibrated in his overcoat pocket. Seven missed calls, two texts and a voice mail. All from Stephanie.

Call me, at 8:32 p.m. 0_0, at 3:17 a.m.

At 3:22 a.m. she had left the voice mail. "Don't be mad. I called that policeman. He didn't answer. I didn't leave a message. I'm sorry."

"Shit!" His voice sounded unnaturally loud. He called her back. Straight to voice mail.

"Steph, if he calls you back, tell him it was a mistake. Say you pocket dialed him or something. My guy is close but it's all going to get fucked up if the cops get involved. Let me know you got the message."

He hung up and dialed another number. "It's me. I need something soon. She's freaking out. I can handle it but I'm going to need something."

He hung up and shoved the phone into his pocket. He decided to walk home. The snow complained like Styrofoam under his feet. The air made his eyes tear. He passed up through the alphabet—Exeter, Fairfield, Gloucester, Hereford, up to Mass. Ave. where he turned left. The buses had started running, taking the first shifters to work. Alex cut through the Fens. The first glow at the horizon came as he walked past the still exterior of the Gardner. He hadn't meant to come this way. His stomach felt hollow. He thought he'd stay up, hit the gym, maybe go to bed early tonight.

Jordan woke up on the couch. The feeling had come back to his arm and his hand hurt like hell. He was famished. It was still light out but the light had softened—he guessed late afternoon. There was a phone on the dining room table next to a manila envelope and the key. Jordan pocketed the key and phone, grabbed the envelope and stumbled down the stairs and out onto the street. The sign on the corner, built into the wall, identified the street, rue Bonaparte, and the arrondissement, the sixième. Fucking Drake.

He allowed himself to be carried by the flow of foot traffic, mostly people heading home from work, it seemed, their heads down, some urgency in their stride. He turned left at rue Jacob, an even smaller street, only wide enough for a single car. Two blocks down he came to a little neighborhood brasserie. Ornate lettering on the awning identified it as Le Pré aux Clercs. The collection of warm smells and gentle chatter of dishes and conversation from inside drew him in.

It was a small place with four tables lining the windows looking out at the street and then, past the bar and down two steps, another room with five or six more tables. Three of them had been pushed together for a large group—Jordan guessed co-workers. They were loud, laughing; several carafes of wine were spread around. Jordan chose the last of the small tables along the window, as far as he could get from the group. As soon as he sat down a girl with an unruly blond ponytail came by and deftly swept the two coins on the table into the pocket of her black apron as she cleared the empty espresso cup and water glass and mopped the table with a couple of swipes from a damp bar towel. She asked him something in French, which he didn't catch, but answered with a hopeful *"Oui, merci."*

She glanced at him for a split second without breaking her momentum and said something else unintelligible as she headed back to the bar. Seconds later a carafe of red wine and a small glass materialized together with a basket of sliced baguette, a white paper place mat and silverware tightly wrapped in a paper napkin. Jordan poured a glass of the wine and opened the envelope.

Justin Butler. Canadian passport with a visa good for five years. Apparently he was from Winnipeg. There was also a Crédit Lyonnais ATM and Visa card with initial password on a Post-it. A sheet labeled CV listed Justin's academic credentials: BSc from the University of Manitoba, MSc and PhD from McGill. Genetics, that was convenient. He finished the glass of wine and, as he put it down, the waitress appeared and refilled it.

"Monsieur?" she said, waiting. When he didn't answer, she said in heavily accented English, "Would you like to order?"

"Oh, of course, I'm s-sorry," he stammered. "Could I see a menu?"

She pointed to a blackboard over the bar with several items scrawled in an angular cursive. *Poulet frites* was the only thing that was both legible and recognizable as a food, not an internal organ sautéed and plated, though he wasn't sure if it meant fried chicken or chicken with fries; at any rate it sounded safe.

"La poulet, s'il vous plaît," he said, nodding toward the board.

"Le poulet," she confirmed and corrected with a smile, and headed for the kitchen humming under her breath, ponytail flouncing.

As it turned out it was a half roast chicken, redolent of garlic and tarragon, the skin bronzed and crackling, the flesh infused with lemon and pepper, served with a heaping plate of perfect slender fries, deglazed pan sauce on the side. Jordan ate with relish. It was comfort food; it was familiar and simple yet elegant and foreign. It was a world away from Tokyo. The only immediate irritant was the man at the next table who lit a particularly rank-smelling unfiltered cigarette just as Jordan's food arrived and continued to smoke throughout his meal. The waitress paid no attention to him and the man pointedly ignored the looks Jordan directed at him.

When he had picked the plate clean the waitress took it away and brought him a small espresso and the bill, which was a tented slip of paper with the number twelve scribbled on it. Jordan put down a ten and five euro coins from the money Sam had left him and stood to go. The waitress pocketed the ten and two of the coins and flicked one more into her apron and handed the last two back to Jordan with a *"Merci, monsieur."* As he passed the next table on his way out he was certain the man blew his smoke right at him.

It was weird. The bitchy wife from the Parrish thing had called in the middle of the night. No message. Herron had called her back around 9:30, straight to voice mail, no call back. He'd been professional, courteous. "Hello, Mrs. Parrish, this is Detective Herron returning your call. I should be around all day. Please call me back if there's anything I can do for you." Not that he was anxious to talk to her again. She'd been a cold fish, the kind of lady who made you feel self-conscious about your shoes and the way you pronounced your *R*s.

Still, it was weird.

42

GITANES

Jordan lay on the couch, folding. The app on his phone was awkward at first compared to the Kinect but soon it had become second nature. At first he had no idea what the sound was—a rising series of digital tones, not really intrusive but annoying if only for the repetition. Alarm? Some kind of timer, maybe? Then it hit him; it was the kitchen phone. Jordan crossed the apartment and picked it up.

"Hello?"

"Jesus, you're a hard guy to reach." Jordan recognized Dennis's voice, the flat Midwestern vowels and clipped military delivery.

"Sorry, I didn't realize it was the phone. I don't get a lot of calls. What's wrong?"

"Nothing's wrong. I'm supposed to find out what you need to do your DNA thing." Dennis was low-key, business as usual, but Jordan knew what it meant. Someone was asking questions.

It had to be Stephanie. She had doubts. The realization knocked the air from his body. Jordan struggled for breath, holding the phone away from him as he turned in a half circle and sank to the floor.

"You there?"

"Yeah, sorry. I was just making something to eat. So what are you saying? You guys *do* want me to age the sample now?"

"Apparently. Sam decided better safe than sorry."

"Right, okay." Bullshit, he thought. He had to think.

"So what do you need?"

"Wow, in Paris? I don't know… I know all the good labs in the States but over here—"

Dennis interrupted, "We have access to a lab. I just need to know what else you need."

Jordan's mind was racing. If Steph was asking questions, what did that mean? He had assumed she must hate him. He knew the cover story—the fictitious girlfriend, the apartment—and all of it so believable the way things had been between them. But now if she didn't buy it, if she kept asking questions? They'd kill her. Parts of him wanted to scream, or run, or to curl up in a ball on the kitchen floor and rock back and forth until it all went away. But one part of him, a small part, cleared a tiny space amid the clutter and noise and went to work. Fundamental principles. Stephanie was a scientist. She knew you didn't prove theories true; you proved them false. Good old Popper. She would look for holes.

Dennis was talking. "Sorry, listen," Jordan said, "it's a pretty long list. Can you come by tonight?"

"Sure. Eight?"

"That's fine." Dennis rang off. Jordan dropped the phone and leaned back against the fridge. A few minutes later the compressor kicked on, and he felt the vibrations through his body. A long list.

"Hi, Mrs. Parrish, this is Detective Herron again, just following up with you, making sure everything's okay. Call me back when you get the message." He clicked off and dialed another number. "Hey, Jules, it's Mike. Got a chance for you to even things up. I need the last twenty-four hours on a number. It's 617…" He looked down at the phone and paged to recent calls. "Sorry, 617-595-3112. Got it—595-3112? No big rush, just email me the log when you get it. We'll call it square. Talk to you." He clicked the phone off. Probably a waste of time.

Dennis glanced quickly over the list before folding it over and stuffing it in his jacket pocket. "I'll pick you up in the morning," he said, standing up.

"Are you serious? You're not going to be able to get all that by tomorrow morning."

"I think we'll be fine," Dennis said.

Jordan looked at him with a half smile. "You're fucking with me, right? What's the joke?"

Dennis clapped him on the shoulder. Jordan flinched but forced the smile to stick.

"See you in the morning, Justin," Dennis said. "It is Justin, right? I lose track sometimes."

Jordan had eaten every meal since arriving in Paris at Le Pré aux Clercs. The waitresses knew him now so he was spared the humiliation of negotiating a new linguistic truce in an establishment where the terms might not be as favorable. The food was basic bistro fare but varied and usually excellent. Depending on how crowded it was he either sat at his end table in the window or at a single table in the back corner of the sunken dining room. His meal times were still pretty random; it had only been four days and the jet lag still played havoc with his sleep cycle. If it was morning, the waitress would bring a pot of coffee and one of steamed milk and a tartine of toasted baguette with butter and a collection of little jam jars—apricot, cherry

and occasionally raspberry or orange marmalade, the last being
the only disappointment.

If it was too late for breakfast, a half carafe of red wine and
a pitcher of water would arrive instead, followed by whatever
the waitresses thought the shy American might like. They had
guessed wrong only once when an order of sautéed sweetbreads
in brown butter had languished untouched for twenty minutes
before being mercifully whisked away and replaced with a more
conservative steak frites.

The Gitanes smoker, for that turned out to be the brand of his
particularly pungent unfiltered cigarettes, also appeared to be a
regular. He was usually there when Jordan arrived, reading *Le
Figaro* and ashing in his saucer or noisily sucking scraps of meat
off the gracile bones of a greasy squab. Jordan made a point of
not avoiding him even though he would in general choose the
table that offered the most privacy. Wouldn't give him the satisfaction. He would take an adjacent table, even leaning slightly
into his nemesis as he squeezed past. For his part, Gitanes never
missed an opportunity to blow his fetid plume Jordan's way or
to simply glower while muttering dark imprecations in his own
particularly phlegmatic French.

He was in his usual spot but Jordan didn't even glance at him
as he slid into his seat against the wall in the otherwise empty
downstairs dining room. He drank a glass of the Côtes du Rhône
but didn't touch the braised oxtail that had appeared as he scribbled a long sequence of *A*s, *C*s, *G*s and *T*s on the paper place
mat. Shaking his head, he crossed the sequence out and started
again. The waitress, a stylish brunette with an asymmetric bob
that reminded Jordan of an old Vidal Sassoon ad, stopped at the
table and said, "You don't like it?"

Jordan looked up and said, "No, it's fine. *Merci. C'est bien.*" She
shrugged and moved on. She had a brief exchange with Gitanes
as she refilled his carafe that Jordan made no attempt to deci-
pher. "Shit," he said, scratching out another sequence of letters.

Gitanes looked over with arched eyebrows. Jordan waved his hand apologetically, saying, "Sorry, sorry, just trying to figure something out. Don't get your panties in a twist."

Gitanes abruptly pushed his chair back and stood up. *Oh Christ*, Jordan thought. The last thing he needed was to get in a fight with some misanthropic old legionnaire. He put his hands up and was strip-mining his semester and a half of high school French for something like an apology when Gitanes pulled out the chair opposite and sat down at his table. Before Jordan could say anything he launched into a guttural monologue. His voice sounded like one of those Tuvan throat singers. Jordan suspected even a native would have trouble understanding him. The cadence of the tale would occasionally rise to a pointed pause, signifying, Jordan assumed, a question, no doubt rhetorical as, after considering his listener for a beat with one eyebrow quivering impossibly high on his forehead, he would plunge right back into the current of the story without waiting for any kind of response.

Jordan smiled to himself. He had misread the old guy. He was just lonely, probably no family, or maybe he had but his wife had died or left him or something. That's why he was always at the café. He began to nod thoughtfully at the pauses, pursing his lips to show understanding and sympathy even though he had no idea what was being said. It didn't matter, did it? Sometimes people just needed to talk things through. Most shrinks probably just sat there daydreaming while their patients blathered on, helped them just the same.

There was another pause. The man looked at him expectantly. Jordan said quietly, "My wife thinks I'm dead."

Gitanes nodded blankly and carried on. At the next break, Jordan said, "My kids, too. I have two, Sophie and Haden. They all think I'm dead. It's crazy—they had a funeral, buried somebody."

Now it was a conversation. Jordan was sure neither understood a word the other was saying, but it still felt liberating, just to be able to talk. Gitanes waved his arm and a fresh carafe of wine appeared.

At one point, the old man's voice rose in outrage and he shook his finger in the air as his eyes brimmed with moisture. The waitress came over and clucked disapprovingly as she cleared the empty carafe and glasses into a bus pan. He lapsed into a sullen silence.

"It all started when we lost the baby. Elizabeth," Jordan said. "It was my fault. I didn't know what to say to her to make it better so I hid. I stayed at the lab and tried to pretend it hadn't happened. And the more I felt guilty for letting Stephanie down, for letting her suffer alone in that house with the other kids, the more I stayed away. I thought I could fix things if the business did well. But of course nothing worked—the company was failing, my family was drifting away. I was so deep in debt and no one knew. I felt completely alone.

"I was going to kill myself. I remember the day I hit on it. It was the proverbial aha moment. Of course. That's the way out, the only way. I know what you're thinking." Gitanes was fumbling for a cigarette, lost in his own thoughts.

"But you're wrong," Jordan carried on. "I didn't chicken out. I would have done it. I'm certain." Jordan gazed over Gitanes's shoulder at the waning activity in the restaurant, his mind going back over those dark days. His jaw tightened and he nodded to himself. He would have.

"But there were problems. If I had done it, the insurance wouldn't have paid out and everyone would have been even worse off. So I called the number. My therapist had given it to me, you know, for emergencies. If things ever got so bad I couldn't go on. And they were and I couldn't. So I called. I had no idea what would happen but I knew I couldn't continue as things were. And then men came and took me away.

"They took me to this place and they made it look like I had had a mistress and we'd been killed in an accident. They made up this whole crazy story. Stephanie must have hated me. They all must have. I'm such a coward." His shoulders started to shake. The old man pushed the nearly empty crumpled cigarette pack across the table. Jordan took one and lit it. He hadn't smoked since high school and then it had been Marlboro Ultra Lights. The unfiltered cigarette tasted sour and thick and made him dizzy and a little nauseous. The paper stuck to his lips and little bits of tobacco on his tongue made him feel like he was going to gag. He stubbed it out, eyes watering, and laughed. "Pathetic, right?" The Frenchman shook his head heavily from side to side as if bringing the judgment of the ages to bear.

43

AUGURING

Julie was quick. Herron opened the attachment. He scanned down the list quickly, his eye immediately drawn to his own number at 3:19 a.m. At 3:17 there was a text to another number and then a call to the same number at 3:22. There was an incoming call from the same number at 5:21 a.m. He quickly scanned up the page. All the calls but two that day were to the same number and none was longer than a minute. Herron picked up his desk phone and dialed. After four rings a voice answered. "Hey, this is Alex. Leave me a message. I'll get back to you as soon as I can." He remembered the voice, the dead guy's partner, Penn, no, Prenn. Slick, used to bossing people around. Didn't like him much, either.

He emailed Julie back. Hey, Julie, you're the best. Now I'm going to have to owe you one. I need to go further back, say, eight months, and can you pull this one for me, too? and he carefully typed in Alex's number.

They were going through dense clouds. You couldn't tell which way was up but occasionally the wing would cleave a discrete wisp and you could see suddenly how fast they were going.

It should have been bumpy but it wasn't. Horizontal streaks of rain striped the window. Someone had scratched the initials TS into the Plexiglas. The seats were old, unchanged since the '70s, and stank of decades-old cigarette smoke. He still remembered when you could smoke on planes.

Suddenly the plane broke through the clouds but something was wrong. They were too low. The jungle canopy was right there. They were at the treetops. He knew they were going in. The image out the window, the section of wing, the dense green canopy laced with vines, froze in his eye, like when the old 16 mm films would jam in the projector at school, the image slightly skewed and undersaturated, fading from focus. He felt no fear, just a curious sense of regret. He felt himself pulling back; sounds became muffled and subdued. He was aware of a violent shaking and, even as the snapshot of the window persisted in his mind, he saw the foliage hurtle by as the plane tore through the canopy. So, this would be dying, he thought impassively as his vision tunneled in, vaguely aware that the plane was cartwheeling now. He was glad there would be no pain.

It was quiet. Then there was a harsh Klaxon from the street and Jordan opened his eyes. It was dark. He pressed the stem of his watch—2:45 in the morning. He was wide-awake, eyes fully dilated; the bottom sheet was soaked in sweat but he felt cold. He pulled up the duvet that had slipped to the floor. The skin on his hand felt tight where the sutures had been. It hurt. Tomorrow would be a busy day; he needed to sleep. He'd never believed that stuff about dying in dreams.

He closed his eyes and tried to recapture the thread. The snapshot of the canopy through the window hung there like a dark pool in the forest. He slipped in.

The snow was melting on the yews hanging over the walk. The sun couldn't reach through the overhanging branches, though, so the pattering drops refroze in the shade. As a result the path was lethally slick. Alex was trying to piece together what he was going to say when he lost his footing. He tried to catch himself and hit the ground hard with his elbow, sending shooting pain up and down his arm just before the back of his head struck the icy brick with a solid thud. He lay still, watching the sun glitter off the ice that sheathed the tiny needles like myelin. A drop of water splashed his forehead and he groaned and tried to sit up. The front door opened and Stephanie looked out. Haden was wrapped around her leg and peering out from behind her.

"Jesus, Alex, are you okay?" she said, picking her way carefully down the walk and helping him up. "I meant to salt it but I got distracted."

He gingerly rubbed the back of his head. "I'll live, probably get a good bump, though."

"Come on," she said, taking his arm, "we'll ice it."

He winced and pulled his arm away. "I slammed my funny bone, too."

"Why's it called a funny bone?" Haden said. "'Cause it feels funny when you hit it?"

"That's one reason," his mother said. "See if you can think of another."

"I don't know."

They made it up the stairs and Alex draped his wet coat over the radiator.

"What is the real name for that bone?" Stephanie said.

Haden thought about it. "I don't know," he said, losing interest in the subject.

Sophie was sitting at the piano in the front room listening and chimed in smugly, "It's called the humerus. Get it?"

Haden rolled his eyes. "Ha, ha."

Dennis drove quickly through the cold early-morning streets. They crossed the river and headed east into the tenth arrondissement. He swung the little Citroën into a lone parking spot across

the street from a bus stop: Grange aux Belles–Juliette Dodu. A
pair of older women with empty mesh bags sat in the shelter,
conversing rapidly. Right behind them was a modern brown
building that appeared to be wrapped in netting. The face of
the building was striped with alternating bands of wide and
narrow reflecting windows. On the sides they were flush but
in the middle they were set back as if a giant hand had peeled
off the ugly shell to reveal the glittering jewel beneath. A small
unobtrusive sign by the door identified the building as the In-
stitut de Génétique Moléculaire.

They entered through plain glass doors and Dennis walked purposefully to the security desk. The guard looked up, and before
he could speak Dennis handed him a folded piece of paper. The
guard opened it and read, glancing once or twice at Jordan as he
worked down the page.

Apparently satisfied, he took a white plastic card from a
drawer and inserted it into a small machine on the desk. He
typed a sequence of numbers into his computer and the card
was smoothly ejected. He handed it to Dennis and said, *"Deux
cent quinze, monsieur,"* and went back to his paper.

In the elevator Jordan saw that most of the floors were devoted to the CEPH. He smiled to himself; the Centre d'Étude
du Polymorphisme Humain had been one of the biggest private labs involved in sequencing of the human genome. They
would be well equipped.

Dennis unlocked the door with the card key. The lab was
small but more than adequate. "How long you going to need?"
Dennis asked, slouching in the doorway.

Jordan took a deep breath. "A while. I'll probably use de-
oxyribonuclease I in a solution with manganese ions to cut the
strands. That should give a pretty random length assortment.
Then I'll have to treat the fragments with mung bean nuclease
to clean up the ends. Otherwise, they could theoretically be
able to tell they were restriction cuts, not natural necrosis—"

Dennis interrupted, "How long?"

"Twenty-four hours, maybe?" Jordan said. "I'm not sure because I'll have to do a gel electrophoresis pass and make sure the strand length distribution corresponds to the hypothetical necrosis. I'll probably do a couple of shorter incubations with the DNase to make sure I don't oversegment... I guess I could PCR up some of the longer strands—"

"Okay," Dennis cut in. "I'll be back with lunch. Get busy because we only have the lab for today." The door smoothly clicked shut behind him.

44

CLOSER

Herron held the two lists side by side. There it was—5:21 a.m., Alex calls Stephanie back. Goes to voice mail, nothing on hers until 8:41. But then Prenn calls another number, a 202 area code. DC. His finger ran quickly up the page, then he flipped to the previous one. There. He circled the number and continued back to the beginning of the record.

He scanned Stephanie's printout. Nothing. Then he went through it again, circling all the calls to or from Prenn. He drew a timeline on the back of an envelope. August 13, Prenn calls DC, and then again early morning on the twenty-fourth, the day after Parrish disappears. Later that day several calls back and forth between Stephanie and Prenn. Through the rest of the fall and winter there's a pretty constant regular flow of calls between the two of them, all hours, sometimes pretty late, Herron noted. Then on February 26 there's a call from Prenn to the DC number. That was Thursday, five days ago. Sunday night things got exciting—the calls and texts, the call from Stephanie to him, Prenn calls DC again and here we are.

Herron sat back in his chair and steepled his fingers, thumbs to his chest and pursed lips resting on the index fingers. Connect the dots. Let's say the wife finds out her husband's fucking the bimbo he's set up in the Back Bay apartment. She's pissed, but she wouldn't just confront him. She definitely struck Herron as being from the dish-best-served-cold school of vengeful bitches. So she bides her time, cozies up to the partner-slash-best-friend. One thing leads to another; nature takes its inevitable course. Maybe Prenn falls hard for her, and she winds him up tight, sells him the "we have to get rid of my husband, then we can be together" bullshit. Right out of some cheesy noir movie.

Now, Prenn, he knows people, he's mister finance; he has to have some interesting acquaintances. He calls his DC connection, maybe the guy comes to town. Prenn calls him a few days later and within hours Parrish's gone. He and his girlfriend wind up in the river dead. And now Prenn and the missus are inseparable, calls, texts all hours. Too easy. That was the thing, though, most people who committed murder got caught. Either because they were stupid or because they figured everybody else was. It was like those kids who shot that liquor store clerk in Revere on New Year's. They were fucking waving the gun and dancing around laughing, then they shot out the CCTV camera and never thought to take the tape out of the VCR. Herron remembered the stunned expression one kid had on the stand when the video was shown, like he couldn't believe it. Fucking douchebag.

This one looked like a slam dunk. He was tempted to dial the DC number, but why spook the guy. He picked up the phone and called Julie. This had to be by the book.

"Hey, Jules, it's me. Listen, there's a 202 on the sheet you just sent over. I'm going to need everything you got on him. I'm going to Trahon now, so I'll have the warrant tomorrow. I think this is a very bad guy."

★ ★ ★

The lieutenant was on the phone but motioned him to a chair. Trahon was all right, street cop, came up through the ranks. Herron knew he wouldn't ask too many questions about where the phone logs came from. But some of the judges could be pricks about shit like that. The last couple of years Herron had seen too many cases thrown out because cops had used cell records off the internet. It was stupid, everybody bought them. Why is it no big deal when telemarketers buy people's information, but then when the police do it to catch some piece of shit who everyone knows is guilty as sin, all the civil liberties pussies start foaming at the mouth? Maybe he should go visit the widow first, see what he could stir up. He got to his feet and mouthed, "It can wait," as he headed out. Trahon shrugged and went back to his call.

Dennis had dropped off a salami sandwich and a bottle of Vittel around noon. He had brought a dinner menu from the brasserie at the corner and Jordan circled the rabbit stew, which Dennis had delivered at six. Other than that he had left him alone. He came back around eleven. "How are we doing?" he asked.

"Okay, I think," Jordan said. He looked tired. "I'm on the third round of DNase. I just want to be sure it doesn't end up looking like I've been dead six years instead of six months so I'm going in short increments. It's a little unpredictable. I've never tried to control the fragment size this closely before. It's tricky…" His voice trailed off. "It needs to be right."

"Yes, it does," Dennis said. Then after a moment, "I can give you until six in the morning but that's it. Got it?" Jordan nodded.

"Have a good night, Doc," Dennis said and clapped him on the shoulder.

As soon as he was alone, Jordan crossed to the BioAutomation MerMade 384, a massive rolling steel apparatus surmounted by a hydra's head of plastic tubing and bottles, and turned the monitor back on. He didn't know if Dennis would have known what the DNA synthesizer was, never mind that it wasn't necessary for what he was supposed to be doing, but he wasn't taking any chances. He unfolded the creased paper place mat from his pocket and, finding his place, quickly continued entering *A*s, *C*s, *G*s and *T*s on the computer keyboard. The MerMade wasn't what he was used to, but the Oligo software was intuitive enough and the machine was actually faster than the synthesizer in Jordan's lab. He checked the progress bar; he was going to make it. Just.

Alex held the Ziploc bag of ice cubes against the lump on the back of his head. It throbbed dully. He looked concerned. "If he calls again, I think you have to answer. Otherwise, it looks like you're hiding something."

"Why don't I just tell him the truth?" she said. "I haven't done anything wrong."

"No, but I have," he said. "My guy will get kicked off the force and probably be prosecuted if anyone finds out what he's doing. I was able to convince him to help us because he owes me but I can't let him go to jail. You agreed to do this my way. Right?"

Stephanie sighed. "I know, you're right. I'm sorry. If he calls again, I'll talk to him." She turned and recrossed her legs. "Why is it taking so long?"

"Just waiting for the right guy to be working evidence. Apparently you can't just walk in there and help yourself. You have to hang in there. It'll happen."

"I'm trying," she said, wrapping her arms around her knees even though it was warm in the kitchen.

He smiled. "I know it's hard but we'll get there. My friend— we'll call him Louis—he owes me. We go back a long way. It'll happen."

She nodded. "Okay." Then, "Why Louis?"

"You know, *Casablanca*. The cop. Working for the Germans but helping the good guys? Nothing? The 'start of a beautiful friendship' guy."

She shook her head. "Nope. Don't think I ever saw it."

"Never saw it? That's impossible," he said in mock horror. "Promise me you'll let me address that. Stat."

She smiled under tired eyes, still hugging her knees close. "Okay."

When he left Stephanie's, Alex tried to call Sam's message drop but got a recording saying the number was no longer in service. There was another number. He flipped through his contacts. There it was, a 307 area code. Wasn't that Wyoming? He'd never called this one. It was listed as "Sam, emergency." This qualified. Stephanie was unraveling. They needed the DNA now. Alex didn't feel like Sam appreciated the delicacy of the situation. He dialed. There was a long delay before the phone rang and then the ring sounded, hollow and filtered. Sam picked up on the second ring. His voice was flat and harsh.

"Hang up and go home, you fucking asshole," he said and terminated the connection.

When Alex walked into his apartment the phone was ringing. Unknown caller. He answered, "Hello?"

"Listen carefully," Sam said. "Boston Police were asking about the other phone number. That's why it's gone. You're the only person who would have called me from there, which means they're looking at you. Home phone is clean still but your cell is shit. Get a burner, and do not, under any circumstances, try to contact me again. Am I clear?"

"I'm sorry. I promise you I never said anything to anybody."

"I'm sure you didn't," Sam said.

"I was just worried about Stephanie. She's going to do something stupid if I can't get her Jordan's DNA."

"She'll have it tomorrow," Sam interrupted, "and if that's not the end of it I will kill that fucking bitch myself. This whole situation has become quite tiresome, Alexander. My gut says to kill them all right now and be done with it."

"You can't," Alex said, almost frantic. "We're so close."

"It's on your head, Alex."

"I'm really sorry," Alex started to say, but the line had gone dead.

45

BIGGER FISH

It was 5:36. Almost there. Jordan checked the electrophoresis gel. Electrophoresis was used to separate DNA fragments by their length. There was a light band, then the dark clump of the bulk of the strands, then another faint band. He separated out the two aberrant clusters and added the remainder to his sample. Done. He took a sterile swab from its paper wrapper and smeared it across the depression in the sample plate before dropping it into one of the plastic evidence bags Dennis had left him. There was enough left for two more Q-tips, so he prepared and bagged those, as well.

When Dennis arrived just after six, Jordan was asleep, slumped against the wall with the three evidence bags in his lap. Dennis shook him roughly by the shoulder. "Wakey, wakey, Doc. Time to go." He took the three plastic bags. "This it?"

"That's it." Jordan nodded.

Dennis dropped him off just as the sun rose. Jordan stumbled up the stairs. He pulled the drapes and fell fully clothed onto the bed.

★ ★ ★

When he awoke it was dark again. Almost 8:30 at night. He'd slept almost fourteen hours. He felt empty, empty in the most literal sense. He remembered doing a fast once when Stephanie had been trying to lose the last ten pounds of baby weight after Haden was born. He had joined in a show of emotional support. After three days of nothing but lemonade with cayenne and maple syrup he had felt the same sort of hallucinogenic clarity he felt now. Everything seemed overly sharp and yet disconnected; it was like trying to navigate the world through a microscope.

He took a long shower. The shower, in the French fashion, was a handheld in the bath.

There was no curtain so Jordan sat cross-legged in the deep, narrow tub. He put the drain stopper in so the tub gradually filled.

When it was full he turned off the tap and lay back in the gray water with everything but his knees and head immersed. The sound of occasional drops from the faucet reverberated loudly over the distant bustle of the city.

When the bath cooled to room temperature he pulled the stopper. The retreating water clung to his skin, reluctantly yielding his body to the air. When, with a slurp, the last of the bath drained, Jordan unsteadily got to his feet and took a clean towel off the stack.

He brushed his teeth. The man looking back in the mirror seemed unfamiliar. He had a set to his jaw and force in his gaze that Jordan didn't recognize. He was thinner as well, and harder. As he got dressed, his stomach gurgled hollowly. He had to eat. He pulled on a white ribbed sweater and his blue peacoat and headed out.

"Mike, it's Julie. Listen to me, whatever you're into, drop it. That 202 is government. I couldn't get any more specific and that's a bad sign. Could be CIA, or NSA, or it could be some off-the-books thing, but whatever it is, it's not something you want to mess with. Let it go. Take care of yourself. I'll see you around."

Herron played the message again, then deleted it. What did that mean? Did it change the story or just mean Prenn hung out with a better class of hitters? Curiouser and curiouser.

"*Ça va*, Yanqui?"

"*Ça va, con,*" Jordan said as he slid into his seat. Gitanes laughed quietly but didn't look up from his paper. Jordan's favorite waitress, Virginie, was working and dropped a basket of sliced baguette and a carafe of wine as she whisked by. The dinner rush was in full swing at Le Pré.

Jordan peeled open a butter packet and slathered a slice of bread. It was the best thing he could ever remember having eaten. He emptied the basket in minutes.

Virginie laughed when she returned with a plate of boeuf chasseur, a rich stew with mushrooms and carrots. "You are hungry tonight?"

He nodded and dove in. It was as if he had never eaten before. She brought a fresh basket of bread and he sopped up the last drops of juice from the plate. He had finished the carafe of wine, as well. Any hesitation he might have had about drinking within minutes of waking up was quickly overcome by context.

The immediate needs sated, Jordan pushed back his chair and sighed deeply. Gitanes was studying him over the top of his paper. Jordan shrugged with a smile and said, "That was fucking good." His eyes felt as though they were open unnaturally wide.

Virginie cleared away the empty dishes and said, "Dessert, *monsieur?*"

"Sure," Jordan said.

"*Et mon calva*, Virginie," Gitanes added.

She returned with two small snifters and a nearly empty bottle of calvados. She poured the glasses and left the bottle. *"Santé,"*

Gitanes said, raising his snifter and giving the clear eau-de-vie a quick swirl.

"Cheers," Jordan returned. The spirit was narrow and hot at first; turpentine sprang to mind. But then it mellowed as the warmth radiated throughout Jordan's body. Virginie put down a steaming slice of tarte tatin topped with a mound of crème fraîche. As Jordan ate, his companion launched into one of his incomprehensible recitations. Jordan nodded when it seemed appropriate but otherwise let the old man's monologue flow into the sea of muddled eddies and currents that filled the restaurant.

It was getting late. The rush had passed, though most of the tables were still occupied with groups lingering over dessert or drink. Jordan's companion, who seemed completely unaffected by the alcohol, waved to Virginie and shouted, "Absinthe, *chérie!*" She made a disapproving face but brought the bottle.

Jordan shook his head. "No, I've seen this movie. It didn't end well."

Gitanes paid no attention but poured a shot in each of their empty glasses. Then he balanced his fork over one and put a sugar cube on it. He slowly trickled water from the little pitcher so it ran over the sugar and into the glass, blooming in a milky cloud. He pushed the glass to Jordan and repeated the process with his own. They tipped their glasses and drank. A flood of memories rose up all at once, threatening to overwhelm his newfound sense of well-being.

"Let me tell *you* a story," Jordan said. "I was drinking this shit a couple of weeks ago in Tokyo…" Could it have only been a couple of weeks? He felt that he had died and been reborn at least twice since that night.

"I ended up almost sleeping with this child prostitute. And then I ran." Jordan glanced up. The old man was fumbling with the pack of cigarettes. He finally shook one out and tamped it against the crystal of his watch. Jordan picked up the Zippo on the table and lit it. Gitanes nodded thanks and sat back, staring off into the middle distance, no doubt lost in his own memories.

"I should back up," Jordan went on. "I told you my family thinks I'm dead, right? I was a biologist once upon a time. Hard to believe, I know. My partner, my best friend, screwed me over. He wanted me gone. I think mostly so he could fuck my wife. Shakespeare, isn't it? And I walked right into it."

Over the next hour, as the customers drifted out of Le Pré aux Clercs, Jordan relived every moment of the past six months. "And last night," he said, "last night I put the message in the bottle and threw it into the sea. But no one will ever find it because I am dead." His head lolled forward into his hands and his shoulders began to shake. He couldn't tell if he was laughing or crying.

Gitanes spoke. It took a moment for Jordan to realize he was speaking English. "After the first glass you see things as you wish they were, after the second you see things as they are not. Finally you see things as they really are, and that is the most horrible thing in the world." Jordan looked up; the old man was turning the empty absinthe bottle in his weathered hands. "Oscar Wilde, I think."

46

LITTON

Litton Labs was in a small office park just off Route 128 in Lexington. It was a low brown building with reflective windows like state police trooper shades. Alex pulled into a spot right in front of the door. The receptionist looked up, startled, when he came in.

"Mr. Prenn, was Dr. Chun expecting you?"

"No," he said. It was quiet. The sound of the expressway was muted to a barely discernible hum. The gray mottled carpeting and overstuffed pair of sofas along the wall coupled with the acoustic tile ceiling seemed to absorb all ambient sound. "Is he around?"

"Yes, sir, I'll tell him you're here." She pressed a button on the phone and adjusted her headset.

"Don't bother, I'll find him," Alex said, pushing through the door to the labs.

Matthew Chun was slurping noodles from a cup of instant ramen while watching columns of numbers scroll down the monitor in front of him. He didn't look up when Alex came in.

"How are we doing?" Alex said.

Chun jumped up. "Mr. Prenn, I had no… Did we—"

Alex waved him down. "No, just happened to be in the area. Thought I'd check in."

"Of course, that's great. Ah, nothing too new to report. This run looks good. So far they're right on."

"Good. Any progress on cloning the algorithm?"

"Some, but it would go a hell of a lot faster if we could compare notes with ROBIN, if we had some understanding of how they were running their model…"

"Sorry. Can't do it. Double blind, we have to be sure. How close are you to matching it?"

Chun glanced down at the screen. "It's hard. Maybe fifty percent. Maybe a little more. We just need more data."

"And if there was no more? Could we still crack it?"

"Why? Why would there be no more? Is something wrong?"

"No, just trying to get a sense for where we are."

Chun looked relieved. "Possible, but we won't know until we really look at the results of this last run. But like I said, we're definitely onto something. I hope you're not having second thoughts."

Alex clapped him on the shoulder. "No chance, Matthew. We're in for the long haul."

Chun nodded vigorously. "Good, good. You know how important this is…"

"I do indeed, don't worry. Just keep me posted, okay? Running ROBIN is a massive expense. The sooner we can automate it, the better for all of us. If you reach a point where you think you have enough data to finish the algorithm, I need to know, understand?"

Chun nodded. "Of course." When Alex left, Chun picked up his soup. It was cold. What had that been about? Genometry had been Litton Labs' sole client for three years, three pretty lucrative years. They were the lead on the PEREGRINE project.

The job was to verify protein folding projections made by another group, ROBIN, and to extrapolate the algorithm ROBIN was using. The method involved designing simple amino acid chain puzzles to tease apart ROBIN's approach. They had no idea who the ROBIN team was but their work had been stellar, miles beyond everyone else. Matthew would give his left nut to be there. They were winning the race; they were going to be the newest bio-billionaires. And now Prenn was talking about scaling back? It didn't make sense.

47

VICHY

Jordan looked at the old Frenchman incredulously. "You speak English?"

"Of course," he said, still idly turning the absinthe bottle over in his hands.

"Why didn't you ever say anything?"

"Why would I? I think you had much that you wanted to say and maybe would have had difficulty saying if you knew you were understood."

Jordan shook his head. "And what were you talking about? Did you think I understood you?"

Gitanes smiled and turned to face Jordan. "No, I was quite sure you did not. I, too, had things I wanted to…how would you say, uncarry. That's not right, but you know what I mean, I think."

"You have me at quite a disadvantage apparently," Jordan said. "You understand, the things I told you, they could get you killed."

"I suppose so," the old man said. "But I promise you, there are far worse things. My name is Michel, by the way. I gather that you are Jordan, who is called Justin sometimes even though it is not your name."

"Nice to meet you, Michel." Jordan laughed, extending his hand. The Frenchman's grip was surprisingly strong and Jordan winced, imagining he could feel the tiny transmitter in his palm grinding against muscle and bone.

"Sorry," Michel said, "I forget about your hand. Does it hurt?"

"Not really, usually I forget it's there," Jordan said. "Do you live in the neighborhood? You seem to be here a lot."

"You are generous. I am here all of the time. You think it must be a sad and lonely existence, no? No, it's true." He went on when Jordan tried to object, "I live upstairs. I own the building so they are very good to me. I come down here because to sit upstairs and listen to life going on below is infinitely more depressing than hovering on its fringes."

"I get that," Jordan said. "I definitely get that. No family?"

Michel pursed his lips and said nothing for a moment. "No," he said finally. "I have no one. And you, what will you do now that the bottle is thrown into the sea as you say? Things are in motion. Where will you go?"

Jordan looked down without speaking.

They sat in silence for several minutes, each lost in his own thoughts. Finally Michel said, "When I was a young man, there were terrible student riots in Paris. The '60s. It was a very confusing time. At any rate, I did things, things that I knew were wrong. I betrayed many of my closest friends. In the end I came to own this building, and another besides, but at a great price. I think other men who did as I did during that time turned to the church afterward but for me there was no forgiveness. I found only hypocrisy." He wrote quickly on the back of a napkin and pushed it across the table. "If it ever should come to pass that I can be a help to you, I would be grateful."

Jordan slid the napkin in his pocket and unsteadily stood. "Thank you, goodbye."

"*À bientôt,*" the Frenchman returned.

As he pulled his coat close against the cold night air, Jordan glanced back over his shoulder and saw Michel sitting in the empty restaurant, lost in his own memories as the two Algerian barbacks stacked the cane chairs and mopped the floor around him.

48

VIDEO KILLED THE RADIO STAR

Kevin Bryce had worked at the Brook House for three months. His cousin Lionel had hooked him up. Lionel had done security there four nights a week for five years. The job had supported him through nursing school. The day Lionel graduated he'd given notice at the Brook House and recommended his young cousin for the job. Kevin had started the next week. It was a pretty cushy job. You just sat at the reception desk and kept an eye on the monitors.

Most nights Kevin did his homework or watched videos on his laptop.

During the day they had pretty girls working reception but at night there was no need to impress anybody; people just wanted to feel safe. And in this neighborhood they felt safer when the big black guy with the gun was on payroll.

The cop came in around one in the morning. He was friendly enough. Brought a couple coffees, bag of donut holes. He was interested in the video system and how the backups were logged.

He asked to see the overnights from the penthouse elevator camera for the past few weeks, and even though he didn't have a warrant or anything, Kevin figured, what the fuck, more exciting than homework. And it made him feel important for a minute.

The detective seemed particularly interested in one of Mr. Prenn's overnight guests, a lady with a ponytail, brown hair. Mr. Prenn had a fair number of girlfriends and the pretty blonde one was there the most, but this one seemed special.

Finally he asked Kevin to copy some of the files to a thumb drive. He slipped him a hundred bucks and left the sack of donut holes.

Stephanie checked her phone as soon as the class ended and the students started noisily filing out. She had heard it vibrate during the lecture and had subsequently found it difficult to concentrate on her subject, the inflationary model. The text was from Alex. It said, I have it.

Can you meet me at Simon's? she texted back.

He replied immediately. sure. half an hour?

See you there. You're the best.

Simon Perry ran the DNA sequencing facility in the Engineering Sciences Lab just across the street from Conant Hall on Oxford Street. He did the bulk of the sequencing for the literally hundreds of doctorate and postdoc projects that were happening at the university any given semester. He was also one of Stephanie's closest friends on the faculty and had done some moonlighting for Genometry in the early days. He wore a pair of half-moon spectacles perched near the end of his refined, some thought disdainful, nose. He made Stephanie a cup of tea in an old stained mug commemorating the first Clinton campaign while they waited for Alex. After handing her the tea, he rinsed out the kettle and made a noisy show of tidying up the lab as if he could keep her sorrow and anxiety at bay with his own constant motion.

Mercifully there was a gentle knock on the door and Alex let himself in. He nodded to Simon and placed the unmarked manila envelope on the counter.

"Right," Simon said to no one in particular. He opened the envelope and drew out the plastic bag. The seal was intact. He put on a new pair of latex gloves and carefully opened the bag to remove the swab. "Epithelial cells?" he asked, looking at Alex.

"I assume so," Alex replied.

"Good."

Alex eased himself down to the floor where Stephanie sat with her back to the wall, arms wrapped tightly around her knees. Without looking up, Simon said, "You know there's no point in your staying here. It's going to be at least a couple of days before I know anything. I'm running the full CODIS, that's thirteen different sites."

"I know," Stephanie said quietly. "I just want to stay for a little while."

Alex delicately reached his arm around her and she allowed her head to rest on his shoulder. The only sound was the occasional scrape of Simon's stool when he shifted his weight to reach across the counter.

49

LA VIE EN ROSE

The grass was brown, dormant; a small group of desultory tourists was clustered around a towering modern sculpture in the middle of the park nestled between Avenue de Verdun and Boulevard Jean Jaurès. Nice in the off-season was a quiet town. Year-rounders went about their daily routines to the steady, measured tempo of beach towns in winter. Jordan felt as if he could have been in Hyannis or Down East except there were palm trees and carved marble where the scrub pines and bleached shingles should have been. The sculpture was an early Venet, a simple arc in black steel canted like the keel of a ship climbing a wave, fighting its way through punishing surf to reach the calmer seas beyond.

Jordan cut through the formal gardens and past the Monument du Centenaire to the Promenade des Anglais, the main drag along the beach. Traffic was light, so he jaywalked across the street, scarcely pausing on the grassy median. The pedestrian promenade was easily as wide as a two-lane country road. In the summer it would be packed with sun worshippers from all over Europe jostling one another with their canvas beach bags, umbrellas and the ubiquitous rolled straw beach mats one could buy at every sandwich shop or from the African vendors who plied the promenade, but now it was nearly deserted. A cluster of light-blue-painted wooden chairs stood facing the sea, angled as though a group of restless ghosts had just pulled them up for a chin-wag.

A stiff onshore breeze numbed Jordan's left ear even as the low sun warmed his face. The Côte d'Azur lived up to its billing, the sea was a striking pale blue under a mostly cloud-filled sky with ribbons of a deeper blue glimpsed behind. The sun was just beginning to sink pinkly into a distant huddle of sullen clouds. The tawdry ball lights of the Casino Ruhl were already on. The casino occupied the ground floor of the Méridien Hotel. Its pink awning and dated decor seemed sad to Jordan, like a faded beauty with too much makeup caught in the daylight.

He crossed at the crosswalk and walked purposefully into the sprawling casino. There was only the Ruhl and the Palais, so he'd leave tonight for the richer hunting grounds to the west—Cannes, Saint-Tropez and Aix-en-Provence. Inside the Ruhl, Jordan made straight for the cage. He walked up to the open window and pulled out his bank card.

"Two thousand, please," he said, sliding the card under the thick glass partition.

"Yes, sir," the cashier, a young man with bad skin and thin spiky hair, said, swiping the card. "How would you like it, Mr. Butler?"

"Two five hundreds and ten hundreds, please."

"Yes, sir." The cashier expertly stacked two piles of green chips with a muted click and swept them into the transfer box. Then he took two black chips from his drawer and slid them in, along with the bank card and a printed receipt. He sealed the box on his end, which unlocked the outer door. Jordan opened it and gathered up the contents.

"*Merci,*" he said, nodding to the cashier.

"*Merci, monsieur,*" the cashier replied, resetting the box.

Jordan walked through the casino, eventually settling on a Vingt-et-un table whose primary virtues were the two dark-haired girls giggling and playing from a shared stack of chips, and the unobstructed view of the surveillance camera on the ceiling.

When he sat at the table, his demeanor changed. He became animated and voluble. It took him three glasses of champagne and forty minutes to lose all of his green chips. He flirted artlessly and shamelessly with the two women. They turned out to be Italian, in Nice for a wedding. When he doubled down on an eleven with the dealer showing six and then lost his last green, he spread his hands as if to say, *What can you do?* and headed somewhat unsteadily back toward the cage. The black chips never left his pocket.

After two and a half hours he had lost three thousand euros and had ten black chips in his pocket. He went back to the cage and cashed out, keeping his head down and his back to the ceiling camera. Five minutes later he was back on the boardwalk. The cold night air cleared his head. The clouds had passed and an impossibly large moon, days from full, hung just beyond the bobbing yachts anchored offshore. A gentle surf lapped at the smooth round stones that stood in for sand along this stretch of the Mediterranean. Jordan walked down another quarter mile to the Palais.

The Palais was a grand white edifice, more in the modern Vegas mold than its faded cousin. The floor rang with the digital cacophony of the slot machines. There was no central cage; the sheer scale of the place seemed to ensure security. The cashiers were in a discreet row on the far side of the casino. Jordan went up to the first open window and bought five thousand, all but a thousand in five-hundred-euro chips.

He ordered a scotch and soda from one of the circulating waitresses and wandered through the casino. He had never understood gambling. From the pensioners at the slots slowly bleeding out their life savings, to the wild-eyed shooters at the craps table, to the tight-jawed poker players waiting for the cards to turn, Jordan had always felt a deep sympathy for gamblers. They struck him as addicts, no better than skid row drunks or junkies in a shooting gallery. They had that same hollow look; the vulgar luxury of the setting only seemed to highlight the despair.

He squandered a few hundred at a crowded roulette table and actually won almost a thousand playing reckless Vingt-et-un. After a couple of hours he was basically even.

Nonetheless he went back to the cashier for another five thousand. After swiping his card, the cashier looked at her screen and with an apologetic smile and said, "I am so sorry, Mr. Butler, the bank wishes to speak to you. Would you like to speak with them, or perhaps another card…?"

She let the question hang. "No, I'd like to speak with them. I'm sure it's fine," he said.

"Very good, sir, just a moment." She dialed, and after a minute on hold, she spoke in quick efficient French for a moment, nodded and, cupping the mouthpiece, handed him the phone under the decorative bars of the window.

It was a cordless handset so Jordan stepped away from the window. "Hello, this is Justin Butler," he said.

"How are you, Jordan?" said a dry, familiar voice. There was no delay; it sounded as if he were down the street. Sam. Jordan panicked for a second and looked around, expecting to see him leaning against a slot machine flanked by his thugs. He wasn't. "I wouldn't have pegged you for a gambler," Sam was saying.

Jordan recovered quickly. "Clearly I'm not," he said, making his voice sound as if he was tipsy but trying to hide it, channeling late-night adolescent returns to waiting parents. "I've been losing." He laughed a little nervously.

"I see that," Sam said.

"Not that much, though," Jordan said. "A few thousand, maybe. I thought I had plenty of money. You said I did."

"You do, Jordan," the patient voice went on, "but not infinite."

"Yeah, yeah, I know. I'm just trying to have fun. Making friends, seeing the country."

"I see. All right, well, enjoy. Just make sure your travels don't take you outside of the country, please."

"I know. I know the rules." There was a moment's silence. "You're not here, are you?"

"No, I'm not. Please pass me back to that lovely young lady, won't you?"

"O-okay, um, thank you," Jordan stammered and passed the phone back. The cashier listened, nodded and clicked off.

"You're all set, Mr. Butler. What denominations, please?"

50

THE PALMS

"Oh, I meant to call you, Officer Herron. I am so sorry." She looked tired, rushing back to her office after class. Even so, she was striking; he'd forgotten how striking. Beautiful face, natural. She opened the door, balancing a stack of books, and Herron followed her into the cluttered office.

"Please sit down," she said, moving a stack of magazines off the chair and stepping behind her desk. "I did get your message, and it was very kind of you to follow up, but if I called you, it was completely unintentional. I do that all the time." She took out her phone and put it on the desk. "I have no idea how but I somehow manage to routinely dial old numbers in my purse. I have one friend who won't answer my calls anymore because of all the pocket dials." She laughed, inviting him to see the humor.

"Would that be Mr. Prenn, ma'am?" Herron said.

She hadn't expected that. She was thrown for a moment. Then she smiled. "Yes, it would actually. Of course you met Alex. That was a very difficult time."

"Yes, I'm sure it was," Herron said. His face was sincere but there was something in his tone of voice, as if he was in on a private joke, that made her face feel hot. "I'm sure he has been a great support."

It was a statement but Herron's inflection suggested it was more of a question. His eyebrows remained slightly arched, inviting Stephanie to elaborate.

She knew she was on dangerous ground but the silence required some comment. "Yes, absolutely," she said, trying to find a safe way forward. "I actually met Alex at the same time I met my husband. They were friends, from school." Herron nodded politely.

"Harvard actually." She flushed as she heard herself; it sounded elitist and condescending somehow. She wondered where the detective had gone to school. Was there a university like West Point or Annapolis for cops? Of course not. Stephanie felt like she was going to laugh out loud. She felt reckless; the whole conversation seemed surreal, absurd. Raised voices from the students outside brought her back.

"How would you describe your relationship with Mr. Prenn now?" Herron asked.

"He is probably the nearest thing I have to a friend." She paused for a moment, looking up at the dusty transom over her office door.

"My husband was my confidant, my shoulder. We were a society of our own. Now that he's gone Alex is my closest link to that society. He's the only other person who knew Jordan like I did, so when I need someone I talk to him. Does that make any sense?"

Herron nodded thoughtfully. "It must be nice to have someone to talk to."

Stephanie looked at him, her head tilted a little to one side. "Of course," she said.

Follow the money. When Herron had first made detective, his partner had been a guy named Jimmy McKenna. He was a couple years from retirement and mostly shuffled around the station with his gut leading the way and his pants threatening to fall off because he had no ass to keep them up. He gestured with a hand that seemed to have a cup of coffee permanently attached, making weighty pronouncements for the benefit of the junior detectives. "Follow the money" had been a particular favorite trope.

Genometry was a very small cap stock traded on the Hong Kong Exchange. Until the recent buyout talk with Pfizer, it was seldom traded at all. However, going back several years Herron saw a pattern of high-volume trades that seemed to anticipate significant moves in the share price.

Surefire tell for insider trading. Bigger company, someone would have noticed. The biggest individual shareholders were Jordan Parrish and Alex Prenn. But they weren't buying or selling. The bulk of the liquid stock was held by Viceroy Interests, a venture capital firm with a Boston address. Time to go to the lieutenant. He'd need subpoenas.

The kids were long asleep when the phone rang. Stephanie was lying in bed with an old issue of *The Economist*. She never seemed to catch up; every week another issue chock-full of no doubt timely and insightful reporting would arrive before she had cracked the last one. Her eyes were rescanning the same paragraph for the third time and she still had no idea what she'd read.

She picked up the handset. "Hello?"

"Hi, Stephanie. I hope it's not too late to call. It's Simon."

"No, it's fine. I was just reading."

"I wanted to call as soon as I knew." His voice seemed a long way away. "It's a match." Stephanie didn't respond. She looked at the way the faded palm trees on the wallpaper visible through the bathroom door didn't really line up where the seam was and wondered that she'd never noticed it before.

"Are you there?"

"Yes, sorry, Simon. Thank you. You're absolutely sure...of course you are, I'm sorry."

"I ran thirteen sites, three trillion to one against a false positive, and that's allowing for twins. I also checked the fragmentation and it was consistent with the date of the accident. Listen, I'm really, really sorry—"

She cut him off. "Please, Si, don't. I needed to be sure, that's all. Thank you for indulging my craziness. You're a prince. Go home, get some sleep."

"Are you okay?" So far away.

"Yes, of course. I'm fine, it's better, really. Good night, Simon."

"Good night, Stephanie."

If she were designing wallpaper, she would space the pattern so that the seam would always fall on the solid tone, not the print. It was maddening.

51

WILLIAM

Jordan walked up Victor Hugo to La Rotonde, the massive fountain and roundabout just up the street from his hotel in Aix. He turned right onto the Cours Mirabeau, a wide pedestrian mall with a narrow street running down the middle. Two rows of plane trees lined the street. It was early so the Cours wasn't terribly crowded yet. The cafés were serving the breakfast crowd and the retail shops were just throwing open their gates and having their walkways scrubbed clean. A couple of blocks ahead Jordan saw the green neon cross of the pharmacy.

Jordan had prepared a list but the pharmacist, a solid woman in her early fifties with lustrous black hair pinned severely back and distinctly grandmotherly spectacles, was eager to improve on it. She suggested an herbal alternative to the antibiotic he ordered. He took both.

Back at the Cézanne, he took an inventory of his purchases. He had a box of ten Miltex disposable scalpels, a box of suture needles and some gut suture, several boxes of gauze, disinfec-

tant, both topical and oral antibiotics and their herbal counterparts, a box of latex gloves, a tincture of iodine, surgical tape,
a large and small set of tweezers and an eyelash curler. The last
item was an improvised replacement for the clamp he'd imagined but had been unable to find.

Everything was spread out on the queen-size bed. The room
was modern and stylish in that cheap way favored by so many
post-Starck hotels. Jordan packed the medical supplies neatly into
a black duffel that already contained thirty-five thousand euros
in tightly wrapped bundles, cashed-out black chips. Money,
hopefully, Sam didn't know he had.

He shoved the duffel under the bed and went down to the
business center. He still had the phone but only used it for the
Foldit app and Maps. He assumed Sam monitored it. The business center, really just a seedy little room with a pair of ten-
year-old PCs with smudged LCD screens, was deserted. Jordan
logged on to a new Gmail account. One new mail.

Neil G. Ives
Re: transport
William, I have spoken with my associate Patrick, who is scheduled
to run a load of Galway sheep to Montmorillon in a couple of weeks,
March 13. Let me know if that will suit your purposes. As to the financial arrangement, Pat would require 5,000 E in addition to our
agreed-upon fee for handling your travel needs. Cash. No bitcoin.

Please let me know if that is acceptable.
Regards, Neil

Jordan hit Reply.

That is acceptable. I will assume travel on March 14.
Best, William

He logged off. It was a little tight but it would work.

★ ★ ★

Lieutenant Trahon nodded impatiently. "Okay, I get it. You sure the partner's fucking the wife?"

"Pretty sure," Herron said.

"And are you going to be able to share the source of this opinion with the judge?"

"Probably not, but the public financials should be probable cause on the insider trading angle."

"Yeah, maybe. Okay, let me see what I can do."

He was good like that. Knew when not to ask too many questions. "Thanks, Lieutenant."

Trahon only grunted and went back to the open folder on his desk as Herron let himself out.

52

THE WESTERN FRONT

Thought you should know, Si confirmed.

    jordan?

Yup. He's sure.

    and you?

Yes, I'm sure, too.

    how's that entanglement thing going?

Don't make fun. I'm trying.

    i know sorry.

One day at a time. But thank you.
Really.

mission accomplished.

Let's get together soon.

lunch?

Haha. Watch it!!

kidding. but yes, let's.

Kk

Alex switched to a different conversation on another phone.

id confirmed. all quiet on the western front. thank you.

53

CONCORD

There was an actual working pay phone just across the street from the Cézanne. Jordan swiped his telecarte and, holding a small, creased napkin up to the light, dialed the number.

"Le Pré aux Clercs, bonsoir," a harried voice answered.

"Michel, *s'il vous plaît,*" Jordan said.

"Un instant," and there was a clatter as the receiver was set down and apparently fell to the floor. Jordan felt a strange sense of comfort as the sounds of the brasserie came down the line.

Then there was a loud clattering and fumbling as the phone was retrieved. *"Allô?"*

"Ça va, con?" Jordan said.

"Ça va, Yanqui." Without missing a beat.

"I need that favor, Michel," Jordan said. "It's a big one. Do you have a pen?"

"Bien sûr."

Once you looked, the pattern was obvious. Viceroy Interests was the main player in Genometry stock. And Viceroy had made a killing. They had anticipated every significant announcement or patent with a major play, and always the right one, shorting the stock right before results of an unsuccessful clinical trial were published, or leveraging their position right before a new patent announcement. Viceroy had made tens of millions over the past seven years. It stank. Herron hadn't ever chased an insider trading case before but this looked like a slam dunk. Follow the money.

But who was Viceroy? The Boston address was a mail drop. Corporate filings indicated a Hong Kong–based office, but according to his contact in the AG's office, that didn't mean shit. It took a couple of days and a few old chits but Herron finally traced the actual ownership to a company called Hessians Global. Hessians was privately held, registered in Lichtenstein. It was a brick wall. Herron sat back in his chair and studied the screen. There was something. The connection danced just out of reach.

He grabbed his jacket and took the stairs. He drove an old white Cadillac. Jewish grandmothers, pimps and him. Drove like a motorboat with a flooded bilge. He put on the radio. WEEI. Sports radio, 850. It was a phone-in show, bunch of idiots armchair-managing the Sox.

Paul from Revere (that had to be a joke, right?) called in to say Papelbon was done and they needed to pick up a new closer before the season opened.

He jumped on the pike and headed west. As he left the city behind, the scenery settled into that dull gray low terrain that Herron found so depressing in the winter. Soon spring would come and the hills would explode in the lush green that was the belated reward for one hundred and thirty-three days a year of rain. The chatter of the radio stilled his mind and allowed it to wander aimlessly. He thought about Christine, then tried not to, which just brought her into sharper focus. He supposed he had loved her. Not that it ever would have worked out, anyway. She was never going to be a cop's wife.

He sped past the Waban exit and saw signs for 128 and 95 North to the Concord Turnpike. Something stirred and shimmered in the darkness. Without his conscious mind taking any part, the Caddy slowed and drifted into the breakdown lane. He pulled the stem in the steering column to turn on the hazards and slid the transmission into Park with a little lurching clunk. He sat quietly as cars whipped by inches away. When trucks passed, the car shuddered. Bits of sand and gravel from passing tires struck Herron's windshield with a spitting sound.

Concord. Hessians… Jesus. How fucking stupid could he be? He banged the button on the glove compartment until it sprang open. He fished out a pad and wrote down the letters. *H E S S I A N S*. Then backward. Then the consonants above the vowels. *H S S N S, E I A*.

There it was. He crossed out the letters one at a time. *S H A N I S S E*. Shanisse Prenn. The partner's stepmother. Fuck. No way that's a coincidence. Hazards still flashing, he pulled back onto the road with a spray of gravel and took the next exit.

It was completely dark. The air had that quality unique to hotels. It was neither cool nor warm; it had passed through so much ducting and equipment it had been stripped of all traces of terroir. It could have begun as a frigid icy blast from the North Sea, or just as easily as a balmy breeze off the Mediterranean.

Jordan couldn't remember where he was at first. The clock radio by the bed said 4:38. A small pad of paper illuminated by the pale green numbers bore the crest of l'Hôtel Anne de Bretagne in Rennes. Right.

He'd been dreaming. There had been a boy. His eyes had been opened wide as if he were screaming but his mouth had been completely still. Jordan knew the boy was being chased by someone and was terribly afraid. But he couldn't remember if he was the boy somehow or if he was the one chasing him. He was on the tipping point of wakefulness. Better to sleep if

he could. He pulled his legs into his belly and counted back–
ward from one hundred as his body almost imperceptibly rocked
back and forth.

54

ANOMALIES

He looked uncomfortable; his eyes darted nervously around her office. Tiny beads of sweat shone on his forehead, partly from the stuffy heat after the chill outside, but not entirely, Stephanie thought.

"Can I get you something to drink, Simon?" she asked pleasantly. "I have—" she opened the brown minifridge beneath her desk "—let's see, Diet Coke…and Diet Coke. Name your poison."

"Nothing, thanks, I'm fine," he said, sounding unsure. Then it came out in a tumble. "Look, Steph, I went back and forth all night about this. I know there's going to be some reasonable explanation and I probably have no business even bringing it up, but at the same time, it's weird and, you know, you're my friend, and Jordan was my friend and I couldn't just let it go and not say anything, you know?"

"No. I have no idea what you're saying," she said with a wan smile, "but whatever it is you can tell me. You know that, Si."

He nodded absently while his fingers pinched a fold of his corduroy pant leg and roughed and smoothed the wale. He didn't look at her. "I sequenced some more of the sample after we spoke. No reason. I just wanted to be, you know, thorough, I guess." His eyes flitted around the cluttered office.

"Anyway, there were some... I suppose you'd have to say... anomalies."

Her eyebrows rose slightly. "Anomalies?"

"Well, yeah, that's what I'd call it. I mean, strictly speaking, *contamination* is probably a better word, but not exactly right, either..." His voice trailed off.

"What did you find, Simon?"

He pushed his glasses up the bridge of his nose. "Sorry," he said. "First there was a substantial amount of P33. That's an isotope of phosphorus used in gene sequencing, radioactive. Obviously my first assumption was that it was local contamination. So I rechecked the original sample. No question, it was there. I'm careful."

"I know you are," she said. "How could it have gotten in there?"

"That's just it, I have no idea. It doesn't make sense. But there was more. There were traces of protein that weren't human."

"What do you mean, not human? Are you saying that it wasn't Jordan? I don't understand."

"No, no, the DNA was from Jordan. Positively. But there was contamination with some kind of animal protein. Again, I have no idea what or how."

"I see, and can you figure out what that animal was?"

"I'm working on it—I think so. But that's still not the strangest part. Like I said, you can write all that off as contamination from outside. But there was something else."

Stephanie struggled to keep her impatience in check. "Go on."

"Okay, I don't know how to explain it. At first I thought there had to be some mistake on my part or with the sequencer, but

I've checked it a dozen times now. There were a large number of strands that had the same sequence, identical, as if they had been PCR amplified or something, and the sequence was a nonrandom repeat that I've never seen before. It shouldn't have been there."

"I'm not sure I get what you're saying."

"I'm saying there was a long repeating section of code in Jordan's DNA that doesn't belong there."

Stephanie felt as if she were peering over the edge of a deep hole. "What was the sequence?"

Simon dug a folded piece of lined paper out of his jacket pocket and opened it. He raised his chin slightly and looked down at the page. "I wrote down the bases—A, T, G, C, T, G..."

"GTG!" she interrupted, leaning forward in her chair, trying to read his scrawl.

He looked up at her. "Yes. How could you know that?"

"You started at the wrong place," she said. Her eyes shone with feverish intensity. "It's CTG, GTG, ATG. The codons for leucine, valine and methionine. LVM. 'Love, me.' We signed a thousand notes to each other that way. LVM. 'Love, me.'" She couldn't speak. It felt as though great hands were squeezing her chest.

He stared at her with a dull quizzical expression frozen on his face. "That doesn't make sense," he said. "Like a tattoo... I don't even think it's possible what you're suggesting."

It was her turn to be confused. "What am I suggesting? I don't get it."

"Well, it seems like you're saying this sequence of codons was something that had meaning for the two of you, and the inference would be that at some point Jordan synthesized the sequence, introduced it into his own DNA via a bacteria or something and that the plasmid was incorporated and replicated."

"Can that be done?"

"Theoretically, I suppose. Ventner watermarked his bacteria—" talking more to himself "—maybe something Jordan experimented with. It would take a while…and why sixty repeats, although maybe that—"

"Simon—" her voice was sharp "—tell me what you think this all means. Please." Softer.

He took a deep breath. "I don't know exactly but I think I have some sense of it. The only explanation that makes any sense is that Jordan must have used himself as the subject of an experiment involving synthesized plasmids. I'm not sure when he was working that angle—my guess, years ago. But it clearly worked. He was on the way to a cure for, theoretically, anyway, any genetic disease. If you can identify the mutated gene responsible for the disorder and synthesize a normal version of it and then have the working copy incorporated into your DNA, you're fixed!"

"So you're saying he used our little code as a test? Or a marker?"

"Maybe. Maybe it was his way of making you part of him. He never told you?"

"No." She gasped as if she'd been holding her breath and her shoulders began to shake uncontrollably.

"Oh God, I'm sorry. I knew I should have left it alone."

She couldn't speak but shook her head.

He came around the desk and awkwardly put his arm around her shoulder. She turned toward him and clutched at the back of his jacket, sobbing into his rib cage. He felt a twinge in his lower back as he struggled to stay upright and still. After a couple of minutes she released him and sat back, wiping her eyes and nose with the back of her hand. Finally she managed to say, "I'm glad. Thank you." Her face was red and damp.

"Ughh, I'm sorry, Simon." She took a deep shaky breath. "That hasn't happened in a long time. Oh God." She laughed and wiped his shirt with her sleeve. "I've gotten you all snotty."

★ ★ ★

Herron sat on the front edge of the sofa; he couldn't imagine settling back into the cushions. The toile pattern in blue on white showed a pastoral scene, a young man pushing a girl on a swing. She is laughing, head thrown back, one bare foot crooked back, the other extended. A second boy is eating an apple with a smile that suggests he has an unobstructed view up the young lady's voluminous skirts. Herron couldn't decide if it was an actual eighteenth-century design or a smirking modern riff, but either way it was clearly a hideously expensive piece. There was nowhere to sit in the house that didn't make him feel big and awkward. He felt as if the smell of his body, an honest sour loam, was despoiling the crisp linen air. He couldn't imagine how people lived in houses like this.

Mrs. Prenn had gone to get her husband. Four in the afternoon and he was apparently napping. Shanisse Prenn was comfortable in her skin, he thought. And shared it happily. She had answered the door in a pair of cutoff denim shorts and a man's plaid button-up with only a couple of buttons buttoned. Her long straight hair was streaked with honey highlights and her skin was an even butterscotch. She was barefoot and seemed to skate over the slick hardwood floors. Radiant heat, he thought. He glanced at the neat group of shoes by the door and started to slip off his Clarks. She stopped him with a careless wave and showed him to the living room.

She had offered him a drink, which he'd declined.

He heard feet coming down the hallway and inched even farther forward on the sofa, standing when Shanisse and her husband, Martin, came in.

"How can we help you, Detective?" Martin Prenn said, extending his hand. He had to be rich, Herron thought. A good twenty-five years older than the missus. Trying to keep it together—well groomed, light blue linen shirt and khakis, also barefoot. Thin lips, tiny eyes. He looked like a cancer patient dipped in Oompa-Loompa orange.

Herron shook his hand, good grip. "I'm sorry to bother you, Mr. Prenn. I'm just following up on the investigation into the death of your son's partner, Jordan Parrish, and wanted to ask you a couple of questions."

"Oh! That was just awful," Shanisse said. Her face took on an exaggerated expression of solemnity. "Traffic accident, wasn't it?"

"Yes, ma'am," Herron said. "That's right. Listen, if this is a bad time, I can come back…"

Martin waved him back to the sofa. "Don't be ridiculous. You're here now. Ask away." Scent of lavender soap and sex. Hence the nap and her obvious good humor. For some reason the idea was disturbing.

"Thank you," he said, retaking his awkward seat. "Are you familiar with a company called Viceroy Interests?"

Martin looked at his wife, who had taken a perch on the arm of his chair, one leg casually draped between his. They both shrugged. "No, never heard of it, why?"

"They are a major investor in your son's company."

Prenn nodded. "Here's the thing, Detective… Harden, is it?"

"Herron."

"Sorry. The thing is Alex doesn't share much with me. Certainly nothing like that. Our relationship is…complicated."

Shanisse idly stroked her husband's longish gray hair.

"I see," Herron said. There didn't seem to be any point digging further here. Sleeping dogs. Why stir shit up? Besides, seeing the stepmom, he had some other ideas why Alex might name a shell company after her.

He stood up carefully, resisting the impulse to smooth out the impression his ass had left on the sofa cushion. "Thank you both. You've been very helpful."

"That's it? We haven't told you anything at all," Shanisse

Prenn said. Somehow her tone suggested disappointment that he wasn't going to stay, maybe have a couple drinks. They could light a fire, and who knows where things might go from there. Herron practically ran for the door.

55

CROSSWITS

Stephanie slept badly. No dreams—at least, not any she remembered. Just a nagging sense that something was wrong, or missing. Something vital was dangling just out of reach. She woke up early. It was still dark. Distant chains on dry snow and the hum of the streetlight. Just after four. Stephanie was wide-awake; her eyes seemed too open, as if she could neither blink nor fully relax the muscles of her forehead. Simon had said the sequence was ATG, CTG, GTG repeated sixty times exactly. *M, L, V.* At first she had thought that he must have been mistaken, but then she had realized that ATG, in addition to coding for methionine, was the start codon for almost every gene in the genome; it was the sequence that initiates transcription. So, maybe, she had theorized, starting with the *M* was just an artifact of the steps Jordan had taken to copy the sequence and introduce it into his DNA. But now, in the predawn stillness, that explanation didn't sit well. Jordan was a meticulous scientist, OCD if she was honest; his experimental work was always clean and elegant. It wasn't a coding gene; it could start however he wanted. He would have gotten it right.

In her twenties, before motherhood had drained the selfish hours from her Sundays, she had been an obsessive crossword solver. She had done the *New York Times Magazine* puzzle over coffee in pen and then lounged away the rest of the day in faded blue Andover sweatpants and wooly socks, wrestling with the London *Guardian*'s cryptic. She still had an app on her phone called Crosswits. It was her cheat of last resort when she got stymied. You entered the letters you knew and question marks where the missing letters were and the program spat out the words and phrases that matched.

Stephanie turned on her bedside lamp—one click, a soft yellow light just strong enough to push through the darkness in a compressed bubble that spilled off her side of the bed and across the carpeted floor to the window. She retrieved her phone from the floor.

She entered "M?L?V?" and the screen immediately offered, "My Love," "Me Love" and "Molave" (which it went on to explain was a municipality in the Philippines). She started moving the wildcards. "M?LV?" yielded "Molvi," no definition suggested. For most of the arrangements the program replied, "I'm sorry, no results matched your query." But one—"?M?L?V?"— gave four. The first suggestion was the rather poetic "O, my love." There were links given to a song by the Cloud Room and "Oh My Love" by John Lennon. Next was "Emil Ivy," a name Google had no citations for. Then the program suggested the rather narcissistic and grammatically dubious "I me love." When her eyes reached the fourth suggestion, Stephanie felt the walls of the room rip suddenly away as her focus tunneled to the letters on the screen. She couldn't breathe. She had exhaled but despite the empty pressure of her lungs it seemed inconceivably complicated to reverse the process, to realign the valves in her throat and sinuses, to compel her diaphragm to drop and create the partial vacuum that would draw the air in and replenish the supply of oxygen to her brain. The cursor blinked patiently next to the words her husband had written in his DNA, had repeated sixty times over and over as if screaming to be heard, and as she read it she knew with an absolute certainty it was true.

"I'm alive."

56

FRANS MAAS

The man came in to Le Vieux Puits, stooping slightly to avoid striking his head on the low beam that divided the bar area from the dining room. The relais was quiet; most of the truckers and tour operators had been and gone. It was the late-afternoon lull; a couple lone motorists had stopped for a coffee to get them to Saint-Malo, and there was one French truck driver talking on his cell phone and marching briskly through a second liter bottle of the local cider. Neil made a note to let that drunk bastard get a good head start before he hit the road again. The man was looking around hesitantly as his eyes adjusted to the dim light. It had to be him. Neil raised a hand and pushed back his chair with a grunt. "Oi, you William?" he said with the deep sigh of a man who could do with four or five stone less bulk on him.

"Yes, Neil?" the man said, putting out his hand. Decent grip. American, it sounded like, okay-looking guy. Didn't look like a poof—white-collar hands, though.

"Yeah. Good to meet you. Have a seat." Jordan took the

opposite chair. "Sorry I didn't wait," Neil said with an apologetic half smile, glancing at his nearly empty plate. "Calves' feet," he added with a little jerk of his chin, acknowledging the anatomically explicit remains. He didn't mention that he'd actually arrived two hours before the arranged meet to make sure there were no unwelcome guests from any of the several potentially interested gendarmeries. It had looked clean.

"You want to order something? Food's better than you'd think."

"No, thank you, I'm fine," the man said.

"Suit yourself," Neil said, pushing his plate away and refilling his glass from the pitcher of cider.

"Did you bring the ante?"

Jordan took a brown paper bag from inside his coat and pushed it across the table. Neil peered inside; a couple stacks of lavender-tinted five-hundred-euro notes hunkered smugly in the bottom of the sack. The bills smelled new. He let his eyes linger an extra moment before rolling the top of the bag shut and stuffing it in his coat pocket. Neil loved money for its own sake. Pat was always on him about that, trying to make him admit that it was the things you could get—cars, houses, women, respect, security—that mattered but Neil could give a fuck about all that. He had what he needed and could take what he didn't. No, it was the money itself, the paper and ink, that he loved. Made no sense but true just the same.

"May I see the truck?"

"Oh, yeah, yeah, of course," Neil said, draining the glass and laboring to his feet again. Not big on chitchat was he. Fair enough; Neil got that. He dug a couple crumpled notes from his pants and left them on the table. "This way."

Jordan followed the trucker out the back door of the restaurant. *Christ, he's big*, he thought. *His leg's the size of my waist.* And yet he didn't seem to have any fat on him, just big and solid.

Even his head was massive, jutting jaw, piercing blue eyes and brows permanently cocked in ironic amusement.

The cab was an older white Mercedes Actros, flat nose, slight curve at the sides. The trailer was covered with a fitted blue tarp with the logo Frans Maas printed on the side in large yellow letters. Neil lifted the tarp in the back to expose a heavy padlock. He opened it with a key at his belt and slid the door open. He stepped up into the trailer and held the tarp for Jordan.

The inside was empty. The trailer was covered but the sides were open slats so a dim blue light filtered through. "So they don't have to open us up," Neil said. "They can shove the end of the detector right up under the tarp. That's how they do it, you know. It's all CO_2 detectors now. Quick and easy. That's why they catch most of 'em.

"Illegals sneak into the back of half the trucks making the crossing. They'd never find them back in the day, but now they got these detectors. If you're breathing, you're busted." He liked that line.

"So how do we avoid them?"

Neil smiled broadly. "We don't, we want 'em to check us. Half the time they'll catch one that's hitched a ride without me knowing. But they have never found one of my customers." He beamed, thick arms crossed over his chest.

Jordan's eyes swung around the empty trailer. Finally he shrugged. "Okay, I'll bite."

Neil nodded smugly and motioned Jordan to follow him to the back of the trailer. He took a short screwdriver from his coat pocket and pried up a section of the floor. It swung open and Jordan saw a pair of shallow compartments, each just high enough to hold a man lying down. At the head of each compartment was something that looked like a scuba regulator connected to a hose.

"You breathe through there—CO_2 gets blown out with the exhaust. Come see the outside." He lowered the floor back into place. From the outside Jordan couldn't see where the compartments could be; the trailer floor was only a couple of inches thick.

"Nice, right?" Neil said. "The floor inside slopes gradually up—you can't tell but it does. By the back of the truck you have an extra foot and a half. Pretty good, eh? Guy who built her out was a fucking magician."

Jordan nodded appreciatively, though he thought drug smuggler a more likely occupation for the previous owner.

"Don't worry, Billy. We'll get you to Dover safe and sound," Neil said, clapping Jordan heavily on the back. For what he was paying, they better, Jordan thought.

57

A NICE FUCKING DAY

Trahon had come through. The lieutenant had gotten a warrant for the Viceroy mail drop and Prenn's apartment, including any computers and files on the premises. It was all tied to the insider trading angle so it wasn't going to make the security camera footage any more usable, but it was a start. Herron pressed the penthouse buzzer and waited. He nodded at the security guard, who gave him a quick glance before returning to his book. Probably the Bryce kid's cousin, Herron thought. The video screen came to life, the image swelling like a bubble, then settling on the face of a clearly just-awakened Alex Prenn.

"Yes?" Voice low and raspy with sleep.

"Good afternoon, Mr. Prenn. Detective Herron. Mind if I come up?"

His face was close to the camera, as if he was leaning against the wall. "Actually, this is not a great time, Detective. Would you mind coming back in a couple of hours?"

"Sorry, sir. I'm afraid it has to be now." He held the folded document up to the camera. "I have a warrant."

Alex didn't react to this bit of information except to nod slightly and say, "I see. I suppose you'd better come up, then." The door to Herron's left buzzed and he walked through it to the elevator bank.

Prenn answered the door in a thick belted hotel robe and socks. He read quickly through the warrant as he led the way to the U-shaped sofa in the sunken living room. "What would you like to discuss today, Detective?"

"Why don't we start with Viceroy Interests?"

"Okay, when we went public Viceroy was an active early investor. When things started to go badly they bought up most of the outstanding shares. They basically own Genometry now. Stuck with it. Other than that I'm afraid I can't tell you much." Alex met Herron's eyes levelly.

"Really? That surprises me, Mr. Prenn. You would think you'd have done more research on your largest investor."

"I tried. It turned out to be very difficult to identify the principals."

"How far did you get?"

"Hong Kong. That seems to be where they're based."

Herron pulled a distressed little notepad from his jacket pocket and started flipping through it. It was an absurd little display, like something out of an old *Columbo* episode, but it gave him a minute to watch Prenn sweat.

"Right, I thought that, too, at first."

"At first? So you found something that suggested otherwise?"

Herron pretended to read from the notebook. "Yes. I traced the ownership of the Hong Kong company to something in Lichtenstein called—" here he fumbled through pages again... wait for it "—here it is. Session? No, Hessians Global, that's it. Any bells, sir?"

Alex pursed his lips and affected a thoughtful gaze, eyes up and left, just where they ought to be if he was searching his midterm memory. A rueful shake of the head. "Sorry, I don't recognize it." Cool as a cucumber.

Herron decided to let that one dangle for a bit. He shut the notebook and put it back into his pocket. "Would you mind showing me your office, sir?"

"Of course," Alex said, standing and leading the way. His office took up almost a third of the upper floor and had probably originally been the master bedroom, Herron thought. Floor-to-ceiling windows took up two walls of the corner room. One side looked out across the Fens and the other down Pond Avenue as it snaked slushily down and around the park, shadowing the stream that bisected it, invisible beyond snowy banks.

An antique table of dark cherry with three large monitors presided over one side of the room while the other was devoted to a wall-mounted plasma, a worn leather sofa and two armchairs. Herron sat down at the computer. The monitors displayed real-time data on several exchanges: New York, London, Hong Kong, Tokyo and a couple he didn't recognize. He opened a browser window and entered an IP address. The direct socket connection was established and the tech guys downtown took control.

"Mr. Prenn, my people are going to go through your system now. Are there any encrypted or password-protected files?"

"I don't think so. If there are, the code would be 78374, probably." He seemed incredibly relaxed. More awake now, almost smirking. They weren't going to find shit.

"Do you have another computer or a laptop here, sir?"

"Yes, my laptop is downstairs. Shall I get it for you?"

"I'll come with you, if you don't mind, sir."

Alex laughed. "I'm not sure you want to do that, Detective. I promise you I'm not going to erase anything."

"Just the same."

Alex led the way down the spiral staircase to the lower level. The downstairs was dark and still, no natural light, just a dull orange aura from recessed lighting in the ceiling, which was lower than Herron had expected. He knew he wasn't really going to hit his head but felt himself involuntarily stooping nonetheless. There was a hallway with a couple of doors at the far end and long sliding doors all the way along one wall. Serious closet space.

Alex opened the door on the left at the end of the hallway and Herron followed him in. It was even darker in the bedroom, almost black except for a sliver of light coming through the heavy drapes. The room was several degrees warmer than the rest of the apartment and there was a heavy, musky smell. Alex touched a smooth metal plate by the door and the ceiling fixtures came on with a gentle hum, gradually rising to a preset golden glow.

Herron hadn't realized the girl was there until she sighed drowsily and rolled on her side. She was sprawled on top of the duvet, completely naked except for a black leather strap around her left ankle that was still attached by a steel ring to a length of chain that disappeared under the sheet at the corner of the bed. She propped herself up on one elbow and met Herron's eyes for a moment before lazily swinging her gaze to Prenn.

"What time is it?"

Eastern European, almost Russian but not quite. Herron was pretty sure she was the blonde from the security video. She was exquisite and utterly unselfconscious. Herron saw the other ankle cuff on the floor at the foot of the bed, attached to a steel rod with some kind of hardware he couldn't really figure out. She had a series of angry welts across her ass and upper thighs and what looked like faded burn marks on her breast and arm. No track marks, he noticed.

Prenn unplugged a MacBook Air from the bedside table and ran his fingers lightly over the small of her back while smiling at Herron like the cat who just fucked the canary. "It's early. Go back to sleep. I won't be long."

"Good," she murmured, pulling one of the pillows into her belly and curling up, hair fanned around her head and one leg straight out, pulling on its restraint. Prenn tapped the wall plate again on the way out and the lights dimmed and extinguished.

Upstairs he handed Herron the laptop. "There you go, Detective. Knock yourself out."

"Thank you. I won't need it more than a day or two."

"Good, my whole life is in there."

"We'll see."

"Yes, well, was there anything else you wanted to discuss? I did have some things I really should get back to." With that smug smirk again.

"Have you seen much of Mrs., rather, Dr. Parrish lately?" Two could play, asshole.

"I speak to Stephanie often. She's had a bad year and we're very old friends."

"I'm sure you've been a great comfort."

Prenn's eyes blazed for a split second before he regained control. "I'm certain my friendship with Stephanie Parrish is outside the purview of your warrant, Detective. If you'll excuse me, I am rather tired."

"Of course, of course." Herron followed Alex to the front door. He tapped the laptop. "I'll be sure to get this back to you as soon as possible."

Prenn didn't answer but pressed the elevator button and leaned against the doorframe, fully back in character, the louche rake, Teflon. As the elevator door slid shut, Herron stopped it with his hand. He knew he shouldn't but he couldn't resist.

"By the way, I met your stepmom the other day. She's a piece of work, isn't she?" He pulled back his hand and the door slid shut. *Have a nice fucking day.*

58

HAYSTACKS

The broker didn't understand; she thought the Canadian wanted to renegotiate the terms and was trying to explain the absolute impossibility of such a thing. "I am so sorry, Mr. Butler, I thought I made it clear. The price you paid was for a year in advance and as you have already signed the *contrat* and taken possession... I don't understand—"

Jordan interrupted with a soft smile, "No, Claire, it's all right. I'm not trying to back out of the deal. It's fine. I am asking if you will find a tenant for me. A sublet. You understand? My work situation has changed and I will no longer be staying in Rennes. However, there are—" he paused and struggled to find the words "—certain tax implications and residence requirements... You understand, I am sure. So I wish to sublet the house. I am willing to rent it for well below what I paid if you can find a tenant who can offer cash. In advance."

He raised his eyebrows as if to say, yes, this is all flirting with the boundaries of strict legality but we are all adults here, people of the world who know how life works. And, of course, as in all such things, there would be financial rewards for facilitating such an arrangement. Best not to speak too directly lest one be obliged as a result to lie to the authorities at some future date... Claire seemed to grasp immediately all the subtext his arched brows meant to convey and instantly brightened, regaining her customary brisk, professional demeanor. And he was certainly not unattractive in a somewhat serious, unfashionable way. And he clearly had money; his bank approval had come through instantly.

She glanced at her watch. "Why don't you let me see what I can do tomorrow and I can come by, say, around six and let you know how it looks?"

He pressed her hand warmly as he got to his feet. "Thank you, Claire. I knew I was right to call you. Tomorrow, then."

Jordan checked his Gmail account.

William,
Confirming pickup at the relais on Wednesday morning at eleven. We will rendezvous with Pat outside of Calais and continue on to Dover on the 21:35 ferry.
Regards, Neil

Good. He typed a quick reply.

Neil,
Confirmed.
William

Sent.

"I know how it sounds," she said. "I'm sure you think I've lost it, rampant denial or something, but humor me for a minute." Simon had a pained expression.

"Listen, you know him. Can you really imagine him inserting a vector permanently into his own DNA with the start codon misplaced?"

Simon just looked at her with an expression Stephanie took as pity for the crazy lady.

"All right," she said, exasperated, "let's just say, for the sake of argument, I'm right. If you were Jordan and were trying to send me a message, how would you do it? You'd wave a flag you know I'd recognize and be able to read. But then what? Come on, Si! Where do we look? He wants us to find it but no one else. Something in the procedure... I don't know. Obviously he doesn't expect us to randomly sift through millions of bases. Damn it, Si, help me. I'm not fucking crazy. He's alive. I know it. And he needs help. Help me!" Tears ran down her cheeks but she ignored them, staring fixedly across her kitchen table at the struggling Perry.

He searched her face, for what? Madness, he supposed. She looked rational, but then crazy people usually did. He took a deep breath, unable to withstand the force of Stephanie's will. "Okay, listen. I'll do whatever you want but promise me you'll stop this and let him go when there's nothing there and all this turns out to be an artifact of a decade-old experiment in vector uptake. I need you to promise me. Otherwise, I'll be guilt-racked forever for bringing anything up in the first place."

"I promise, Simon." She smiled and took his hand between hers. "I knew I could count on you."

"A better friend would have nothing to do with this."

"Not true. I couldn't ask anyone else. I need you, Si, and you're coming through like you always do."

"What does Alex think?"

She paused. "I haven't said anything to anyone else yet. I think we should leave it between us for now, don't you? You don't want everyone thinking we're nuts."

He nodded.

She plowed ahead. "Come on, it's a puzzle. You love a good puzzle. Imagine you want to hide something in plain sight for someone who knew to look. How do you do it?"

He sighed, knowing when he was beaten. "I'd use a marker."

"What do you mean?"

"Well, for example, in your crazy scenario I would use the bit we found—the ATG, GTG, CTG sequence—to flag any other sequence I wanted to be found."

"And is there a way to search for that string in the sequence?"

"Of course," he said. "You'd make a probe, an oligo of the complementary sequence with a radioactive marker. The probe would stick to the sample DNA wherever that exact sequence occurs."

Her eyes bored in on his. "How hard is that?"

"Not hard, we do it all the time."

Her eyes asked the question.

"Slow down," he said, "our DNA is around three billion bases long. A sequence that short is going to turn up all over the place. Even assuming there's anything to your theory and we're right about the marker, it's still a needle in a haystack, a haystack full of other needles. There's no way."

"But you'll try," she said. "Thank you."

"No expectations."

"You'll see."

59

NEEDLES

God bless the interwebs. Jordan signed off on the deal with Claire's tenants, an English couple, newly empty nested, arranged to buy a Chicago PD Taser (only used once!) and took a Streetview walk through Hoxton Square, familiarizing himself with every inch of the neighborhood around the Exit Strategy office, all from a seedy little internet café in Brittany. He had really wanted a gun, but with French firearm laws the way they were, it didn't seem worth the risk. The Taser would do.

He'd have to see Claire to get the money; she'd been chilly since he'd failed to capitalize on her celebratory mood Saturday night. She'd come late, bearing champagne and a faxed letter of intent from the empty nesters. She popped the cork as she slipped out of her pumps and into the depths of the fire-facing sofa. When her stockinged foot teasingly nudged his thigh for a second refill he got a generous view up her skirt. Her face fell when he got up minutes later with vague apologies about the hour. Probably for the best, though, he thought. Less likely to gossip about a transaction with such an anticlimactic ending.

Checklist getting shorter. Tomorrow he'd see Claire, drive to Laval to pick up the Taser and figure out how to lose the car. T minus thirty-six hours and counting. He prayed Stephanie had found the message. And understood it. He couldn't think about that. It was too late to stop now; the Rubicon was far behind. They'd be there.

Herron slammed down the phone. Both computers were squeaky-clean. The histories had been selectively purged. The weenies had managed to follow the IP trail as far as some Russian server that had been used as a proxy and no further. Trahon had said there was heat from undisclosed heights to back off if nothing turned up. Probably related to the DC phone. Smug son of a bitch was going to get away with it all. He didn't give a fuck about the insider trading—that was a circle jerk, rich stealing from the rich—but Prenn was going to get away with murder.

Herron shook his head. What kind of people were these? Prenn is fucking his partner's wife and making a fortune by torpedoing his own company. That's not enough so he finally kills the partner who's off banging his own mistress—win-win for Prenn and the merry widow. Hell of a neighborhood. He stood up and grabbed his coat off the back of the chair. He'd return the laptop himself.

Simon had been right about one thing, lots of needles. The probe was picking up dozens of matches. He had to isolate each one and sequence it individually. Stephanie had written him out a copy of her college code with the consonant equivalents for each of the twenty coded amino acids. Simon ran each sequence just until he hit a string of bases that didn't correlate to any amino acid. It usually didn't take long; by the seventh base he was usually looking at intron junk.

The twenty-third hit was different.

After the key sequence it read "ATG, TCG, TCG, AGG, AGG, TCG." This sequence repeated sixty times before giving way to random bases. Methionine, two serines, two arginines and another serine. Simon grabbed the list and scribbled on a blank sheet "mssrrs." Jesus Christ. He dropped the pen. "I'm so sorry, S." Fuck, fuck, fuck. It could be true. Or it was a coincidence and he was losing his mind, too?

It took him two hours to find the next one. "Dnttrstnbdy." Again, sixty repeats.

"Don't trust anybody."

He called Stephanie.

60

SHEEP

When Jordan pulled into the parking area behind Le Vieux Puits, he saw Neil's truck idling. The exhaust billowed in the frigid early-morning damp. Jordan could smell the sea. The coast was just a mile or two to the northwest. Neil was on the phone, sitting in the open door of the cab. He nodded in greeting as Jordan pulled up and snapped the phone shut.

"Mornin', Billy. Ready to hit the road?"

Jordan nodded. Neil climbed down and walked around to the back of the truck. He raised the door and pulled the ramp out with a metallic clatter, startling a cote of doves nesting under the eaves of the shuttered hotel. Jordan drove the rented silver Peugeot up the ramp and into the truck. He climbed out. Neil had already stowed the ramp and was sliding wedge-shaped blocks behind the wheels. Moved fast for a big guy.

"Put the parking brake on, mate," the trucker snapped. Efficient, calm, reassuringly professional. Jordan pulled up the brake and shouldered the black duffel. It was heavy and awkward.

Besides the Taser, the surgical supplies and a couple changes of clothes, it was almost entirely cash. With the year's sublet from the empty nesters and his combined poker losings he had a little over 250,000 euros in tightly wrapped bundles. Enough to get them somewhere safe.

"You can put your gear up front, then give me a hand with the car, all right? Cheers." Jordan wedged the duffel under the glove box in the cab and came back to find Neil struggling to wriggle his substantial torso under the Peugeot's front end to attach a hook and chain.

"Let me do that," Jordan said.

"Yeah, better idea," Neil said with a husky laugh. "I'd probably get stuck and then where'd we be, eh?"

Jordan worked his head and shoulders under the car and Neil passed him the hook. "Try and get it 'round a solid bit of frame, yeah?" Jordan did and Neil tugged and grunted his satisfaction before taking up the slack in the chain and locking it down. "She ain't going anywhere," he said with a firm push on the fender. "Let's make a move."

For three hours they drove in silence. Jordan was lost in his own thoughts and only vaguely registered the small towns they drove through—Verson, Pont-l'Évêque, the outskirts of Rouen—places that conjured up cheese and cathedrals in Jordan's memory. They had a simple sandwich of ham on a buttered baguette and an espresso at a medieval stone inn with a faded Stella Artois sign.

As they turned onto the E402 just north of Abbeville, Neil said, "Reckon I got to ask. None of my business, I know. Feel free to tell me to fuck off."

"No, it's okay," Jordan said. He felt light, almost euphoric. What he was doing was crazy, impossible, but he was doing it. And it could actually work, couldn't it? It had to. Stephanie would have to find the message; she was the only one who could. She would know what to do.

His feet rested on the lumpy duffel, so his shins bumped on the glove compartment when the lorry bounced. They were driving through immaculately groomed farmland now. Pastures as far as the eye could see on either side of the narrow two-lane road. You knew you weren't in Kansas. Farms in the states had a symmetry, rectangular fields with tight, even furrows, efficient like a GI's flattop. Here, there was a casual charm, a sweep to the rows and a little wild growth, like graying locks peeking out from under an artist's wool cap. The French, raised on Monet and van Gogh, knew a thing or two about bucolic beauty; even the most functional barn or silo was situated for maximum aesthetic effect.

"Shitty divorce," he said. He saw Neil's eyebrow arch a little higher. "No, really. Very, very shitty. Kids, money, unpleasant. I don't want to go into too much of it but it's bad. Bottom line is I need to get back into England and my ex can't know I'm there. That's the big thing. And she's the kind who'd know. It's her money."

Neil nodded. "So you got kids in England?"

"Yeah."

They drove in silence. Jordan leaned his head against the window. The low hum of the road filled his ears and he drifted until Neil's voice brought him back. "And the sheep?"

Jordan sighed. "You're not going to believe it. This is where it really does get crazy."

"Try me."

"Okay." Jordan reached over and showed the trucker the scar on the back of his hand.

"And…"

"I had a skiing accident a while back and broke my hand. Had to go to the hospital. While I'm under, the crazy fucking bitch gets the doctor to implant something in me, like a tracking device or something."

"Fuck you." Neil laughed, shaking his head. "I was going to believe you, too. Now I know you're full of shit."

"I know, it sounds insane but it's true. You can feel it. There's this hard little bump in there and ever since that happened she's always known exactly where to find me. It's fucked up."

"That's paranoid crazy bullshit."

Jordan shrugged. "Maybe, still."

Neil thought a minute. "I still don't get the sheep."

"Well, if I just take the thing out, she'll know I'm onto her, right? So I'm going to cut it out and put it in the sheep. That way she'll think I'm still in France. Get it?"

Neil abruptly swerved the truck onto the narrow shoulder and put on his hazards. "Get the fuck out!"

Jordan put his hands up. "What are you talking about?"

"How fucking stupid do you think I am? You're either completely full of shit or completely out of your mind. I don't know which and I don't care. I want nothing to do with you. Someone's after you, I believe that. Americans, French police, whatever, it's too big for me. I get caught with some Syrian kid it's a fine, maybe just a wrist slap. I think helping you could get me killed. Take your shit and get out. I'll leave the car up the road."

"No, wait," Jordan said. "Listen, please. It's nothing like that. I promise. I'll pay double. I told you she was rich."

Neil searched his face, jaw working furiously. "Seventy-five thousand."

Jordan nodded. "Okay."

Neil's eyes widened. "You have that much?"

He nodded again.

"I want it now before I drive another foot."

Jordan pulled out the duffel and opened it on his lap. He pulled out a stack of bundles and passed them to the driver. "That's sixty. I'll give you the last fifteen in Dover."

Neil picked up one of the bundles and riffled the edges. His eyes gleamed lupine in the gray light. His smile was cold. "Okay,

Billy boy, we have a deal. Do yourself a favor, though. Don't tell me any more fairy tales. I never liked 'em. Just tell me to mind my own fucking business." He put the truck in gear and slowly pulled back onto the roadway. He glanced quickly in the rearview mirror before flicking off the hazards. He texted someone. There was no reply.

No one spoke again until they passed a sign for Calais and Neil took out his phone and made a call.

"Oi. You here?"

Jordan heard a muffled voice on the other end. Couldn't make words out. Then Neil said, "Yeah, five minutes. Cheers."

He turned onto rue Nationale and then a half mile later onto an unnamed road that ran behind a low brown warehouse. If there was a nowhere between Calais and Sangatte, this was the middle of it. Perfect for what Jordan had to do. There was one other truck in the parking lot, a livestock carrier. Its lights were on. Even though it was only three in the afternoon it was almost completely dark.

Neil pulled around so the two cabs were side by side with the bodies pointed in opposite directions. He rolled down his window. "Pat, Bill. Bill, Pat." Pat Murphy was a big, athletic guy with thick black hair and a boyish face. Jordan guessed he was pushing forty but he could have been fourteen save the laugh lines around the eyes.

"Nice to meet you, Billy." His accent was thick working-class Irish. He hopped out of the truck and came around as Jordan opened his door. Jordan climbed down. Something was wrong. It was too quiet. The sheep, he should have heard them. He walked to the back of Pat's truck and looked in. Black. Empty.

He turned around with a puzzled expression. "There are no sheep."

Pat shrugged with a funny little smile. "No. No sheep." Then he hit Jordan. He knew how to fight; his feet were grounded. The blow came out of his legs, short, efficient movement. Jor-

dan felt all the air go out of him. His eyes popped as he doubled over. He couldn't get a breath. Then the next blow came.
Pat caught him on the cheekbone. It felt like he'd been hit with
a hammer. A shock to the jaw, sharp pain, ear and cheek. He
tasted blood in his mouth. The left side of his face was numb.
Finally he managed to gulp for air. He looked up to see another
left coming at his body. He just managed to turn so it caught
him in the ribs instead of the stomach. There was a crack and
searing pain tore across his side.

"Fuck!" he screamed and rolled to the ground. Pat's boot
caught him in the small of the back. He heard the heavy foot-
falls as he rolled and caught a glimpse of his attacker's face. Pat
was grinning, his face flushed bright red and his tongue stuck
out slightly as if it were too big to fit in his mouth. Jordan rolled
toward the truck but Pat grabbed his jacket before he could slide
underneath.

"No, you don't," he panted, cuffing Jordan's right ear with
an open hand and pulling him to his feet before slamming him
back against the truck and pinning him with a steel forearm
against his throat. He was pressing against the windpipe and
Jordan's vision started to go dark with bright flashes of light,
like little fireworks. He clawed with his free hand at Pat's face,
which just enraged the trucker. He kneed Jordan repeatedly in
the groin without releasing the forearm press. Jordan twisted
frantically, finally turning his neck enough to suck a tearing gasp
of air. His mouth was pressed against Pat's fist. He bit down as
hard as he could.

With a bellow of pain the larger man ripped his hand back
but Jordan held on. His neck cracked as it wrenched forward
and he felt a pop in his mouth and pain and blood filled it. He
assumed a tooth had pulled out. Pat meant to kill him, he was
sure. He couldn't let go.

Pat readjusted his free arm and put Jordan in a headlock with
their legs intertwined, hunched over. Jordan heard his breath-

ing in his ear, guttural and savage. "Neil! Get him off!" The pressure increased on his neck, and Jordan felt like his head was going to explode. He bit down as hard as he could and twisted his head to the side. There was a terrible scream and he felt the thing between his teeth separate with a harsh grinding sound. Something was tugging at the corner of his mouth like a string. Pat's grip loosened and Jordan twisted away and the stringy thing snapped. They were separated by a couple of feet and Pat was holding his hand and screaming. Blood was rhythmically pumping through his fingers and occasionally bubbles would form, swell and pop with a sticky slowness. Jordan had something hard and rubbery in his mouth and he spat it out. It took a moment to realize it was the top half of a finger. It rolled under the tire of the truck and Pat fell to his knees, his bleeding hand pressed to his belly as he dug with the other hand.

Suddenly there was a stinging sensation in Jordan's leg and his entire body went rigid. It felt like every muscle was contracting as hard as it could. He collapsed to the ground, unable to move. He saw Neil walking toward him with a vicious smirk, holding the Taser.

"Nice toy you got here, Billy." He touched the trigger and Jordan's body contorted again.

Neil kicked him in the stomach and ribs repeatedly. Jordan heard another rib snap like a rifle shot. Neil kicked him in the face, splitting his lip. Blood filled Jordan's mouth again. He couldn't move or protect himself. He was going to die. Then headlights swept the parking lot as someone pulled around the side of the warehouse.

"Shit, we gotta go," Neil yelled to his partner with one last kick at Jordan's face as he pulled the Taser darts out of his thigh and emptied his pockets.

"What about my fucking finger?" Pat screamed, blood-flecked foam flying from his mouth.

"Bring it. We'll go to hospital, see if they can put it back." Neil was laughing. "Put it on ice or something."

"Ice?" Pat screamed. "I don't have any fucking ice!"

Neil climbed up into the cab of his truck. "Then put it in your fucking mouth, keep it wet."

Pat wiped off the bloody finger and tucked it in his cheek, looking for all the world like a redneck with a good-size chaw. He picked up Jordan's head by the hair and spat in his face, then head butted him right on the bridge of his nose. There was a brilliant flash of white light and then darkness.

61

CASABLANCA

Stephanie was crawling out of her skin. Alex had brought a bottle of something red and expensive. They watched the movie all together in the living room, plates of spaghetti and turkey meatballs balanced on their knees. Finally, during the scene where Humphrey Bogart and Ingrid Bergman finally kiss, Haden fell asleep curled up at the end of the sofa with his head on Stephanie's lap. She looked down and Sophie was asleep, too, leaning back on the sofa with her mouth open, chin slack. Stephanie paused the movie.

"Help me bring them upstairs, will you?" Stephanie asked as she stood up and heaved Haden over her shoulder. When both children were tucked into Sophie's bed, Stephanie said, "I should really hit it, too. I have an early day tomorrow."

"Come on, it's almost over," Alex said, restarting the movie and refilling their glasses. She was going out of her mind; she was desperate to talk to Simon, to see what else he'd found.

Don't trust anybody. That was the message. Simon had been

shaken. No question of believing her now. But what did it mean? She couldn't focus on anything. The day had been endless. She needed to know more. She wanted to trust Alex, to confide in him, tell him everything. But she couldn't. Don't trust anybody.

And *I'm so sorry, S*. The other message Simon had found. What did that mean? Sorry for what? What had he done? Did he mean about the girlfriend, the whole secret life? Or was that even real? If he was alive, who could say what was true? It was overwhelming. She blew her breath out, venting her impatience and frustration.

"Sorry," Alex said, taking his hand from her shoulder. She hadn't even noticed.

"No, it's not you. I was thinking about this situation at school. It's just annoying."

"Do you want to talk about it?" he said.

"No, I don't want to think about it. It's ridiculous."

"Okay." On-screen Bogart was watching the plane with Victor and Ilsa taxi down the runway.

"I've seen this movie twenty times," Alex said, "and I still well up at the end every time. You know," he said as Rick and Renault walk into the mist, "they shot two versions of the ending. No one knew how it would end, whether Ilsa would leave with Victor or Rick. Hard to imagine it any other way now. And of course when they made it the war was still going, everything was up in the air. Crazy, isn't it?" The credits rolled by.

"See," he said, "1942." She followed his finger—MCMXLII—and did the quick calculation in her head.

"Yeah," she said distractedly. "I never knew that."

MCMXLII—1942. What was it, something... Then it hit her. She felt her gorge rise so suddenly she almost choked. She jumped to her feet and ran to the kitchen; she almost made it.

She threw up half into the sink full of dishes, but chunky vomit—pink with wine and tomato—splattered the floor and the cupboard.

"Jesus, Steph, are you all right?" he said.

She pulled away. "Yeah, sorry. I don't know, the wine, maybe. I'll be okay. I should go to bed."

Oh God, keep it together. He must hear her heart hammering in her chest. Her mouth was dry and sour, her stomach acid and still rebelling. Sixty repeats. Always sixty. Jordan had a reason. Roman numerals. LX. Sixty. LX. Alex. Jordan had made it part of the flag; it was that important. Alex. Who did this? Alex. And she'd almost told him. All the memories flooded back— the looks, the comments, the feelings she'd had and filed away. She didn't question it for a moment. She had learned to trust her gut; it had been pretty clear this time.

She wet a dish towel and started wiping up the vomit. "I'm okay, Alex, really. Please. I'm just going to go to bed. I need sleep. I'll be fine." She forced a weak smile. "I promise."

"You won't let me help you clean up and—"

"No. I'm much better. I just had to get it out. I feel so stupid. Don't make it worse."

She felt like she was going to fall over. She gripped the counter so hard her fingertips went white.

"Okay," he said and leaned to kiss her forehead.

She turned her head. "Good night. It was sweet of you to come over." Her face felt cool and was beaded with sweat.

When the outer door closed she fell to her knees and retched convulsively. There was nothing left to throw up but bile and spit. Her head throbbed as she pulled herself shakily back to her feet and ran the cold water in the sink. She splashed her face repeatedly until she felt her heart steady and her breathing settle into a manageable rhythm.

The kitchen phone was an old-fashioned wall mount with a long coiled cord. It was a ridiculous Luddite antique but she loved it. When she spoke on it she would try to get all the twists out by working them back toward the handset. The repeated worrying of the cord had made the coils flabby and the cord twined on itself in a lumpy plait. Her fingers went to work as she waited for Simon to pick up. It was like knitting; her mind played no active role in the brisk dexterous manipulations.

"Hello?" His voice sounded frayed. Not just exhausted but disoriented. She realized how thrown he must have been by the revelations of the past day and a half. His ordered world had been destroyed just as hers had. How could you adjust to a reality where dead people sent you messages in their genetic code and you couldn't talk about it to anybody except the dead man's wife who until yesterday had been a widow? And where was the dead man now?

"Hi, Simon, it's me," she said.

"I see that. There's nothing new. I'd have called you."

"I know. I'm not calling to bug you. I figured out the sixty repeats. It's roman numerals, LX. It means 'Alex.' He wants us to know it was Alex."

The line was silent. Stephanie could feel him thinking, putting himself in Jordan's place.

Finally, "Right."

There was a weariness in his voice, a resignation, an acceptance of the absurd new rules in this absurd new world he found himself in.

"We're not crazy," she said quietly.

From the backyard, the kitchen looked like an amber aquarium, its large bay window bulging out of the boxy clapboard. The low incandescent light shone warm and liquid through the clear cold air outside. The yard was dimly shadowed in moonlight scattering off the ice-crusted snow. A single set of boot prints led to the fence where Alex stood under a sickly elm watching Stephanie twist the phone cord around her fingers.

62

FEDA

He couldn't see. There was pain but he couldn't tell where; it seemed to be everywhere at once. Slowly it began to localize. His head. There was a sharp long burning running from the back of his head down his spine. His face felt swollen and the left side of his lip and the left cheek were numb, though a dull throbbing ache seemed to emanate from somewhere in that area and radiate through his head in waves. He tried to move his fingers. The right hand twitched with a jolt of fresh pain but the left seemed frozen in a loose fist. He tried to turn on his side but the searing fire that ripped across his chest made him cry out. He heard a strangled croaking sound from just off to his right and realized it must have been him. He strained to open his eyes. With a sound like masking tape coming off the roll, his right eye opened a little. He was peering through strings of pus. The view was unintelligible. Light from somewhere, fuzzy. Some shadows. One of the shadows separated from the rest and hovered just in front of him, blocking out most of the light. A voice.

"You are hurt, Amerikaayi." Young, just a child. A boy. "Drink this." Jordan felt pressure against his face and a warm liquid ran down his throat and the side of his face. "You must sleep." And he did.

"Hey, Steph, it's me. Just checking in to see how you are. I hope you're feeling better and, ah, I guess that's it. Give me a call when you get a sec so I don't worry." Another call was coming in. He clicked over.

"Mr. Prenn, good morning. This is Detective Herron."

"Hello, Detective. How can I help you today?"

"I just wanted to return your laptop, sir."

"Well, I'll be here all day. Drop it off anytime."

"I'm right downstairs, sir."

"Of course you are," Alex said with a grim laugh. "Come on up."

"Nice of you to call in advance," he said, opening the door.

Herron held out the laptop. "There was nothing on it," he said, eyes sweeping the apartment casually, "but you knew that. My guys said the history had been selectively purged."

Alex smiled. "You know, sometimes my girlfriend surprises me with her resourcefulness. There are things I like to keep private."

"Of course," Herron said, smiling in return and placing the laptop on the console. "Can I be totally candid with you, sir? Off the record?"

"Sure." Alex nodded, crossing his arms and leaning against the wall.

"Let me tell you what I think." Herron kept his tone conversational, almost chatty, no point in going fishing in an aircraft carrier.

"I think you and Stephanie Parrish have had an ongoing relationship, probably for quite a while. And of course your partner had his own little side project. I'm thinking you knew about his but he had no idea you were banging the missus." Alex didn't say anything but shifted his slouch a little lower on the wall.

"For a while I thought he found out and freaked, but now I don't think so. I think you were planning on getting rid of him for years. You manipulated the company's stock price to make yourself rich while leaving him almost busted. Meanwhile you've got him insured up the ass. So when he's gone your girlfriend gets rich and you two can be together. Of course, you have to wait a decent period so no one thinks anything's funny. How am I doing so far?"

"Incredible. Please go on," Alex said.

"Okay, feel free to jump in if I miss something. So you and the missus hire someone to make the hit while the Professor and Mary Ann are having their lost weekend on the Cape. This bit's a little off topic, but if I had to guess I'd say you had a hand in encouraging him to take that little trip, maybe even pretended to cover it up with the lovely widow to be." Alex nodded in mock appreciation.

"As far as I can tell, your hitter is DC, maybe a freelancer. He's tough to get a bead on. Though, between you and me, I think I got a good picture of him coming up here so, maybe, fingers crossed." At this point Herron was pretty sure he caught a ripple in Prenn's bland facade.

"I'm a patient man, Mr. Prenn. And there's no statute of limitations on murder. This isn't over. I will be your shadow, your constant companion. Oh, and by the way, and this is none of my business, but does the widow know about the hookers and the bondage shit? She doesn't strike me as the kinky type. Too uptight. Never know, though, I've seen it all. Now your step-mom on the other hand…"

Alex put his hand up. His face was calm but serious. "That's enough. You've got a lot of speculation and theories. If you had anything else, you'd arrest me. The reason you don't have anything is because there's nothing to have. This whole lively little fantasy is just that. Pure fantasy, untainted by the merest hint of anything as prosaic as the truth.

"You have no idea who we are. I admit, there are aspects of my life that aren't entirely PG, but that's not a crime. You've got it all wrong. I loved Jordan. I would never, ever have done anything to harm him. I don't give a shit if you believe it or not. It's the truth. You have taken a pile of partial information and conjecture and woven a picture that I'm sure you believe to be true, but it isn't. Stephanie Parrish and I are friends. No more, and if you knew her at all, you would see how absurd you look trying to paint her as a killer." He shook his head.

"I feel like you're a decent guy under all this tough-cop bullshit. And I know I rub a lot of people the wrong way. But I'm asking you as nicely as I know how to let this one go. Let it be. None of the scenarios you're imagining are true. However, some of the people who've turned up in your little net are people truly best left alone. And some of the others are innocent, innocent people who will get hurt despite never having done anything to anyone. I implore you, Detective, walk away."

In spite of himself Herron almost believed him. He wanted to say, *Hey, if the murder and stock manipulation thing doesn't work out, you might want to think about a career in Hollywood*, but thought better of it. Left it at a simple "Have a good day, Mr. Prenn," as he stepped into the elevator.

Alex let out a deep breath when the detective had gone. He hoped he'd been convincing.

Herron had a lot of it wrong but not enough.

Thirty-four Hoxton Square was a nondescript two-story white brick building just off the park. There were two separate entrances; a flight of stairs led to the formal front door and a small wrought-iron gate guarded the entrance to the lower level. Originally that door had been conceived as a service entrance, then, in the 1970s, the lower floor had been converted into an independent unit. Over the past thirty-five years it had served primarily as a psychiatrist's office. The doctor's successful practice had eventually allowed him to buy the building. He had kept the lower unit as an office while living in the upper rooms with his young Italian lover, a former patient. In the end the doctor turned out to have been neither a terribly good psychiatrist nor a very good judge of character as the boy had bludgeoned him to death one night with a plaster reproduction of a Greek kouros.

Exit Strategy had taken the entire building over in the mid-noughties. The upper floors were tastefully done in Edwardian furnishings and housed the offices. The lower level was never seen by the clients and was decorated in timeless Pentagon gray. The innards of the company were here out of sight of its more presentable face above.

Sam was at a terminal when Dennis rapped on the doorframe. "Ah, you're back. Good. How was Dubai?"

"Fine. He's coming in, nowhere else to go at this point. Saudis told him to go fuck himself."

"Of course they did. Self-righteous pricks to the last."

"Listen," Dennis said, "I got a call this morning from Washington. Someone ran your picture through CIA facial recognition. People are unhappy."

"Who ran it?"

"Don't know, but I got the picture." He pulled a folded piece of paper out of his jacket pocket.

Sam studied the shot. It was taken from above, grainy low-res. Security camera, it looked like. Then he recognized the hallway. "Son of a bitch. Fucking Prenn."

63

WELCOME TO THE JUNGLE

Voices, nearby. Hushed, urgent tone. They were arguing. His left eye was a nonstarter but his right opened a little. He saw a group of people across the room. They were dressed in a motley assortment of parkas and sweatshirts as if they'd just come from a giveaway at the Goodwill. Everything still hurt but in a manageable, compartmented way. He tried to turn his head and groaned. The voices stopped and they all turned to look at him. A young boy separated from the group and rushed to his side.

"You are awake, Amerikaayi."

As his eye focused he took in the room. It was basically a lean-to made of tarps, scrap plywood and tires. The dirt floor was swept clean and the chinks in the walls were filled with rags and balled-up T-shirts. Seven stern faces gathered around his cot. They looked Middle Eastern, dark complected; the men wore beards and the women's heads were covered.

"I am Feda," the boy said. His eyes were bright, his face smudged with dirt.

"Where am I?" Jordan croaked.

"They call this the Jungle," Feda said.

"What jungle," Jordan said, struggling to stand.

"No, no, you mustn't," Feda said. "You must stay inside. You won't be safe out there."

"My bag," Jordan cried.

"You had no bag, Amerikaayi. You had nothing. My father found you three days ago. By the parking lot. You were badly hurt. You kept saying you were sorry. And other things I didn't understand."

Jordan fell back onto the cot. That was it, then. A quarter of a million euros, his phone, his clothes, passport, wallet, everything gone. Why had the trafficker turned on him? He'd checked out. Dozens of successful crossings. No intercepts, no complaints. According to the chat rooms, way safer than the Eastern Europeans. It didn't matter now. He closed his eyes. All gone.

He wasn't aware of having fallen asleep but it was dark except for a guttering lantern in the corner that cast the boy's shadow like a twitching monster across the tarp ceiling. Angry voices on the other side of the doorway.

"You must eat," the boy was saying. Jordan smelled charred flesh and something yeasty and rich. And something brighter, herbal. Mint, maybe. Feda laid a plate on the wooden crate next to Jordan's cot. There was a scorched flatbread, long like naan. It was dotted with blackened bits of finely chopped meat. Jordan realized he was famished. He sat up despite the protest of bruises. Feda offered him a pale tea in an old vegetable tin.

It was warm and spread heat throughout his body even though it tasted like weak, bitter, thrice-used tea bags with a hint of old mint. He ate with his hands; the bread singed his fingers but he didn't care. Feda watched him eat, refilling his tea when it was empty. His shrunken stomach was soon full. Jordan offered the boy the last of the bread. He took it and ate it slowly; his eyes closed almost reverently. Jordan noticed for the first time how thin he was.

"You're hungry," Jordan said.

"Sometimes, yes."

"Why do you feed me if you haven't enough food for yourself?"

"You are a guest."

"Where is this jungle? Who are the men outside? How did I get here?"

"I told you, my father found you. You were hurt so he brought you here."

"Here..."

"This place has no name. Many people live here in the woods all around. This house is the hujra—you know, for guests."

"What is the language the men are speaking?"

"Pashtun."

"Pashtun," Jordan said. "Where is that from?"

The boy smiled. "My tribe is Afghan. Some of the others are from Pakistan. There are also many, many refugees from Syria. They are trying to make the crossing. Many people."

"You are Afghan?" Jordan asked. "How do you speak English so well?"

Feda smiled again. "There was a man in my village who lived for a long time in your country. The Jirga decided he should teach English to all the children. They thought it would be wise to understand our enemies and that children could get closer. And, of course, it would be easier for the young to learn a new language."

"But I'm American," Jordan said. "Why are you helping me?"

"You needed help," Feda said as if the question was silly. "Pashtunwali, it is the law." He thought a moment. "It is the way to heaven. It is honor." He seemed more satisfied with this word. "This is a sacred thing."

"Even if that man is your enemy?" Jordan said.

"Of course," Feda said.

"So, if a man tried to kill your family and you found him hurt on the road, you would help him?"

"Of course."

"And yet on another day, if we met somewhere else…"

"Maybe it would not be the same."

Looking at his face, still softly contoured, not a trace of facial hair, Jordan found the contradictions impossible to reconcile.

"How old are you, Feda?"

"Twelve years."

"And when I am better, when I am healed?"

"Where would you want to go?"

"To England."

Feda nodded. "Everyone wants to go to England. It is difficult."

With a loud snapping sound the tarp that covered the doorway swung back and a man with a gray turban and fierce brows strode into the hujra. He had a long face and a thick gray beard with a single streak of dark black. He had round glasses and his eyes were dark and intense. His face was wind burned. Beneath a green army surplus coat that seemed tight in the shoulders, Jordan could see several looped scarves and a black Guinness sweatshirt. The man stood over Jordan, eyes flickering over his injuries, assessing him while he spoke quickly to Feda. He had the presence of someone used to being obeyed.

When he finished speaking, Feda said, "My father welcomes you. He says you are hamsaya. You are under our protection."

"What's he playing at?" Sam said. It was late and the heat had cycled down to its night setting.

Dennis looked up and arched a brow.

"The Angel says he's in Calais but his phone is crossing into Belgium. He's not stupid. What the fuck is he thinking?"

Dennis grunted something noncommittal. "I don't like it. It doesn't make sense."

Manny at the other terminal cocked his head. "Maybe somebody stole his phone."

"Maybe. I don't like it. Any of it. I want eyes on him."

64

OUR MAN IN SOUTHALL

Jordan was alive. She didn't question this. Alex was somehow responsible. But where was he and what was she supposed to do? Was she in danger? Were the children in danger? Why hadn't he just called her, or written? Stephanie felt her conviction slip away moment by moment as the irrationalities of the situation pressed down on her.

The phone's ring made her jump. It was Simon. He sounded tense. "Stephanie?"

"Yes, Simon. What is it? Did you find more?"

"Can you meet me?" he said.

"Of course. I can be there in half an hour."

"No, not here." He sounded frightened.

"Okay. Where?"

"You remember the place you and Jordan took me out to when I first started?"

"You mean—"

"Don't say it," he interrupted. "Just tell me if you remember."

"I remember," she said.

"One hour." He hung up without waiting for her response.

Jesus. What could he have found that would scare him like that? Stephanie reached for her phone. She'd need someone to get the kids from school.

The Abu Bakr Mosque in Southall, just west of London, was a nondescript redbrick building that looked more like a school than a house of worship. Dennis met Yaqut Zar Wali in his small spare office just behind the prayer hall.

"*Pakheyr*, Dennis."

"*Salaam*, my friend. It's been a long time."

They embraced the way men who have fought together do.

Zar Wali offered a chair and poured chai. They didn't speak until both had sipped their tea and had a couple sugar-coated almonds. Then Zar Wali put down his cup and folded his hands on the desk in front of him.

"What can I do for you, my friend? I am deeply grateful for the opportunity to repay the great debt I owe you."

"There is no debt, my friend. You owe nothing. I ask only for a favor as one friend asks another. There is a man. We believe he is among your friends in Calais."

65

MR. ROBINSON

Aid workers from La Belle Étoile provided lunch for the camp. The line formed early. By eleven the crowd of men outside the converted truck was volatile. The Syrians, Pakistanis, Africans, Afghans and Iraqis clumped together in hostile groups, each jostling for position near the still-shuttered window from which the food would be distributed in another hour or so.

Jordan kept his head down and tried to hold on to his little piece of ground. He was at the edge of a group of around a dozen of the men from Feda's tribe. He was almost a full head taller than most. Almost no women or children were in the queue.

When the window opened, the goal was to grab as much of the bread and soup as you could and pass it to the outside. Height was an asset. There was a noise from the food truck and a wave seemed to pass through the pack. Jordan stumbled, then regained his balance. A man just ahead of him turned and snarled something Jordan didn't understand. His lip curled back from his teeth and he spat in the dirt at Jordan's feet. Jordan raised his

hands, palms out in what he assumed was the universally understood sign for peace.

This seemed to enrage the man. His thick black brows rose,
then knitted in fury over glittering dark eyes with yellow, blood-
shot whites. He yelled something at Jordan, then looked around
for confirmation. The crowd of men seemed to open and flow
around so now Jordan and the man were in an open space.

The man seemed to expect a response. A murmur of assent-
ing voices rose in the crowd.

Everyone was looking at Jordan now.

"I'm sorry, I don't understand you," Jordan said, trying to back
away but hands pushed him forward toward his livid adversary.
His hand brushed the sleeve of the man's jacket as he fell to one
knee. The man grabbed a handful of Jordan's hair and pulled
back to look into his eyes. Then he spat full in his face. Jordan
felt a spray across his forehead and eyes and a thick rope of saliva ran down the side of his nose. It smelled rancid, like decay
and tobacco. Jordan wiped his face with his sleeve and tried to
stand. He felt an odd impulse to laugh. The situation seemed
too bizarre to be truly dangerous. He reached out his arms again
and tried to turn away from his attacker.

He heard the sound of the knife sliding out of its sheath and
the sharp intake of collective breath from the crowd.

The man said something low and menacing. Jordan heard
the word *Amerikaayi* and turned. The knife was long, serrated
along the top. The handle was wrapped in tape but the blade
gleamed as it danced lightly in the man's fingers. The circle of
men around him widened as his enemy closed. Jordan backed in
a slow circle but everywhere hands pushed him back. The blade
swung; it was an awkward inside-out movement, but it caught in
Jordan's parka just under the shoulder. It opened a long gash in
the fabric; tufts of gray-white down puffed at the cut. It missed
his skin but he'd felt the blade nick at his shirtsleeve. Reflexively he clutched at the spot with his other hand. No blood. He

swung his head wildly, scanning the crowd. The men looked grim; a bloodlust was on them. No one was going to help him.

Just then there was a roar to his left and the crowd parted. Two men stepped through. Jordan recognized one from Feda's father's tribe. Jordan's assailant said something to them without ever taking his eyes off his prey. Then without warning he leaped at Jordan. Jordan threw his hands up to protect his face. There was a deafening explosion as the man crashed into his chest. Then a terrible stillness. The man felt unexpectedly light as he lay across Jordan's body. Something hot was soaking Jordan's sleeve and hand, and his ears felt like they had cotton stuffed in them.

Then someone screamed. A woman's voice. Then pandemonium. The man's body was pulled away as strong hands grasped Jordan and pulled him to his feet. People were running in all directions. The smell of cordite was thick and bitter. A man cradled the limp body of Jordan's attacker. He had a black beard and was screaming at the sky. Men clustered around him. He met Jordan's gaze across the clearing. His face distorted in a snarl of pure hate. One of his front teeth was gold. A strong hand grabbed Jordan's pant leg. "This way." Feda. Jordan kept his head down and followed the boy into the woods. No one paid any attention; the show was now the standoff between the men from Feda's tribe and the dead man's.

Feda led him down a path where the brush had been beaten down by countless feet making their way through the makeshift tent city. There were crude lean-tos, neat regular huts made of scavenged trash, even mattresses grouped together in the open air. In front of them some women were cooking flatbreads on makeshift stoves made from the convex sides of old oil drums.

There was a low cement building with peeling green paint and a faded Red Cross sign.

Feda led him inside. The sharp ammonia smell made Jordan recoil. The latrine was a long trough with a drain on one side and a trickle of water coming in at the other. There was a faucet that swung out over it. Feda turned this on and Jordan rubbed his hands underneath the stream. The blood ran in a pink ribbon down the latrine. Jordan took off his coat and washed the blood off as well as he could. The down where the sleeve had been cut was flecked with red.

"Are you cut?" Feda asked.

"I'm fine," Jordan said, wringing out his blood-soaked sleeve.

"This time," Feda said somberly, "I think it will be hard to protect you here, maybe. That man, Azir, if he is dead, there will be much trouble. You saw his brother, with the gold tooth? He is called Qhaywaan. And there are others. Maybe easier to get you to England."

Jordan froze. "Really?"

"Maybe. Come."

Feda led him farther through the woods, which finally opened out onto a beach. The beach was teeming with Eritrean men walking aimlessly, some smoking, some staring out over the choppy gray sea. A few briefly considered Jordan and Feda and, judging them no threat, continued their meandering perambulations.

"Stay here," Feda said. Jordan walked to the edge of the water. Tiny waves lapped at the sand. He could see land on the other side. A white wavy band. They weren't kidding about the Dover cliffs. They looked so close he felt like he could stretch his arm out and touch them. A giant ferry with P&O in blue letters on the side was passing parallel to the beach. Jordan could hear the low throb of its engines as the bow started to swing away from shore, froth foaming at the stern. The ferry's course took it directly away from the beach so it seemed not to move at all but rather slowly shrink as the sea between it and the shore expanded.

Jordan hadn't noticed Feda's return so he was startled when

the voice beside him said, "Tomorrow night you will be on that boat."

Jordan looked down. Feda was watching the dwindling ferry with a wistful look. After a moment, he sighed and said, "Come."

The shoreline curved around to reveal a collection of huge rusted buildings and cranes. An abandoned shipyard. They clambered up a collapsed breakwater onto a dock. At first it seemed deathly still as they walked away from the gentle static of the water but then gradually Jordan became aware of murmuring and creaking sounds all around. They were on a narrow walkway between two massive metal buildings. There were train tracks sunken into the asphalt and, along the building on the right, a row of massive rusted pipe sections on scaffolding about three feet off the ground. Each was about twenty feet long and four feet high with sealed ends and periodic outgrowths of short round pipe facing the ground that made them look like miniature submarines on their backs.

Suddenly a head popped out of the nearest pipe and looked around. It was a young Eritrean boy. When he saw Feda his eyes opened wide and he yelled, "Feda!" The head disappeared and a second later the boy dropped out of the pipe feetfirst.

"Ghedi," Feda said before conferring with the boy in a language Jordan didn't understand. He turned to Jordan. "You will stay here tonight. It will be safer for you, I think. Azir's brothers…"

Jordan nodded as he looked dubiously at his new home. "I need you to get a couple of things for me."

66

BEN

Sunny's Diner was almost empty. Simon, wearing a Red Sox jacket and cap with dark glasses, had taken a booth near the back with a view of the door. Stephanie slid into the facing seat. "Since when are you a baseball fan?" she said.

He slid a sheet of paper across the table. "Yrbngwtchd" was written in dark blue pen and above it he'd scribbled "a e i o u y." A maze of little lines plugged the vowels in.

"You're being watched," she murmured under her breath.

"Yeah. Unless you can find something else, I'm afraid so. Listen, Stephanie, I…" He faltered, looked at his hands on the table. "I have to be honest with you. I thought this was all bullshit. I mean, him being alive. I figured, okay, maybe he messed with the code in his own DNA as part of an experiment years ago but that was it. But I have to tell you, I'm scared now. I liked it much better when you were the crazy widow and I was the patient, long-suffering friend." He laughed sourly.

"I ran the odds of coming up with the phrases we've found

through random mutation, you know, the proverbial monkeys with typewriters, and it's fucking millions to one. He's alive, or at least he was when this was coded, and he's sorry, he's scared, scared for you and the kids, and he knows you're being watched. If this is how he's reaching out to you, I can only assume that he's in serious trouble, as well." Stephanie listened patiently, her eyes darting to the letters on the page when he paused but she didn't interrupt.

"I care for you. You guys have been great friends to me. But I am, in the end, a coward. I'm an academic geneticist." That bitter laugh again. "It doesn't get any more sand-kicked-in-the-face than that. Anyway, what I'm trying to say is I can't do this anymore. Whoever's watching you must be watching me now, too. I want to help but I'm not a hero." He looked her in the eye for the first time. "You must think I am the lowest."

"God, no, Simon. I'm the one who's behaved badly. I had no right to drag you into this. There just wasn't anyone else. I should have gone to the police, probably."

"I think if you had you'd be dead already," Simon said.

"Maybe," she said. "I don't know. None of it makes sense, but I had no right to involve you. And, of course, you're right. Stop messing with this. We know enough to know that." She twisted a lock of hair around her finger. "We probably shouldn't speak for a while. The kids go on spring break next week. I'll take them somewhere."

"I'm sorry," he said, looking down.

"No, I am. You *have* been a hero, you know." She squeezed his hand and slid out of the booth. "Goodbye, Si."

"It was rabbit, by the way," he said. She stopped with a quizzical look.

"The foreign protein in the sample, it was rabbit." He didn't look up as she left the diner.

Jordan woke in total darkness. At first he thought he was back in the capsule in Tokyo. Colder, though, and the floor was harder and curved. Then he remembered. Ghedi's family was huddled together on the other side of the pipe. They had been gathered around a smoldering coal fire. Jordan had tried to explain the danger—the gases would collect in the pipe with no way out, driving the air out and killing them all, and indeed the fire seemed to struggle in the oxygen-poor atmosphere—but the Eritreans spoke no English at all and had only smiled warmly at everything he said.

He heard one of the babies stir and the mother murmured to it. There was a rustle of movement and then all was still again. The thick iron of the pipe seemed to muffle sound within as well as blocking all sound from outside. He stared at the spot where he knew a simple sheet of cardboard covered the hole that served as the front door. He couldn't see a trace of light so it must still be dark outside. He should try to sleep. He'd need it. He focused on his breathing and tried to slow the beating of his heart.

In the dream he was running, pounding down metal stairs that descended into the darkness. He was being chased, no shock there. And then he was awake but the ringing footsteps went on. He rubbed his eyes. It was day. The pipe was empty. Diffuse light shone up through the hole in the floor. Someone was tapping. He slid closer to the opening. He heard a voice, Feda, calling, "Mr. Jordan, Mr. Jordan." He scrabbled along the floor. It was too low to stand, and he'd struck his head hard the night before, misjudging his crouch in the gloom. He lowered himself feetfirst through the hole and dropped to the ground, blinking in the glare of the day.

Feda had a stick in his hand. Jordan assumed that was what he'd been hitting the pipe with. Next to him was a box and a little bundle. "I brought what you asked for," he said, looking quite pleased with himself.

"Perfect," Jordan said, peering into the box. The rat was as big as a cat, fat with a sleek clumpy gray coat. Its eyes gleamed with malicious intelligence. A survivor. "You're sure they swim?" he asked.

"Of course," Feda said as if the question was ridiculous.

"Good." He closed the box. Feda had poked several holes in the top and he could see the rat twist around inside as he set it down. It was surprisingly heavy. "And the knife?"

Feda handed him a knife wrapped in a filthy cloth. It had a thin blade, almost a stiletto.

Jordan ran it over his thumbnail; a translucent shaving curled up effortlessly. "Good. Needle and thread?"

"That was difficult. This was all I could find. I think the needle is for mending shoes." That sounded right, Jordan thought. The needle was thick and curved. It would have to do.

"Did you eat?"

"Last night. Ghedi's family was very generous."

"Here." Feda handed him a chunk of day-old baguette and an apple.

Jordan sat down on the ground to eat. He tore off little bits of the bread and poked them through the holes for the rat. When the bread was gone he took a bite of the apple. It was a little mealy but sweet. He opened the lid of the box. The rat blinked up at him, sniffing the air. Jordan held out a little piece and the rat took it delicately with his teeth, then sat back and held the chunk of fruit between his paws as he nibbled around it.

"What are you going to do, Mr. Jordan?" Feda asked.

Jordan smiled. "If I tell you, you won't want to help me and I'm going to need help."

"I won't harm anyone," Feda said firmly.

"I'd never ask you to. I think me and Ben here are the only ones at risk."

"Ben?"

Jordan laughed. "Stupid joke. Bad movie. Doesn't matter.

Let's go, get it over with." He shut the lid on the rat's box and stood up.

Feda gave him a scarf to wrap around his head. "Perhaps you should keep your head down."

"Is it done?"

"No, not yet," Dennis said. "He is there. Someone is helping him. But Zar Wali says it's just a matter of a day or two."

67

THE BOG

Jordan tore one of the T-shirts into strips. He used the other to wipe down the long trough urinal. Then he balled it up and plugged the drain. He opened the spigot all the way. Looked like it would take ten to fifteen minutes to fill. He checked to make sure the door was locked, then let the rat out of its box. He let it wander the floor freely as he bit little pieces off the apple and arranged them around himself on the floor. He watched the rat as it first circumnavigated the latrine, hugging the cement wall and sniffing the air.

After a couple minutes the rat came back to where Jordan and Feda sat on the dirt floor. It took a piece of apple and ate it. It was remarkably unconcerned, Jordan thought. The sound of the water running into the trough had changed as the bottom became completely submerged. It had lost its percussive quality and become more of a constant drone. Jordan offered a piece of apple from his hand and the rat took it. As it chewed, Jordan reached out and touched his back. The rat pulled back with a scrabbling of claws on dirt but didn't go far and momentarily returned to take another piece of fruit.

Jordan tried a new tack. He held out a piece of apple, but when the rat tried to take it he held on so the rodent was obliged to eat out of his hand. Then he touched it again while it ate. It flinched but allowed the contact. Jordan stroked the back of its head and then ran a finger down its back. The rat's fur felt oily and thick and there was a spongy layer of fat above the muscle and bone.

"Check the water level," he asked Feda.

Feda slowly stood, keeping a wary eye on the rat. "It's about this deep," he said, holding his hands about six inches apart.

"Okay, almost there. Are you ready? I'm going to need a little help in a minute." Feda nodded uncertainly, his eyes wide.

"Don't worry," Jordan said, keeping his voice low and even. "It's going to be all right."

He laid out several strips of the torn T-shirt on the ground like stripes on a flag and gently led the rat over them. When he was satisfied with the rat's position he slowly lowered his right hand onto its back, talking all the while in gentle reassuring tones, and then, without warning, he slammed the hand down, pinning the animal against the floor. The rat twisted its neck around, frantically trying to bite, its eyes rolled back in fear and fury, tail lashing and twisting around Jordan's forearm. He used his first two fingers to prevent the head from lifting.

"Quickly, tie him to my hand," Jordan said through clenched teeth. He hadn't been prepared for the ferocity of the rat's response. It took all of his strength to keep the creature pinned down. He could tell if it got its legs under it again, he'd lose it.

Feda, pale but determined, tied the strips of T-shirt tightly around the back of Jordan's hand. When five strips were tied, pressing the rat's back into his palm, Jordan felt it suddenly go limp. He could feel the animal's heart pounding, its sides heaving.

"Okay, okay," he said. He was panting, too, and his forehead shone with sweat. With some effort he slowed his breathing and blinked the sweat out of his eyes.

"Turn off the water," he said. Feda did. It was suddenly deathly quiet. Jordan's breathing seemed to reverberate off the cement and he could hear a ratcheting sound, almost like a cat's purr, from the rat, and the odd drip of water into the trough.

"Knife." Feda handed it to him. Fear, awe and confusion fought for the upper hand on his face. Jordan looked at the rat's hind leg. The fleshiest part was high up, almost on its back, a round soft-looking ball of muscle. He took one more deep breath to steady himself, whispering, "Here we go," under his breath, and cut.

The cut was about an inch long and almost as deep. He made it with the point of the blade in one quick stroke. The rat screamed. It sounded like a small child. The shrieks echoed in the close space. Jordan stood up. With its legs no longer pinned to the ground the frantic animal twisted and flailed, trying to turn its body over so it could get a purchase on Jordan's arm. He plunged his hand into the trough. Blood bloomed from the rat's hind leg like crimson smoke in the water. He pressed the rat against the bottom, the claws grated over the metal. He pushed down hard to keep the hand still. With the tip of the knife he lightly traced the scar from where the Angel had been put in and then he cut it open.

Searing pain shot up his whole arm. He almost blacked out. He leaned against the side of the trough, blinking himself back, breathing fast and loud through his nose. He heard Feda cry out in Pashtun, seemingly from far away. So much blood. His hand disappeared behind thick billows. He dragged the rat up the trough to the clear water. He had to work fast. With the end of the knife he tried to dig the tracer out. He could feel it hard against the tip but he couldn't get any purchase on it.

The knife scraped against a tendon and Jordan cried out, a

deep guttural involuntary groan. "Feda," he cried, "you have to help me."

The boy was sitting on the ground with his arms wrapped around his knees, tears running down his expressionless face, shaking his head.

Jordan dropped the knife. It hit the bottom of the trough with a ping. He couldn't see it through the water now tinted red to the point of utter opacity. Screwing his eyes shut, he slid his thumb between the rat's thrashing body and his palm. He pushed up with the thumb as hard as he could and shoved his ring finger into the fresh wound. He felt the glass chip, hard and smooth, unnatural. The middle finger of his right hand jerked spasmodically as he pushed against nerves and tendons. He got under the Angel with his fingernail and with a little sucking release it was free. He couldn't see anything; the blood flow from his hand had redoubled and the efforts of the drowning rat were making a pink froth of the water.

For a second he had it as it floated free. Then it was gone. Frantically his left hand swished through the water. Nothing. The rat's struggles had subsided. Just twitches of the forepaws.

Everything was quiet. Slow drips from the faucet. Jordan's head sagged forward. The water sloshed gently down the trough in red waves. Then he felt it, something small and smooth brushed against his thumb as it rested on the bottom, clutching the rat. He swept the free hand in and there it was. Glass scraped against metal. He pinched the chip between his thumb and middle finger and swiftly slid it into the incision on the rat's haunch, pushing it as deep as he could into the muscle. He ripped the rat out of the water. It was deadweight. The water-logged carcass hung off his hand, heavy and dripping. It reminded Jordan of the dead squirrel he'd found in his gutter one year during the annual cleanout. He had been throwing handfuls of sodden dead leaves up onto the roof when the little body had rolled out, swollen and bloated.

"No," he croaked. His voice was gone. He'd gotten this far. Not like this. He pressed the rat against the ground and pushed down sharply, compressing the rib cage. After the third compression a flood of pink water ran out of the rat's mouth and it sputtered. Its tail snapped from side to side. "Quickly, Feda, needle and thread. You have to do this."

The boy nodded grimly. Jordan showed him where to start stitching up the rat's leg. "What about your hand?" Thick blood was pumping steadily out of the wound and running in rivulets down the side of his thumb and into the rat's coat.

"Later. The rat."

"What was in your hand, Amerikaayi?"

"It doesn't matter."

Jordan heaved a great sigh of relief when, halfway through the stitching up, the rat seemed to come back to himself and succeeded in twisting around and biting Jordan's finger and raking his forearm with the claws of its uninjured hind leg. The pain was nothing to the relief that the rat would apparently survive.

He pulled his hand out of the bloody harness and succeeded in getting the struggling rat back in the box. He wrapped a strip of shirt around his hand to slow the pulsing flow of thick blood. There was the sound of raised voices from outside and someone pulled on the locked door. Feda looked fearfully at Jordan and said, "We must hurry." He pulled the balled shirt out of the trough and the bloody water started to twist down the drain with a metallic sucking sound. He put the wet T-shirt and the discarded strips in the box with the panting rat.

"Please put the kafiyah back on," the boy said. Jordan loosely wrapped the scarf around his head with his good hand and Feda tugged the front of it down so it hid most of his face. Someone banged angrily on the door and Feda yelled something in Pashtun.

"Come, walk like you are sick," he hissed. He opened the door and Jordan followed him outside, bent over with his bloody hand pressed to his belly. Two Arab men were arguing outside. One shot Jordan and Feda a filthy look and walked into the latrine. The other was a man from Feda's tribe. He took Jordan's elbow and guided him into the woods as Feda spoke to him quickly under his breath.

68

GO WITH GOD

The widow came out of the diner and turned left. Her shoulders were hunched up, hands jammed in her coat pockets. She didn't look at Prenn parked across the street, slouched low in the seat of the black A6. As soon as she rounded the corner he got out and quickly crossed to the diner. What were they up to? Herron thought. Tag teaming somebody? Then the answer hit him—the widow had another guy in play. Maybe a double cross, or just a simple love triangle; throw in the hooker, make it a square, or what the hell, stepmom makes a pentagon or a pentagram, whatever you call it. This was good. He would love to be a fly on the wall in there but Prenn would make him in a second. He opted to settle for a look through the window; if he could tag the third wheel, maybe he'd lead somewhere.

Prenn was in a booth with his back to the window. He was sitting across from a skinny black guy in a Red Sox cap and jacket. They seemed to be having a friendly enough conversation. They clearly knew each other. Herron went back to his car and waited.

Prenn came out alone, crossed to his car and drove off. Herron waited for Red Sox. He came out a couple minutes later and walked right by the cop's window. Herron got out and fell in behind him, following him down the stairs of the Kendall Square T station. He took the Alewife train two stops to Harvard Square and, Herron trailing half a block behind, continued up Mass. Ave. to Cambridge Street. He walked past the science center and took the walkway to Oxford Street. A couple of blocks up he turned into the Engineering Sciences Lab, a gray cement anachronism of '70s modern amid the dominant Georgian brick.

Herron pretended to study the directory as Red Sox nervously paced by the elevators. The elevator arrived with a discomfiting thunk and a muted chime. Herron put his arm in as the doors were sliding shut. He re-pressed the already illuminated button for three and gave Sox a curt nod before watching the numbers climb. Herron walked ahead down the hallway, but when he heard a door open behind him he waited a beat and glanced over his shoulder. Suite 322.

Back in the lobby his finger ran quickly up the directory—322: Gene Lab. Dr. Simon Perry.

Nice to meetcha, Doc.

Stephanie was late for class. She was digging through the disarray on her desk and didn't hear Alex come in. He cleared his throat and she jumped. "Jesus, Alex. You scared me." She did look pale.

"You've been avoiding me," he said with a smile, leaning against the doorframe.

She forced a matching smile as she stuffed the whole pile of papers into her briefcase. "Sorry. It's just end of term insanity. We go on spring break next week and it's all a little crazy right now."

She brushed a loose strand of hair behind her ear and squeezed past him. "Walk with me," she said over her shoulder. "I have to get to class." Her heart was pounding in her chest.

"I came by earlier," he said casually. "You weren't around."

"I wish I'd known you were coming. I had a meeting," she said.

"Ah," he said. "I figured you'd gone out to lunch or something."

"No such luck. Just a student."

"Of course," he said.

He walked with her across the courtyard and held the door. "Don't be a stranger," he said.

"I won't, I—I'll call you," she stammered and awkwardly kissed his cheek. "Promise."

He watched her walk down the hallway with a thoughtful expression.

Sam unfolded the fax again. Pretty low-res, no way they made an ID unless they already knew who they were looking for. He remembered the day he had gone over to Prenn's. How did security footage from Prenn's building end up in DC, bumping into locked doors and disturbing sleeping dogs? He traced the curve of his lower lip with a fingertip.

He pulled out his phone. "Good morning, Dennis. I need you to take care of something else."

"There is a truck," Feda was saying. "It is heading to Marseille— vegetables from England, all in cardboard boxes. Your friend Ben will be fat and happy." Jordan nodded. Feda handed the box with the rat to another Pashtun boy, who tucked it under his arm and headed off down the path.

The rag around Jordan's hand had completely soaked through and blood was dripping steadily on the dirt floor, making a rust-colored slurry. "I'm sorry," he said. "I need another cloth or something." He cupped his other hand to catch the drips and went outside. Feda's father was standing outside the hujra in conversation with two other men. They stopped talking when Jordan came out and looked at him with hard eyes. Feda's father saw the blood-soaked rag and took Jordan's wrist. He unwrapped the wound and looked at it. There was no expression on his face, just a bland thoughtfulness. Without looking up he barked an order and Jordan heard a reply from inside. A moment later one of the women came out with a small cooking pot, a light cotton shirt and a jar of oil. Outside, two women were cooking flatbread on an oil drum stove. At a word from Feda's father they gathered their things and hurried away with downcast eyes.

The woman from the hujra tore the cotton shirt into strips and put most of them into the pot. Then she took a burning stick from the fire and lit them. She gently fanned the pot as the cotton burned to ash. Then she poured in some of the amber oil and muddled it to make a thick gray paste. She took the remaining strips and soaked them in it. Satisfied, she nodded to Feda's father. He called to Feda, who came running. There was a quick conversation. Jordan saw Feda's eyes go wide for a moment.

"My father says you must stop the bleeding. This is the only way. He is sorry."

"What do you mean, what is the only way?" Jordan said.

Before he could react the men had pushed him to his knees beside the incandescent half oil drum. The tribal chief seized Jordan's wrist with an iron grip and turned his hand over and then pressed it right on the drum as another man stepped behind and put his hand over Jordan's mouth.

Jordan screamed as the flesh of his hand seared and cauterized, but even as he did he registered with some surprise the almost complete absence of pain. If anything there was a sensation of extreme cold, nothing more. He smelled it, like meat searing on an iron skillet, and heard it, an angry sputtering hiss, but felt nothing. After a long second his mouth was released and his hand was lifted from the drum. He caught a glimpse of red puddled flesh already blistering; it looked like wax just starting to set. He watched as a bystander, someone present but not materially involved. Then, slowly, the hurt came. It was like a sound that was too high to hear but was now falling into the audible range; first just a high whisper, then building to a piercing whine, descending through a shriek to a howl and finally to a deafening, all-obliterating roar.

He gasped, his eyes bulging, dry heaving, his whole arm suddenly consumed by fire. The woman wrapped the cotton-ash-paste-soaked rags around his hand with quick, efficient movements, tying the bandage off and tucking the ends under. Jordan pulled the hand to his belly and rolled to the ground, rocking and moaning. He heard the men talking, their voices unconcerned, as if they'd already forgotten him. After a couple of minutes he came back into himself. The pain had peaked but then had settled. He didn't know if it was the poultice or just a temporary respite, but while his hand still burned like hell, it was at a level he could handle. He found that he could push the pain down in his mind and wall it off. He started to shiver uncontrollably. Then he felt hands on him, pulling him roughly to his feet.

He was half carried, half dragged. He lost track of distance, of time. All around there were hushed voices. There was a banging sound and he had a sense of going up a steep incline. Then he was in the back of a huge truck. Several flashlights played crazily around the interior.

Packing crates were stacked everywhere like giant toy blocks. Jordan was led to the back of the truck. One of the crates had been pried open. There was room for five men if they stood back to front like forks in a drawer. Jordan leaned back against the hands that pushed him forward. He heard Feda's voice high and clear through the babble.

"Mr. Jordan, Mr. Jordan. You must go. The ferry is about to sail. Friends will release you in Dover. It will be all right. It will be all right."

He was coming closer. "You must go now. Go with God, Amerikaayi." Jordan saw his face for just a moment before he was pushed in, pressed against a bony man who smelled sour and bitter, and then, with a bang of wood on wood, the light went away.

69

LUCKY MAN

At the end of the lecture as Stephanie was stuffing her notes back into her briefcase, Reina Nordstrom, one of her graduate students, came up, leading a thin boy with bad skin and oily black hair that hung in lank bangs over his face.

"Dr. Parrish, this is Tommy, the friend I told you about."

Stephanie looked up. "Hi, Tommy." He looked about as you'd expect, she thought. "Reina told you what I need?"

He didn't meet her eyes but flipped his hair with a practiced jerk and nodded while focusing somewhere just over her right shoulder.

"Just need a picture."

"It needs to look real," Stephanie said.

"It will be real. My friend works for the DMV. It'll look exactly like any other license." There was a ring of professional pride in his voice. "When you take the picture, go to Kinko's or something and get a passport photo on white background. I can change the background color but it looks bad if you don't start clean."

"Okay, I'll get it to Reina tomorrow. How much is this going to cost?"

"Five hundred." He was looking down at her feet, the hair once more flopped over his eyes. She was sure he wasn't charging the high school kids that. She wondered how many people had died in car accidents caused by alcohol his work had made available. She nodded.

"All right. I'll give her the cash, as well." He seemed to inflate as she accepted the price. "Thank you, Tommy. Nice to meet you."

"Yeah, no problem." A final bang flip and he turned for the door. Reina gave Stephanie an apologetic smile over her shoulder. Stephanie shook her head and smiled back. No more than she expected.

It was like being buried alive. It was impossible to move. His shoulders were turned and his hips were pressed against the back of the crate. He was breathing shallowly through his mouth because when he breathed through his nose the smell made him gag. Air was getting in—if it wasn't they all would have been dead already—but the thick smell of sweat and the rotting teeth of his coffin mates was unbearable. Jordan tried to take his mind away. He'd taken a couple meditation classes at the Y a lifetime ago, and while he'd decided it was all a little too flaky for him, he did remember the sense of timelessness the practice had given him. He could feel his heart beating and he concentrated on slowing and controlling its rhythm.

The two men at the far end of the crate were murmuring quietly. Jordan couldn't tell if they were talking to each other or praying, though he suspected the latter as there seemed to be none of the natural give and take of dialogue. Suddenly the crate lurched. Jordan's head slammed against the wood before he

could brace with his arms. They were moving. The truck must
be heading for the ferry. The murmur from his left paused for
just a second and recommenced. There was a regular side-to-
side sway as the truck drove. Turning was worse. At first Jordan tried to lean back against it, instinctively fighting to keep
the crate from falling over, but soon he saw the futility in that
effort and surrendered to the buffeting forces.

Then, with a lurch, the truck stopped. There was a muffled sound from outside and then a sharp crack and a shard of
light as a crowbar burst in just above Jordan's head. With a few
quick pulls the side of the crate was ripped open and Jordan was
blinded by four or five flashlights. He turned his head and raised
one arm to protect his face. Someone grabbed his bad hand,
making him cry out in pain. He was pulled roughly out of the
box. His legs were unable to support him at first and he stumbled but several hands grabbed him and pulled him to his feet.
He looked back at the crate and saw the four men inside yelling in confusion as several figures he couldn't make out shone
lights in their faces and pushed them back in. Within seconds
the side was back up and nailed into place. Jordan still heard the
muffled voices of the men inside.

There wasn't time to think. He was pulled roughly out of
the truck and watched it drive away as he was hustled into the
back of a rusted-out black Citroën. The driver was a man in
his midthirties, full beard and intense, glowering eyes that constantly flashed to the rearview mirror to look at his passenger. He
snarled something in Pashto and drove on, headlights catching
the trees, dangerously close on either side of the unpaved single-
lane road. Jordan was pretty sure he was going to be killed. He
would give them one hell of a fight, though. He wasn't afraid.
Which was funny; he realized now he'd always been afraid.
Afraid of losing something or missing something, but now, probably as close to death as he'd ever been, he felt nothing, no fear
at all, just a mild impatience, a desire to get on with it.

With a skid of tires on gravel the car stopped in a little pullout. Several men came out of the woods and surrounded it, scanning the area. The lights switched off. The door opened and Jordan heard Feda's voice with a mixture of confusion and relief.

"Come quickly, Mr. Jordan, change of plans." Jordan climbed awkwardly out of the backseat. Feda was there and took his hand.

"Quickly."

He led him through the trees to another dirt road. There was a small tan Renault idling on the shoulder with an older white woman in a green sweater and little round glasses standing next to it. She smiled at him. "*Ça va*, Monsieur Jordan?"

French, looked like someone's granny, but she had a jaw like a bulldog. She offered a hand and he took it with his uninjured left. Thin skin, prominent veins but a firm grip and calloused palms.

"This is Maman," Feda said. "That's what everyone calls her. She is going to take you through the tunnel. There is a train. The man who was killed, Azir, one of his brothers was in the crate with you. They were going to kill you. A man was bragging about it and my father heard about it. No one will find out you are not in that crate until they open it in Dover." He smiled, seeming to relish the image.

"You can trust Maman."

Maman opened the trunk of her car and pulled up the carpet to reveal a hidden compartment cut into the backseat. Jordan looked at the tight faces of the men and nodded. He gingerly squeezed his body into the space. He was lying on his right side with his knees pulled halfway to his chest. The compartment was padded with old blankets and seemed comfortable enough. He craned his head around and found Feda's eyes.

"Thank you," he said.

"I think you are a very lucky man, Mr. Jordan," the boy said. Then the carpet was pulled over him and it was dark.

A moment later he heard the car start and saw that there was a slit along the side of the seat back right at his eye level. He caught a glimpse of Maman in the rearview mirror before the interior light went out. Her mouth was set. He strained but all he could see was the odd flash of white as a tree caught the head-lights and the green glow from the speedometer.

After a few minutes the ride became smoother as the car turned onto a paved road.

Streetlights swept the car's faded interior. Jordan blinked to focus. Maman switched on the radio, syrupy strings and a French crooner. She smiled and her eyes twinkled with some happy, distant memory.

70

CURIOSITY

Julie Seward walked home as usual. It was just over half an hour from her office in the J. Edgar Hoover Building to the small Georgian house she shared with two cats and, once in a great while, a gentleman caller. She realized with some alarm that it had been almost a year and a half since the last time the cats had had to share her attention. It wasn't that Julie was unattractive or had difficulty relating to men; it was just that the job, at least at this point, seemed to take all of her time and energy. She was a researcher for the FBI. She wanted to make Special Agent but that meant finishing her degree at night while still working a sixty-plus-hour week. She was tired.

She walked up Independence, along the side of the Capitol Building, then right on Pennsylvania and left onto North Carolina Avenue. Her house was two blocks up in the middle of a quiet elm-shaded street. She fumbled in her purse for the keys that always seemed to worm their way to the very bottom. She cursed silently under her breath as she opened the low wrought-iron gate and gingerly picked her way up the narrow walkway. The front light was out again, making the uneven brick treacherous in her low heels. She dug out her keys and opened the heavy door.

The hall light was out, too. The streetlights were still on and she could see lights on in the house next door. What a pain in the ass. Her hand groped along the wall for the switch that turned on the living room lights. Her foot slipped on something slick on the floor and something warm and wet brushed against the side of her face. Reflexively her left hand grabbed the door-jamb as her right swung up to protect her face. The arm struck something soft and heavy. There was a muted gurgling sound.

"Jesus Christ," she screamed as she flailed in the dark and slipped to the floor. On her hands and knees she crawled into the living room and found the wall switch. The lights came on, blinding her momentarily. It took a moment for her brain to make sense of what she was seeing. The hook of the coat hanger had gone in through the back of the cat's head and come out its mouth, holding the jaw open in what looked like a crooked snarl. The hanger had been looped over one of the arms of the brass chandelier in the foyer. The cat's belly had been cut open and something that looked like link sausage hung out, dripping blood on the floor. The blood had smeared where Julie had slipped in it. The pool ran all the way to the stairs. The animal was still alive. One hind leg spasmodically pawed the air as if trying to get purchase on wet marble. Her open eyes met Julie's, pleading. She was trying to make some sound but the hanger had clearly destroyed that capacity. Blood bubbled at the exit wound.

Something clicked in Julie's mind. The raw panic receded and a clinical detachment took its place. She kicked off the pumps and smoothed down the skirt as she stood. She grabbed a side chair from the living room and stood on it, cradling Ruby's body as she gently lifted the hanger off the chandelier. She felt the cat's hind leg continue its fruitless pedaling against her jacket.

She murmured softly to her as she carried her to the sofa. She looked away as she tried to nudge the sausagy thing back where it belonged with her elbow. "Shh, shh," she whispered, "there's a good girl."

The front door was still ajar, keys dangling from the lock. No cars were on the street and it seemed unnaturally quiet in the house. A sound from the stairway made her heart skip. She hadn't considered the possibility that whatever monster had done this was still in the house. Panic tightened her throat and squeezed her chest. Then she saw Buster, the other cat, a gray male, come slowly down the stairs, tail high, the tip flicking nervously from side to side. He ran his cheek and body along the rails the whole way down. He quickly crossed the foyer, delicately skirting the pooled blood, and came to her. Julie knew he'd be hiding under her bed if anyone was still in the house. He meowed accusingly while rubbing himself against her legs. Hungry. She was late. Buster seemed completely unaware of his companion on Julie's lap.

Ruby's breathing was shallow and her eyes were wide. She was dying. Julie knew it and knew there was nothing she could do except try to ease her suffering. She cradled her head and grabbed the hook of the hanger just below where it entered. With a firm turn of her wrist she twisted the hook out. Ruby's eyes stretched even wider and her mouth opened in a silent scream, then shut, pale pinkish fluid beading at the exit wound. Julie dropped the hanger, startling Buster. Ruby's eyes relaxed and found Julie's and the tip of her tongue poked out of her mouth. For a second she looked perfectly normal and peaceful, then her body hiccuped. She got a faraway look in her eyes and was gone.

Julie took off her jacket and spread it out on the couch. She laid Ruby on the jacket and went into the kitchen to feed Buster. She mopped up the blood in the hall, then poured herself a big tumbler of Maker's. Ruby was still; it looked like she was smiling and squeezing her eyes shut. Her body was cold; she didn't feel real, the weight felt wrong. Julie wrapped her up in the coat. She was scared, but more than that she was angry. This had nothing to do with her. She took out her phone and dialed Michael Herron in Boston. Herron picked up on the first ring.

"Hey, Jules. How's it going?"

"Not so well, Michael. In fact it's been a pretty shitty evening so far." Through the cell latency she heard him start to speak, but she cut him off. "No. Don't say anything. Just listen. I just finished cleaning up the blood from one of my cats who was gutted and hung up by a coat hanger through her head. She was still alive, Michael. She's dead now, thank you very much. No, no, shut up and listen. This is on you. I've been thinking it through. This was a warning, you know, curiosity killed the cat, right? But I'm thinking, what the fuck have I been working on that could stir up a hornet's nest like this? Nothing. There's only one possibility and that's you. Either that phone number you had me run or one of those pictures I tried to ID for you. And I fucking told you, too." Her voice was rising, the composure slipping as she spoke.

"I fucking knew it. When that DC number came back cold I told you to back off. Goddamn it, Mike." She was crying in earnest now. "So we're done. You got it? No more little favors for old times' sake. Nothing. You hear me? I don't want to hear from you. Got it?"

Herron may have answered but she had already clicked off.

Matthew Chun refreshed the page for the umpteenth time. Nothing. ROBIN had gone completely silent. No new data in days. He should call Prenn but it was nerve-racking talking to him lately. He'd give it one more day.

In the basement of the building on Hoxton Square, Sam frowned. The FBI girl had gotten the message. But she hadn't called Metro. She'd called some cop in Boston, Herron, the guy who'd handled the Parrish case. It made no sense. That case was closed.

What the fuck was he up to? What did he know? It kept spreading. This cleanup was turning into a bigger and bigger mess.

At a certain point the upside didn't matter. That was the thing with gambling. You had to know when to walk away.

71

TRAIN

For a while they drove smoothly, then the car performed a series of long turns before coming to a complete stop. Maman's window rolled down and Jordan heard her converse briskly with what he assumed were the immigration police. He couldn't understand the conversation but it seemed light and familiar. Maman laughed out loud a couple of times. He heard the trunk open and froze under the carpet but after just a couple of seconds it slammed shut. And then they were moving again. He couldn't see anything but they made a couple more long turns, heading downhill now. Then there was a metallic clatter as they drove onto the train that would take them through the Chunnel. The sound echoed in the close metal enclosure. The car drove another slow thirty or forty feet and then the motor switched off and Jordan heard the throaty rasp of the parking brake.

Maman glanced in the rearview mirror and gave him a quick encouraging smile. In less than an hour they'd be in England. It was happening. Ready or not. He wished there weren't so many unanswered questions. What kind of security would there be at Hoxton Square?

And who would actually be there? And the biggest question of all: Had Stephanie gotten his message? Had she understood? It was too late to turn back; the coaster was over the top. He had to trust her. Everything depended on it.

Fifteen miles in, as the train sped sixty-eight meters under the English Channel, there was a tap at Maman's window. Maman rolled it down. *"Oui, monsieur?"* She cried out in protest as the man reached into the car but the cry was cut short when he opened her throat with a long knife. Jordan saw a spray of blood in the mirror and then Maman collapsed out of his view. The driver's door opened and the man got in, pushing Maman's still body roughly aside. He leaned down and found the trunk release. Jordan heard the trunk open and another voice behind him.

Adrenaline flooded his body. In seconds they were going to lift the carpet and find the compartment. The man in the car got out to help his companion. Jordan clawed at the tiny gap he had been looking through while pushing back as hard as he could with his legs. It wasn't working. His right leg was asleep and the angle was wrong; he couldn't get any leverage. He felt the carpet slide back and heard an excited cry behind him. With one last desperate effort he slammed against the seat back and felt something give. The entire backseat of the Renault collapsed, spilling him into the car. He rolled, seeing light and two surprised faces behind him. The one with the knife looked familiar. He recovered first and came around to the side. Jordan lunged for the door lock and hit it just in time. All four doors locked with a satisfying click. Eyes wide, he stared through the window at his attackers. They'd have to try and come through the trunk if they wanted him. They'd be headfirst and crawling. He would make them pay.

The man with the knife said something to his friend and smiled wickedly at Jordan as he held up the keys and the key fob.

The fluorescent light glinted green off his gold tooth. Qhaywaan. He pressed the button once and the front door unlocked. Jordan lunged for it and as he did he heard two clicks and all the doors unlocked. Jordan rolled on his back and kicked out at the left rear door with both feet. The door hit Qhaywaan in the chest and knocked him to the wall. Jordan didn't wait to see what kind of damage he'd done. He pulled open the opposite door and dragged himself out. He heard yelling as he sprinted down the narrow aisle past the long line of cars. As he ran he saw fear and confusion on the faces of all the vacationers. Car doors locked and mothers pulled their children down. He saw a sign for stairs at the end of the front car. He pushed himself and ran hard. He had put a dozen car lengths between him and his pursuers.

He took the stairs three at a time. The upper level was just like the one below, a long line of cars stretching out of sight. He saw a lavatory on the right side and sprinted to it, aware of the pounding on the stairs behind him. It was occupied. They were close. He hit the ground and rolled under a muddy green Range Rover. He saw their feet as they reached the upper level. They split up, each taking one side. They moved quickly. Jordan looked under the cars and saw that there was a Sportster four cars back that he'd never fit under. So he started worming his way back toward the men. They were scanning under vehicles as they went but hadn't seen him yet. A car door opened toward the front of the train and Jordan saw a brown work boot step onto the floor.

"Oi, you lot," a voice boomed. Northern, sounded like a big guy. "How about fucking off, eh? People trying to sleep."

The man with the knife snarled something and kept working his way up the line.

"Wot did you say, you fucking cunt?" the man said, slamming his car door and walking back toward them. A woman's voice, shrill from inside the car. "Shut it, Kim. I'm gonna teach these Pakis some fucking manners." Jordan could only see feet as the two Afghans converged on the brown boots. There was a momentary scuffle. Jordan used the distraction to wriggle as close to the fighters as he could. This was an area they'd already checked.

"Jesus Christ! You motherfucker!" the man yelled. "You cut me. I'm going to rip your fucking head off." More screaming from his car, almost right above Jordan. He apparently lunged at the man with the knife but was too slow. He must have been hit in the face because next he was on all fours with a thread of bloody spit hanging from his lip. He turned his head slowly and looked right at Jordan underneath the car. He seemed puzzled. Then the knife went in between his shoulder blades, all the way to the hilt. Like a bull at the conclusion of the torero he went down. His head was inches from Jordan's. The Afghan pulled the knife out. There were screams and the sound of doors locking down the train.

The men quickly moved up the line to where they had left off, ignoring the hysteria in their wake. When they came to the occupied lavatory they converged. Jordan had made it to the front of the car right by the stairs. He just needed a second. Qhaywaan kicked the lavatory door. Then put his shoulder to it. Jordan tensed under the front car. Just as the lavatory door collapsed and both men reached in to seize the hysterical girl inside Jordan slipped into the stairwell.

He held his breath and listened. He didn't dare look. He heard the girl screaming, people yelling. No footsteps, though. He hadn't been seen. He ran quietly down the stairs to the lower level. People's eyes met his, then looked away; they were frightened. He knew the Afghans would be back once they'd swept the upper deck. He ran down the line, trying to think, trying to push the adrenaline down. It had saved him but he needed to be clear now.

Around the middle of the train, he saw a big Ford SUV. He ran a few cars past it, then slid under and worked his way back.

The clearance was high. As quietly as he could he worked his body up into the space between the suspension and the drive-shaft. He was pretty sure he couldn't be seen. He just had to hold on for the twenty or so minutes it would take to reach the other side of the channel. He wedged himself in and waited.

A few minutes later they were back. The way he was positioned he couldn't see anything but he heard their voices over the constant clatter. He tensed, waiting for them to pass but they didn't. Several more minutes ticked agonizingly by and still nothing. Then there was a deafening blast. It sounded like a bomb had gone off. As his ears recovered he heard screaming from all around. Almost instantly, black choking smoke filled the space. And heat. It rolled up the train car in waves. The smoke triggered an alarm and a bright green light started to flash in time with an electronic siren that rose in repeating whoops. It was utter chaos. Then the train started to slow down. And then, eleven miles from the station at Folkestone, it stopped.

72

HELL

"Parrish's on the move."

"With our friends?" Sam said.

Dennis shrugged. "Zar Wali hasn't said anything."

"Which way is he headed?"

"South," Dennis said. "He's making good time."

"Alive and well?"

"Apparently. Does this change anything?"

"Don't know. Let's see where he goes."

The rat, full almost to bursting, chewed its way out through the corner of the box of Wentworth baby lettuces and blinked in the bright sunlight. His leg was scabby and ached some but otherwise life was sweet.

This was hell. Flames, smoke, heat. People were screaming; several started their engines as if they were going to drive out. Jordan had no idea where the Afghans were. People started to climb out of their cars. Once it started, the panic had spread and soon everyone was out of their vehicle and pressing to the rear of the train car. Jordan dropped to the ground and peered up the aisle. They had blown up Maman's car. It was engulfed in flames and the cars closest to it were clearly in danger. A woman's voice was speaking over the intercom. It was impossible to tell what she was saying but she spoke calmly in English and French—had to be the emergency evacuation instructions. A lot of good that was going to do, Jordan thought.

He stayed put. After what felt like hours but was probably no more than a couple of minutes, there was a new beeping noise and a rumble through the carriage as the rear of the car slid open like a giant garage door. Men from the train crew were outside yelling in English and French for people to evacuate. Passengers surged out into the tunnel. Jordan waited until the train crew sweeping the car had passed him, then slid out and joined them. They escorted him and one other man they'd found passed out in the back of his car to where the rest of the passengers stood huddled under harsh emergency lights. Jordan didn't see the Afghans anywhere. He had to get away. The mass of people offered no real protection. And even if it did, he'd be evacuated back to Calais; the burning train was between them and England. He worked his way to the edge of the group. Some people were yelling, trying to be heard, trying to find each other; others stood silent and dazed. No one saw Jordan slip into the tunnel away from the lights and break into a light jog back toward France.

A couple hundred yards up the track he saw a door with a green light over it. It was heavy steel and had a large vertical handle. There was a red sign next to it saying Service. Jordan looked back down the tunnel and saw that the passengers were being organized into two long lines and they were heading his way. He pulled the handle across and there was a loud hiss of air. The door pushed in but it felt like someone was inside pushing back. It took all his weight to force it open. There was a rush of air coming out. He realized they must pressurize the service tunnel. He stepped in and the heavy door swung shut behind him, the hiss of air rising to a high whistle before it sealed. He was in a small tunnel lit by red emergency lights. He yawned to pop his ears. He jogged down the shaft, which opened out into a larger service tunnel. This ran parallel to and between the two main tunnels. It was well lit and empty. Not for long, he was sure. The tunnel curved gently to the left. If he could get far enough before the train crew got there or rescuers arrived he might be clear. He started to run at a brisk but sustainable pace.

The only sound was the rhythmic slap of his shoes on the cement and his breathing, three steps to every exhalation, two to every in. His mind surrendered to the rhythm. Images flashed through his head, running up and down the hills of Roppongi, around the Charles in Cambridge, through his old neighborhood in Somerville, chasing his dad's receding shadow.

He looked back over his shoulder. Nothing there and he was pretty sure he couldn't see the door he'd come in through. Things were looking up. Then his luck got better still. There was a car. Not exactly a car, more of a glorified golf cart. The vehicle was parked in a little recess in the tunnel wall. It had a Mercedes logo on its hood. He stopped. It had to be an emergency vehicle; no way it was going to need a key. Sure enough, just a start button. He pressed it.

Nothing. Then he stepped tentatively on the accelerator and the car leaped forward. Of course, electric. He pulled out into the tunnel and floored it. Not Mercedes's best work. He could run faster. But this would save his energy. He'd ride until he couldn't.

He heard something. At least he thought he did. He released the accelerator and the car came to a smooth silent stop. He strained his ears. Over the constant rush of air through the tunnel's ventilation system he heard something else, a low hum and the whisper of tires on cement. Someone else was driving in the tunnel behind him. Probably rescue workers. But why come this way? They were past the train. He craned his neck and stared back down the tunnel. Another service car came into sight a few hundred yards back. Even from this distance Jordan was pretty sure it wasn't rescue personnel. He swore under his breath and punched the pedal. He had a head start.

73

PALM SUNDAY

Two miles farther, the tunnel opened out into an enormous switching cavern. The constant light of the service tunnel gave way to a steadily pulsing emergency light. Jordan saw two sets of rails cross, then disappear into black tunnel mouths on the opposite side. He was debating the next step when he saw headlights flickering in the continuation of the service tunnel. That made up his mind. Rescuers were coming from the English side. He jumped out and moved swiftly into the concealing shadows in the vast cavern.

He'd wait for the rescuers to pass and continue on foot, that way he could move faster and go down any of the three tunnels, leaving his pursuer to guess. He worked his way mostly by feel to the far left wall. Each time the light strobed on he'd map out the next few steps in his mind. He had just reached the wall when three trucks burst into the tunnel. They were moving fast. The first two were outfitted to fight fires; the last looked like an ambulance. As the ambulance passed with a last

rush of air Jordan heard a sound from the France-bound tunnel mouth behind him and turned just as the Afghan leaped.
It wasn't Qhaywaan. Jordan just had time to turn his shoulder
so the knife slid past his ear and struck the cement wall with a
spark and a bright clang. He was knocked down but rolled to
free himself and scrambled back to his feet. He kicked at the Afghan's knife hand and was awarded a grunt of pain and the sound
of the blade skittering over the floor. He ran, hand against the
wall in case he tripped. Looking back he saw his attacker frozen
on the ground, searching for the knife in one flash, standing in
the next and chasing him again in the next. He was younger
and faster. And he had the knife. With each burst of light Jordan
scanned the cavern for an answer, a door, a weapon. Then he
saw something, maybe fifty yards down. There was some kind
of tool on the wall, like a long tire iron with a socket on one
end. Ignoring the fire in his side and his ragged breathing, he
ran faster. He tore the iron off its mount and turned right, out
toward the middle of the cavern. The Afghan followed close.
Jordan could hear his breathing. He tried to move in a different direction each time the light went out.

The adversaries circled each other in a strange little hopping
dance. Each vying for positional advantage.

The Afghan lunged in the dark, missing by inches. Jordan
brought the iron bar down with all his force. He hit something.
The man groaned and when the light came on Jordan saw him
on one knee clutching his shoulder. He swung again but missed
in the dark. Jordan tripped on the train track and fell sprawling across the other man. He frantically rolled clear as the light
came on freezing the blade in midarc. In the darkness he heard
it strike cement just next to his ear. He swung the bar, feeling
once again solid contact. The illuminated Afghan was bleeding
profusely from his temple and seemed stunned. Jordan stood and
when the light came on again he took aim and swung with all
the fury and fear and rage in his body.

There was a sickening moist cracking sound and he felt his weapon shatter something brittle only to expend the rest of its force sinking into something more yielding underneath. The entire right side of the man's face seemed to have collapsed, giving him a surprised expression. He wasn't moving. Jordan swung again. He struck somewhere near the shoulder and something snapped underneath the skin and muscle. Somehow every blow seemed to stoke Jordan's anger. He swung again and again, the exertion making him cry out with each blow. He saw the damage he was inflicting as a series of snapshots in the strobing light. His hands and arms were soaked in red and the Afghan's head was an unrecognizable mess of blood, bone fragments and tissue.

And then it was over. Jordan felt the passion suddenly drain completely out of him. His sweat-soaked body felt cold and all of his muscles were spent. He let the bar drop with a clatter to the floor. His chest heaved and breath came out in ragged gasps. Tears streamed unnoticed down his face. He had to keep going. There was still another pursuer out there. He picked up the knife and stuck it gingerly in his back pocket.

He chose the left tunnel and started to run. His legs felt like deadweight but he forced himself to keep moving. The only light came from dim fixtures on the wall every fifty yards or so. He ran on the relatively flat space to the left of the track. His shoes echoed loudly. He couldn't plan ahead; he had no idea what he'd do when he reached the tunnel mouth. He'd figure it out when he got there. Then he heard a bloodcurdling scream from behind him. Sorrow and rage in equal parts. Grief and bloodlust. Qhaywaan had found his companion. Jordan froze and leaned against the wall, breathing as quietly as he could manage. A minute later he heard a yell like the baying of a dog on a scent and footsteps coming hard down the tunnel. Fuck. How had he known which one? In the quiet he heard a thick drop of the dead man's blood splatter on the ground. Of course. He'd left a fucking map.

He ran. It was too hard; he was too exhausted. He wasn't
going to make it. Nowhere to hide. Then there was a ladder, really just rungs set into the wall leading to a hole just big enough
to squeeze into. He climbed. He went in headfirst, no way to
turn around. If he was caught up here he'd have no way to protect himself. He pulled himself several feet into the black shaft.
He was sure he couldn't be seen from below and hopefully it
was too dark in the tunnel for the blood to give him away.

He lay still, listening to his heart beat. The slap of feet on cement echoed down the shaft, close now, heavy, even breathing
right below him. Then there was something else, a vibration, a
distant rumble. Air started to stir around his ears. Then a stiff
breeze blowing from his feet past his head. The rumble grew
louder. His ears popped. Then he understood. He was in one
of the pressure relief ducts. It must run all the way to the other
track. When the trains came through at high speeds it gave the
air somewhere to go. He inched forward. The duct sloped gently
up. The noise grew louder and the wind was now rushing past
him. Then the train was hurtling by just behind him with an
angry suddenness and the walls seemed to shake and the roar of
the wind through the duct was deafening. And then, just as suddenly, it was over and the train was receding and a light breeze
was pulling back the other way, drawing fresh air that smelled
faintly of the sea past his face.

He had to keep going forward. His ears strained in the darkness. If he let his imagination go he could almost feel Qhaywaan
crawling up the shaft behind him. Fighting down the panic he
used his elbows and the bent tips of his toes to worm his way
through the narrow enclosure. He squeezed his eyes shut and
took a deep breath. A clew of worms, a slither of snakes, a bed
of eels. After running flat for a while the shaft pitched down
as he inched his way forward. Then, like a newborn coming
into the world, he finally squeezed out of the pressure duct on
the southbound side. The tunnel was quiet, several miles south

rescuers were putting out the fire. They would find Maman's body, so badly burned her true cause of death would never be known. He walked on along the track and after what seemed like only a few minutes he saw a gray light up ahead. Twenty minutes later he walked out of the tunnel mouth. The sun was just rising in Folkestone. It was Palm Sunday.

74

BUZZING

Stephanie glanced at her notes. She was lecturing on Hawking radiation. She'd given this lecture a few times, and for the most part it flowed even though her mind was completely preoccupied. Reina had come in late, causing her a few minutes of panic, but as she'd taken her seat she'd flashed Stephanie a quick thumbs-up. She had the fake ID.

The body was covered in nasty welts and burns. Some of the burns were ringed with black, scorched flesh. When she was found, her eyes were wide-open. A pair of underwear was balled in her mouth, most likely to muffle her screams. Her blond hair was tangled and knotted as if she had twisted from side to side for some time. She was spread-eagle. Her hands were tied to the bedposts with black stockings and her ankles were bound with leather cuffs chained to the bed frame. The first detective on the scene at the Marlboro Street brownstone, Delguidice from Homicide, was puzzled by the stockings as he had found a second set of chained leather cuffs tucked between the mattress and box spring at the top of the bed.

The ankle restraints were only intended to keep her centered; her legs were kept fully spread by a steel rod attached by a second pair of leather anklets. Another steel rod extended up from the spreader, terminating in an inserted conductive dildo. The genital region was horribly burned. "Christ Almighty," Delguidice said, shaking his head. This wasn't kinky sex gone wrong; someone had deliberately tortured this girl to death.

Herron's hood snagged on the yellow police tape as he stooped under. "Hey, Scott, what do you got?"

"Not sure, it's pretty fucked up. Lieutenant said you knew the place."

"Yeah," Herron said. "Parrish. Dead guy, couple months back. Kept his mistress here on the company dime. I think the company still holds the lease." He walked around the bed to see the girl's face. "Damn, Scott. I think I know your girl, too." *Think, shit.* He'd know that body anywhere. It was the blonde from Prenn's place. No question.

It didn't make sense. Maybe the widow found out? No, that was crazy. No way she did this. It was him. Herron felt it in his gut. He didn't know why but he knew his guy. Prenn must have snapped. Fucking loony tunes. He was a killer. When he didn't get what he want he lashed out.

"Scott, let me know what you get for prints. I think I know who did this. In fact, I'm pretty sure. Call the lieutenant. He'll give you the story. I'm going to pick the bastard up."

Just like on TV: small room, big mirror, table and a couple chairs. Alex watched the cop in profile in the mirror. Fischer was talking, calm, controlled. The cop looked like he was going to have an aneurysm. He kept trying to ask Alex questions directly but Fischer kept swinging him around. He was probably the best and certainly the most expensive criminal attorney in

Boston. The cop was saying something, a question, but Alex didn't hear him. He saw the expectant face, spit in the corner of his mouth. He could feel the hostility. The guy wanted to reach across the table and grab him. It didn't matter, nothing did. His ears were buzzing, a low constant sound. He couldn't hear anything the cop was saying or, for that matter, Fischer's responses; it was all a dull distant murmur.

He had to figure this out. Breathe. The Bolshy was dead. Sam. Had to be. And framing him for it, but why? Eventually the cops would find Vanessa and then he'd be in even deeper shit. She'd have him killed. Pimp's first commandment.

"If there's nothing else, Detective," Fischer was saying, making a show of pushing his papers together and stuffing them into his briefcase.

"Mrs. Parrish? She find out, tell you to end it hard?" That came through. Alex looked quizzically at the detective; his mouth started to open.

"Alex," Fischer said, forcefully pushing his chair back, "we're done here. Detective, if you decide you have cause to charge my client with a crime, perhaps you'd be so kind as to call my office. Otherwise…" Fischer looked into the mirror. The cop kept staring at Alex. Neither said a word. Alex got up and followed his lawyer out of the station. None of it made sense. His head started to spin as they walked down the steps of the precinct building. Fischer caught his arm.

"Are you all right?"

"Yes, sorry."

Fischer studied him for a second. "Go home, Alex. Get some sleep, have a meal, take a shower. You look like shit. If anything happens, I'll let you know. I don't think they'll try anything like that again. They've got nothing and no business dragging you in. Let me take care of the police. You take care of yourself."

And then his lips were just moving. And there was only the buzzing.

75

THE BAD THINGS

It was so obvious. It was almost silly. Stephanie stood in the CVS aisle shaking her head. The shelves were full of baskets, green plastic grass, eggs of every impossible hue and bunnies. Candy bunnies, fluffy stuffed bunnies, chocolate bunnies, some solid some semi and some completely hollow. The rabbit with its prodigious reproductive vigor was a pagan symbol for spring, fecundity, rebirth; the symbol that had been appropriated and laid over the Christian story of Christ's rebirth and the implied renewal of the soul through faith. Easter. That was the when. Jordan had put rabbit protein in the DNA sample because it would be impossible to miss.

She had a date. A date with her husband on Easter Sunday, just a week away. It was a date she was not going to miss. She just had to figure out the where. The phosphorus had to be the key. Unless Simon had missed something, that was the only other big flag in the sample. She needed to dig, she thought as she pulled up to the house.

Alex's car was parked out front.

Her heart started to race. Calm down, keep it together.

He was smoking a cigarette. She'd never known him to smoke before. Ever. He ground it out in the street when he saw her car.

"Jesus, Alex, you look terrible. Are you okay?" she said, straining to sound calm. He did look bad. Drawn, exhausted. "Come on in. I have to put this stuff away." He followed her into the house, looking around warily. As she busied herself putting the groceries away he paced the kitchen, then suddenly grabbed her by the arm and turned her to face him. His eyes were red rimmed and swollen.

"Are you fucking Simon? I need to know." His voice sounded raw and dry.

"What are you *talking* about?"

"Let's cut the bullshit, Stephanie. There isn't any time. I would have loved to keep everything slow and easy but it's too late."

She was scared but she struggled to keep herself cool and affected an expression of utter bewilderment.

"Alex, what are you talking about? You're freaking me out a little."

He was close, towering over her, his grip tight on her arm. "I saw you with him. A couple of days ago at Sunny's. After you left I talked to him. He said you had just run into each other but he was lying. And I could tell he was nervous. Like he knew about us and was afraid to tell me you were seeing each other."

"Alex, listen to me. Simon is just a good friend. There has never been anything more in our relationship. I felt like I owed him something, an explanation or an apology for all my hysteria around confirming Jordan's DNA. He was a mensch—he really hooked me up. I know he was up late rushing that through for me. Anyway, I just wanted to get him lunch and let him know how much I appreciated it." Alex was about to interrupt but she cut him off.

"And yes, I think he is a little intimidated by you. You make him nervous. So I'm not surprised if he got a little flustered."

He wanted to believe her; she could see it in his face. But he was struggling. And the grip on her arm wasn't getting any looser.

"What did you mean when you said there wasn't any time?" she said.

"I was arrested this morning." Stephanie's eyed widened. "Someone I used to know was killed and I'm being framed for it."

"Oh my God," she gasped. "But that's ridiculous. You didn't do anything." She tried to make it sound more like a statement than a question.

"It doesn't matter. I think I know who did it and why. If I go to jail, I'm dead. If I don't, I'm dead." He laughed, a humorless chuckle. "I'm pretty fucked."

"But that's crazy," she protested. "Go to the police, tell them what's happening."

"It won't make any difference. These people can get to me anywhere. These are powerful people. I did a deal with them a while ago and it went wrong."

"This is about money?" she cried. "I have money—what do you need?"

That little laugh again. "No, it's not about the money. I can't really explain it." He looked into her eyes. "It's complicated. I need to disappear, just drop off the grid. And I will. But listen—" he took a deep breath "—I want you to come with me."

Holding both of her arms now. Desperate.

"Alex, slow down. Please. You're scaring me. You're talking crazy. Whatever has happened, you can fix it. I know you can. And you know I care for you but this is all just happening. I need time."

She flinched as he slammed his open hand on the birch cabinet. She heard the tinkle of bottles inside.

"I'm sorry, I'm sorry." Pleading. "You have to listen to me. There isn't any more time. I wish there was. This is it. Sometimes you have to take the leap. I'll make you happy, I promise." A pause. "I need you, Steph."

He leaned to kiss her. Behind her she heard the steady drip of what smelled like sesame oil from the cabinet onto the granite countertop. What would he do if she refused? She buried her head in his chest and put her arms around him. Think. Think. His lips brushed her hair. His hands encircled the small of her back, pulling her closer, then sliding inside the waistband of her skirt. She could feel him pressing against her and his heart hammering beneath her cheek. He roughly pushed the skirt down and pulled the cotton aside. His breathing was raw. She felt numb with fear and revulsion, paralyzed. She didn't think she could stop it now. This man she'd known almost half her life, who was somehow responsible for her husband's kidnapping or whatever the hell it was, was going to rape her in her own kitchen.

She eyed the knife block by the fridge. She couldn't. She sank to her knees in front of him.

He tried to pull her back up. She looked up at him. "No, I want to."

She took him in her mouth. He groaned and leaned back against the island. His fingers lightly twisted in her hair.

Her mind divided in three. While one part performed the motions that she hoped would buy her the time she'd need and another lay curled up in the dark like a little girl with her hands over her eyes waiting for the bad things to go away, a third part of Stephanie's mind, calm and detached, began to trace the faintest outlines of a plan.

76

CASH

Zoe Cameron couldn't understand what was going on. The freeway was absolutely gridlocked. Cars were backed up for miles, it looked like. She had to get back to Paris. She was going to take the first train. It was Eric's birthday tonight. She absolutely could not miss it. He was the cutest guy she'd ever seen, let alone dated. They'd met at a house party at Sonia's. He had this shy smile and that adorable French accent. And he'd liked her. It was crazy. It was absurd trying to start a relationship with someone who lived in another country but, ooh la la, it was hot, too.

She tried to tune in to the radio station that the signs said had up-to-date Eurotunnel information but the radio in her piece-of-shit Nissan was worthless. She'd thought about getting a new one but what was the point of having a radio worth more than the car you put it in? All she could get was good old BBC1. They were playing Akon. She loved him. He was adorable.

She didn't hear the car door open and nearly fainted when

the bum got into her passenger seat. He was filthy and smelled so bad she almost threw up. His face was swollen and cut and there seemed to be bits of blood all over him. He had a beard and was dressed in typical bum clothes; nothing fit and it was all gross. He stank of smoke and BO and, worst of all, his right hand looked melted or something. A horrible smell was coming from it, too. Zoe thought maybe he was a leper, though she didn't really know if there were such things anymore.

"What the fuck are you doing?" she screamed.

"Shh, I'm not going to hurt you," he said. American accent.

"Get out of my car! You can't just hop in people's cars whenever you like." She was going to go with bitch. Weren't bums usually crazy and more likely to be scared of you if they could see you weren't scared? Then she saw the knife. Long and wicked looking. And, worst of all, covered in blood. Wet blood.

She started to cry. "Oh, no, please…"

"I told you, I'm not going to hurt you. I just need a ride."

"Whatever you want. Just don't hurt me."

"What's your name?"

"Zoe." Sniffling. Looking at him out of the corner of her eye.

"My name is Jordan, Zoe. I need you to make a U-turn. We're going to London."

Alex tried to pull away but she held him. And then he came with a moan of disappointment and a shudder and the rage seemed to melt away. He tried to raise her face but she pressed it to his stomach. He lowered his head and she heard him sobbing softly into her hair. "God, I have loved you."

She stood up and hid her face in the curve of his neck. "I just need a couple of days, Alex. I need to get some things together."

"All right. Two days." He turned her face to his. His eyes were shining, manic. "We're going to be okay. All of us. I promise you."

She nodded, then took a deep breath. "I know."

★ ★ ★

He was telling her the whole story. Alex, the kidnapping, Tokyo, Paris, Calais, even the killing in the tunnel. She had been rapt, asking for clarification occasionally but mostly just listening. The time had flown. They were in the suburbs, Darenth, just south of London. Almost there.

He'd eaten an apple, the only food she'd had in the car, and now his stomach was in turmoil. He'd had nothing to eat and now he was violently cramping. It felt like appendicitis, like someone was stabbing him in the gut with hot knitting needles.

"Pull over please, Zoe. I have to get out for a second."

She swung onto the sandy shoulder and braked. He opened the door and half fell out of the car. The side of the road fell off to a drainage ditch. He retched as he slid down the hill. Nothing came up but bile mixed with a little blood. Pink foam clumped in his beard and ran down to the dirt in viscous strings. He was struggling to clean himself when he heard the door slam. He looked up to see Zoe lock it from inside. He saw his reflection in the window. He looked completely deranged. She hadn't believed a word. Come to think of it, he probably wouldn't have, either. She mouthed, "I'm sorry," as she pulled away.

Two new voice mails. The first was from Vanessa.

"Alex. I hear the police have let you go. It doesn't matter. You are a dead man. You understand?"

It was business for her. Alex understood. If she couldn't protect her girls how could she justify her piece? No point in trying to protest his innocence; it wouldn't make any difference.

The next message was from his father. Second unsolicited call from the paterfamilias in a decade.

"Hi, Alex. It's…your father. Ah, just got a message from your friend, said he was meeting you here this afternoon. I, uh, must have missed *your* call. Delighted to have you, of course. Just let us know when you're coming. Shanisse can whip up a little lunch or something. Okay, talk soon."

Shit. What did that mean? Could Vanessa have already made a move? Or Sam… The call had come in almost an hour ago. Alex called back.

"Hello, you've reached the Prenns. You know what to do." Her voice.

"Hey, Dad. This is important. You may be in danger. Get out of there. Whoever called you is not my friend. Get out and call me." He took a deep breath. "I'm really sorry."

He clicked off. He called back again and hung up when the machine answered.

The manager of the branch stood and shook her hand. His suit had a thin, forlorn quality.

His grip was weak and clammy.

"Miss Rosales tells me you want to close your account, Mrs. Parrish." Stephanie nodded. "I can absolutely take care of that for you." He motioned her to a seat facing his desk.

"Has our service been lacking in some way? You've been an excellent customer and we'd love to keep your business if we can. Perhaps you'd like to speak with one of our Diamond Group wealth managers. They can provide a range of services for higher net worth individuals like yourself."

Scripted. He reminded her of a character from *The Office*. GED, scrapes with the law, community college, one foot still in the gutter, she thought; then, with the next breath, yeah, but look where all the Ivy League bullshit's gotten us.

"No, the service has been fine. Just moving."

"We have branches in twenty-seven states, ma'am," he offered eagerly.

"No, thank you," she said and folded her hands on her lap, hopefully indicating the end of the conversation.

"Okay." He shrugged. "Where would you like me to transfer the funds?"

"I'd like a cashier's check. Made out to cash, please."

He stopped typing. "Mrs. Parrish, I'm sorry, there's over a hundred thousand dollars in this account. That seems like a very large amount to be carrying around."

"Don't worry. I'll put it somewhere safe." She smiled at him.

As she left the branch with the check folded in her purse she wondered if the manager was already on the phone to his friends. This would not be the day to get mugged.

77

NAUGHTY

Alex made the drive to Concord in forty-seven minutes. It would have been faster but traffic sucked.

The car skidded on the gravel driveway. Martin's ridiculous Ferrari was in the garage next to a brand-new, forest green Range Rover. Alex assumed that was Shanisse's. So, both home, no other cars.

He walked quickly around the outside of the house. No sign of forced entry. The dogwoods were just starting to bud and Alex could hear the little stream that ran behind the stone wall babbling brightly, flush with meltwater flowing down from Gold Hill.

The front door was unlocked. Alex pushed it open. The house was still. It had a peaceful drowsiness. Sunlight shafted in at a low, late-afternoon angle.

"Hello?" His voice sounded small and hollow. He found his father in the living room.

Martin Prenn's pants were pulled down to his ankles. He was

kneeling, shirtless, bent over the arm of the sofa. He looked like he was praying. His backside was covered in straight, thin red weals and a trickle of blood had dried on his inner thigh. His hands were tied behind his back with a cable tie, the plastic kind the police use in lieu of handcuffs.

His eyes were bulging, wide-open, and something bright red was in his mouth. With his leathery tan he looked for a moment like a Damien Hirst riff on roast suckling pig complete with apple. As he got closer Alex could see that the apple was really the fat end of an absurdly large red rubber dildo, the rest of which was responsible for the odd distortion of Martin's throat. A red-flecked studded leather strap lay on the floor beside the couch. The sharp edge of the strap's buckle was stained red. It had probably been used to carve the crude block letters on Martin's back. *NAUGHTY.* There was almost no blood where the word had been cut. Then Alex saw the other side of his father's head and understood why.

There was a small hole in the middle of his forehead and the right side was completely blown away. The sofa cushion was soaked in blood and salted with bits of bone and brain tissue. The gun lay on the coffee table beside the sofa. He picked it up. Alex found he didn't have any feelings for this brutalized thing that had been his father. He felt neither sorrow nor horror. His senses seemed heightened and everything moved with a stately clarity as if he were walking on the ocean floor in an old-fashioned diver's gear, tether and air hose snaking lazily to the surface.

He held his breath and strained to hear any movement in the house. Nothing. He walked as silently as he could down the hallway to his father's bedroom.

"Just sign here, and here, Mrs. Levine," the Citizen's bank manager said, indicating two *X*s on the account docs. "Great.

You're all set. We'll issue you a temporary debit card now and you should receive your permanent card in a couple of weeks."

"Thank you," Stephanie said. The fake license had been accepted without question. She had deposited the cashier's check for $137,684.19 in a brand-new account under the name of Jessica Levine. There was a packed suitcase with clothes for her and the kids in the trunk of the car. And a new pay-as-you-go cell. It was time to go. Somewhere he'd never find her.

Herron pulled in behind Prenn's sleek Audi. He eased open the front door. All quiet on the western front. Then something red caught his eye in the living room.

He stood over the body, clenching his jaw, shaking his head. Prenn was one sick, fucked-up puppy. Herron pulled his gun and moved softly toward the back of the house.

Shanisse's wrists were tied to the bedposts with black stockings. She was naked save a pair of suede fringed boots. She had been tortured just like the hooker; the burn marks looked like bruises against her unnaturally tanned skin. Her body was completely hairless except for a tiny strip of singed stubble on the pubis. Herron searched the rest of the house; Prenn was gone.

78

LONDON

The Comfort Inn at O'Hare was a dump. The room sported a queen bed with a fuchsia-and-lavender floral bedspread and a pair of greenish-brown armchairs in front of cream blackout curtains. Stephanie had ordered up a cot for Sophie but it had never come. The kids were watching TV while Stephanie scanned the internet for information on phosphorus.

P33 was the name of the isotope Simon had found. It was also the name of a state road called Jaunpiebalga in Latvia. That seemed like a stretch. There was no free-occurring phosphorus anywhere, too reactive. It was used in explosives. Could she be on the completely wrong track? She glanced at her children laughing on the bed at something in the show they were watching. They hadn't questioned anything when she'd told them they were leaving for spring break early. They had dutifully given their fake names to the TSA guy at the airport. She'd only told them she didn't want to be bothered and they'd nodded solemnly and done what she asked. It was a game. Spy versus spy.

Phosphorus was discovered by Hennig Brand in Hamburg, Germany. That was promising.

She wrote *Hamburg* on the Comfort Inn pad. Commercial phosphorus is derived from apatite. The homonym would have appealed to Jordan. She scribbled it down. Apatite is mined in China, Russia, Morocco, Florida, Idaho, Tennessee and Utah. An area in Central Florida called Bone Valley is the largest producer. She added Bone Valley to her list and sat back with a sigh.

"Momma, look!" Haden cried suddenly. "Uncle Alex is on TV." Stephanie froze.

Alex's mug shot was in a box in the upper left corner of the screen. The reporter was standing outside his father's house in Concord. The front door was blocked off with yellow police tape and uniformed officers were swarming like ants in the background. He'd killed them both. Massive manhunt. Police were confident they'd make the arrest within hours.

The pain in Jordan's belly was unrelenting. It eclipsed for the moment the dozens of other pains that clamored for his attention. He felt weak and his belly was distended. It occurred to him he could be simply starving. He didn't recognize his own reflection in shop windows. His face was gaunt and his hair and beard were wild and matted. People on the street gave him a wide berth and avoided making eye contact.

He found a treasure trove in the trash behind an off-license in Bromley. A cardboard box full of wrapped Cornish pasties. Their sell-by date had come and gone, but when he opened one it smelled okay. He wolfed it down, filling his pockets with several more. The dense meat pie felt heavy in his stomach but the needle-sharp pain retreated. He felt new energy as he studied the posted bus map. He was close.

Karmic payback, he thought. A lifetime ago when he and Alex had just opened the lab on Dunster Street, they used to toss the leftover donuts from their Friday morning meetings in the trash behind the building. Alex would always argue for a reduced order but Jordan would insist on the full double dozen, saying, "The bums gotta eat, too."

He crossed the Thames at Tower Bridge. Tourists scattered as he passed the Tower of London and a Fabergé football of an office building called the Gherkin. The sun set as he turned from Great Eastern onto Curtain Road. A few blocks up he passed the Hoxton Pony and crossed Old Street. He was there.

There was a single security camera over the outer door. Jordan sat on the steps of the building across and down the street. The sun set at 7:44 p.m. In three hours no one went in or out. Foot traffic on the street was light. A lone woman with a small boxer wove delicately up the block. The dog came over to sniff at Jordan but his owner, a proper, fashionably dressed matron, tugged him back with a sharp jerk on the leash and crossed the street.

Jordan shook his head. He'd come this far and had no plan for the last twenty feet. He could hardly stroll across the street and ring the buzzer. Jordan watched couples return home, flushed from a night on the town, voices a little too loud and confident. And later still, single people returned, most with a hunch of disappointment in their unsteady carriage. The streetlights cast long shadows and he hugged himself against the chill. He opened another meat pie but this one smelled decidedly off.

By three it sounded like the city had finally downed its last blowsy nightcap and stumbled off to bed. Except for the low drone of distant motorway traffic, the urban version of cosmic background radiation, it was utterly still. He heard a lone car approach from blocks away. There was something not quite right in the rhythm of the engine, as if there was a murmur, a hiccup in the simple two-stroke syncopation. The green Vauxhall parked in an open spot just before the Exit Strategy building.

Two women got out; each had a large green bucket with rags and cleaning supplies. West Indian, maybe. They were in the middle of a conversation; one was laughing brightly in a tone that suggested her merriment was at another's expense. Across the street Jordan stiffly pulled himself to his feet. Cleaning ladies. Could be going into any of the buildings, but maybe… He moved to the curb.

They bypassed the lower gate and walked up the steps of the main entrance to number thirty-four.

Jordan affected the lurching roll of a drunk and swayed down the middle of the street. In his peripheral vision he saw the cleaning ladies enter the code on the keypad at the door and heard the buzz as the lock opened. Laughter rang in the night air and breath wreathed their heads as they pushed the door open wide and walked in. Jordan had managed to weave as close as he dared and now he ran and took the stairs in two, lunging for the closing door. He got two fingers in before it could shut. Cold steel pressed against his knuckles. He held his breath and counted to ten. He was lying across the top step with his fingers in the bottom of the door. He was probably visible in the security camera but what were the odds anyone was looking at this hour. He heard the cleaning ladies' voices from several rooms away. He slid noiselessly in, allowing the door to click shut behind him.

79

IN IT

Holding his breath, he listened. The cleaning ladies were upstairs, still laughing and chatting. Clearly they weren't worried about disturbing anyone. It was warm. He scanned the ground floor. There were three large offices coming off the central foyer. They were done in a tasteful Edwardian style, perhaps too tasteful. It felt professionally decorated; there was no individual personality to any of it. It all seemed neutral and expensive, reassuring for the clientele, Jordan imagined.

The stairway curved slightly to the left. Jordan went up the first few steps and saw a hallway upstairs with more offices, smaller but equally well-appointed. He remembered references in Terry's email to "the basement." He looked for stairs leading down. He walked down the hall that ran down the center of the building toward the back. The left side was taken up by a long conference room, done, surprisingly, in mid-'90s hotel-business–center teal melamine. The right side had a washroom, a coat closet, a kitchenette and, finally, a locked steel door with another keypad.

That would be the one. Jordan grabbed a chair from the conference room. Standing on the chair, he was able to loosen the hallway and kitchen light bulbs. He replaced the chair and crouched just inside the kitchen between the wall and the microwave rack and settled in to wait.

He heard the cleaning ladies work their way methodically through the upstairs offices before coming back downstairs where they split up and quickly dusted and vacuumed the three front rooms. One of the girls came to the back and flicked the light switch. She let out a small grunt of irritation when nothing happened, then crossed to the conference room. Jordan saw her run a damp cloth cursorily over the table and straighten a chair before she clicked off the light and closed the door. He held his breath and pressed himself deeper into the shadows but she went back toward the foyer and, minutes later, he heard the front door open and then shut. He was alone.

He opened the small refrigerator. Somewhere between urban office and bachelor apartment. A few bottles of Veuve Clicquot, a six of Stella and a solitary take-out container. He opened the white box and sniffed tentatively. Some kind of curry. He hungrily shoveled it into his mouth with his fingers.

He heard the front door and pressed back into the shadows. Heavier footsteps. One person, almost certainly male. Feet mounted the stairs. Jordan watched the ceiling as the footsteps made their way almost directly above him, then stopped. He didn't dare move. The man was on the stairs, and then footsteps were coming down the hall toward him. Jordan pressed deeper into the shadows but it was no use; he thought his stench must have given him away. Then he heard the light switch click once and again. There was an exasperated sigh and suddenly a man came into sight, framed by the light from the foyer. His face was in shadow but Jordan recognized him immediately and his heart started hammering as his eyes went wide. Sam. The familiar sweep of gray over horn-rims, tan slacks and sensible shoes. He was looking down, reading something on his phone. He walked right past the open doorway to the kitchen. He stopped at the keypad to the basement door and just stood there reading. Sam was so close he could reach out and touch him.

Suddenly Sam clicked off the phone and entered a code on the keypad. There was a metallic sliding sound and he pulled the door open. As Sam reached in to turn on the lights Jordan stepped out of the shadows. Sam looked at him with a puzzled expression as if he'd just materialized out of thin air. For a split second no one moved. Sam stood with his right hand still near the keypad and his left reaching through the doorway. Jordan grabbed the edge of the door and slammed it as hard as he could on Sam's arm. He heard the phone clatter down the stairs and Sam groaned. Before he could pull his arm back Jordan threw all his weight against the door. He was rewarded with a strangled cry. Jordan stepped back as Sam's right arm swung around to block him. He pulled out the knife and stood across the hallway. "Parrish?" Sam said incredulously.

Jordan didn't say anything. He saw Sam studying his face, glancing at the scarred right hand, confirming.

"It is you." Then his eyes lit up. "The fire in the tunnel."

"Not my fault," Jordan said. "Let's continue this downstairs, please."

Sam pushed the door open and gestured with his right hand. "After you." His left arm hung limply by his side.

"No, you first, I insist," Jordan said, switching his grip on the knife. "And please don't make me kill you. I will if I have to."

Sam studied him for a moment and nodded. "I believe you might."

80

EXIT STRATEGY

The basement level at 34 Hoxton Square seemed smaller than the upper floors. There was a long central room with a conference table ringed by smaller offices. The desks and fixtures looked like they'd all been bought at a Pentagon garage sale. Gray metal with tan accents. Jordan had appropriated an office in the middle, equidistant from the stairs they had come down and the front entrance. He stood hunched over the terminal. Sam sat. His arms and legs were tightly duct-taped to the chair. His left arm was noticeably swollen and his glasses were askew on his nose.

"What's the plan, Jordan? What are you going to do? This can't end well, you must know that," Sam was saying.

Jordan didn't respond.

"You know what will happen. To your family. And it will be your fault. You aren't leaving us any choice."

"Shut up," Jordan snapped.

The log-in screen had no separate field for username or password, just a single blank space with a blinking cursor.

"Let me go now and we can try to work something out, Jordan. Security is going to be here any second. The building is constantly monitored."

"I doubt that," Jordan said. "I don't think you want anyone else to know what goes on here and the people you work for have no reason to threaten you. They need you."

He typed Terry Allison's password—*"a-r-s-e"*—*tik-a-da-tik*.

The screen revealed a root directory, Unix. Figured. There was a separate Windows partition. Jordan navigated to it and booted into Windows. Seven, never upgraded. So much for security.

"Bravo," Sam said. "Terry always was a little lax. But what's it going to do for you? You need to stop and think, Jordan. You are killing your children."

Jordan whipped around and tore a length of duct tape off the roll and wrapped it over Sam's mouth.

He scanned the directory system and opened, then copied, several files. Then he opened Chrome and logged on to Gmail. He sent an email, attaching the files he'd copied.

"Now we wait," he said. He leaned back against the wall, too uncomfortable to sit. Sam stared at the screen. A few minutes later there was a ding and a new email in Jordan's in-box. There was no subject. Jordan opened it and smiled.

It said, Ça va, Yanqui?

Jordan hit Reply and typed, Ça va, con, and hit Send.

He ripped the tape off Sam's mouth and swiveled the chair so Sam was facing him.

"So here's where we are. My friend has received a series of Excel files. He has confirmed that they contain information on the identities and whereabouts of many, if not all, of your current clients. You will not be able to find him. The account I sent them to is already gone."

Sam said nothing but continued to watch Jordan with a wry smile.

"While I assume these are probably not very nice people," Jordan went on, "I have no interest in outing anyone. I just need some insurance. I need to know I'll be left alone. Do we understand one another?"

Sam nodded. "Very well, I think."

"I think it would be best," he went on, "if Jordan Parrish stayed buried. I'm sure you of all people can provide me with documentation for some other identity."

"Of course," Sam said. "Your wife has gone missing, by the way," he added, watching Jordan's face.

Jordan tried to keep his face still. He didn't want to give any more away but his heart was bursting. Stephanie had disappeared. She'd gotten the message in the bottle and understood. She was coming.

"Ah, you knew. I see. You *are* full of surprises this evening."

"I have a question for you," Jordan said. "How long ago did my partner approach you about getting rid of me?"

"Quite some time," Sam said. "For what it's worth I tried to dissuade him but he could be…convincing."

"Could?"

"Our mutual friend has become somewhat of a liability."

Jordan took this piece of information as if it were a foreign object inexplicably turned up in an old suit jacket pocket. He held it up in his mind and turned it this way and that, trying to figure out where it fit into his evolving worldview.

"I'm afraid he was drawing a great deal of unwanted attention," Sam said. "It's unfortunate."

Jordan nodded as if this were explanation enough.

"I'll need money," he said finally. "I thought we might augment what's left of mine with funds from some of your more—what's the word?—let's say ethically challenged clients."

Sam tentatively flexed his left arm and winced as he nodded. "Oh, and I could use some clothes."

81

HARRODS

Natalie M'Bute paused by the smoked salmon. There was a life-like sculpture of two peacocks facing each other over a plain peahen. She assumed they were fighting over her. Wasn't that the way of the world? She smiled to herself. Cradling her green Harrods bag, she elbowed her way past a couple of tentative Englishwomen and commanded the attention of the young man behind the counter. He was in his early twenties and very attractive, she thought, in an earnest, son of a cabbie sort of way. The food halls at Harrods were the one bit of menial shopping she truly enjoyed doing herself. She usually sent Celeste out to do the rest of the errands but every Friday she would have Mahdi drive her to Harrods and circle the block while she stocked up on delicacies.

She had a weakness for seafood: Kumamoto oysters, Scottish salmon and, of course, Russian caviar. All chased down with bottles of Krug. Of course, it wasn't just for her. She had to take good care of the general, or Abdi as she was now supposed to call him. An absurd thing. His name, *Obah*, meant *king* in Yoruba and *Abdi* was a word for a servant. Natalie snorted in derision. Her husband, a servant. That would be the day.

The boy came back with the salmon wrapped in thick brown paper. "Anything else today, ma'am?"

"No, thank you," Natalie replied with an imperious nod. "Good day."

She found an open seat at the oyster bar and ordered a dozen of her treasured Kumamotos and a Buck's fizz while she rested her feet. Two fizzes later, feeling sated and a little sleepy, she texted Mahdi and asked for her bill. She paid with her Barclays card.

The girl came back a couple of minutes later, somehow managing to look apologetic and impertinent at the same time.

"I'm so sorry, Mrs. Samuels, your card has been declined. Would you like to try another?"

When the second card was declined, people said Natalie's outraged screams could be clearly heard three floors away in Men's Shoes.

One loose end, Herron thought. The widow closes a checking account with $137,684.19 in it. That same day—surprise, surprise—a new account is opened at a Citizens branch in Somerville with a cashier's check in exactly that amount. The account holder is one Jessica Levine. Mrs. Levine and two children flew to Chicago that night. Credit card records place her at the O'Hare Comfort Inn. Follow the money to the widow. Follow the widow to Prenn.

Alex had killed his own father and stepmother. Jesus. And every policeman in Boston was looking for him. He would never find her now. Stephanie tried to inventory her feelings on the subject but they darted away like minnows. She'd tackle that one later. She had more pressing questions. Three days to Easter. Where the hell was she supposed to be going?

Slow down. Start at the beginning. Wikipedia. She read it out loud.

"'Phosphorus is the chemical element that has the atomic number 15 and the symbol P.'"

P. It was too obvious. That's why she hadn't seen it before. Occam's razor, Jordan's favorite old chestnut from Philosophy 101: *Entia non sunt multiplicanda praeter necessitatem.* "Entities must not be multiplied beyond necessity." In other words, the simplest solution is almost invariably the right one.

It was just P. The single letter *P.* Jordan couldn't have made it any plainer.

She wouldn't need to search through the vowels; she already knew. There was a picture in her purse.

82

PAIA

Mary Star of the Sea was just off the Hana road in Paia on Luna Lane. It was the only church in town. Paia, on the north coast of Maui, was spared almost all of the tourist overrun that was the blight of the southern coast. Most of the residents were unreformed hippies or hard-core surfers. It was a tradition to hit the 4:00 a.m. Easter vigil before heading out to Jaws, the massive break on the east coast of the island for a dawn ride. Father Ray lit the small pile of wood chips in the bowl as he recited the opening prayer. Then he lit the new Paschal candle, a four-foot cylinder of pure white. At first the flame wouldn't take, but as the wax around the wick melted it sputtered and caught.

"The light of Christ," he said.

"Thanks be to God," the congregation responded.

Father Ray lifted the candle and walked toward the chancel. The congregation followed. Twice more he stopped and proclaimed, "The light of Christ," and twice more they responded.

He stopped in front of the altar and turned. The members

of the congregation came up one at a time and lit their candles from the Paschal candle. The congregants had small white tapers pushed through Dixie cups to catch the wax. Stephanie guided Haden's and Sophie's hands as they lit theirs. She was worried about Haden igniting his candle. She knew Sophie didn't need her help but didn't want Haden to feel slighted.

They filed back to their pews and sat for the reading. Stephanie looked around her. The candlelight made a warm dappled pool. The faces of the young surfers seemed so earnest and guileless. Half of them looked just like the traditional depictions of Christ with long brown hair and trimmed beards. Several were already in their wet suits, though Stephanie had opted for a simple flowered dress and the children were dressed in the best she'd been able to piece together.

Father Ray read from the Book of John. He told the Easter story of how Mary went to the place where Jesus was buried and found the stone had been rolled aside. As she is weeping Jesus comes to her and she mistakes him for the gardener.

"'Jesus said to her, "Do not hold on to me, because I have not yet ascended to the Father. But go to my brothers and say to them, 'I am ascending to my Father and your Father, to my God and your God.'" Mary Magdalene went and announced to the disciples, "I have seen the Lord"; and she told them that he had said these things to her.'"

Then a girl with ironed blond hair sang and played acoustic guitar. The congregants sang along with the Alleluias, perhaps the only word in the liturgy that seemed equally plausible in both Latin and Hawaiian.

At the end of the service Father Ray led the congregation outside and they headed for home or for the beach in groups of twos or threes, their candles flickering in the distance like little constellations fanning out from the church. Stephanie and the children walked down the Hana road. Behind them Anthony's

Coffee was shuttered tight but the light was already on at the Fish Market.

They turned left down Lolo Lane, a dirt road lined with ramshackle houses, many with chickens already scratching in the predawn gloom. Forty-three Lolo Lane was on the left just before the road petered out into a little path that ran between a couple of houses and down to the beach. It looked small and unprepossessing from the road but when you walked inside it revealed itself, a sprawling six-bedroom with magnificent Pacific views from every room.

The house had been built in the '60s by Brian Nelson, a contractor who had made a killing putting up hotels along Maalaea Bay. When the boom had subsided, Nelson had moved back to California. His youngest son, Sandy, eventually grew up and went to Harvard, where he lived for two years in Jordan's co-op in Central Square. Sandy had magnanimously offered use of the family home on Paia to all of his housemates. Jordan had taken him up on the offer only once, years later. He and Stephanie and their two young children had spent an idyllic week lazing by the pool, watching sea turtles surf in the break and playing Monopoly way past the children's bedtime at the flaking white wicker table in the den.

Stephanie nursed her coffee and watched the sky shift from gray to pink to blue. Haden and Sophie had fallen asleep, curled up together on the sofa. She watched the light blanket rise and fall with their breathing. What would happen to them? Doubt began to seep through the cracks and gaps like smoke from a basement fire. Did she really believe that Jordan was alive? Not only alive but coming here to meet them? It sounded crazy. And based on what? Translating his junk DNA with some silly code they'd shared when they were practically children. If ever a fantasy reeked of desperate wish fulfillment and self-delusion this was it. Wasn't it far more reasonable to believe that she had, driven by her own grief and loss, *found* his message the same way dime-store clairvoyants find messages in tea leaves or inscribed by the pointer on a Ouija board? She'd been so certain, but now, an ocean away from home, it seemed absurd. She finished the last dregs of the now-cool coffee and set the cup down. She'd know soon enough. And perhaps, when he didn't come, she'd finally be able to let him go.

83

HERRON

The Levines had checked out but the trail was still warm. Mrs. Levine had used her MasterCard to book three one-way tickets to Hawaii. They'd flown from O'Hare to Denver, then Denver to Seattle and finally Seattle to Kahului/Maui.

Herron wasn't prepared for the air. It had a soft warmth to it with none of the crisp brine or the wet-blanket weight of its Atlantic counterpart. He took off his light suit jacket, feeling suddenly self-conscious, rumpled and pasty. His breath smelled rank, fermented airline coffee and scrambled eggs with some sort of dense biscuit that now sat like a deadweight in his churning stomach. When he had been a child his father had joked that he wanted his gravestone to read "Dan Herron. Never went to Hawaii, never wore blue jeans." It hadn't in the end. Just the name and dates. Beloved husband and father. That was a good one.

At the Enterprise counter he was greeted by a guy and a girl, both young and attractive, dark skin, brilliant white teeth. In fact, all the locals seemed absurdly good-looking. Relaxed, smiling, fit. Weren't they supposed to be bloated on Spam or something? It seemed like either brilliant or lousy marketing, Herron couldn't decide which. Who wanted to go on vacation and feel like the ugly American? On the other hand, the departure lounge was full of vacationers headed home and they all seemed pretty tan and mellow. Maybe that was the pitch: if you stayed in paradise long enough you turned beautiful and happy, too.

He opted for the Jeep Grand Cherokee. Put it on his personal card. You never knew when you might have to off-road it. Leilani traced the route to the South Island on the map. All Herron had to do, she explained, was follow the Mokulele Highway, which cut straight across the neck of the island like a necklace, or a garrote, he thought.

Haden woke up hungry. No surprise there. Stephanie cut up a fresh pineapple and sliced some mango. She had another cup of coffee as the kids devoured the fruit by the pool. Watching them play, Stephanie was struck by how much better they both seemed. Coming here had been good for them. The tension had broken. Something about the change of venue, or maybe it was just that their frozen mother had finally begun to move again. The direction didn't matter; the sense of purpose was everything. They would be all right. There was light.

Sophie taught Haden how to dive. First they sat side by side at the edge of the deep end. Then she showed him how to hold his arms over his head, hands overlapping and pointed, arms pressed over his ears. Then, on her clear, decisive three count, he leaned forward and plopped into the water. He came up, sputtering, "Mom, Mom! Did you see?"

"I did. That was amazing," she said.

"Look. Look," he cried as they did it again. By the time the sun cleared the row of palms and struck the patio directly, Haden was standing on the edge of the diving board, knobby knees shaking as he tipped off into a perfect cupped belly flop. So-phie laughed hysterically but he was beaming when he surfaced.

"You gotta go in straight," Sophie said. "Pretend you're holding a thousand-dollar bill between your ankles." She bounced lightly off the board and entered the water with the merest ripple. Two hours later Haden was diving nearly as well as his sister and both children's lips had started to turn blue.

"Everyone out of the pool. Let's get dry, get warm and go grab lunch," Stephanie said, tossing the three-year-old Thanks-giving *Saveur* aside and grabbing towels.

Lunch was mahi-mahi burgers at the Fish Market and gelato at Ono's after. It was the same every day. She was low on cash so Stephanie paid with her new debit card at Ono's.

Half an hour after she swiped her card, an email flagged Urgent hit Herron's phone. Ono's Gelato, Paia. Sent from a numbered dot-gov account. He was burning through a lot of favors, Herron thought.

84

SUNSET

After lunch the kids wanted to go to the beach but Stephanie told them she was tired and wanted to stay close to the house. Not that she expected anyone to show up. She was certain now. It had all been a fantasy, a fantasy fueled by grief and denial. She was beyond all of that now. Call it due diligence. She was just seeing the thing through.

Haden caught a lizard and Sophie helped him make a terrarium in a shoebox. The box would periodically shake and jump as the kids pored over a thousand-piece puzzle of a van Gogh self-portrait. Stephanie left them and went outside to sit and watch the waves.

As the sun finally rejoined the sea, balancing on edge for an impossible moment before breaking the surface tension and beginning to sink slowly beneath the long swells, she poured herself a glass of white wine and walked down the cement stairs to the beach. There was no sand here, just uneven rock studded with black volcanic boulders and slick tidal pools. The land had begun to shed its heat and the flow changed to a light offshore breeze that blew wisps of Stephanie's hair into her face.

She sighed deeply as she watched the great orange ball dissolve into a stain across the water. Tomorrow she'd have to figure out what their next step would be, but it would wait. She'd think about that tomorrow. She smiled, picturing Vivien Leigh in *Gone with the Wind*, resolute before the painted backdrop of Tara.

She was about to head back up to the house when she saw the tiny figure just rounding the point, picking his way carefully over the rocks. Some trick of foreshortening made it seem that he could walk indefinitely without ever getting any closer. She couldn't make out any features but he seemed to favor his right side; there was a slight hitch in his walk. Finally, she could discern light-colored trousers and a darker shirt, facial hair, maybe. Then, as he followed the swing of the shoreline, he disappeared from sight for several minutes. Waves lapped at the shore with a light slap and a yawning retreat. Time was suspended.

Then he reappeared, closer now. He was painfully thin; his shirt hung on his frame.

Bearded. He was protecting his right arm; he used the left to brace himself against the boulders but kept the right close to his side. She searched his face, squinting her eyes in the failing light. He was no more than a hundred yards away now. He looked up and their eyes met for the first time. They were different. The shape…they seemed a little wider and maybe more rounded. But there was a familiar light in them. A light she hadn't seen in a long, long time.

85

BAREFOOT

The girl at Ono's looked at the picture with her face scrunched up, twirling her hair. Picture of concentration, mostly for his benefit, Herron thought. "Yeah, maybe," she said. "Two kids, right?" More deep thoughtful consideration. Herron was pretty sure she was a stoner. And pretty sure she was scared enough of getting busted to tell him whatever her limited intellect thought he wanted to hear. *Useless* in a word.

"Thanks, you've been very helpful," he said, taking back the picture of Stephanie Parrish and tucking it into his pocket. The interview at the Fish Market had been much more productive. The waiter, a cocky surfer kid, deep tan, pale blue eyes with a shock of streaky blond hair that kept falling over one eye, had recognized Stephanie immediately.

"Oh, yeah, I remember her, yesterday lunch." He'd said it with a smarmy smile that left no doubt as to why his memory

was so reliable. "Pretty lady, came in with kids, barefoot, sa-
rong and a one piece."

That was the handy bit. Barefoot. More than likely walked.
Lived close, then. It wasn't much but it was what he had.

86

YOU'RE HERE

She had come. He wanted to run, crawl, drag himself across the lacerating rock and bury his face in her hair. All this time. How had she done it? All at once he was overwhelmed by the enormity of what she must have endured. He picked up his pace and almost immediately tripped, just catching himself on one of the razor-sharp ridged volcanic boulders. He saw her start and reach out her hand. Carefully again he carried on, judging each footstep and handhold. When he looked up again they were only twenty yards apart. His hand throbbed and his heart was hammering in his chest. And then the space was gone.

"You're here," he said.

"I'm here."

He had no idea what to say—the hundreds of times he'd played this scene in his mind and he had nothing. He took in her face, the tiny wrinkles at the corners of her mouth, the clean line of her brows, the strong jaw and the eyes. Their color was indescribable, a warm green interspersed with tiny puddles of deep blue and soft brown, and they glistened as though she were about to cry but at the same time seemed so calm, serene, accepting, so full of love and patience. He reached out with his left hand; it shook slightly. He touched her temple, right at the hairline, and gently tucked a wisp of hair behind her ear. Her hair was soft and light as corn silk under his rough fingertips.

And then it came, in a rush.

"Oh God," he cried, falling against her. "I'm sorry. I'm so, so sorry." All the strength that had propelled him and kept him going since France fell away.

Stephanie's wineglass fell to the rocks and shattered as she flung her arms around him. She felt his tears hot on her neck. She ran her fingers through his hair and held him as he sobbed. He was a baby in her arms, too weak to stand. As she held her husband Stephanie felt something inflate inside her, swelling until it must break, rising through her chest and then bursting out of her as she gasped for air. And then she was crying, too, squeezing him as hard as she could as her body tried to make sense of what her mind couldn't yet accept.

It was several minutes before either of them could speak, before they became conscious of themselves again. Finally he straightened up and held her face in his hands.

"How did you—" she started to say.

"It doesn't matter," he said. "You're here."

She laughed. "*You're* here."

He was so thin. She tenderly unwrapped the bandage around his right hand and winced when she saw the melted flesh of the wound. She searched his eyes. He smiled.

"Momma!" The scream came from far away. The house. Sophie. They both froze for an instant before Stephanie started scrambling across the rocks toward the stairs. Jordan followed a step behind, oblivious to the scrapes and bruises.

87

HOME

Stephanie and Jordan finally reached the top of the stairs and scanned the yard frantically. "Sophie!" Stephanie screamed. "Haden!" There was no answer.

Alex stepped out of the sliding door. His arm was wrapped around Sophie's neck. Her mouth had been taped with gray duct tape and her hands were taped together behind her back. Her eyes were wide with terror. He had a long kitchen knife.

"Hello, Stephanie," he said with a smirk, then the smile froze on his face and turned into something uglier. "Oh, *and* the prodigal husband. This is awkward. Three's a crowd, eh?" Sophie's eyes swept to her father and went even wider.

"It's okay, baby," Jordan said. "Everything's going to be okay."

"I'm actually not completely sure it is, partner," Alex said. "You should have stayed dead."

"Exit Strategy, the number, Dr. Rosen… It was you all along, wasn't it?" Jordan said quietly.

"Oh, wait, don't tell me, I know. I love that movie. *On the*

Waterfront, wasn't it? 'It was you, Charlie, it was you.' Brando, right? 'I coulda been somebody…'" Alex laughed with a forced heartiness that seemed out of place, like he was picking up a round at a sports bar. "Don't try to pin your troubles on me, pal. I never encouraged anyone to do anything they weren't already predisposed to." He leered at Stephanie as he said this.

"Bullshit. I trusted you."

"Guilty conscience, maybe. You had it pretty good for a while, didn't you, partner? But you never appreciated any of it. Right? Too busy wallowing in self-pity. Poor, poor Jordan. Isn't life just so fucking unfair?" Saliva was clumping thickly at the corners of his mouth and spraying as he spoke, the pitch and volume continuing to rise.

Jordan inched forward, measuring the space between them, trying to angle between Alex and Stephanie.

"But not you, right? You were Mr. Mellow, happy with the cards life dealt you."

"Life gave me shit but I made the most of it. Shall we continue this little reunion in the house?"

Jordan flashed a look at Stephanie. He almost imperceptibly shook his head. "That doesn't sound like the best idea. It's beautiful out here."

Alex forced his elbow under Sophie's chin. "I think your daughter's a little chilly."

Stephanie screamed, "Stop it!" but froze when Alex tightened his grip. Sophie moaned, partly in pain and partly in fear. Her wide eyes darted back and forth between her mother's face and the face of her father's ghost.

Jordan's jaw worked as he continued to inch forward, eyes fixed on his former partner's.

"Why didn't you just kill me?" Jordan asked.

Alex laughed. "You were too close. So close…"

"What are you talking about?"

"The models. You were better than ninety percent. We had to know how."

Jordan froze. "What do you mean? I thought the labs were coming back random..."

"I lied. Shorted the stock. Everybody's up your ass when you claim success, but tell them you got it wrong and no one thinks twice about it. And you, Christ, you were born ready to believe you'd fucked it all up." Alex's voice was shrill.

Jordan's eyes darted from point to point, like someone dreaming, putting it all together. Years, years. His life.

"You fucking bastard... Why?"

There was a flicker of motion from inside the house. Alex turned to follow Jordan's eyes just as Haden crashed screaming through the open door swinging a brass poker like a baseball bat. It would have caught Alex just above the ear but the little turn caused it to glance painfully but harmlessly off his shoulder. The knife spun into the grass. Alex snarled and whipped around, releasing his grip on Sophie, and viciously backhanded the boy. Haden flew a foot in the air and was unconscious before he hit the ground.

"Haden!" Stephanie screamed and ran to him as Jordan hurled himself on Alex. He drove him back against the sliding glass door, which cracked loudly as tiny lines radiated out along the pane, but it didn't break. As they fell to the ground, his fingers clawed for some kind of purchase but Alex's body seemed smooth and slick like hard wet rubber. Finally he grabbed a fistful of shirt and tried to hold him far enough away to get a good shot at his face. He felt Alex's knee drive into his stomach as his fist hit something hard. Alex cried out and Jordan felt a sharp pain in two of his fingers. As he pulled back to swing again, Alex got his legs to Jordan's chest and kicked out hard, sending the lighter man sprawling. Then he scrambled to his feet and grabbed a folding lounger and slammed it across Jordan's side, the aluminum frame bending easily around his hip. Jordan brushed it away and came on. The bandage had come off his hand and it was throbbing. It felt like one of the fingers was broken. He saw a flicker of fear in Alex's eyes.

"Bastard," Jordan spat between ragged gasps. He was crying. He didn't know why.

Everything. He would kill him. Alex was backing away and his heel caught the edge of the grass. He put his arm out to steady himself and Jordan rushed him again. Lowering his head he hit him hard and low. They went down together, Jordan on top. Jordan hit him again and again. The broken fingers protested with each impact but the pain seemed to come from somewhere far away. He saw Alex's nose break and erupt in a fountain of blood, then his lip split. His shoulders felt so heavy. Then he realized Alex was laughing. Staring right at him, laughing. Making no effort to defend himself.

Jordan stopped hitting him.

"I'm sorry," Alex said. "I was just thinking." It came out with bubbles of blood and snot and spit as he struggled to clear his lungs and speak. He coughed. He mumbled something else but Jordan couldn't hear what it was. He leaned closer.

"I was thinking about that funny little noise your wife makes just before she comes." Jordan turned his head to look at Stephanie. She was bent over Haden, looking at Alex.

"You bastard," she said.

Jordan felt all the air go out of his body. Alex head butted him as hard as he could. There was a burst of blinding pain and he was falling. Then Alex was clawing through the grass. With a triumphant howl, he closed his hand over the knife and wheeled on Jordan, who was struggling to his feet.

The blade slashed through the air and cut a clean line across Jordan's chest. Jordan felt nothing. Alex hit him hard on the cheek with the knife handle and, as he started to fall forward, he buried the knife to the hilt in Jordan's shoulder. It felt like ice, radiating from the shoulder down the arm. Jordan turned his head to one side, quizzically like a parrot. He seemed unable to control his body. He fell to the grass. It felt cool and soft against his cheek. Alex kicked him repeatedly in the ribs and legs. He was screaming but Jordan couldn't tell what he was saying. He heard a rib crack and felt something warm and salty fill his mouth. The grass looked so green. He realized Sophie was only feet away. She lay where she'd fallen, hands still behind her back and mouth still taped. The tape diaphragmed in and out with her frantic breathing. Sweat beaded her forehead. Her eyes were blinking furiously and wide with horror. Jordan tried to smile, to reassure her. To say "It'll be okay, baby. Don't worry." But he couldn't seem to work his face.

Alex grabbed the handle of the knife and pulled it out. The ice turned to fire, fire that burned everywhere at once, and Jordan passed out.

Panting heavily, Alex wiped the blade on the grass. He grabbed a fistful of Jordan's hair and pulled his head back, exposing the throat. He had just raised the knife when the poker caught him between the shoulder blades. He roared in pain and ripped it out of Stephanie's hand and flung it across the lawn.

"You are a cynical little cunt, aren't you, Steph? You knew he was alive. You were coming to meet him? Jesus fucking Christ!" Alex laughed. "Fucking bitches. All the same. I should have known. I should have fucking known."

Stephanie looked frantically around. He was nodding and mumbling to himself as he scrambled to his feet and advanced on her. Pink saliva streamed from his split lip and left a splotchy trail behind.

"How did you find us?" she said.

He laughed, pink bubbles foaming at the corners of his mouth. "Haden's phone. I found my friends."

She nodded. Of course he'd kept it. For the games. He

couldn't have understood why it mattered. She tried to circle toward the house. Drawing him away from the children.

"We would have been all right," he said. "Why couldn't you just let it go?"

"You're sick," she said, backing slowly toward the open door. They both saw the poker at the same time.

Stephanie was closer. Her eyes darted from the poker to Alex to Sophie. "Fucking bitches," he snarled.

Stephanie dove for it, rolling as she hit the ground. Alex shifted the other way and, as she came to one knee with the weapon clutched in her right hand, he stepped hard on Sophie's hair, pulling her head back to the ground and eliciting a muffled scream.

"Don't, please," Stephanie cried. She slowly laid the poker down.

Without taking his eyes off her, he reached out with his left hand and grabbed it. He stood back upright, lazily spinning the knife in his right. "You know what a male gorilla does when he defeats the silverback?" He prodded Sophie with the tip of the poker.

"Please," Stephanie whispered.

"He kills the juveniles. Makes the females more—what's the word?—receptive." He used the poker under Sophie's chin to turn her head so she faced up at him.

"Alex," Stephanie said, "listen to me..."

He spat, red and thick. Some of it sprayed Sophie's hair. "Too late for that. You lie. You cunts all lie." He used his foot to roll Sophie on her back and shifted the knife in his hand.

"No!" Stephanie screamed.

The 9 mm hollow-point shell slammed into Alex's left shoulder. The initial impact swung his body back toward the door. The shell flattened and expanded as it tore through the subscapularis muscle and shattered the glenohumeral joint. Alex felt like he had been punched hard. The poker hit the ground with a hollow thud. He swung around, confused. Herron stood up from his blind on the steps to the beach.

"Drop the knife," he yelled, sighting down the Glock, held in two hands as if he were on the range. Alex looked at him dully and shook his head. It was too absurd. He staggered toward Stephanie, his left arm useless at his side and his right still clutching the knife, fingers convulsively clutching the handle.

The second bullet struck Alex just above the right eye. The point shattered the supraorbital ridge, then opened like a flower. The temporary cavitation caused a sudden pressure against the optic nerve that Alex perceived as a brilliant flash of pure white light. The knife fell to the cement but Alex didn't notice.

The now-mushroom-shaped shell tunneled through the prefrontal cortex, losing velocity as it went, finally coming to rest in the middle of Alex's parietal lobe. He felt no pain but the brilliant white light persisted. Within the light a figure took shape. She reached out to him with willowy arms. He moved toward her with no conscious effort. He could smell her skin, like cocoa butter and the sea, and something else that was uniquely her own. And then he was in her arms, his head nesting perfectly in the hollow just below her clavicle. Her breast, smooth and resilient, pillowed his cheek. And her hair. It flowed over and around him, making a bower apart from the world. His eyes closed and he breathed her in as a sea of shining chestnut and auburn swept across his face. Shanisse's voice was warm and humid in his ear. "Welcome home, sweet boy."

88

MEMORIAL

At first he thought he was back in Washington, at Exit Strategy, the crisp sheets, the steady beep of the monitor, but then he saw Stephanie. Her feet were tucked underneath her on the hospital chair and her hair fanned over her shoulder in a soft wave. A collection of trashy gossip magazines spilled from her chair to his bed. She was asleep. The clock said just after two and it was dark outside the window. On the other bed in the room Haden and Sophie were sleeping curled up together. Haden was in a hospital gown and Sophie in a sweatshirt and jeans. Haden's mouth was open and occasionally he twitched in his sleep with a little snort.

Herron was downstairs in the Maui Memorial gift shop trying to find a toothbrush among all the chocolate-covered macadamias when the man with the gray hair and horn-rims tapped him on the shoulder. He looked vaguely familiar, maybe from the plane or the rental car place.

"Detective Herron?" Herron looked up blankly as the man extended his hand. "I've so looked forward to meeting you. Please call me Sam."

AFTER

Stephanie emptied the contents of her purse on the veneered wood table in the G5 as it cruised thirty-five thousand feet above the Pacific. Jordan sat beside her and Sam directly across. Sophie and Haden were sprawled asleep on the long couch that ran down one side of the jet. Sam's fingers quickly sorted through the contents. Hair ties, wallet, makeup bag and a lone lipstick, lip balm, rubber bands, crumpled receipts, napkins from several different sources, a travel toothbrush (never used) and a collection of scraps of paper and detritus. He made a couple of piles. Then he opened the wallet and removed everything except the cash. He tucked all the cards into his pocket and sorted through the paper pile. He plucked out a picture. Stephanie and Haden on the beach. He turned it over. S&H, Paia. He smiled and folded the picture before slipping it into his pocket.

"Sorry," he said.

He grabbed the wastebasket from under the table and was beginning to sweep all the papers into it when Stephanie reached out to seize one folded lined green sheet. Sam took it from her and unfolded it. "TGG TGG! CTG GTG, ATG." He studied it for a moment, then looked at them with a quizzical expression.

Jordan had taken Stephanie's hand and they looked at each other with glistening eyes. Sam nodded and pushed the sheet across the table. Stephanie refolded it and slipped it into an inside pocket in her purse. As Sam swept the last of the paper into the bin he picked up a little wadded-up paper. He smoothed it out and saw it was a tiny, precisely folded baby rat—no, a possum. He chuckled to himself. Then he saw the faint pencil marks through the faded paper. Using his pinky fingernail and squinting through his glasses, he carefully unfolded it and smoothed it out. Jordan's face was expressionless. Stephanie glanced at him and back to Sam. Sam saw the number and nodded to himself. He folded the little piece of paper over and licked his thumb. Then he rubbed the paper between his thumb and forefinger until it was completely gone.

Nice people, Dorothea Allen thought. That house sat empty so long you didn't know what was going to happen. Dorothea assumed it was a house flipper who'd gone underwater and defaulted. Times like these, banks were likely to wait it out, too. But then the new people moved in. Weekend move, quiet. Didn't have hardly any stuff, neither.

Kids started school Monday morning first thing at Pressey. Both parents walked them. Held hands like in the old days. Sweet. They had started clearing out the yard. It had gone wild while the house had sat empty. They worked together side by side, and sometimes they'd stop what they were doing and just look at each other. Didn't see people in love like that real often, not with two kids and going through all the things you go through in this world.

They must have made a ton of money sometime 'cause nobody seemed to have a job or anything like that. That's the way it was sometimes these days, though, or people just worked from home. What was it called? Telecommuting. Sweet, though, the way they looked at each other. Like they counted every day a gift.

★ ★ ★

Matthew Chun opened another beer. Fuck it. Litton Labs was an empty shell. He'd had to lay off almost everybody after the whole Genometry thing blew up. And they'd been so close. The alert ding from the workstation startled him. It had been deadly quiet. Even the background hum of the servers, the usual ambience at the lab, was missing. He glanced at the screen, then did a double take, the beer bottle hovering just above the counter, beads of condensation running onto his finger. ROBIN was back online. Folding.

★ ★ ★ ★ ★

ACKNOWLEDGMENTS

I used to see acknowledgments in books and think, how could there possibly be so many people involved in what is essentially a solitary endeavor? Okay. I get it.

First there is family. Alex, Georgie and Harry—thank you for inspiring all of the best bits, both in the story and in me. Nana, Pete and Sal, Cybele—you were my earliest and most supportive readers and editors. This time it's really done. Promise.

Then there are friends. When the earliest, clunkiest iteration of this story was done, I sent it out to everyone I knew who had been foolish enough to say something like "Oh. You've written a book! I'd love to read it." That'll teach you. Some of you not only waded through the entirety of it but managed to get what I was going for, better than I did at the time. I am eternally grateful. As I am for the loan of many of your names. Real-sounding names are impossible to invent. Thank you. You know who you are.

Thank you, Dr. Carl Heilman, for helping me sound like I knew what I was talking about, Carolyn for making him do it, and Tommy Cohen for being our consigliere.

But most of all, I am indebted to my friends at the Table. You were there every step of the way, literally from the birth. You gave support when I needed it and led me out of every hopeless corner I painted myself into; you always knew the wheat from the chaff. Kathy, Jill, Shelly, Andrea, Brett, Frank, Roy and Leslie, we wrote this together. I am beyond lucky to have had you all there.

Which brings me to Claudette Sutherland. You are surely godmother to this, my first. It was your dumb idea after all. I had a little movie pitch and you said, "Hey, why not make it a novel?" And down the rabbit hole I followed. You were the greatest cheerleader, tour guide, champion, critic, editor and mentor a new writer could have possibly asked for.

Thank you.

When you think you've finished a book, there's this funny moment when you nod to yourself, say, "Okay, now what," and tick it off your to-do list, where it's been nagging you as long as you can remember.

I had no plan. Then Jill and Brett introduced me to the extraordinary Adam Peck. Adam is the reason any of these words are out in the world. He managed to convince Stephen Barbara at Inkwell that there was something in the story. Stephen walked me through the rewrite that finally pulled the main threads of the story together and then got it to Peter Joseph at Hanover, the exact embodiment of my dream editor. I have been singularly fortunate in having these three voices guiding me in finding and refining the story hidden within my earlier drafts. The editorial process is a revelation. ("Ohhhhh, *that's* what it's about.")

And then there were the real writers, Christopher Reich, Daniel Wilson and Michael Tolkin, who were kind enough to not only read my book but to write nice things about it to hopefully convince you to buy it.

So yeah, it takes a village.

Song clearance acknowledgments:
Senses Working Overtime
Words and Music by Andy Partridge
Copyright © 1982 BMG VM Music Ltd.
All Rights Administered by BMG Rights Management (US)
LLC All Rights Reserved Used by Permission
Reprinted by Permission of Hal Leonard LLC

Clearing one lyric use was such a surreal experience and such a testament to the utter byzantine absurdity of the music business that it needs its own little section.

I was advised to cut the chapter using lyrics from XTC's brilliant "Senses Working Overtime." I was warned that clearing lyrics was a nightmare. But, I protested, I am a musician. This is my world. I know these people. Whatever the email equivalent of tut-tutting and patting someone on the head is, I did it.

I had no idea.

The system, if you can call it that, for clearing song lyrics for use in fiction is completely broken. It should be a source of some shame to music publishers (though I remain unconvinced that this is a quality they in fact possess).

At any rate, it is only because of the invaluable help of Franne Golde, Paul Fox, Curt Smith, Roland Orzabal, Chris Hughes, Carol Childs, Tracie Butler, Andy Partridge and, most of all, Jake Lowry that the song, and the smutty interlude it accompanies, ever made it to these pages. I'm grateful that it did.